NA'AMEN GOBERT TILAHUN

Night Shade Books
New York

Night Shade books may be purchased in bulk at special discounts for sales promotion, corporate gifts, fund-raising, or educational purposes. Special editions can also be created to specifications. For details, contact the Special Sales Department, Night Shade Books, 307 West 36th Street, 11th Floor, New York, NY 10018 or info@skyhorsepublishing.com.

Night Shade Books® is a registered trademark of Skyhorse Publishing, Inc.®, a Delaware corporation.

Visit our website at www.nightshadebooks.com.

10 9 8 7 6 5 4 3 2 1

Library of Congress Cataloging-in-Publication Data

Names: Tilahun, Na'amen Gobert, author.
Title: The tree: a novel of the wrath & athenaeum / Na'amen Gobert Tilahun.
Description: New York: Night Shade Books, [2018]
Identifiers: LCCN 2017036138 | ISBN 9781597808903 (paperback)
Subjects: | BISAC: FICTION / Fantasy / Urban Life. | FICTION / Fantasy / Contemporary. | FICTION / Fantasy / Paranormal. | GSAFD: Fantasy fiction.
Classification: LCC PS3620.I496 T74 2018 | DDC 813/.6—dc23
LC record available at https://lccn.loc.gov/2017036138

Cover illustration by Charlie Bowater
Cover design by Claudia Noble

Printed in the United States of America

This book is dedicated to all of those people who provided support and helped me survive a very difficult year, especially my mother, Marlene Gobert Last, and my friend Julian Shendelman.

I love you all and could not have done this without you.

MANHATTAN

# MARIAN

"Do you see anything?"

"Give me a second, damn it."

"Sorry, sorry. Just nervous."

Marian sighed and glanced back to smile at Lester. It was his first mission as a full-fledged Agent. She couldn't blame him.

Marian closed her left eye so she could see more clearly through her right, which was currently in the building across from them. She grunted as the eye rolled along the dusty floor. It was painful. That feeling of one bit of dirt in your eye? Multiply it by fifty and spread it over the circumference of the whole eye and you might have some idea. She had been trained for this, though—the pain was simply another thing to be dealt with.

She saw nothing of note as her eye rolled down a dark hallway. Then she spotted the small crack of light. She maneuvered her eye towards it and grunted as she squeezed it under the threshold.

"Bastard piece of shit," Marian spat.

Lester chuckled but kept all other commentary to himself.

Marian's eye rolled into a bright room that looked like an assembly line of Clive Barker's nightmares. People hung limp in chains along the wall, their mouths melted shut, twisted, scarred masses of flesh and blood. Huge hooks pierced their arms and calves, dripped red life onto the floor.

She avoided the liquid as much as she could as she rolled forward. The room was cavernous; it looked as if a fourth of the building had been hollowed out to make it.

She heard something. All of her senses were linked into this tiny representative part of her. The sound resolved into speech, a language she recognized the rhythm of even though she could not understand it: one of the Ante dialects with intonations beyond the hope of any human throat. The notes of almost song rose high enough to make Marian wish she could plug her non-existent ears. Someone came around a corner and she slammed against the pillar, hiding in the small pool of shadows. The two beings that turned the corner were impossible to mistake for human. The first was huge, topping seven feet. It had two legs that bent three times, back-and-forth and back again, and then ended in cloven hooves. The torso was thick and covered in dark-black matted fur, and it had three arms, one emerging from the middle of its back. The arms were covered in the fur as well. They ended in hands with two pairs of opposing digits. There was no head, but Marian saw hints of facial features under the torso fur.

She knew of this Ante. It called itself Burning Metal because one of the first humans to touch its skin had burned off three of her fingers. Later she said it felt like burning metal. The Ante had taken that as its name and refused to answer to anything else. It was one of the leaders of Anoan and it was here in Manhattan without passing through a known gate or registering its presence with the Agency.

The Ante moving by Burning Metal's side looked to be made of metal. It shone a bright silver that reflected the light. It was more appendages than body, with long, thin, jointed legs that resembled a crab's, which exploded out of its core at every angle. Marian could see none of its main body, if it even had one. She thought it might actually be technology of some sort, but as the two beings moved past the pillar, she saw that the silver skin was rippling with scales. It passed close enough for her eye to break what she was seeing down to heat and light and aura and color and she sensed the life in the being. She had noticed that the Ante's arms were moving but as it got close she could see that all of its limbs were busy taking notes. They were each paired off, one holding a small reflective surface that another limb tapped on.

This was not good. None of their queries of Anoan in recent weeks had elicited a response and here was a prominent member of its Ruling Courts walking through this house of horrors.

"Shit." She whispered it, but only because her throat was suddenly too tight. Her mouth had lost all moisture and she could not make a louder sound.

"Lester, listen. You need to be ready to move," she whispered.

"What?"

Marian opened her left eye and swayed at the double vision she was suffering. She took a deep breath and fought down the nausea.

Lester looked very young and nervous. She wanted to comfort him. This was supposed to be a milk-run to ease him into the job. New or not, though, they were both representatives of the Agency right now, and they would not fail. She would not let them.

"Just listen. Something really bad is happening. I need you to fly back to Headquarters, as quickly as possible, and report to Agent Andre."

"But I'm not supposed to fly, especially at night."

"Listen to me. That doesn't matter right now. This is more important."

Marian was distracted because her eye was still carefully following the pair of Antes and most of her attention was on not getting caught. The downside of her position in the building was that there were tables and shelves all about and she knew something was happening on them from the way the two Antes bent over them to observe but she had no way to see them from the floor.

"When I say, you will go to Agent Andre and you will tell her we have a Red Button Issue. Do you understand?"

Lester's hands were shaking, but he swallowed, straightened his back, and nodded.

"I understand. Focus on your other part. I will guard you and wait for your order."

If his voice wavered a bit, Marian still smiled at his show of spine. She closed her left eye again and focused wholly on the building.

She passed into the next room, well behind the two Antes, but close enough to keep them in sight. There were piles all around her, some of metal bars and screws and odd silvered frames, but others looked disturbingly like hands and legs and other human parts. She was not close enough to discern whether they were actual meat or imitation but from a distance they looked all too real.

Too late she noticed the silence; the footsteps behind her had stopped. She rolled her vision around, only to see darkness and feel slick scales grabbing her up.

"Well, what do we have here?"

The English was liquid in a way that made her realize how ugly her own voice was.

"I believe it's a little spy." She was lifted toward the wall of hair; the heat of the closeness was unbearable, and she cried out in surprise and pain.

"Hmm . . . a little eye to spy."

Marian screamed as she was squeezed until she burst apart. All awareness of the inside of the building was now gone. She was back on the roof, her hand pressed over her empty socket, which had begun to steadily leak blood and fluid.

"Lester. Go. Now," she gritted out.

To his credit, Lester hesitated only a second before lighting up. The flames that crawled across him had a sickly yellow tint that denoted his fear and nervousness. Once his body was completed engulfed, his flesh disappeared, and he was nothing but a roiling mass of fire floating in the air. The stars behind him were dimmed by his brightness.

She saw the outlines of the beings coming for her against his light.

"Now. Hurry!"

He shot straight into the air and she saw some dark, flying shapes turn to follow, but she knew they would never be able to catch him once he really got going. The other figures continued straight at her as she forced herself to her feet. Her sight was not the only thing Odin had blessed her with, but right now she would have killed for the mastery of sorcery that her mother had possessed, or the battle fever that had killed her cousin. What she did have, though, was her connection with death.

She dove at the first shape, hand still covering her bleeding socket. As she moved, though, the bleeding slowed as the blood froze. Her body released steam into the air, the coldness of death now running through her veins. The first Antes screeched at her touch. The sound was so loud she staggered back in surprise.

Her movements were fast but not fluid. Her body jerked and cracked as she channeled the realm of Hel through her body. The world faded to the bright red of heat and the dark gray of cold. Whole rainbows of color bloomed where the two met. Her fists pounded into flesh that snapped like wood. She was grabbed by tentacles that slicked her upper arms with fire. She roared. Marian did not expect survival. She only wanted to give Lester enough time to get away.

"I will take care of her." Suddenly bands of burning heat clapped onto her wrists. She did not scream but wanted to. Instead she bit her tongue until her mouth filled with blood. The world swam in her vision and she was facing the torso from inside the building. "This must be the rest of our little spy."

Burning Metal was fearsome up close. She could see the cruel smile through the rough black fur. The air around him radiated with heat and something more sinister, a feeling that penetrated the cold of death. She screamed in his face. It was the call of a raven. A scream of defiance.

There was a flare of even greater heat and Marian was blown off of her feet and Burning Metal was the one screaming. The calls of the other Antes joined in. Calls of pain. Marian rolled onto her back, tilting her head to take in what was happening.

Lester had come back. He was burning white against the night, his fire almost incandescent. Even as she looked, her remaining eye watered and his image blurred.

"No." She whispered it. The foolish fucking boy! She rolled over and rose to her feet. There were other forms surrounding them. She had to turn her head to take them all in. Ten figures in a loose circle around her, Lester, and Burning Metal. They were all crouched and cowering, holding onto burned limbs that glowed red in her sight. Lester at least had taken out the others but she could see that he was failing against Burning Metal. The fire of his body was wavering. He was unable to maintain the super-heated temperature for long. She saw him struggle to lash out with his fire. He flared brighter, but only for a moment.

Marian knew she had to go. This was bigger than him; bigger than all of them. One of the Antes in the circle had fallen to the ground and now lay still; Lester must have hit something vital. She rose to her feet slowly but none of the others noticed or moved in her direction. They were all staring at Lester and Burning Metal—a fight that became more and more one-sided as she watched.

She dove for the non-moving Ante and it was only after she had tumbled over the edge of the roof that she heard one of the others cry out in warning.

Now it was time for the hardest trick; she had only ever done it a handful of times, and it had cost her dearly the last time. The cost didn't matter, though—only getting the message through mattered.

Because of her other injuries, it was painful. She screamed as her body turned inside out, as her mind split down the middle again and again, smaller and smaller. One mouth crying out in pain became five, became fifteen, became thirty.

Marian forgot a lot. She forgot her human body. She forgot that she was falling. She forgot her fear, but she did not forget that she had a mission. An unkindness of ravens rose into the sky in a squawking, crying crowd. They did not like flying in the darkness of night but they had to. As they rose into the sky they heard a dying scream behind them.

The ravens did not know why the sound of it made them call out in unison. They only knew a pain tight in their chests, even as their heads were decidedly pointed away from the source.

# ZEBUB

# LIL

Lil sent her awareness through her body, taking stock of her arms and legs. She felt the potential in her muscles, and the curve of strength. She also took stock of the missing pieces of her body: The stumps of lost toes. The stump of lost tongue. The divots in her face and body where pieces had been cut away. She felt the small bits and pieces of magic that grew inside her body; magic that she had picked up here and there. Most of her magic took not internal power, simply study and hard work—the right combination of intuition, skill, and concentration. Unfortunately, so many of these magics required exact equations or motions that she could not recall perfectly, and a simple mistake could cascade out of control too quickly.

There were other magics, though. Narrower, and more focused ones that Mayer had not deigned important enough to teach. She had an affinity for some, though, and had taught herself from the books in Kandake.

A pain shot through her heart at the thought of her old home, now lost to her, but she shook it off and returned to her body.

When she was finished . . . when she knew every piece of her body . . . she reached for one of the magics resting inside her. She visualized them as small lights and this one pulsed a red/black as it became larger in her mind.

Blood magic. Many ‘dants used it daily in small ways—light healing, blessing homes, finding family. It was the last one that interested her the most right now. The light filled her vision and she flung it out of her in two separate threads, one for Min and one for Davi.

She followed the threads. Her vision blurred as her spirit was pulled from her body. Moving along the threads, she passed over the ruins of The Out and over the territory of the Court of Predators and Instincts, where 'dants lived among animals that would tear apart those who didn't belong, and occasionally those who did. She flew over the territory of the Court of Mists, which was shrouded as always. She moved faster and faster. The blood of her sibs calling her closer until she slammed into a wall.

Her power dissipated. The momentum was gone and she had just enough time to see she was above The Drowned before she was snapped back to her body, gasping. When she had her breath back she let out a cry of inarticulate rage and stood up. This was not the first attempt she had made to find her sibs in the last two six-days. It was not even the tenth, but she had had hopes that this attempt would be different. Her strength was returning to her, and blood magic excelled at family bonds. She had to face the fact that something or someone was blocking her from finding them.

Lil paced back and forth, her stride wobbly from the loss of toes and her new sense of balance. The Nif in the corner, whose numbers seemed to grow larger everyday, chittered softly to each other and every once in awhile one leaned forward to coo in her direction. They had slowly become more vocal. She didn't know what it meant, but she did know she found the pity in their voices annoying.

There was a knock on the door. She had not expected her cry of frustration to go unheeded but she had hoped. Only Kima or Uchel would come to her. The others in the house were wary or openly hostile. Lil did not care what any of them thought. She was thankful for their help and owed them for that, but their personal opinions meant nothing to her.

The door opened and Lil paused to watch Uchel enter.

The older woman moved quickly for one of her obvious age. She also had some experience with power—potions mostly, given the foul liquids she kept trying to to make Lil swallow.

"You are supposed to be resting."

Lil rolled her eyes so hard they ached for a moment. She swung her arm out to gesture at the bed, ignoring the sharp pain that burst across her chest.

"I understand, but if you move too soon, you will only injure yourself more."

Lil sighed. Uchel was right about normal healing. But Lil was not normal. She had not been "normal" for quite some time, even if she was only now realizing it. She pressed her hand against her shoulder where the fresh wound sat. The wound of her own making. It was a simple carving; a working rooted in blood and pain. The Osirii equation was not the most effective magic for healing, but it did have minor healing capabilities, in addition to its main purpose of allowing the user to adapt to missing limbs faster than normal.

She sat on the bed and faced the old woman who had her head lifted in the air, nostrils flaring.

"You've been using power."

Lil narrowed her eyes at the woman. Perhaps she was more than a potions maker after all.

"You know that using power will speed your initial healing but you will hurt for longer. The small aches will last."

Lil knew this. This was what she hated most about losing her voice. She could not interrupt others when they explained things she already knew.

"You were looking for your siblings, weren't you?"

Lil saw no reason to hide it, so she nodded.

Uchel let out her own sigh and sat beside Lil on the bed. She reached over and grasped Lil's hand, her fingers closing over the palm and touching the scar where her pinkie used to be. Lil refrained from shaking off the touch only because she did not have the strength to be disrespectful.

"Kima has our people out listening for any information about them."

Lil barely kept from rolling her eyes at this. She had been in her room for most of her time in this home but that did not mean she was ignorant. As soon as she had recovered enough to use a little power she had begun gathering information about "The Resistance," and she was far from impressed. The fact that the Antes of Zebub had no idea there was any resistance to be spoken of was not a good sign. From what she'd been able to find out, they confined themselves to smuggling 'dants between districts, and possibly out of the city itself.

There were five of them in the house, and that seemed to be the main group: five against hundreds of thousands of millennia-old beings with enormous power. Of course they wanted Lil to join them.

Uchel reached for her quickly, and before Lil could stop her, she pulled the fabric covering her shoulder aside, revealing the ragged symbols cut there. Lil had cut it with her left hand, so it wasn't as clean as she wanted, but it worked.

"Osirii's equation? Really?"

Lil froze, partly in shock at Uchel's brazenness but mostly in shock that the woman knew the symbols on sight. Uchel stood and pushed on Lil's injured shoulder. With a soft cry Lil moved back and fell across the bed. She reached up to slap the woman, pain and anger pushing her past any hesitation. Uchel caught her wrist. Either Lil was still very weak or Uchel's strength belied her age and apparent frailty.

"You are my patient, and I do not take kindly to those under my care injuring themselves further."

Lil slowly reached for the stylus and pad of paper in the pocket of her robe. The back of her hand brushed against the root and she shivered at the pulse of power that flashed through her skin.

*It is taking Kima entirely too long! The Hunt is out there after my sibs and my allies. I don't have time to just lay here.*

The old woman read her words with no change of expression.

"You must be patient. They will find your siblings . . . and the Antes."

The distaste in Uchel's voice was another reason Lil would rather be searching for them. Kima had not blinked an eye at Lil asking for news of Arel and Jagi. However, Uchel and Assan, Kima's second-in-command, had not been able to hide their disgust and judgment. As for the other two occupants of the house, every time Lil had seen Quinn and Hlani they had been wrapped up with one another; Lil knew little of them.

"If you are to be of any use to us, you must heal."

*I told you all. I owe you my thanks and I will help if I can, but I have more important goals than fighting Antes right now. What good is resistance if all of Corpiliu is devoured?*

Uchel hummed but said nothing. Lil was not surprised; the darkness had apparently not made many forays into this part of town, and by and large the 'dants here viewed it as a problem of Antes. Lil had not realized that the attacks had been concentrated around the Athenaeums until Kima had showed her the map they used to trace the attacks. She had tried to argue that no matter what it looked like now, things were coming, and the darkness would spread. But it was hard to be emphatic when there was no tone to her words; only letters on a page. Lil was forever surrounded by people who put their own agendas before what needed to be done.

Then there were Davi and Min. She knew that her sibs were alive; she would have felt otherwise when using the blood magic, but there were plenty of things that they could live through.

*I need to leave this room. I have nothing to do here but worry and think. Neither are helpful for rest. I need to move about and be useful.*

Uchel seemed to be thinking about it. Even without her approval, Lil was reaching the end of her patience, but it would be easier without having to sneak past everyone.

"Let me think on it," Uchel said as she turned to the pile of Nif in the corner.

Lil watched closely. None of the 'dants here had interacted with or even acknowledged the Nif so far.

"You will make sure she does not leave that bed."

Some of the Nif seemed to stand taller. They chattered at her and Lil could hear the affirmation in the sounds. It was a brilliant move. The Nif had saved Lil's life and the last thing she wanted was to upset them. Uchel threw her a smile as she left the room, which Lil met with a grimace.

The Nif watched her carefully and she knew she could press the matter. They could not actually stop her. Well, they could try, but she doubted they would be willing to physically stop her and risk adding to her injuries. She sighed and reached into the pocket of her robe, pulling out the bag that contained the root. She opened it and poured the bones onto the blanket in front of her. The Nif in the corner made a long cooing sound in unison.

The bones chased each other across the bed, each attracting some and pushing away others until there was an abstract pattern laid out before her. She had done this before, and while the patterns always had similarities, they were not the same. She reached under her mattress for the loose papers—a few pages squirreled away from every pad they gave her. Finding a blank one, she quickly sketched out the pattern in detail, just as she had with each before.

When she was done, she picked up one of the bones and tossed it lazily into the pattern, and the stones rearranged themselves around the new vector. She watched them and wondered about the movement. She left the bones and laid out each of the drawings she had made, in chronological order. She stared at the first and second, looking at where the stones had moved and the patterns began to emerge. Perhaps it was not the placement that mattered but the movement of the stones? She studied the pages, trying to figure it out, until she fell into dreams.

The sound of a knock woke her from slumber. She looked down at the bones and pages scattered about her bed and gathered them all quickly, putting them away as Uchel entered. Lil glanced out the window and saw that night had fallen.

"I must go to the night market and Assan, Quinn, and Hlani are out. Would you like to accompany Kima and me?"

No, Lil wanted to be out looking for Min and Davi. She wanted to hold them in her arms. But anything was better than staying in this cursed room, so she simply nodded. Uchel placed a pile of clothing that Lil had not noticed onto the bed.

"Dress. Then meet us in the main room."

Lil dressed quickly. The clothing was shades of gray and black, meant to blend in with the burnt trees. She put on the pants and shirt, and pulled up the hood to hide the places where her scalp was raw and red where her hair had been pulled from it. She hesitated before putting the root in her pocket.

The Nif had been having some loud, piping conversation in the corner, and when she looked down six Nif had gathered around her feet. Three circled each foot, and touched the tips of their bodies together. They began melting into each other while spreading over the flesh of her feet.

Lil stared at the new shoes she wore that were not shoes before shrugging and leaving the room, ready to be outside the walls.

# ARELAREL & JAGIJAGI

They were all going stir-crazy. In two six-days they had not left the building at all. The Hunt rode the streets still, looking for them.

"Close your fist. Slowly." Arel stood behind Min, hands on her shoulders, while Jagi crouched in front of her, guiding her through the exercise. Slowly the fingers made of ice cracked and moved and closed one by one.

The air grew colder, but not unbearably so.

"Good girl."

Min smiled, despite the sweat gathering at her hairline and dripping down her face, freezing like icicles on her chin, before finally falling. They looked like some abstract ice-mask but she did not react to them.

"Now, keep your fist closed, and I want you to think about the temperature around you."

"Too warm."

Davi's hand tightened around Jagi's neck and his knees dug into the Ante's sides. Jagi could not fault him his nervousness; this was where it had often gone wrong the other times.

"Is that your whole body or just the arm telling you that?"

There was a long pause and Min's face twisted into a frown as she tried to figure out the answer.

"It's the arm."

Arel and Jagi shared a look over the girl's head.

"Is the arm doing anything else? Telling you anything else?"

Min frowned again but this time there was no revelation to clear the confusion from her face. "How would I be able to tell?"

"Any thoughts that do not feel like your own?"

Min frowned harder and the air around them became cooler. "But they're just thoughts in my head, how do I track where they came from?"

Her eyes opened and Jagi could see the fear in them.

"Do not worry, little pup." He made sure to use the nickname as it calmed both her and Davi. "This arm is a part of you now. A gift from your sister, and she would never give you something you could not handle."

Min still looked scared but her nod was solid and unwavering.

"I want you to concentrate on bringing the cold back inside your limb."

Min licked her lips, the warmth of her tongue melting some of the ice, and focused her gaze on her frosted limb. Slowly the chill left the air and the limb went from frosted to clear and perfect ice. She carefully flexed the fingers, and there was no cracking and shedding of frost this time.

"Good pup."

"Yay!" Davi let go of Jagi's neck to raise his hands and cheer, and promptly slid off of Jagi and onto the floor. He lay there, still cheering for his sib.

Arel smiled and held up the glove. Min lifted her hand and Arel pulled the shoulder-length glove all the way on. It was spiraled with an uneven gray that showed small imperfections. It looked as dangerous as it was. They had made it themselves; the two of them weaving their separate filth into a powerful gauntlet to hide her new limb while the pups slept between them.

They were in the House of the Madame's common room. They probably should have done this in their private room but they could not stand to be cooped up another minute. Someone tried the door and knocked loudly when they found it locked.

"Coming." Jagi rose from his crouch making sure that Arel was pulling on Min's jacket, fully hiding her arm from sight.

It was the two 'dant companions of Byron. They had had little contact with the three 'dants, who were the only other long-term residents of the House of the Madame. It was clear that they were running from something as well, and a mutual bond of silence and lack of curiosity had been agreed upon without a word spoken. Jagi nodded at the two as they entered. These 'dants moved oddly; he had noticed it in the glimpses he had gotten of them. There was something in their stance that confounded him. Where had he seen such a stance before?

He looked over at Arel, who shared the same quizzical expression. Then it came to them. Mayer. Riana. Krezida. They had all had that cock to their hip and that stomp to their feet, but only in their own Athenaeums. It was confidence. Arrogance.

Never had he seen 'dants approach them with such confidence in the lines of their bodies. Arel pushed both Min and Davi behind him, onto one of the cushions. Arel and Jagi watched and waited.

The man, as 'dants reckoned it, spoke.

"We have not been properly introduced. I am Bastion and this is Melisande." He gestured to the woman, who bowed her head.

"I am Joni and this is my brother Rau and the children of one of our servants—Zasie and Vala." Arel spoke quickly and Jagi nodded along to the cover story they had invented and drilled into the pups.

"Interesting," the one called Melisande said and moved around Arel to get a look at them.

The apertures on Arel's torso snapped open and his tentacles teased out, a clear warning.

Some of the confidence dropped from the 'dants stance. Arel and Jagi had thought the other guests were from some smaller city they had not heard of, but now Jagi was beginning to wonder if they were from one of the breakaway 'dant-only settlements.

The woman backed away with her arms slightly raised but the smile on her face was mocking. Arel and Jagi shared a look. The man draped himself over one of the cushions opposite the children and the woman moved to stand behind him. Arel sat on the cushion on one side of the pups while Jagi took the other side.

Min looked back and forth between them and heaved a sigh.

"What can we do for the two of you?" Arel had tried to bleed the aggressiveness from his voice, but it was still there.

"What are you two running from with two children of another species?" Melisande clucked her tongue as she spoke.

Jagi frowned. "What concern of that is yours?"

"Tell us," she ordered.

"Excuse me?" Jagi was doing his best to keep his temper. To have a 'dant order him about so? It could not be borne. The only reason he had not attacked the man and ripped his spine from his body was the attention it would bring. Jagi and Arel had one priority right now: keep

Davi and Min safe until they could reunite with Liliana. And beyond that, even. If they were being honest, they would protect the pups as long as they could.

"We're just so bored," the one called Bastion whined, and Jagi did not reach over and snap the boy's neck, though the image brought him comfort.

"Yes, well, that is something you should bring up with The Door. I'm sure there's all manner of diversions they would be happy to provide."

Bastion smiled at them as if it were all some joke and Melisande placed her hands on his shoulders and slowly sank onto the cushion behind him. Jagi felt his own apertures open and the skin over his third eye tensed. He was able to keep it shut only through a supreme act of will. He did not like these two 'dants.

"Why are you here then?" If they were so clearly going to break their silent agreement then Jagi felt no reason to honor it.

"We were hoping you would offer us some entertainment."

The alarms were ringing in Jagi's head and he rose, acting before Arel could, for once.

"I am sorry that you foolish children seem to have us confused with some traveling players. We are not here to entertain you."

"Oh, but pretty, pretty, please." Melisande's voice rose into a horrible high pitch, meant to imitate a child, Jagi guessed. It sounded like blades grinding sideways against each other.

Jagi gestured behind him. Arel rose, as did Davi and Min.

**"Sit down."**

This time both 'dants spoke at once and there was something else beyond their voice, some echo.

Jagi bent his knees to comply. Then he stood again, his third eye finally snapping open. He whirled around. Arel was also standing, but Davi was sitting obediently, his hands in his lap. Min was sitting as well, but there was a tension in her thighs and a frown on her face, as if she would rise at any moment.

"You dare?"

Jagi stepped toward them and both of the 'dants looked shocked. Foolish things. Bastion scrambled to his feet and moved behind the other one. They spoke in unison again.

**"Stop."**

Again Jagi felt the urge to do as they said, but this one passed even quicker than the first time, and he took two steps closer.

The door to the common room flew open and Byron flung his body between Jagi and Arel and the two 'dants, who belonged to him.

"Please, I apologize on their behalf."

Jagi felt his teeth grind and he could feel the press of Arel on his side as he came up alongside.

"They attempted to use powers on us." The idea that they had thought their puny powers would have any lingering effect on an Ante was insulting. The only thing Antes feared was Babel, and these two had no command of that. Though perhaps the darkness should now be added to that short list. "The punishment for that is death."

Byron turned to the two behind him and whispered something that neither Jagi nor Arel could hear. The two immediately fell to their knees and bowed their heads. He turned back to Arel and Jagi and bowed his own head but not so far that he could not see them.

"I understand, but they are new to Zebub, and new to their power as well. They are foolish and only meant to entertain themselves. They meant no harm."

Arel placed a hand on his shoulder but Jagi shrugged it off. The fear he had felt had turned to anger, and he wanted these 'dants to fear him. He wanted them to know that they lived at his sufferance, and then he wanted to kill them for threatening those who were his.

Their lives were saved by the small hand that slipped into Jagi's. He looked down at Davi who was staring back at him. He smiled down at the pup he had come to love as his own and saw that smile returned. He would not kill these 'dants. Not in front of Davi and Min at least.

The Door came to the common area at a run. They were wearing a sheath of bright green fabric that shimmered and split into pants at their legs. Their hair was curled and held tinges of burnished gold in the dark depths that matched the sandals they wore. They looked at the the three 'dants.

"Out."

Neither Arel or Jagi had thought that a Door would or could speak in such a way. Their voice thundered through the building and echoed in the room. The very walls seemed to pulse with their vibrato. It reminded him of the way the Athenaeum had reacted to Mayer.

Byron and his two followers hurried out. Arel and Jagi looked at The Door as they spoke quickly and clearly.

"The Hunt is going door to door now; it is only a matter of time before they reach this house and begin to search."

Arel stepped forward into Jagi's vision. Jagi was happy to step back and bend down to lift Davi into his arms to comfort them both.

"Do you have a way out?"

"Yes. Right here, in fact. There is time, though. Is there anything you need from your room upstairs?"

Arel and Jagi both answered in the negative. They had brought nothing with them and in their time at The House had accumulated nothing.

The Door nodded and walked over to the wall. They reached into the side of the green sheath that left their shoulders, neck, and arms free of fabric. They came out gripping a knife. It was thin and glinted in the light. The Door touched it to the small seam between two planks of wood on the wall, sinking it an inch in. Then they pulled the knife out of the wall and slammed it through the palm of one of their hands. Davi cried out and buried his face in Jagi's neck. Everyone else was silent.

The Door pulled the knife out but there was no blood on the blade, nor was any gushing from the wound. They could all clearly see the cut and the blood flowing inside but it did not spill over the edges of the wound. The Door held their hand up, spreading their fingers as far as they would go. The seam they had marked with the knife began to widen and gape before them. The Door turned their hand sideways and the two planks on either side of the opening turned sideways as well, making the gap just big enough for them to slip through.

"Go. They shall not find this passage. It will lead to another House of the Madame, the one closest to the Ruling Courts. It has already been searched, so you should be safe there."

Arel and Jagi met each other's eyes and nodded. Jagi hurried through with Davi in his arms, Min scrambling behind them without a word. Arel stayed behind for a moment. He looked at The Door.

"I thank you."

"You are welcome. It is my duty."

Arel narrowed his eyes.

"All the same, if this is a trap, we will survive and we will come back and make you pay."

The Door's beautiful, wide eyes became luminous, their full lips stretched into a wide smile, their golden skin glowed.

"I would expect nothing less."

# LIL

Lil had only seen The Out from her window, so her head snapped to and fro as she followed Uchel and Kima through the black woods. The three sisters rode high in the air tonight, and the light they shed made the broken blackness of the trees and lingering ash glow. She and Kima blended in somewhat with their gray and black. Uchel wore a pure white dress with long sleeves brought in by a belt of braided black and gray. The hem hung to the ground and dragged in the ash and dirt, but picked up none of it.

"It is a lovely night for the market," Uchel said, and Lil could hear the smile in her voice. She moved faster than Lil, which was a given, but also faster than Kima.

Lil stumbled slightly under the weight of the two baskets she carried. She knew they were nothing compared to the three that Kima had strapped to her back and each shoulder, but the weight of them, light though it was, pulled on Lil's injuries. It made her more aware of her missing toes and the new way she was forced to balance her weight. It made her stomach and sides ache for pieces of muscle that had been removed along with her skin.

Lil refused to show the strain. Her focus narrowed as they walked; less attention on the environment and more on pushing her healing body. The woods were all the same anyway. Just broken and burned trunks with small hints of green in the skeletal branches that arched above. Until they came suddenly to a clearing, and Lil stumbled in shock because now it was bright as day. She looked up. The blackened branches here had more bits of new growth peeking through. They were taller and thicker as well, and reached farther up, interweaving over the clearing. A perfect circle was kept clear in the center of the canopy and the light of the three moons shone through, somehow amplified, making the clearing bright but not extending beyond the circle of trees. The light had been invisible to Lil until they stumbled into it.

At least fifty 'dants bustled around under the light. Tents and tables were set up in four concentric circles with enough space between them that customers could move from circle to circle easily.

They were approached and stopped by two figures in head-to-toe black. Their faces were covered with masks of the same color, and their eyes were protected by wide lenses that glowed green in the night. They let them by immediately, nodding to Kima and Uchel, but staring at Lil with suspicion as she passed.

Lil tapped Kima on the shoulder and gestured back to the dark figures, raising her eyebrows in question.

"Yes, I know them."

She said no more on the subject, so Lil assumed they were part of Kima's "Resistance."

Lil longed to ask about this clearing and the power that obviously ran through it, but her hands were full and she could not write anything down. She caught Uchel's gaze and tried to gesture up and all around with her head.

"There are a few places like this in The Out. Places sacred to those who lived here. Before they were all killed," Uchel explained.

That had not been what she wanted to ask. Lil already knew a little about those who had lived here. They had claimed to have been in the woods forever, and to have never been chained by the Antes. They had lived quiet lives and kept themselves apart. No one knew what had finally pushed the Antes to attack them, but attack they did, and murdered most of them, scorching the forest black in the process. Lil also knew that some had survived. She knew Mayer had helped send them to another city. Lil had been only seven cycles at the time, but they had looked no different from the other 'dants as she watched them crouch in a forgotten corner, weeping and begging Mayer to help them.

Her head ached at the thought of her mentor and she quickly pushed him from her mind.

The power to create this clearing might explain the Antes' reaction, though. No one but Antes could manipulate the very living flesh of Corpiliu, or so Lil had always been taught, though 'dants had access to many smaller magics, and the Holders and their apprentices had access to and training in much larger magics. However, none but Antes like those from the Court of Sorrows and Riches, the Antes that grew the pink living houses from the very ground, were supposed to have this kind of power.

They walked to a table in the fourth and most central circle.

"Right here is fine," Uchel said, already laying out a thickly woven blanket over the surface of the table.

Kima and Lil set down the boxes of herbs and Uchel heaved her large bags onto the table as well. Uchel immediately began to unpack and arrange all that she had brought.

"Thank you. I am fine here by myself. You should go off and explore." Lil looked around and realized Kima had already melted into the bustle of the night market. The old lady was smart and realized that no one would approach with Lil hanging around the table. She nodded and gave the woman a rueful smile before leaving. She did not go far, though, and, weaving among the stalls, she made sure to keep an eye on Uchel's table.

She watched for a while and realized that many of the customers that came to the table bought nothing. Not to say that Uchel did not have customers; the supply of herbs was steadily depleting. But most came up, talked to her for a moment, held herbs in their hands, and then put them down and walked away. Members of the Resistance, no doubt, but how odd that they spoke to Uchel instead of Kima. Was it for convenience? It could be for secrecy, but Lil got the feeling that most in the Out knew what Kima and her group did, so why hide? Unless they were hiding the truth from her, and Uchel was actually the leader.

"What are you doing?"

Lil let out a gust of air at the voice behind her and turned.

Assan stood, too close, his hands clenching so tightly that the amber skin of his knuckles looked like it might split. The scars on his chin made it look like he was always frowning and suspicious. It did not help that, as far as Lil could tell, he actually was always frowning and suspicious.

She narrowed her eyes at his question.

"They may trust you, but as far as I'm concerned—"

Lil turned away from him. She knew what he was going to say. It wasn't the first time he'd said it, even if those times had been loudly outside her door to someone else. He grabbed her arm. She spun around, ready to speak, forgetting she had no tongue.

Ignoring the pain that welled up in her at the memory, she braided the two center fingers of her right hand together and curled her thumb and third finger in. She hoped it would still work with her missing pinky. She knocked the curled fingers in the center of his forehead, holding the image of pure, blank, whiteness in her mind's eye.

The grip on her arm went limp as his eyes clouded over. She backed away from him and moved into the crowd, which was growing larger. As soon as she was far enough away he would wake, no worse for the wear, but out of her space.

She moved from booth to booth for a while, taking in their wares. The proprietors always looked at her oddly. She noticed that most others greeted each other by name. Most likely they did not get many new faces at the market. No one moved to stop or question her, so she ignored their stares.

At the center of the concentric circles that made up the market she felt darts of tight pain across the skin of her neck. She recognized the feeling from when she was around Mayer, when he first taught her other branches of power, or used them himself: Power, 'dant power. The ten shopkeepers beside Uchel that made up the center circle were all very different. All ages. All shades of skin and hair. They had nothing in common with one another, other than that each of their tables or tents held a distinct feeling of power. And they all stared at her with wide eyes and their hands clutched at various items she assumed were charms or idols of power.

She approached each table, nodding at each shopkeeper in turn. She had no intention of purchasing anything and in fact had nothing to barter with. She only had her knife and the bag of the root, neither of which she was willing to trade.

Most of the tables had infused items for sale. Stones with different properties that shone with power were watched over by a girl barely out of her childhood. Two older men watched over a table that had feathers to improve speed and swiftness of the mind. She moved among them, holding her hand over the items in question until she recognized the intention of the object. She then tried to reverse engineer how she would create such an object.

It reminded her of the tests that Mayer had occasionally thrown at her without warning. And she needed to build up her knowledge.

So much of her study from the last few years had been in Babel. Now she was stripped of her most potent weapon and left with only half-remembered larger-power-workings and smaller magics.

For speed she could have used any of the feathers as long as it was whole. Then she would have bathed it in a mix of herbs and eaten it. That would have made the speed longer lasting, though it would take a couple days to prepare. Alternately, she could have used her knife to carve a crude drawing of a bird into her flesh and then threaded the feather in and out of her skin alongside the image.

Blood magic was fast and dirty. Pain was an important part.

Only at the very last table did she stop, surprised. The person behind the table was tall and wide, the skin she could see between glove and sleeve a light brown. She could see nothing of their face, as it was covered in a carved wooden mask. The mask had no features, simply dark holes for the eyes. The robe they wore was a dark brown, verging on black, and seemed to move on its own. She thought it wind at first, but then noticed the lumps moving underneath, bulging the fabric oddly before disappearing.

The table was littered with various knots of wood that looked completely natural, as if they had grown that way. No matter how closely Lil looked she could not see an end to any of them. Each seemed to be a continuous twist of wood.

"We have many wares that would interest a Holder Apprentice."

Lil jerked back. No one had called her that since coming to The Out. Even Kima and Uchel just used her name.

The proprietor held up their hand palm out and Lil took note of the odd symbol in the palm of their glove. A spiral in the center with eight arrows pointing inward, hemming it in. "Do not worry, young one. We mean you no harm."

Lil raised an eyebrow at that. The symbol tickled something in the back of her head. It belonged to none of the Houses or Courts of Zebub. She would recognized those immediately. She reached for her pad and stylus.

*How did you know who I was?*

The figure laughed, and it was a light giggle that seemed to echo with a number of smaller voices that came from under the robes.

"There is little that happens in Zebub that we do not know." The figure rose from their seated position and Lil could see that they were exceptionally tall. She could see the wideness of their belly and hips as the loose fabric of their robe clung to them. They reached over the table and their gloved hand moved over all wares on the table before stopping. "This one."

They picked a beautiful knot composed of two woods; one a silvery-white, the other a dark, deep brown. They curved around and into each other, looking like a heart from one angle, a knot from another, and a hand from still a third.

"Birch for rebirth, Oak for strength," they said, and held out the piece. "Take this. It will help you soon enough."

Lil hesitated and stared at the proprietor.

"Come along child. If I were to betray you, do you think I would do so here, in front of all these people? If I were going to betray you I would have already told the Courts where you were this whole time."

Lil touched the knot of wood, lightly, with one finger. There was some power thrumming through it to be sure, but it did not feel antagonistic. It also did not feel positive. The energy was simply there, uncaring one way or another about her. She clutched the knot of wood in her palm and slipped it into her pocket along with The Root and her other belongings.

"Now, go and explore what you were interested in. You have much to learn."

Lil nodded in thanks and began to back away. She let her hand rest on the wood in her pocket, feeling the warm thrum of life and power. She kept the person in her line of sight until she had no choice but to turn, and they stared at her the entire time as well. At least she assumed they were staring.

Slowly she made her way out of the center and moved closer and closer to the edge of the clearing. She hesitated, made even more cautious by the mysterious encounter, and paused as she overheard the proprietor of one of the outer booths speaking with a customer.

"I heard she's the one the Courts are hunting."

"Who is she here with?"

"Uchel."

There was silence then, and Lil wished she could see the expressions on their faces.

"She must know what she's doing."

"I don't know. Bringing a hunted here?"

They grumbled for a bit longer but provided no useful information for Lil, and eventually she moved to the edge of the circle of the light, anxious for a closer look at the trees that formed the border of the clearing. There was power in them, but it didn't spark across her skin like the other 'dant magics. Instead this was like a hum in the air; constant, half-heard, and achingly familiar, but Lil could not place it. She stepped out of the circle of the light and into the near-complete darkness of the forest surrounding them. There was the immediate feeling of being watched that happened when surrounded by darkness. Looking up, she could make out the trees that formed together to protect the clearing. Waiting for her eyes to get used to the dark she slowly traced the branches down until she singled out one of the trunks.

Lil moved deeper into the darkness to study the tree. There was something about it that called to her. She ran her hands over the bark. Ash and soot quickly covered her palms. Lil could still feel the power in the tree. It moved through the tree but the tree was not the source. The source was somewhere attached to it. When she focused on it she immediately felt the shock of Babel in her system.

Babel. Written.

She shimmied through the brush moving around to try and catch a glimpse of the symbol. When she finally took it in, it was much as it had been at the entry to the Vault. As soon as she saw the carving, the meaning of the word glowed in her mind: GROWTH. She could think of a number of pronunciations that could fit with this symbol but of course she had no access to any of them anymore.

She moved to the next tree and examined it. As she was moving her hands over the the rough surface of the bark the feeling of being watched increased. Whereas before it had been a nagging feeling, now she felt as if a knife was about to be plunged into her back. She stopped and looked around, seeing nothing until she looked down.

Eyes, dozens of small eyes, watched her from the underbrush. They glowed white and reflected the pieces of moonlight that made their way through the thick canopy here. She stayed still and the eyes simply watched for a moment before every one of the bright reflected spots shifted to the left, as if they were all watching the same thing. She darted her eyes in that direction and caught a hint of movement.

What was coming through the woods was like nothing she had ever seen. Its flesh blended into the shadowed night even better than the clothing she had been given. She could barely see it as it moved slowly toward her. Every few steps it stopped and, when still, it became almost invisible. She froze, tracing its movement as best she could.

The hint of shape she made out was similar to a ‘dant, but there were other shadows around its head that said it was anything but. It could be one of the rarer Antes; either rare in Zebub or rare altogether, but some tightening of her stomach and a sense of foreboding made her doubt that.

Lil backed toward the light, all the while reaching for her knife. It was meager protection but better than nothing. She purposefully grasped the blade of the knife, letting her blood flow along the edge of it. In her mind she imagined the older ‘dant symbols for blood and fire. The language was old. Though not as old as Babel, it was no longer used and still held power in the lines of it.

She tried to hold back a grunt as her blood turned to flame at the site of the cut. There was no actual flame or light when she glanced down, but she could feel from the heat that she held unprotected flame in her palm.

Lil would probably never know if it had been the scent of her blood or her barely withheld grunt as her hand burned, but whatever was in the forest with her let out a small growl. She moved closer to the tree, hoping to blend into the shadows, but she could see the small ripple of movement as the thing's head followed her. It took a step forward, closer to the light, and she saw more of its form.

It was almost as tall as she was, but wider in the shoulders and chest. Its skin was black and glittered slightly in the light. It moved forward and she stumbled to put the tree between the two of them. She could make a run for the clearing but there was no guarantee that the thing wouldn't catch her in the short distance. Even now she heard it moving toward her. After looking around, she clamped the knife between her teeth and began to climb up the trunk in front of her.

She discarded any consideration of quiet for speed and managed to make it two of her body lengths up the trunk before the thing came around the trunk itself. She held on tightly as it slammed its body into the tree, which swayed wildly. She heard no calls from the clearing. No questions. No fear. They could not hear what was happening, despite being only a few feet away. Lil assumed this was somehow related to the powers of the tree ring. The thing slammed into the tree again and her hold began to slip.

She could not stay up here forever. It would knock her down soon enough. She could not call for help. Even if they could hear her, she no longer had her tongue. She could certainly not fight it. Not injured as she still was. Even as she held on to the tree trunk she could feel her wounds reopening with each of the creature's blows.

She looked down as it made another run at the tree, and was barely able to hold on this time. It turned to walk away for another attempt and Lil took her chance, dropping directly onto the thing's back. The impact knocked her breath free and she nearly dropped the knife, but she wrapped her limbs around it and held on as it crashed back and forth trying to dislodge her. She felt cuts open in her back as extra limbs whipped around, trying to pry her off.

She reached for its face with one hand that still burned with blood and fire. She tried to claw or burn its eyes out but all she felt was something smooth like glass and slightly damp and sticky. She made a fist and slammed it down on that part and the thing went crazy. So it did have eyes after all, simply different ones. It slammed to and fro and finally headed directly toward the ring of trees.

They crashed into the clearing, Lil clinging to the thing's back like a limpet. Immediately people ran in every direction. She glanced up and saw Kima running her way, which surprised her, but she had no time to think about it. She pulled the knife from her mouth and brought it down, striking again and again. It scored the black armor but did not pierce it.

"Lil, let go!"

Lil didn't want to obey the voice, but her arms were weak and aching and so, almost of their own volition, they released the neck of the creature, and with its next heave she went flying directly into another warm body.

"Get off me!"

She recognized Assan's voice and struggled to free herself from the tangle of limbs they now found themselves in. Lil rolled off of his body and moved to her feet. People moved all around her screaming, gathering their wares, trying to get away anyway they could. Assan cursed as he rose to his own feet. Now, in the light of the clearing, Lil could see the dark glittering skin of the thing clearly. She could see the large jaw open with its hundreds of needle-like teeth. She could see its large two-toed foot and its four-fingered hand. She could see the two extra appendages that sprouted from the thing's shoulders; they had numerous joints and ended in sharp points.

A loud blast reverberated through the clearing, and then another. Lil glanced at Kima and saw the woman fending off the thing with a long-bladed knife that did no damage Lil could see. Kima's other hand held what Lil assumed was a pistol. She had never seen one before, though she had seen drawings and photographs. 'dants in Zebub had always been banned from possessing or using them, and Antes didn't need them. The shots from her gun seemed to knock the creature back even if they didn't cause it any pain.

Assan was on his feet as well, pulling another pistol from somewhere in his pants. She was closer so she could see the way it was patched, different metals and clamps holding it together. She watched the blast twist the creature around. In the light of the clearing she could confirm that this was no Ante. This was something created. Its body looked whole and well proportioned but she could see the seams in its hide; the places where things had been almost-perfectly attached.

The cut in Lil's palm had already healed over, tight and pink. Blood magic tended to take care of itself. So she cut into her fingertip until the blood flowed freely and used the red liquid to write on the blade of her knife again. In the same old 'dant language she painted symbols for piercing and breaking. She moved quickly while it was distracted by Kima's attack.

Lil moved behind the creature and struck, plunging her knife into the narrow seam that she could see between arm and torso. The knife stuck there as the thing hit her and she went flying again, this time into a table. More of her wounds were open. She could feel the small trickles of blood. She reached for her stomach and felt the lump of the root still secure in her shirt and something else. The knot of wood. She pulled it out and stared at the leaves and acorns that had begun to sprout from it.

She looked up.

Kima had stopped using the gun. Lil watched as she threw it behind her to where Uchel stood. The older woman immediately began to fuss with it. Kima meanwhile moved as quickly as possibly, dodging the arms and other limbs focused on her. Assan had moved behind the thing and was lining up a shot.

Lil looked down at the quicky growing wood in her hand and ran to Assan as quickly as her body would allow. She pulled on his arm and he rounded on her.

"What do you think—"

She made a sound in frustration and slapped him across the face. He froze and she used her grip on his arm to swing him back toward the fight. She pointed at the hilt of her knife, still sticking from the thing's shoulder blade.

Assan stared at her.

"Are you kidding me? That's impossible."

Lil simply pointed again.

Assan sighed and rubbed his free hand over his face, watching as Kima did her best to hold off the thing.

"Okay, I'll try, but you have to get it to be still for long enough to line up the shot."

Lil nodded and headed for Kima and the thing. She could see that Kima was slowing and it would only be a moment before the thing killed her. She moved to its other side and picked up some larger stones from the ground. Lil forced the wound on her hand open again and called the painful fire back to her hand but this time she pushed it into the rocks rather than letting it rest in her hand.

The rock exploded when it struck the thing, knocking it forward. It turned and moved toward her. She held up the second stone and it hesitated. Assan took the shot in that moment and she knew he had succeeded as the creature let out a loud high-pitched scream.

Its body shook and limbs reached for Lil, who rolled out of the way. She hissed as she rolled onto the bleeding wounds on her side. The thing turned back to Assan and Lil forced her weary body to rise. Reaching into her pocket, she pulled free the knot of wood and one of the pieces of the root from its bag of velvety darkness. As the thing slammed Assan down to the ground and wrapped its hands around his neck, she reached them and pushed the knot of wood and root into the wide gash of pink in its armor where her knife had been.

Lil dredged up whatever raw power was left in her exhausted body and slammed it into the creature's wound as well. It let go of Assan and turned to reach for her but she had already fallen to the ground and rolled away. It did not follow. It had more important things to worry about.

Its body shook and shivered, but since it was facing her, Lil did not see the moment it started. She did see the branches that began to curve around its shoulders, though. And the bark that began to grow over its form. The thing tore at the bark with hand and spike but it did not matter. The tree continued to grow at a rapid rate. Soon the bottom half of its body was covered and rooted into the ground. The bark was an odd mix of light and dark just as the knot had been. As its face was covered by bark the thing met her eyes and Lil could swear she read sorrow and thanks in its gaze.

As the tree finished growing around it, Lil smiled and passed out.

# BYRON

Byron ran his fingers through his hair over and over. He had no idea what he was doing anymore. There had been a time when there was a plan and a purpose, but he'd come so far since then and he worried he had lost his way. Ruth's spirit had faded, no longer there, inside him, ready to offer advice. Now only her power remained entwined with his own. He was alone.

He turned back to his ill-chosen allies. They were reclining on the couch, their injuries healed, and their arrogance returned. Byron regretted his decision to grant them some small measure of his power. He had not wanted to leave them unprotected and Ruth's power was easy to parcel out to others.

"You fools. I told you over and over this is a different world in more ways than just looks."

"We were booooooored."

This was the only thing that Bastion and Melisande had said since he had saved their worthless lives. The Antes were obviously on the run from something. Why else would they be in the House of the Madame in the majority 'dant neighborhood of The Drowned? Even if the Hunt had not been loose in the streets since he arrived, he would have noticed the oddity of it.

He snapped his fingers and they both screamed and slumped off the couch, boneless and limp: the power that he had laid into their bones was now ripping itself from their frames. He pulled the power out halfway and then allowed it to snap back into their bodies.

They made little noises and began to gulp air.

"You will listen to me."

They both continued to gasp, and he stomped over to them.

Crouching and reaching forward, he grabbed them both by their hair and brought their faces close to his own.

"Let me make this very clear. You are only of use to me if I can rely on you. If you do not listen to what I say I will have no problem stripping you of my power and leaving you on the streets to die horrible, painful deaths."

There was fear in their eyes, and a growing hatred. He was used to hatred, but he knew it meant their usefulness was now on a deadline. They would turn on him. Though not tonight.

They both nodded and Byron abruptly released them so their heads fell back against the floor with painful thumps. He looked at them. Even in this moment he did not know why he had brought them along. A part of himself he was long used to ignoring tried to inform him that the reason was loneliness, but he turned his attention away.

There was no way to change what had to be and therefore no point in feeling bad about it. Instead he focused on their next step. His contact should have gotten a message to him by now. The continued silence left him worried.

"My allies should be arriving very soon," Byron said.

"You've been saying that the whole time we've been here." The words were somewhat disrespectful but the tone was subservient enough, so he merely stared at Melisande until she looked away.

"Yes, well, the presence of the Hunt has most likely made it difficult for them to make contact."

Byron had left the House of the Madame since they had arrived, though he had forbidden the two of them from doing so. He had walked the streets and seen the patrols of Antes, moving through the city. He'd also seen both species leaving every day in small clumps. The Antes had a plan, he had no doubt. The humans did not, as far as he knew, so why would they be packing? Where did they think they could go?

He had many questions but no way to satisfy his curiosity until he was contacted. In many ways, he had the Organization to thank for making contact with his allies in Zebub. The time he spent under their . . . reeducation had left him with a lot of time wishing to be outside his body. With power, sometimes wishes came true. By the time they had deemed him ready to serve as a useful tool for the

Organization? He'd already had his own contacts. His own plans. His own destiny.

If his own world would treat him so harshly, then his world needed to be changed. And no world had ever been changed without a few sacrifices along the way.

The Door knocked and stuck their head in without a welcome. It was their house after all.

"The Hunt has arrived. You will all come down for an inspection."

Before they left, Byron shot Melisande and Bastion a look.

"You will say nothing in front of The Hunt. You will pretend you have no voice or I will rip my power from your bones. Then I will rip your bones from your body."

It was a crude threat, but they were crude followers. They moved to the main room of the House and saw The Door looking stunning as always, a bloodred sheath of fabric wrapped about them that matched the drawn lines on their hands and delicate bare shoulders. They stood facing over a dozen Antes. Byron recognized half of the forms in front of him—the ones that were similar to other Antes who had crossed over on his watch—but the other half he had never seen before. They encompassed every shape and size; there were two figures barely two feet tall that looked like masses of red twine, tangled and dripping blood, that had been twisted into vaguely arachnid forms; a giant golden serpent sporting a human face; a wheel of eyes and a cyclone of air; a ruddy-skinned giant hovered in the back, its face dominated by one large circular eye that constantly watered and leaked. Some were blocked from view by the ones he could see but Byron assumed their presence based on the odd glimpse of limb or eye as they shifted.

Byron felt the shift in the air as Bastion and Melisande went stiff behind him. He could feel their eyes boring into his back, as well as the tension and fear they both now radiated. Perhaps he had been wrong to shield them from the outside. A little fear would have been more useful than his unheeded warnings.

"You are currently the only guests in the building. They would like to ask you some questions."

Byron did not bat an eye at being called the only guests. The Door met his eyes without fear and Byron doubted there would be any evidence to contradict The Door's story.

"Of course. As the Ruling Courts wish," Byron answered, voice steady.

He glanced back at Bastion and Melisande and let his power flow into his voice.

"My servants will of course cooperate as well and do whatever I say."

Both of them nodded decisively. He could see the anger and resentment in their eyes. Granting them a trace of his power would make them more aware of when he used it but there was no room for any dissention now. He deliberately did not close the loop of power. He could have given the command duration or limit but leaving it open like this kept it linked to him. He would have to maintain it from his own power but it would release only when he allowed it.

The wheel of eyes rolled forward slowly, circling him.

"This is Killa'ila," The Door said as they stepped back.

*And them.* The voice sounded in Byron's head and he showed none of his surprise.

The Ante's eyes all flicked to Bastion and Melisande behind him.

"They are mine. Not very smart, but I cannot abandon them yet. They may yet be of some value to me. They know nothing that I do not know."

The mass of eyes came closer, stared into his own with a dozen of its own of varying colors and shapes. It was not the odd ones that made Byron uncomfortable, not the eyes that looked like jewels or the one that looked like lips wrapped around eyes rather than an eyelid. No, it was the more human eyes that shook him. The dark brown eyes that reminded him of Matthias, and the black one that made him think of Ruth. He fell into those eyes and was back in the house with Ruth, both of them naked and painted with each other's blood.

Sacrifices were made.

Then he was back in the opulent, gold-accented room, and the wheel of eyes was rolling away.

*They know nothing of the ones we hunt.*

The other Antes took its word and slowly began to file out. Some looked back at Byron and his minions, but he had no experience interpreting the many different faces and expressions. The Door, however, was smiling, and Byron got the feeling they had known how this whole thing was going to turn out all along.

Two of the Antes stayed behind even as the others left. One resembled a heptagram balanced on one of its points, made of something thin, white, and furry. The other was the golden serpent with the human face. Its face looked like a stereotypical pornographer from the seventies; a large bushy blond mustache adorned its upper lip. Its cheeks were spotted with tufts of hair and the smile on its face was pure smarm.

The serpent spoke clearly. There was no cartoonish hiss to its words. Just a dry airless quality as if they were said with little breath behind them.

"We apologize for the wait, Byron of San Francisco. The Hunt is taking precedence, but we are aware of your presence and your failures."

Byron straightened and opened his mouth to defend himself.

"I'll have you—"

The serpent spoke over him as if he had said nothing at all, rising up on the coil of its tail so that it towered over all of them. "There have been failures on this side as well. We have lost the girl. The old man is now a necessity instead of a liability."

Byron nodded.

"There is more planning to be done. We will come for you this evening and escort you to a safer space."

The heptagram said nothing. Byron wondered if it could even speak. Both of the Antes turned toward the exit and paused when they saw The Door standing there.

The serpent studied The Door for a long moment and The Door, who it seemed they all had forgotten was still in the room, simply stared back and made no move one way or the other. The serpent swayed back and forth but The Door simply raised an eyebrow until the serpent finally flung itself out the door. The heptagram unfolded itself into a long thin rope of white fur and followed.

The Door studied him for a moment.

"So you will be leaving soon." It was not a question but a statement.

Byron nodded and turned to his minions, carefully closing off the power still flowing to them, allowing them free will again.

"What was that?" Melisande whispered it.

"Which part?" Byron asked.

"We know you said there are other things here but—we didn't think they would be—" Bastion tried to finish the thought, but struggled himself.

"So alien?" Byron asked. Now that contact had been made some of the tension in his shoulders eased. "Back to the room now." He had forgotten The Door was there once. He would not do so again. They were playing a game of their own and he had no idea what it was. He was sure that the two Antes he had run into earlier were the ones being hunted, but the Ante covered in eyes had somehow not seen the knowledge in his head.

Was it something to do with the ritual? With Ruth's sacrifice? There must have been a reason that image hit him so strongly as it delved into his mind. Once they were ensconced in their room again, he turned to the two humans.

"You will say nothing about the earlier incident with the two Antes and the children to anyone. Do you understand me?"

He did not lace his voice with command. He thought about it but decided that this would be a test. They had no contact, and no one to tell. But if they tried he would know it was time to dispose of them. Even if The Hunt had not been looking for the two Antes from earlier, which he highly doubted, they were running from something, and that kind of knowledge was always valuable to someone.

He had no illusions about the deal he had made or the trustworthiness of those he had made the deal with. He had a little leverage but this could mean much more. Byron was no fool. They would cease to be allies as soon as he outlived his usefulness. They were using each other, though he was sure the Antes believed him to be sincere. It was part of his charm—a more subtle effect than the one they all saw him use—and one he was thrilled to know also worked on Antes.

For now.

# SAN FRANCISCO

# ERIK

How do you avoid a ghost?

Distraction and a good dose of "la la la, I can't hear you!".

Eventually Daniel got tired of his constant silence and would leave. Erik had enough to deal with and the emotional toll of having his dead ex around was stifling and distracting, to say the least. The guilt was still crushing and, according to Matthias, was most likely what was affecting his healing powers. He certainly had enough to do without dealing with the emotional fallout of Daniel's death. The time for crossing over into Zebub was approaching rapidly, and he was becoming more and more nervous.

He filled his time reading as many files as he could get his hands on, both from the Organization and the Agency. Reading the files from the two competing bureaucracies was intriguing. Both had extensive files on The Blooded inside and outside of their respective groups. The differing cultures and priorities came through in many small ways in their reports. The Agency was focused on controlling information and limiting exposure, and given its governmental connections, it was far more rigid and hierarchal, and very concerned with policy and procedure. The Organization seemed more concerned with gathering power and knowledge—as protection against the Agency, or for its own sake? Given the trust issues so many independents seemed to have towards the Organization, and recent revelations about hidden connections to The Angelics, this seemed like a legitimate question. The less strict culture that the Organization fostered meant it was more than likely that individuals in the Organization had competing and hidden agendas. This was one reason why an outsider like Erik had been given so much power—to ferret out just how widespread the hidden alliance with The Angelics was.

Erik read the files on himself first, of course, followed by all the people he knew. There had really only been two big surprises in those files. One was the revelation that his grandma had been pretty big in the Bay Area Blooded scene during the fifties and sixties. Reading about her exploits . . . well, he had learned a lot but also had a lot of questions.

The second surprise was less positive: Tae had been lying to him. The boy he'd been prepared to call a friend wasn't weak and in need of training to compensate for his lack of power. In fact, the Organization had yet to find an upper limit to his powers. Since he had learned this, all of his texts from Tae had gone ignored, which was why when the theme song for *Buffy the Vampire Slayer* rang through his room, he didn't move.

Only when he finished reading the entire file on the Anzu bloodline did he look at the screen.

It was from Matthias. Another part of his life that Erik would rather avoid. The last few days had been difficult between them, as they struggled to find a balance between former Counselor and Aspirant to . . . friends? Something else. It had been easier to limit their interactions to business only. Not that their relationship hadn't always been business, but Erik made it a point to ignore hints of anything else now. Matthias was clearly not interested, and Erik would not continue to feed into some impossible happy ending.

daya and i are on our way over

Erik sighed as he read the text from Matthias and the doorbell rang downstairs immediately afterward.

He met his mother in the entryway.

"It's probably your grandmother. It would be just like her to show up a day early to catch us off guard."

"I think it's Matthias and Daya, actually." Erik replied.

Immediately his mother's shoulders lost some of their tension. He hurried to the door as she disappeared behind him with a call out:

"I'll leave you to it."

Erik wondered why she was leaving. His mother had sat in on every other meeting related to the Agency, which she and his grandmother would be in charge of in his stead. He shook his head. It was probably nothing. Every time she did something odd now Erik wondered if it had some connection to her powers manifesting? She was still so secretive about what gifts her awakening had granted her.

He opened the door to Matthias and Daya, the latter with a bag over her shoulder made of dark purple velvet. Erik stared at her for a second. They had not truly spoken or been in such a small group together since their blow-up underground. He held no ill-will towards her—they had both been under massive stress. But he still did not like how she had spoken to him or the things she had implied. He nodded at her, keeping his face blank.

She returned the gesture although the blankness quickly turned to a grimace as she looked over at Matthias.

"Can we come in?" Matthias asked.

Erik moved to the side and let them into the entryway.

"What do you guys need?" Erik asked, his eyes being drawn back to the bag. There was something about it that made him uncomfortable. "Where's Elana?"

"We didn't want her around for this."

Erik put his back to the door and looked at them both. They were hovering carefully out of reach. He rolled his eyes. "For what, exactly?"

"Let's talk in the living room." Matthias smiled.

Erik rolled his eyes again. If he kept doing it he was worried they would end up permanently pointing in the wrong direction. He gestured toward the kitchen, as a small act of defiance, and followed them in.

"First off, is he here?"

Erik knew who Matthias meant and he shook his head, using the motion to take a final glance around the room. Sometimes Daniel snuck up on him and by the time he noticed the ghost, he always had the feeling Daniel had been watching him for a very long time.

"Good. We're still worried about him."

Erik was worried too but he also didn't doubt that the ghost was Daniel. He was worried about what death had done to Daniel.

"So, we want you to do something for us."

Erik narrowed his eyes. "What?" He sat down at the small table and they sat across from him.

Daya putting the velvet bag on the table between them. The bag was lumpy and oddly shapen and he could smell the faint scent of wet dirt.

She pulled it open and took out a white plastic plate that was stained yellow along the edge and covered with painted symbols. Then she reached in again and pulled out a skull.

"Shitballs." The skull looked fake to Erik because it was so white. Skulls weren't that clean and pearly, were they?

"This is an old working. We went to visit my Tia Heloise to get it. Neither of us have this kind of specialty," Daya explained.

"What are you guys talking about?" Erik asked.

"The dead," Matthias answered.

"Yeah, I got that part. What about the dead?" Erik snarked back.

"This will allow us to speak with the spirit of Daniel," Daya said.

"We can already do that, though," Erik said slowly.

"This will summon his spirit into this vessel." Daya patted the skull, which she carefully placed on the plate facing Erik. She then pulled out a scrap of orange fabric, stained with blood, then a handful of seeds and a white candle.

A suspicion started to build.

"So, any skull will do for this?" Erik asked.

They looked at each other and lowered their eyes.

"Solange in an elevator! Really?" Erik looked at the skull in front of him, now sure it was Daniel's. They both just looked at him and waited for him to say yes or no.

Daniel's body, along with most of the other dead, had appeared after the destruction of the tree. Whatever explanation had been given to his family Erik didn't know. They had made it clear that they had no interest in allowing him to attend the funeral. Erik could not blame them, even if it was for the wrong reasons. Daniel was dead because of him. He did not deserve to mourn with those who lost him, because someone had turned Daniel into a weapon. A weapon aimed at Erik.

"I guess if you went to all the trouble of grave robbing, how can I say no?"

He saw Matthias grimace at his tone and looked to Daya, who did not meet his eyes as she lit the candle.

"Put your hands on the skull."

Erik hesitated for only a moment before doing what she asked.

"And call out his full name."

"Daniel Crispus Moorehead."

They all waited. Erik felt weird doing this in the middle of the day in his yellow and white kitchen. It should be midnight in a graveyard, right? When the skull rocked back and forth under his hands he yelped and jumped, his chair sliding back a foot. The skull shook back and forth again, slowly rocking and rotating on the plate, taking in Erik, Matthias, and Daya.

*What am I doing in this vessel?*

The voice was Daniel's but it was truly dead, no emotion or inflection to the words at all. The skull spun again and its empty sockets focused on Erik.

*Were you this desperate to see me again? I would have returned shortly. Or was this for them?*

Words that would have been flirtatious or mocking became menacing and ominous when stripped of all tone. Erik looked at the other two.

"Well, what was the point of this?"

They both ignored him and Matthias focused on the skull, which swung around to face him as he spoke.

"What is your name?"

Erik frowned at the question but held his tongue.

*Daniel Crispus Moorehead.* There was a pause. *Ah, now I see.*

Erik looked at the skull as it turned its empty eye sockets on him and answered the question on his face.

*I cannot lie like this.*

Erik looked to Matthais and he would not meet his eyes though Daya did so defiantly. Erik felt a flare of anger, not because they had done this but because they hadn't filled him in. Did they trust him at all anymore?

"What exactly are you two looking for?"

Neither of them answered him and, rather than repeat his question, he sat silently as they began to question the skull. He sat there as they asked questions about his relationship with Daniel. He sat through the recounting of Daniel's death, from Daniel's perspective; the dry emotionless voice reciting the terror that Daniel had felt. It sent shivers up his spine.

"Are we done yet?" Erik asked, his tone clipped.

Matthias looked at him and winced at whatever was showing on Erik's face.

"Almost. Just one last question," Matthias replied.

Daya interrupted. "But—"

"Daya. One more question."

She made a face but leaned back in her chair and didn't push it any further.

"What are you doing here?"

The skull shook for a moment.

*I am here to watch over Erik.*

It should have been an "awwwwww" moment; instead, when it came through the non-existent yet somehow scratchy throat of the skull on the table, it turned into an "oh Jesus, fuck no" situation.

"On whose orders?"

*No one's but my own.*

Daya and Matthias shared a look and then Daya snuffed out the candle and the skull very lightly clattered back down, but shattered the plate anyway.

"Tia said that might happen. She's gonna make me work that off for sure."

Matthias snorted. Daya packed up everything she had brought and left with a goodbye for both of them. He and Matthias were left facing each other, alone. The awkwardness descended almost immediately. Matthias broke the silence before it stretched too long.

"I'm meeting with a few independents from Oakland in an hour, would you like to come along?"

"Yes."

They headed toward the door, on more solid footing now that they had a mission to focus on. Matthias had been taking Erik around, introducing him to as many of the independents around the Bay Area as would agree to meet with him. After all, he was an eighteen-year-old who had taken over the office of one of their enemies. He really couldn't blame some of them for being cautious.

They got into the Mini Cooper that Erik was pretty sure Matthias just considered his now, and Matthias guided it out onto the street. He saw a couple of photographers in the yard and frowned at them. He hadn't had much problem with paparazzi lately. A stern warning from people in dark suits did wonders in scaring most off.

Matthias was silent until they were on the Bay Bridge and Erik busied himself by gently feeling out the forces around the car. Now that he was aware of it he found it soothing to fall into the easy rhythm of the speed and the mass of the car cutting through the air resistance.

"You should forgive Tae."

"I will. Eventually," Erik responded immediately.

"It's not his fault he's not trustworthy," Matthias responded.

Erik raised an eyebrow at him. He was mad at Tae for lying about the level of his ability but Erik realized it wasn't completely rational. They had barely known each other. Why would Tae tell a practical stranger everything about himself? It still stung.

"He's a seer." Matthias shrugged as if that explained everything.

"Yeah. I'm gonna need you to elaborate on that."

"Seers don't have the best reputation. They can see a lot, but they're not necessarily the best with interpretation and they become . . . focused on their vision, either trying to make it come true or trying to avert it. It makes them chaotic."

Erik nodded as they pulled off the freeway and turned into west Oakland.

"I'm not saying he would actively hurt you or anything, but he won't put your relationship first."

Erik looked away. "Well, who does?"

They rode the rest of the way in brittle silence. They parked on the street and walked into a small diner called Pretty Lady. As they entered, the older Asian woman behind the counter smiled at them and gestured for them to take a seat.

"We're actually meeting some people," Matthias answered.

She nodded and went back to serving those at the counter. Erik looked around and knew who they were here to meet as soon as he saw them. They were seated in the back-corner booth. Physically they weren't dressed differently than the other customers; they were smiling and joking with one another, and they hadn't noticed Erik and Matthias yet.

There were three of them, two Black women and a Native man, all dressed similarly in jeans, boots, and t-shirts: things they could move in easily. As Matthias approached them, they looked over almost in unison. They smiled warmly at Matthias, but as they spotted Erik, the smiles became more practiced. False.

Erik nodded to them as he moved to sit in the booth opposite them.

Matthias seated himself next and one of the women spoke.

"So, this is the 'Primo'?" Her hair was crafted into a faux-fro-hawk pulled and slicked up. She had dark skin and eyes and a round face that looked joyful but had hard edges. As Erik looked at her he felt a force around her. It was almost alive. It felt like being watched. The gaze felt predatory and cunning. Animal-like. Sometimes it hovered over the woman's shoulder and sometimes it was at her feet.

Erik flinched at the title—Primo. He wasn't used to it, and he knew the Organization had meant it as an insult. At first it sounded like a joke, but they were basically calling him a prima donna. He didn't know what it was supposed to prove except that some of the members of the Organization had the maturity level of junior high boys. He wasn't insulted by it. He just thought it sounded ridiculous.

"Yes, Citrine. This is Erik."

"I heard he was young but damn, he can't even drink yet." The man had a heavy Southern accent, which Erik hadn't expected to encounter in Oakland. He had gorgeous dark skin and a heart-shaped face. His hair was dark and up in a man-bun, which automatically killed any attraction Erik might have felt. He caught a hint of a tattoo coming up from the collar of his shirt. It looked like a piece of map, with lines that crisscrossed each other in thick black ink.

"I can drink just fine."

"Not legally."

Erik shrugged. "What the hell has the law done for me lately?"

The man laughed and pushed his hand forward. Erik shook it; his grip was firm but the man didn't play that macho bullshit of trying to hurt the other person.

"Amen, brother. I'm Samuel."

Erik hated the assumed familiarity of being called brother, but did not let it show on his face.

"Nice to meet you."

The last woman looked younger than the other two. Closer to Erik's own age. Her hair was down in two long side braids that reached her waist. She cocked her head to the side and studied Erik. He met her gaze and held back a yelp as her eyes slit vertically in the middle and started to peel back to reveal pure-gold orbs.

Then she blinked and they were gone and her head was no longer tilted. If Erik's last month had not been so completely unbelievable he might have thought he imagined it.

"I like him," she said to the other two and turned her attention back to Erik. "I'm Reina."

"Erik."

Then their attention was on Matthias.

"Well, you called this meeting, Matthias," Citrine said with eyebrows raised. "Did you just want to show off your former Padawan here?"

Reina snorted.

Matthias ignored both and simply started the spiel. Erik sat there as Matthias explained about the darkness, the fight in the mall, and the fact that they were going to the Angelic's home turf. Erik sat through the exclamations of surprise and horror and the automatic denials. He had heard it all before. Matthias was spreading the news around, trying to get the information out. He had also been encouraging people to work together more.

After the first meeting Erik had attended he asked Matthias why he was doing what he was doing. Matthias had explained as he drove them back into San Francisco proper.

"I hate to admit it and if you ever repeat this I'll just call you a liar, but the one thing the Organization really does have going for it, and the Agency too for that matter? It is that they have a singular focus and goal. Independents sometimes form long-term cells but they're rare, and all too often our paths rip us apart again. War is coming. If we survive I don't want the Organization and Agency to take control just because they're better organized."

Erik had nodded at that and begun to accompany him regularly.

Erik was shaken back to the present as Daniel came through the wall of the diner and hovered over the three independents across from them and screamed, "What the fuck!"

Erik did his best not to react to the voice that only he could hear. The last thing he needed was to start speaking aloud and look like he was already cracking under the pressure, or worse, have to explain about Daniel. He didn't need to go back through it for a second time today.

"I mean really, you just sat there and let them use my skull for some weird ceremony?"

Erik winced. Matthias noticed his movement and glanced over with a question in his eyes. Erik shook his head and gestured for Matthias to go on.

"What exactly did you think you were going to learn?"

Erik jumped, allowing his hand to fly to his pocket. He pulled out his cell phone, tilting it so that no one but he could see the screen and quickly pressed it against his ear.

"Yeah. Hold on for one second."

He turned to the rest of the table. "Sorry, I have to take this outside. I'll be back as soon as possible."

Matthias looked confused but got up and allowed Erik to slide out of the booth and head out of the diner. Once outside, Erik turned his back to the large windows that made up the diner's street facing walls. Daniel floated in the center of his gaze, still in his prison jumpsuit.

"What the hell? You know I can't answer you in public," Erik said.

Daniel rolled his eyes and floated closer. "I was in the middle of some important shit when I just faded from existence."

"Important shit?" Erik narrowed his eyes at the ghost. "What important shit were you up to exactly, when only I can see you?"

"I never said only you could see me, I just explained why you could. And who said that my business was on this side of the veil?" The words were hissed out.

They stared silently at one another for a while. Erik gave in first this time. He was right anyway. That young woman Zaha had been able to see him.

"They showed up at my house without telling me their plan. I just decided to let them go through with it."

Daniel was silent for another minute before he spoke, his voice much gentler.

"I'm sorry. I shouldn't have snapped at you."

"Yeah, I'm busy now anyway. I'm leaving in a few days."

All expression dropped from Daniel's translucent face, where Erik kept his gaze focused. Daniel was still in the prison jumpsuit and still with the ripped-up chest. According to Elana he should be able to control that by now but Erik didn't want to bring it up, so he just kept his eyes away from it.

"Are you coming with me?"

Daniel was silent and just like that began to fade away. Erik took a deep breath and went back into the diner, schooling his face to show nothing. He slid back into the booth, this time on the outside. Matthias looked and him with a sad smile as if he knew exactly Erik had been talking to.

"You weren't on your phone. Who were you talking to?" Reina asked bluntly.

Erik sputtered and hesitated as he tried to come up with something. "How did you know?"

Reina smiled. "Part of my power is I can feel energy really well, see it even. I know what a cell-phone call near me feels like."

They were all looking at him now, eyes narrowed and lips pursed. Matthias stepped in.

"He was talking to one of our allies. That's neither here nor there. What I'm here for is to let you guys know that something big is coming, and we need to be able to call on each other if we need help."

Slowly the three independents looked away from Erik and back at each other. The expressions on their faces tilted this way and that as they had a conversation through that alone. Finally Reina turned to them. "Okay, we trust you, Matthias. You've got a good rep; if you say some big and ugly darkness is coming to eat us up, it seems better to believe you and hope you're wrong than the other way around. What do you need?"

"Nothing right now and this goes both ways. While we're gone consider the resources of the Agency in San Francisco at your disposal," Matthias offered.

They all looked pretty suspect at that.

"Hettie Jayl and her daughter Dayida are going to be taking charge of it while we're gone," Erik explained.

"Hettie's coming to town?" Citrine asked, a smile lighting her face for the first time.

The other two were also smiling widely and Erik couldn't help but ask.

"You know my grandma?"

They were looking at him in unison again but their expressions were far less hostile.

"Hettie's your grandmother?"

Erik nodded and the reception in the booth became warmer. Suddenly they were treating him as if they were the best of friends. They stayed, talking about contacting each other when in need and just shooting the shit for another half an hour. It wasn't until they were back in the car heading across the bridge that Erik asked.

"Why do they all know my grandma?"

Matthias smiled. "Hettie was a big deal. Still is. When she was here she worked for the Organization but was always willing to help anyone who asked. She was a powerhouse. Maybe the most powerful Blooded in the city. Those guys? Hettie probably helped their parents as well as them. She was like an old-school knight. She would help anyone who needed her services, no matter who they were."

He went quiet and Erik thought about what Matthias had said. It fit with the things that he had read. He loved his grandmother but he didn't see her much. They had been in L.A. most of his life and then by the time they moved up to the the Bay Area she had already left and was traveling the world. He saw her at least once or twice a year but only for a few days before she was off again.

"Then your grandfather died."

Erik looked over at Matthias. His grandfather had died before he was born. All he knew was that his grandma had really loved him and still got this sad look in her eyes when she talked about him. His mother was the same way. She couldn't talk about her father without crying and so Erik didn't ask.

He barely knew anything about the man.

"He wasn't Blooded, as far as anyone knew. He went crazy one night and attacked your grandmother. She had to kill him."

"Holy fucking shit," Erik whispered.

"No one knows the details but Hettie blamed the Organization for it. She quit them the next day and became independent. She stayed in the Bay Area for a while after that but most knew it was only a matter of time before she left. They'd lived here their whole lives. Every street held a memory of her husband."

Erik nodded and they were silent all the way back home.

# HETTIE

Hettie smiled at the stewardess as she stepped off the plane. The woman, fully thirty years her junior, blushed. She moved down the ramp slowly, allowing the young woman to take in her form. She still had it. She moved through the airport swiftly. She had not bothered to bring any luggage but her carry-on. The bright turquoise of her dress and head wrap were their own camouflage. People would remember the shapely older woman in the bright blue but no real details about her.

She walked out of the airport and took the first cab she saw.

"Take me into the city, just drive around for a while. It's been awhile since I've been back and I need to take a look around."

The man was young and his pale skin was riddled with red scars from childhood acne, which he tried to hide with a patchy black beard that simply made it look worse. Under it all she could see a sort of rugged appeal. A harsh handsomeness. He opened his mouth to protest.

Hettie lifted her sunglasses and the dark black of her eyes met the light brown of his and pulled him under. She smiled and let her awareness fill the car. His eyes went wide with worship. She could smell his arousal. She hated to be so forward with her power but she didn't have the time to argue.

He took her into the city past San Francisco State University. The car curled through the hedge-bound streets where the wealthy pretended the rest of the world did not exist. She lowered the window and took deep breaths through her nose. The sea was all over this city. It was one reason she loved it. Even in the dead center of the city, as far from the water as you could get in San Francisco, when the wind was right she could still smell it. She felt its pull. She had not returned to the city of her birth except for very brief visits. Grief and the changes she had seen coming to the city had driven her from the place she loved. She'd gone west to the ocean, spending more time over water than on land in the last twenty years.

She could spend an hour or more simply driving around and reacquainting herself with the city but there were important things happening. She had one stop to make before it all began.

"Take me to the Columbarium," Hettie said quietly.

"Yes ma'am, but they're already closed for the day," the driver explained while giving her a wide smile.

"I know. It's fine. I just need to pay my respects."

"Of course." He nodded and turned back to the road.

"Can you put on the radio?" She did not want the silence to fill the time before her visit.

"Of course. Any requests?"

"Anything."

To Hettie's delight, the rest of the ride was filled with classical music.

She tipped him generously and sent him on his way. Her effect on him would fade with distance and time. The main building was already closed but she wasn't going to let that stop her. She placed her hand over the lock on the door and concentrated until the metal begin to crumble beneath her fingers. She reached through the new hole in the door. The only evidence of the lock's previous existence was the streaks of red rust that stained the wood where it had been attached.

She opened the door and walked inside. It was not hard to find her husband. Hettie could find it in the dark if need be. She traced her fingers over the engraved words.

Z.J. JAYL 1945–1999.

He had been a wonderful husband and father. She'd always suspected he was Blooded but he never awakened. She'd had his initials used rather than his full first and second names, though his mother had fought her on it. Z.J. did not like his full name. Zachariah Jahzerah was a mouthful but his mother had thought biblical names would protect him from something she could or would never name.

It was one of the reasons Hettie thought he might have been Blooded. One of the lines that disappeared into a miasma of self-hatred and denial. Maybe he would have awakened if the Organization hadn't interfered. She frowned thinking of them, but then smiled at the coup her grandson had pulled on them.

Hettie lowered herself to her knees, keeping her hand on the plaque, and let a prayer slip from her lips. A prayer to her ancestors. A prayer for her husband. A prayer to the spirit that had granted her a measure of her power and grace. When she was done, tears ran down her face but sunk back into her skin when they reached her chin. An endless cycle.

She left the building and made her way to the street and hailed another cab. It was time to see the rest of her family.

When the car pulled up to her daughter's house she took a deep breath, pulling her power back into herself. She had swum in Mami Wata's waters so long that even when not actively calling, she leaked all over the place. Dayida could always see it and it tended to put the girl on edge. Hettie thought she should just get over it, but Dayida had not welcomed advice from her for many years. Maybe not ever.

She knocked on the door, and in seconds her only child was standing before her in the doorway. She and Hettie were of a height; taller than average. If Hettie had done one thing right with Dayida it was to show her daughter that their height and their wide shoulders were beautiful, and not something to hunch and hide.

"Hettie."

Hettie sighed.

"Dayida."

She did not try to hug her daughter but stepped inside when Dayida gestured her in.

"Where is Erik?" Hettie asked.

"He's out with Matthias now but should be back in a little bit. They were off to meet some independents for introductions."

Hettie nodded and looked at her daughter. She had never been that close to Dayida. Raising her had been Z.J.'s job, and when he died, well, Dayida had been mostly grown anyway. Hettie's powers provided for most of her needs and she had neglected Dayida after Z.J.'s death. Her daughter's presence reminded her too much of the father who had desperately wanted a child.

There had been no coming back from the rift and most would find it shameful that Hettie didn't try that much. Hettie did not but others would. She was happy to take some of the blame but she had never really wanted children. That was all Z.J. Hettie had only ever wanted to help others. That was her calling. Not child-rearing.

"How have you been?"

Dayida pressed her lips together before answering. "Okay. I have a show coming up."

"That's great."

They were saved from more awkwardness by the entry of her grandson and Matthias. Erik came in the door, looking left and right, as if expecting someone other than his mother to be inside. When he saw Hettie, his eyes widened with delight and he moved to embrace her.

"Hey Gram."

"Hello, baby. I'm so proud of you! Only awakened for a little more than a month and already killed an Angelic and took over the San Francisco branch of the Agency."

Erik smiled and shrugged, hugging her again.

"It's so good to see you, Gram." He pulled away suddenly and Hettie glanced to the side to see her daughter frowning at them both.

She rolled her own eyes and pulled Matthias into a hug.

"Hey, Ms. Jayl."

"You know to call me Hettie."

Matthias smiled and rubbed his neck. The boy was always uncomfortable calling her by her name. She spared him and turned back to her grandson, putting her hands on his shoulders and drawing his attention back.

"Tell me what's been going on here, because I have news."

Erik quickly filled her in on everything. His phone call had been purposefully vague, but he filled in all the details she asked about as they moved to sit in the living room. Matthias and her daughter left and came back with tea.

Erik had never been allowed the luxury of being a child, but now her grandson was actually acting as an adult. She could see the strain of the transition in the corners of his mouth and the tightness around his eyes. It was a lot, to go from being responsible only for yourself to being on a frontline fight for everyone's lives. He had minimal training but, from what Hettie was hearing, great instincts.

"The darkness has already made inroads in our world," Hettie said with no preamble.

Matthias's teacup clattered onto its saucer and Dayida's hand shook as she took a sip.

"Where?" Erik asked, his eyes closed.

"Kiev, Madrid, Morocco, and New York, that I know of so far. The exact location doesn't matter, because the attacks eat a few people, in one case a building, and disappear soon after. As it is, both the Organization and the Agency are trying to keep it quiet. Everyone wants the answers to be somcthing 'normal,' so most are being routine building demolitions. That smokescreen will only last so long, though, and it's only a matter of time before someone labels one of the incidents a terrorist attack. And then . . ." Hettie trailed off and Erik swallowed. "On top of all that, something more is happening in New York City. Something is picking off people, Blooded and non, at very rapid rates. More than the darkness would account for. In addition, they've lost contact with their mirror city—Anoan."

"And you didn't let anyone know about this?" Dayida asked, voice tight.

Hettie turned to face her daughter. "I let those I trusted in each city know, and they will spread the word to those who need to know," she answered.

"How do you even know all this?" Dayida asked, voice raised in challenge.

Hettie let her power flow to the surface, knew that her irises were changing color from their natural brown to the dark blue-black of deep water, the glow of adapted life sparking and dying randomly in their depths.

"Where the water flows, I am there. Where it rains, where people cry, even in piss and spit, I am there. I am the waters of life." Then the power left her eyes and she let out a laugh at their stunned expressions. "I'm kidding. Mostly. I went through all of the cities on my way here. There were things I needed to check on in person, since who knows how long it will be until I am traveling again. I have allies in each, though many of them in New York have gone missing."

"Fuck." Matthias was up and on his phone. They all watched him walk out of the room.

Hettie let the boy go and turned to Erik. The smile she had for her grandson was always genuine. She had not taken to motherhood, but grandmotherhood she took to like a duck to water. Perhaps it was because she saw more of herself in Erik. The need for something bigger. The embracing of the new and different. She saw herself at eighteen.

"So, a berserker, but a smart and self-healing one? You get the healing from me, you know. The healing touch has always been my main gift. I don't know where the other stuff comes from, though. It could be your grandfather."

She saw Dayida flinch out of the corner of her eye but plowed on.

"I always suspected his family was Blooded, but at some point they began rejecting it and replaced it with intense religious fervor. They were quick to talk about witches and unnatural powers. I could never figure out the bloodline though."

"They think I inherited it from Robert."

Hettie could not help the combination of snort and laugh that escaped her. "Well, at least that boy was good for something in the end."

"Oh, he was good for something else too, right Mom?" Erik asked with a pointed look at his mother.

Dayida glanced back and forth between Hettie and Erik. To Hettie's eyes it looked like she was trying to decide which one of them she wanted to punch first.

"Erik, there's no need to tell her anything," Dayida said through clenched teeth.

"Mom. Matthias and I are going to be gone for who knows how long. Someone should know. Someone that's here with you, and since you're going to work with Grandma at the Agency, it only makes sense."

Dayida looked angry but Erik continued.

"I'm not telling you what to do, Mama. I'm just saying that you might need someone to know. Just in case."

Dayida sighed and nodded, giving in.

"Mama's awakened," Erik said.

Hettie felt her mouth drop open. Her power came to the front and she centered herself in her body, reading its water. Next, she stretched out and felt for her grandson. There was something of her water in him, though it felt odd, faint and waning. The rest of him felt like pressure and wind and force; an invisible wall of kinetic energy, as if the water in his body were not water at all but lightning. Then she stretched for her daughter, reaching out to read the water in Dayida's body and she felt heat, a burning so hot that water became steam.

"Oh my," Hettie breathed.

"Don't be too excited, Hettie, I'm not of your line," Dayida snapped.

"I can sense that, but that doesn't mean it didn't come from me. I've got a couple lines in me, you know. But it could be from your father as well. How has it manifested? What is the bloodline?" Hettie asked in a rush.

"She doesn't—"

"Erik." Dayida snapped his name in that way all mothers have; a way that said he was treading too close to a line and he was not too big yet.

Erik went quiet and stood up.

"I'll leave you two to discuss it," he said.

Hettie gestured at her cheek and Erik gave her a kiss. He leaned over and did the same for his mother before leaving.

"What don't you do, Dayida?"

Dayida sighed. "I don't know what my powers entail exactly. I've been draining them through Robert's body and now through my painting. I haven't allowed it to manifest."

"Dayida, are you kidding? You know that's not healthy. The more you deny the power its expression, the stronger the explosion will be when it does come out." Hettie kept her voice steady but the worry in it was clear, even to herself.

"I know."

"Do you?" Hettie was standing now, though she didn't round the table or approach her daughter. "You endanger everyone in this house; maybe even in this city. You risk more lives than just your own. Why would you do this?"

"I saw what the power did to you," Dayida whispered.

The answer made Hettie pause before asking.

"And what exactly did my power do to me?" Hettie felt they were approaching the heart of their issues. She could feel what was coming, like a tidal wave, ready to swallow them both. She could think of thousands of things she would rather do than have this conversation, but this wasn't about what she wanted; it was about what Dayida needed.

"It made you kill father," Dayida answered after a long pause of her own.

And there it was. The heart of the anger that simmered between them, the reason for the chasm neither crossed. Hettie sighed and lowered her shaking hands to the tabletop. "You know that's not true. I killed your father because he attacked me; it had nothing to do with my power."

"But why?"

"He went mad." Hettie bit her bottom lip. She wished she had more to tell her daughter but even almost twenty years later, she had yet to figure out what exactly had happened. One day her Z.J. had been his normal sweet self, and the next he was a rampaging monster, coming at Hettie with a knife.

To this day, she had no idea what had caused him to go mad, though she suspected the Organization. The Maestro, who had been in charge of San Francisco's branch, had been a blood purity proponent. He had not liked that the most powerful Blooded in his district was married to someone "so boringly human" as he had said. She had tracked the man down later but he'd died without revealing anything. She was still sure he had known. The arrogance in his eyes, and the tilt on his lips when he died hinted at something. He went to his watery grave proud of himself and that she could barely stand.

"You're a healer, why couldn't you heal him?" This came out more wail than question, as if Dayida wasn't just asking Hettie but the universe itself for the answer. Hettie caught movement outside the room and looked up in time to see Erik ducking back out of the doorway.

She approached Dayida and sat in the chair next to her.

"I would have if I could have, but my healing works by understanding, and I didn't know what was wrong with him." She moved slowly. Dayida was nervous and there was no telling what could trigger an outburst of power.

"I've spent most of my life learning all I could of the body and how it works, so I could be the best healer possible. It wasn't enough to save my husband." Hettie looked down at her hands, lined and covered in dozens of tiny scars, but flexible and supple. "I had to kill him with these bare hands. Do you know what it can do to a healer? To kill?"

She glanced up at Dayida who was looking at her, silent but calm and answering the question with a shake of her head.

"It has nothing to do with power and everything to do with state of mind. When your father died I had been a healer for more than half my life. All healers have the potential to kill. The body is so fragile. It takes little to go from helping to harming. Every healer deals with the possibility differently. Some follow a strict moral code and some have a more malleable one. Some will heal anyone, and some heal only certain people. Some never use their power, and some only use it to kill."

Hettie tore her eyes away from her hands and looked more closely at her daughter's face. She was seeing another face in its stead.

"I had never killed. I would defend myself, but it is simple enough to incapacitate without killing. Your father was mad when he attacked me; screaming, and frothing at the mouth. Such pain. I was able to catch him off guard, knock him out, and bind him in water. I do not know how he woke up or got free of my bindings. I tried to freeze him in place; to flood his muscles with lactic acid. It should have given him cramps, and stopped him where he was. Instead it triggered a reaction. Whoever did it knew what I would try. They booby-trapped his blood. He burned from the inside out. I could have saved his body. Maybe. But his mind would have been gone. He would have been a shell. Empty and waiting for something to fill it."

She reached over to take Dayida's hand but her daughter flinched away from her touch. Hettie stopped, disappointed but not surprised. It would take more than one moment to cure the distance and distrust between them. Hettie wasn't sure they had time or that she had the energy to even try. Also Dayida wasn't completely wrong about the changes that had occurred to Hettie, as she wallowed in her power more often than she did not. She was different than she had been. She had changed because she had to. But also because she wanted to.

She was no stranger to killing anymore.

"Are you going to be able to work with me, Dayida?" She asked.

"Are you going to keep pushing me?"

Hettie didn't know how to answer that because she didn't know what it meant. Dayida seemed to feel pushed by her very presence and she had no intention of dulling her connection to her source. She had no intention of making herself weak again. Of letting herself be caught off guard.

"I can only be myself, Dayida."

"Me too."

"No, my dear. You haven't ever been yourself, but you're on your way." Hettie rose and went to look for her grandson before Dayida could reply. She was already out of the room when she realized that this was what her daughter had most likely meant by *pushing* her. But it was the truth and it was long past time Dayida heard it.

# ERIK

Erik left his mother and grandmother alone to speak. He entered the hall to see Matthias with the b'caster—the Organization's techno-magik communication device of choice—attached to his face, hands texting on his other phone. Erik took out the phone the Agency had provided for him. There were no names in the contact list, except for two—Tassi and Yonas—his two liaisons. The rest were all titles and numbers that were entirely too long.

While listening to Matthias whisper-yelling at someone in the Organization, Erik scrolled down to the listing for Regional Director: West Coast and called.

The call rang five times, then there was a click and three beeps and it began to ring again. This time it rang three times followed by one beep and was picked up.

"What do you want?"

Erik narrowed his eyes.

"Hello. Who is this?"

"You don't need to know any names." The voice was a deep contralto with a slight accent. It put Erik in the mind of old Hollywood starlets who had their foreignness blended out of them as much as possible.

"Well, do I need to know when Agents start disappearing?"

There was silence for too long and Erik's temper finally snapped. He pushed back the power that flared in his core but let it bleed into his voice, making it sound like he had gargled with sharp stones.

"Listen. I don't give a shit about your secrets until they begin to endanger those around me. And keeping attacks against us secret? That definitely qualifies."

There was a small sniff from the line but when the voice spoke some of the arrogance had left it.

"We don't know much and right now it's limited to New York and so there was no need to tell you."

"How many Agents have gone missing?"

There was a sigh, then. "Over two dozen at this point."

"Goat-fucking-shit." Erik cursed and rolled his eyes, before closing them and putting his face in his free hand.

"God, I hope this was a top-down decision and not just you being stupid and withholding information."

There was a huff of breath and then a dial tone. Erik was already pulling out his personal phone and dialing the Organization, Hu specifically.

The phone rang and rang but no answer. The voicemail had no spoken message, just a beep.

"Hu. Call me back. Now. I am entirely tired of this bullshit." Erik pressed "End Call" on the screen too hard and another tiny spiderweb of cracks grew across its surface. It was only a matter of time before the phone became unusable.

"No point. Hu's disappeared, as have fully a quarter of the Maestres," Matthias's voice interrupted.

Erik turned to see the other man looking at him.

"Are you joking?" He finally asked.

Matthias shook his head in response, and then spoke into his b'caster. "Yes, Luka. What news about New York?"

There was silence as Matthias listened and Erik watched his cheeks lose their color and his eyes close. Erik played with the bracelets around his wrists, a gift from Matthias. The cold touch and weight of them calmed him.

"And the answers from the other offices?" Matthias asked

Matthias closed his eyes at whatever answer he received.

Erik breathed calmly and waited for Matthias to finish his call.

"You let us know right away if anything changes."

Erik heard the slurping sounds of the b'caster retracting and waited for Matthias to speak.

"The Organization office in Manhattan has lost over half of their Blooded in the last two weeks, but not to the darkness. They've been lost to a swelling number of Angelics. They've moved the majority of their people off the island and scattered them across the other four boroughs."

"You are fucking kidding me."

Matthias gave a mirthless smile before he closed his eyes and brought the fingers of his left hand up to rub them.

"New York's mirror city went silent and then the streets were filled with Angelics. I mean, not literally, or I'm sure the news would have talked about it. They're managing to keep the non-Blooded out of the loop for now but it's only because the Angelics have mostly sequestered themselves somewhere they can't locate. It's only a matter of time before this gets out. Then—" He shrugged.

Matthias didn't have to say anything else. War, then. Open war between humans and Angelics, with bodies lining the streets by the hundreds, warheads and magic going head to head over populous areas. And all the while, in the background, whatever the darkness was would be slowly eating away at them.

Erik cursed again. "Well, the Agency has had at least twenty-four of their people go missing and they didn't think I needed to know, because it's happening on the other side of the country. I wonder if they would have told me if it was happening in my own backyard?"

Matthias shrugged. "No proof that the Agency was being truthful."

"What do you mean?"

"They've never been trustworthy. Just because you've been conveniently granted a place in their ranks doesn't mean that you are one of them."

Erik rolled his eyes at Matthias. He was smart enough to know that. He had been learning the subtle rules and punishments of being considered an insider/outsider his whole life.

Matthias continued. "Can you really blame either side? It's stupid as hell but you're now a part of two factions that have been fighting in some way or form for longer than anyone alive remembers. The way they see it, you didn't earn your place with either of them."

"I get it. I even get why. But the fact of the matter is, they're both facing a greater threat than me!" Erik shouted.

Matthias nodded in agreement. "That's the thing about power. Maybe you start out to protect others, or help run things fairly, but eventually you start to like power for power's sake. You become proud and convinced that you'll always remain in power. That nothing can challenge you.

"The Organization and the Agency view you with distrust. They've known you for weeks. It is easier for them to assume that you are a plant for the enemy and everything is lies, instead of imagining something they can't control."

"True. Even the Organization sent Tae to spy on me from the beginning." Erik couldn't help the hint of bitterness that leaked into his voice.

Matthias sighed and reached forward to still Erik's hands, which were still playing with the metal around his wrists.

"We can't have this discord between you two while you are in Zebub. We'll be dealing with enough outside threats without us falling apart from the inside."

"I know. I plan to talk to him tomorrow at the meeting," Erik answered.

Matthias nodded. They had all planned to meet; those who would be leaving for Zebub in less than a week. To meet and talk through research and prep.

"This news changes things," Matthias said quietly.

Erik nodded. He agreed. Leaving this world behind to try and save it was much easier when you weren't worried all hell was going to break loose in your absence.

"We might have to call off the trip," Erik said reluctantly.

"You will still go," said a voice behind him. Erik turned to face his grandmother.

"Gram. I can't leave—"

"Oh yes you can. You think your mother and I can't handle a little war? We been handling worse since before you were born." Hettie moved in close to his face.

His mother came up behind Hettie, having heard everything, and nodded her head.

"You need to go. This is an opportunity and you can't pass it up. You need to figure out if New York is an isolated incident or if it's the beginning of something bigger. Remember, their world is being devoured. Maybe they're looking for another world to take over. I'm not sure this world could survive another war of the descendants." Grandma Hettie put her hand on his right shoulder.

Erik knew she was right. He turned his head.

"Matthias?" He asked.

"Yeah." The man seemed to be shaking off his fear. His face was still grim as hell but there was more color to his cheeks.

“We’ll fill in Tae, Elana, Elliot, and Daya on all this tomorrow at the meeting. Then we’ll decide.”

“Sure,” Matthias nodded.

His mother came up on his other side.

“We can handle this. I promise,” she said quietly.

“It’s not that I think you two can’t handle it. If you work together.” He let that hang in the air for a beat. “I just feel like I should be here. I’m probably one of the most effective fighters we have.”

“You’re more than that, son. Remember that. You’re more than just your fists,” Dayida said seriously.

“I know.” He smiled at her and then hugged his mother and gram separately.

“You’re right. In the end it changes nothing,” Erik added. “We knew there was danger and others would work against us and that’s still the case. Our reasons for going haven’t changed. We’ll do more research and train as much as possible.”

# DAYIDA

Dayida's life had changed drastically in the last few weeks. The illusion of being a normal mother and artist had been torn away violently and ripped into tiny shreds. There was no going back. She was not foolish. Dayida knew that when secrets started to be revealed, many others could, and often did, come tumbling out. So she had spent the days leading up to Erik's departure in the conflicting position of wanting to spend time with him but also wondering when everything would be revealed. When would she have to explain herself?

She'd stayed in her studio, painting more and more with the power thrumming through her shoulders and upper arms. She was always at the center of the paintings now. Sometimes she was leading a party into battle and sometimes she was surrounded by others who would not look at her and always, always, she looked isolated and alone. Her painted image was often wrapped in faded cloth, with feet ripped and bleeding. An infinite sadness welled up in her when she looked at those portraits.

Dayida kept these paintings covered, in one corner of her workroom. These she would not put in shows. If she had her way no one but her would ever see them. She wanted to destroy them but whenever she got close to doing so a chill shot through her body, so rough and thorough it felt like her body was about to shake apart.

Dayida locked her workroom when she left.

She had managed to avoid Hettie after their conversation the night before, but when she exited her studio Hettie was waiting in the kitchen sipping a cup of coffee. She held up the mug.

"Would you like some, Yida?"

"No, thank you. I don't drink caffeine anymore." She tried to keep her voice neutral but the smirk on her mother's face let her know that it hadn't worked that well. "Where's Erik?"

"He already left with Matthias. They said they had some stuff to take care of before the meeting. So it looks like we're riding together."

Dayida could not bite down on the sigh of frustration. She saw Hettie roll her eyes as she drained the rest of the mug.

"Are you ready?" Hettie asked, all attempts at levity gone from her voice.

"As I'll ever be," Dayida grumped back.

"You've always been a delightful child," Hettie said quietly as she gathered her purse and made sure that her purple headwrap was secure. She wore a matching kaftan that clung to her curves and fell all the way to the floor. Dayida herself was in dark gray jeans and a yellow button down that was liberally splattered with black and red paint. She had no intention of changing.

"And you a most nurturing mother," Dayida replied.

Her mother only smirked at the rejoinder. Dayida grabbed her keys from the counter and gestured for Hettie to proceed her out of the door.

The thing attacked them as they were on either side of the car, about to get in. Hettie saw it first.

"Yida, down!"

She was not in the habit of listening to Hettie but the tone of her voice made Dayida react instinctively. She dropped to the ground. The crunch of metal exploded above her and she glanced up to see her attacker trying to pull itself from where it had gone through the car door. She rolled underneath the car and she pulled herself out from under the other side, near Hettie.

"You okay?" Hettie asked.

"Yes."

The thing finally freed its "arm" in a screech of metal and glass that tore the driver's-side door nearly off the hinges. It reared back and Dayida got a look at the thing. It towered over them, its body long and thick. It had only the one "arm," with three stubby grasping digits in the center of its "torso." There were hundreds of smaller legs lining both sides of its body. It looked like a gigantic millipede, all of its body a shiny black color.

It let out an odd cry and curled its body into a ring, launching itself over the car. Hettie pushed Dayida to the side. As she landed on the ground, she heard another screech and looked up to see the thing slowing in the air as it fell. The air around it was becoming colder, whiter, and visible with the chill her mother was summoning. Hettie's face looked strained and her hands shook as more and more cold coalesced.

Water and cold, as far as power was concerned, were two very different elements. Not many bloodlines were able to control both and the fact that her mother was able to affect ice at all was a testimony to Hettie's level of power and will.

But Dayida could see that the thing was adapting. Its black skin was glistening brighter and brighter and there were cracks in the ice that was forming between the thing and her mother. Cracks that were widening.

The ice shattered and the thing plowed into Hettie.

Dayida snarled and the power flowed into her shoulders. They became tight and coiled with power. Even as Hettie yelled and pushed at the thing on top of her Dayida was already rushing forward. She grasped her fists together and swung them up in the air. She jumped as she got closer using the momentum of her running and leap to add to the power of her strike as she brought her hands down.

The black surface of its back cracked and it let out a howl that echoed through the neighborhood. It spun, almost too fast to follow, and lunged for her. All of a sudden, the power in her shoulders swelled and raced down her arms. As she held them up to shield herself her fingers felt like they had burst into flame and she screamed even as she watched what looked like molten metal flow from her fingers and form a wall that the monster hit and bent with its impact.

Then just as fast the metal melted back into her hands.

The thing was still alive, though curled in on itself and shivering. There was an odd breaking sound mixed with the gurgle of water and Dayida saw the ground beneath it begin to break apart and congeal with moisture. She glanced at Hettie, who was staring at the creature. Her eyes were a dark stormy blue from lid to lid, as she called water up through who knew how many miles of earth.

The ground beneath the creature turned first to mud and then became more and more liquid as the thing sank into it. It disappeared from sight and eventually all she could see was mud. Then it was just a patch of brown dirt in the center of her driveway.

"What the hell was that?" Dayida asked, breathing hard.

"I have no idea. It didn't resemble any Angelic I've ever heard of. Are you okay?"

"Yes," Dayida said absently, too in shock to say anything more. She stared down at her hands. The light brown of her palms was an angry, blistered red. There was no pain and as she watched, the skin slowly lost the tinge of red and returned to its normal healthy brown. She did notice that all of her blemishes, all the scars and moles and spots on her hands, had been burned away. The skin looked the same but it felt tight and new.

"You've got a powerful gift, Dayida," Hettie said.

She nodded, still staring at her smooth, youthful hands when the ground began to rumble. Dayida and Hettie looked at one another with wide eyes.

"Move," Hettie breathed.

They both scrambled around the car, as far from the patch of dirt as they could. It exploded into a geyser of mud that shot into the air and covered both of them. The thing came out of the ground with a roar that shook the driveway. The top of its tumescent body moved back and forth, as if clearing what passed for its mind. Then it went still and focused in their direction.

It moved quickly, body squeezing beneath the car, upending it through the air as it reared to its full height on the other side. It tried to strike, but found itself beaten back by a blast of water shooting from Hettie's fists.

"I can't do this forever," Hettie called.

Dayida knew this. Even as she watched, her mother's skin turned dry and her cheeks sunk in. Hettie was using the water in her own body for this and there wasn't enough for long without hurting herself.

"Can you suck it dry instead?"

Hettie looked over at her with hooded eyes. "Yes."

There was a wealth of emotion in that one word. Stories that Dayida might never know. Pain she would never be allowed to touch. Despite their problems she did not want to willfully subject Hettie to pain. Unfortunately, she didn't see another choice.

"Do it."

Hettie took a deep breath. "I need to be touching it."

Dayida nodded. "I'll distract it."

Even as Hettie stopped her spray Dayida was running to the side of the creature, yelling and drawing its attention to her. It lunged forward. The top half of it moved fast while its base was stationary. She dropped to the ground, and felt the grasping digits of its arm tangle with and yank out a chunk of her hair.

She screamed but at the same time another voice cried out in pain. The cry was nothing human. Notes that would tear a human throat to shreds undulated between the ranges of Barry White and Mariah Carey and beyond. The screech of pain had nothing of humanity in it.

But if that was the case why did its pain find an echo in her own chest?

Dayida staggered to her feet and away from the sound, doing her best to clutch at her ears and bleeding scalp. She looked back as the wail shrank in volume. Her mother was behind the creature, hands planted on its bottom half. It was undulating and striking at her; Hettie's kaftan was covered in rips, but her face was flush and full. Her skin was lush and dewy.

The creature, in contrast, was not looking well. It shrunk and shriveled in on itself as it was drained of whatever liquid was in its body. The blackness of its body got brighter and its skin began to flake off. Its movements became sluggish and slow.

Power coursed through Dayida once more and this time she was ready for the metal to emerge and she actually wished for a shape. The metal responded to her wish. The broadsword was heavy and lethal looking, crudely shaped but with a wicked serrated edge. She brought the edge down on the thing and it shattered in an explosion of glass and something dark and wet that smelled of burning fuel and sizzled where it touched their skin.

She looked to Hettie and saw that she was fine. Any cuts she received from their foe already healed into perfect brown skin. Dayida walked closer to her and looked down at the creature's shattered remains. The pieces glittered in the noonday sun.

They were silent for a long moment before Dayida spoke.

"He looks similar to the thing that Erik described attacking him on his first night awakened. The one they could never identify. That one was shaped like a human but the same material. The same shattering."

Hettie was nodding but still looking down at the pieces of the thing. Finally she spoke.

"This is not right. Aside from whatever that thing is, it attacked in broad daylight where anyone could see it. It doesn't make sense."

Dayida looked down at the dead thing that had attacked them, and then up at the cloudless sky. She looked around at the curtains that were swaying as people darted away, and the doors that were opened just a crack.

"What should we do?" Hettie asked, her eyes moving, tracking the same things as Dayida.

"I'm going to call Erik. Let's get whatever pieces we can off the street and into the house."

They gathered all of the larger pieces and anything they could sweep into impromptu pouches made from folded clothing. When they were loaded down, Hettie created a quick flash of water down the driveway to sweep the rest into the storm drain, and away from them.

# ERIK

Matthias had picked him up early in the morning. They spent the day going to visit every single independent who would agree to meet with them. They warned them all about the disappearances in New York, and helped set up agreements between some of the disparate independent groups, so they would all have someone to call for help if necessary.

Everywhere they went, Erik was subject to scrutiny at best, and hostile glares at worse. Matthias had insisted he be there, though. These people needed to at least see him before he left. He couldn't let himself be some blank slate, onto which the Organization or the Agency could project whatever lies they wanted.

It had been exhausting but he felt that at least some of the people he met could be called on if he needed help. They were on their way to see one more independent before the meeing with the Agency when Erik's phone went off. He saw his home number displayed and was tempted to silence it. His mother was likely calling to complain about having to ride with his grandmother. But even now, with the power he wielded, the idea of silencing the phone when his mother called filled him with a childhood dread.

"Hey Mama, sorry—"

"Erik. Get back here now. Something attacked us in broad daylight," she interrupted.

Erik put his hand over the receiver and turned to Matthias. "Home. Now."

Matthias nodded and gunned the engine.

"Are you and Grandma okay?" Erik asked.

"Yeah, we're fine but the neighbors definitely saw something."

"Shit, Mom. We'll be there soon. Stay inside and stay safe."

"What happened?" Matthias asked as he took a corner entirely too fast.

"First, slow down. They're safe but we won't be able to help if we get into a wreck."

Matthias grimaced but his foot eased off the gas a bit.

"Thanks." Erik released the death grip he had on the "oh shit" bar. "They were attacked by something."

"An Ante?"

Erik thought about it. "They didn't say, but I don't think so. Gram knows an Ante when she sees one and Mama definitely said some-*thing*."

"That's not good," Matthias muttered as he merged onto Geary Street.

"Or it's actually really good," Erik countered.

Matthias just glanced at him with an eyebrow raised.

"It means that we've touched a nerve somehow. Something isn't happy with what we're doing so we must be doing something right."

Matthias let out a chuckle. "You know that's not normal, right? The belief that if you're pissing someone off you must be doing something right?"

Erik shrugged with a small smile. "Didn't say it worked for everyone. Just for me."

"You're special," Matthias said.

"I know. That's why you love me." It slipped out before he could stop it.

"Right." Matthias's voice was empty of anything.

And just like that the energy in the car turned from jovial to uncomfortable silence for the rest of the ride.

They hurried down the driveway, but not so quick that Erik didn't notice the itch of being watched creeping across his back and the feeling of silent observation that now surrounded the property. It wasn't just their neighbors that were watching. Erik was used to being watched but this was altogether different. There wasn't just greed and curiosity in the air. There was malice as well.

"You feel that?" Erik asked.

Matthias nodded. "We're being hunted."

"Let's get inside. Now."

They moved quickly and Erik made sure to lock the door behind them.

"Mom? Gram?"

"In the kitchen!"

Erik hurried to them with Matthias hot on his tail.

The two women hovered over the dining room table, which was piled high with what looked like broken black glass. Erik recognized it almost immediately. From the look he shared with him, so did Matthias.

"What did it look like?" Matthias asked.

"Like something that a person who watched too much Cronenberg as a child and developed a horrible fear of millipedes might conjure in a nightmare. Including one grasping arm in the middle of its body," Hettie explained.

Erik shuddered. So, nothing like what had attacked Matthias and himself in shape, though they were made of similar material.

"Did you ever figure out what that thing was?" Erik asked, turning to Matthias.

"No. I asked everyone I could think of and no one had even heard of anything like it."

"I don't like the sound of that. Gram? Any ideas?" Erik asked.

Hettie hummed and sifted the mess of glass on the table with her fingers and hummed.

"Whatever I pulled from its body wasn't water. At least, not only water; there was enough in it for me to affect it, but I'm lucky my body filters out the poisons. Otherwise . . ." Hettie trailed off and shrugged her shoulders.

"Can you be anymore specific than just *poisons?*" Erik asked.

"What do you mean?"

"Is there anyway to tell if it was a natural or artificial poison?" Erik asked.

"I don't think so." Hettie shook her head. "My body doesn't work that way. Mami Wata's blessing protects me from poison, and from pollution alike . . . but as for what it was?" She shrugged.

Matthias turned to face Erik fully.

"What are you thinking?"

"Nothing yet." Erik only had suspicions, and he didn't want to say anything until it was more than just a hunch in his belly.

"Well, can I get some of that?" Matthias asked already reaching into one of his numerous pockets for a small plastic baggie.

"Why?" Dayida asked, even as she moved aside and gestured for him to take what he wanted from the pile on the kitchen counter.

"I have some friends whose interests lie at the intersection of magic and science. I think analyzing this would be something that they would be interested in and it might give us some answers."

"Answers would be good," Erik stated.

"We do have one answer at least. We now know one manifestation of your mother's power," Hettie said.

Erik looked up in shock. "We do?"

Hettie nodded, a small smile on her face. "She can manifest metal and form it into weapons."

They all turned to look at Dayida who was looking back at them blankly. Her fingers were tangled together on the table as she wove them together and apart over and over.

"It wasn't horrible," she finally said.

Erik turned and met both Matthias's and his grandmother's gazes. This was the closest his mother had come to accepting her powers. He changed the subject back to the creature before anyone could push her farther.

"Who do we call, though? This could be one of the Agency's experiments, or one of the Organization's millions of secrets, or an attack from Zebub. We can't really trust any of them, and if they were the ones behind it, do we really want them to know we survived?"

No one had an answer for that.

"Tell them both," Hettie said. "If they knew to attack us, they'll probably have someone watching to see if we survived. They both need to know, so they can protect their own people. But don't give any more details than necessary. And let them both know you're telling the other group. If either one of them is behind it, that will keep them on edge and make them cautious."

"Good idea." Erik nodded. "I'll have Patrah tell the Organization and I'll call and alert the Agency after the meeting. Which, speaking of . . ." He glanced at the clock on the wall then looked back at his Mom and Gram, at the rips in their clothing and the mysterious stains. They looked down at themselves.

"We'll go change and then we'll all go together," Hettie said.

Erik nodded as his Mom and Gram headed in different directions without looking at each other. Erik sighed and looked over at Matthias, who shrugged.

"It's better than I thought it would be."

"I know. I just—" Erik stopped. He didn't want to get into it, but he did feel the longing for a family of some kind. He had always been fine with the father that became hostile and the mother who was absent. But he was starting to realize he had always longed for more.

Matthias stared at him for a moment then reached forward and placed his hand on Erik's shoulder. Erik did not shrug him off, but pressed into it instead, taking the comfort he'd denied himself. Matthias opened his mouth to speak, but snapped it closed as Hettie re-entered the room—a vision in a white shirt, headwrap, and jeans. Matthias removed his hand, though she stared at them both in silence until Dayida returned. When she returned she took them all in for a second before speaking.

"Are we ready to go?"

Erik simply nodded and led the way, not bothering to check on them. They piled into the Mini Cooper, Erik sharing the smaller back-seat with his mother while Matthias drove and Hettie watched them all in the mirrors. No one spoke. Erik allowed himself to sink into the feeling of speed as they careened through the streets in a cocoon of quiet.

# MELINDA

Patrah was making her practice before they left for the meeting. Melinda was asleep on the floor of her living room, with Patrah snoring softly beside her. At the same time, they were both standing in the room, their forms invisible and intangible except to another dreamer.

When she didn't think about it, the whole thing became natural. The dreaming that overlaid her living room was a swath of dark blue. Melinda held the image in place and slowly reached out with one hand and let her fingers sink into the blue.

"Good," Patrah said quickly.

Melinda pulled her hand free, staring at the thin threads of blue that clung to her fingers. She could not feel it in the traditional sense. It didn't feel cold or wet, but it did drip like water.

"Now, picture what you want it to become. You've done this before."

Melinda nodded and slowly forced the dreamstuff to bend to her thoughts. It dripped from her fist and formed the base first, then the round platform it rested on, and then a pole rising up, and at the top a bowl lined with buildings and streets. There were intricate details; small streetlamps dotted corners and lit up intermittently. Small figures could be seen walking down navy streets and peeking out from behind cerulean curtains. Cars moved down the minuscule streets and there was a slight noise in the air: conversations that were too quiet and high-pitched to overhear.

"That's great. You've got movement and sound working," Patrah said.

Melinda looked up and smiled at Patrah who had conjured a small rose into her fist, the petals fluttering in an imaginary wind. Her Mom watched from the other end of the room, hands clasped in her lap, smile lighting up her face. Her Meema had declined to watch, saying it gave her too much anxiety, but then Meema didn't have awakened Blooded in her immediate family, unlike Mom, who had grown up with sisters and parents all calling on their powers in front of her.

Of course, Mom couldn't actually see into the dreaming, so she had no idea what they were doing right now, but the love that radiated off of her made Melinda smile wider. Patrah spoke and drew her attention back.

"Now let's see if you can bring it out of the dreaming. Remember what I said?"

Despite Melinda's nod, Patrah went over it again.

"I want you to keep the image of that in your mind. It is part of you. Part that should come back from the dreaming, just as your body does."

Melinda nodded again and when Patrah said nothing else she spoke up.

"I'm ready."

"Are you sure?"

Melinda held back a sigh. "Yes."

"Okay, I'll go first. With my rose."

Melinda watched as the form of Patrah slowly broke apart. Wisps of her moved through the air, rose, and broke apart. Instead of the blue dreamstuff returning to the space around them it flowed with the rest of her into Petrah's prone form. Patrah woke, and sat up. The rose glowed in her hand, translucent. Sunlight shone through the blue petals and cast shadows in every shade of blue across the room. As Melinda watched from the dreaming it began to fall apart, unable to exist in the waking world for long.

Melinda started to do the same, using the breathing exercises Patrah had taught her. She felt herself in two places; the dreaming and lying on her living room floor. She concentrated on the second sensation; the rug under her neck and the one braid that was under her body and pulled uncomfortably. She slowly let go of the dreaming until it was paper-thin and she could barely feel that tug of it.

Her body was more and more real and she could feel every part of it. She could feel the model, too. It was coming through fine, forming to her right. Then, at the last minute before waking, she felt it ripped from her hands and mind. It didn't feel taken from her. Rather, it was as if she had run into a barrier that would not let the model through.

She sat up with a gasp and her Mom burst into applause simply for the fact that she woke up. Melinda felt nothing but disappointment. She had had it, but it had just slipped away like nothing.

"What went wrong?" Patrah asked.

Her Mom stopped clapping.

"I don't know. I had it but at the last minute it was just gone."

Patrah looked confused. "Do you want to try again?"

Melinda nodded determinedly. She looked to her Mom who smiled at her encouragingly.

They lay back down and went through it all again; the breathing, the waking in the dreaming, the conjuration and creation, and then the waking.

The results were exactly the same as the first.

By the third time the hesitation on Patrah's face and in her voice was sounding like disappointment to Melinda. Melinda felt frustration well up inside. She could do this. She knew she could. So why was she finding it so hard?

She nodded at Patrah's instructions again but did not listen to a single word. Patrah's way was not working. If she was going to make this happen she had to do it her own way. Once they were in the dreaming and she had her model created again she slowed down her breathing again but instead of feeling for her body she felt for the model. It was right beside her.

Then she felt around it. Unlike the other things she had made in the dreaming this model felt heavy and weighted. It felt like something real. Instead of waking herself up she concentrated on the model, imagined the way the cool metal would feel under her fingers, the way it would dent the rug as it rested there. The way that the summer sun would heat it up. The lights working and the people moving and everything that made it a city.

She did her best to align the model she could see in the dreaming with the one she was imagining. She thought of them as one; one thing in two spaces that needed to be one again.

With a large *pop* that Melinda felt rather than heard, everything changed.

The model wasn't in the dreaming anymore. She looked at the model resting on the floor and her slumped body next to it. As soon as she laid her eyes on her body she felt the tug to rejoin it, to become whole. It was strong but not overwhelming. Then Patrah's form next to her awoke with a shout. Melinda lost her concentration and was swept back into her body. As her eyes fluttered open, though, she saw the model. It was still there.

"What did you do?" Patrah was staring at the model that now sat in the middle of her living room. It was not blue or translucent. Instead the base, pole, and bowl were a shining silver with dimples and whorls as if echos of the human fingers who had sculpted it. The city that sat in the bowl was a kaleidoscope of color—blacks and blues and greens and yellows and reds.

It looked like a real city.

That's when she noticed the movement. The cars. The people. They had come through too and they were moving to and fro as if nothing was out of the ordinary.

"It just felt like the right thing to do," Melinda whispered.

Patrah was just staring at the model as the lights twinkled and the tiny people went about their lives. Mom had moved from the couch and was kneeling by Patrah, while Meema was standing in the doorway, some sense calling her in from the other room.

"Patrah, what is it?" Her Mom asked.

Patrah turned to look at Mom with wide eyes. "Elise . . . she didn't just bring something from the dreaming into the real. She turned dreamstuff into reality. That's. . . ."

"Unusual?" Her Mom supplied.

"I would have said impossible. She created something. Not building or alteration or even destruction but actual creation from the ether of the world." Patrah stopped and turned to look at Melinda, who had been growing more and more nervous as the conversation went on.

"Did I do something wrong?" She tried to make her voice steady but it shook in any case.

"No, honey, no." Her Mom was across the floor in a second, pulling her into a warm embrace. The scent of lavender and lilac surrounded her: her Mom's favorite scent. She felt her body relaxing. "Right. Patrah?"

Patrah finally looked away from the model and back at Melinda, taking in her frown and nervous expression.

"No. Of course not, Melinda. You didn't do anything wrong. I was just surprised."

There was something in her voice that let Melinda know Patrah wasn't sure of what she was saying, but Melinda nodded anyway. Patrah had already turned back to the model, her eyes now tracking one of the small humans that inhabited the city.

"We need to go to the meeting. Elise. Jeni. I need you two to do something for me."

Her Meema moved further into the room over to where Melinda was still wrapped in her Mom's arms. Meema placed her palm on Mom's shoulder and met Patrah's gaze.

"What do you need?" Meema asked.

"Move this somewhere out of sight, but be careful. As far as we know right now, those little humans are living, breathing people."

Melinda felt her Mom's breath catch from where they were pressed against each other.

"We can do that. We'll be careful. How about the garage? We only use it for storage and there are no windows to the outside," Meema suggested.

Patrah nodded. "That sounds good. Don't tell anyone about this. No one at all."

Mom spoke up. "Who would we tell?"

"I don't know, but it's important that no one knows about this until we figure out what it really is and what it means."

Melinda did not like the feeling gnawing into her belly. They all said it was okay. That she had done nothing wrong. But they were all acting the other way. She knew they weren't lying, exactly. But there were things that they weren't saying out loud. Melinda was young but she wasn't dumb. She knew that adults often hid things. There was only one adult she trusted to tell her the truth.

She was going to talk to Erik about this, no matter what Patrah said, but she nodded along with her mothers and hurried to put her shoes on so that they could make their way to the meeting.

As they left the house her mothers stood in the doorway with their arms wrapped around one another, waving.

They would go back to packing as soon as Patrah and Melinda were gone. The weeks at home had been nice but Patrah had to help with the Agency when Erik was gone and thought it would be easiest if they stayed at the headquarters. Her mothers had gone ahead and invited themselves, which Melinda was happy about. She didn't know how Patrah felt about it, but she'd agreed to it.

As Patrah drove down the street Melinda looked out of the window as they crossed a street and moved from fog to bright sunshine. She hoped it was a good sign.

As Patrah drove down the street Melinda looked out of the window as they crossed a street and moved from fog to bright sunshine. She hoped it was a good sign.

# ERIK

They found parking right in front of the building, like always.

The lobby had been returned to its immaculate gold-and-white splendor since the slaughter. It looked the same as the first time Erik had walked in, except for the garden, which had been completely uprooted at his request. He had watched as those beautiful, mutant trees had been dug up and burned.

Where the garden had been there was now more white marble flooring, brighter and newer than the rest of the floor.

Only a few feet inside the door Melinda was standing with Patrah, Daya, and Elana. The three women were talking while the girl was fiddling with her phone until she looked up and caught sight of him.

"Erik!" She ran to him. He knelt down to meet her and wrap her in a hug. Melinda pressed her cheek against his and she spoke in his ear, softer than a whisper, so the sound was almost just breath.

"I need to talk to you."

Erik squeezed her tighter to show that he heard her.

"Hey sweetie, how are you doing?" He asked.

Melinda pulled back and smiled. "I'm okay. I miss you though."

"I know." Erik frowned. "I'm sorry I've been so busy lately. There's a lot to get done."

Melinda nodded. "I know."

"How about after the meeting I take you out for ice cream or something. Just you and me?" Erik looked up at Patrah for approval and saw no suspicion as she nodded.

"That sounds great." Melinda lunged and hugged him around the neck again.

"Where are you going to be during the meeting?" Erik asked. He would share anything with Melinda that she wanted to know, but being in the meeting itself might be too overwhelming. He distantly remembered meetings from his youth, where all the adults talked over him and ignored his contributions. Erik would never do that, but some of the others? It was better that she have something else to entertain her.

"I asked Zaha to spend the time with her," Patrah answered.

Erik's gaze followed her head tilt to the front counter where Zaha sat behind the desk. Tae was leaning over it to speak with her. He watched them for a moment, noting the small smiles on both of their faces.

Erik shook himself and looked back to Patrah.

"Good. There's some stuff we're gonna share in the meeting that I need you to report to the Organization afterwards, while I take Melinda out."

She looked at him curiously but simply nodded. He turned to Elana who was smiling softly.

"How are you doing, Elana?"

"As well as can be expected," she answered, the smile dropping.

She looked away, most likely thinking about her remains, and the betrayal of the Organization not telling her.

"Betrayal is hard to process." His eyes automatically sought out Tae again.

"Erik," Elana sighed, following his gaze.

"I know, I know. Don't worry. I'm going to talk to him."

Elana nodded and moved over to join her girlfriend in conversation with Matthias. Erik sighed. No time like the present, he supposed. He patted Melinda on the shoulder and walked over to the reception desk. Zaha noticed him first and her eyes went wide and darted around, obviously looking for Daniel. When Zaha didn't see him she actually met his gaze and gave him a small smile.

Tae noticed and turned. When he saw Erik, his whole body stiffened. It was the first time they'd seen each other since the meeting at the Organization's base in Brisbane a couple of weeks ago.

Tae's face showed sadness before he closed his expression off. Erik knew that trick well. Had been using it all his life.

Erik tried a smile out as he closed the distance between them.

"Tae, can I talk to you in private, before the meeting?"

Tae nodded immediately. "Yes."

Erik turned to everyone else in the lobby. "We'll meet you in the meeting room in a little while."

He waved and they moved off to the back of the lobby where a number of smaller offices lay empty.

"I'm sorry," Tae blurted as soon as the door closed behind them. In the silence that followed, Tae leaned back on a desk that sat in the room, while Erik paced back and forth in front of him.

Erik finally sighed. "You don't have to apologize."

"Obviously I do, because you've been blowing me off," Tae said, anger creeping into his voice.

"You're right. And for that I apologize. I needed time to think and I didn't want to talk in case I said something I was going to regret later. I should have let you know what I was thinking."

Some tension left Tae's shoulders and he stood straighter.

"The truth is that when I figured out you'd been spying on me, I was pissed as hell. But you didn't owe me anything then. You didn't know me from Adam and it's ridiculous to think you owed me any loyalty."

"Doesn't mean you feel any less betrayed," Tae whispered, crossing his arms.

Erik gave him a small smile. "True. But I know what it's like to be stuck between two choices, neither one of them good. As for lying about how strong you are?" Erik shrugged. "I can't say I wouldn't do the same thing. Never tell a potential enemy your strengths and weaknesses."

"But you're not an enemy, you're my friend," Tae argued.

"I know, but I wasn't at the time and I get that." Erik nodded.

"So you forgive me?" Tae asked.

"What I'm saying is that there's nothing I need to forgive you for." Erik explained, shaking his head.

"Yes, there is. I should have told you when we started to become friends."

Erik closed his eyes for a moment. This was more difficult than he thought it would be. Tae wasn't wrong. Just because he understood why Tae had done what he'd done didn't mean he wasn't hurt by it.

Tae stopped Erik's pacing with a hand on his arm and Erik turned to face him.

"I see so much, Erik. All the time. With my whole body. All I can do is try to figure out which paths will make the good visions come true, and try to stave off the bad ones for as long as possible. I make a lot of mistakes but all I can do is try again and again. It's exhausting. I think you understand that." Tae paused and they shared a quick bitter smile before he continued. "The feeling that the whole world is resting on your shoulders? That it's up to you and no one else? It makes it hard to trust others."

Erik nodded. "Here's what we're going to do. We fake it 'til we make it."

Tae raised his eyebrows.

Erik continued. "We start acting like friends again and the forgiveness and trust will come back in time. Those things don't just reappear when you want them to, but we can work on building them back up." Erik looked away for a moment. "This is hard for me too. I haven't had real friends in . . . well, a long time. But I do remember one thing. Friends are supposed to forgive each other when they fuck up and honestly apologize. We both fucked up. We do our best to forgive each other and we move on."

Erik held out his hand and Tae slipped his own into it. They shook twice before Tae simply pulled a startled Erik forward into a hug. They both sank into the contact; a tactile reaffirmation of their connection and friendship.

When they pulled away Erik leaned on the desk next to Tae, their hips touching.

"So . . . Zaha?" Erik broke the comfortable silence.

Tae blushed. "I like her."

"I can see that." Erik let the smile drop. "How is she doing, though?"

Tae looked down at the ground for a moment before flicking his eyes back up to meet Erik's questioning glance. "She's okay. She still hasn't heard from her friend Carlie so she's worried, obviously, but there don't seem to be any after-effects from almost getting dragged into the darkness."

Erik hummed a non-committal note. Other than being able to see Daniel, of course. "Have you guys gone out yet?"

"No. We're going slow. She doesn't like that I'm two years younger than her and she's a little cautious about dating a non-Muslim. She says her family will be fine with it but both people she's dated before were Muslim. We're going slow."

Erik shrugged. "Good idea. Think things through before you make a choice you can't take back."

"My ears are burning! Is someone talking about me?" Daniel's voice rang out as he floated in through the ceiling.

Erik stiffened and Tae immediately noticed.

"What going on?" He asked, tensing himself and looking around.

Erik silently turned to face his haunting. The expression on his face was enough.

"Daniel," Tae stated.

Erik nodded. "Go join the others. I'll be up there in a moment."

"By yourself?" Tae asked, glaring back and forth with a look of intense concentration.

"That remains to be seen."

Tae left without another word, closing the door behind him.

"Daniel," Erik said

"Yes, Erik?"

Daniel's ghost faced him, still in the outfit that he had died in. Still horribly injured. Erik noticed something else this time. His eyes were sunken in farther. Not a lot, but enough for someone who knew his face intimately to notice. His skin was still translucent but the brown of his skin was grayer. What was happening? Did Daniel even know? Would he tell Erik if he asked?

"What are you doing here?" Erik asked instead.

Daniel crossed his arms, lying back on empty air so he mimicked Erik's posture against the desk. It made the edges of the hole in his chest pull and flex. It took Erik a moment to pull his gaze away from the sight of his failure.

Daniel smirked and looked away. "Just because I think this is a very stupid decision doesn't mean that I'm not going to come with you."

"Will that even work?" Erik asked.

Daniel shrugged and smiled. "It's worth a shot isn't it?"

"And if I said I didn't want you to come?"

Daniel met his gaze and Erik refused to look away; refused to give in. Daniel was the first to speak.

"Look, Erik. What do you think you can do to stop me? And haven't I helped you so far?"

"Debatable," Erik muttered.

Daniel snorted. "I led you to your friends. I want to protect you. That's why I don't want you to go on this trip. If you insist on going through with it, though, I'm definitely coming along. You'll need me."

"To do what?"

"Be the eyes and ears you need, where no one else can see," Daniel said.

Erik was silent. He had no idea what to say. He could not deny that Daniel would be useful. He would also be a distraction and could cause tension with the others.

"Didn't Matthias and Daya's little trick convince you that I'm here to help?" Daniel asked.

Erik wanted to nod but he had gone over it too many times in his mind. If it was really Daniel, which he still believed, then yes, they could use all the help they could get. But if it wasn't Daniel? If it was something darker and more sinister? Then he'd be inviting an enemy into his camp. The truth was that neither of these things really mattered. Daniel was right. There was no way to stop him. Better to not antagonize him and just agree to it and keep a close eye on him.

"Fine, come along. You might be of some help."

Daniel smiled. It was the same bright sparkling smile that Erik still remembered from their time together. He returned the smile as he pushed off of the desk and headed for the door.

Daniel's voice sounded from behind him. "Also, if you do happen to die? Well, it would be nice for us to be together again."

He stumbled. There it was. The moment of uncertainty. Was that the same dark humor that Erik had always loved? Or was that real malice in Daniel's voice? How much did the man blame Erik for his death? More than Erik blamed himself?

Erik refused to respond and left the room with the chill and blankness that Daniel exuded at his back. Zaha and Melinda were behind the lobby desk playing on the computer. The others had likely already headed up to the meeting room. He moved across the lobby, waving at Zaha when she looked up. Erik saw the moment Zaha spotted Daniel. Her eyes went wide. The paling of her skin was more obvious against the silver and pale teal-patterned hijab she wore.

He looked back and saw the wide, chilling smile that Daniel was giving her. He tried to give her an encouraging look until Melinda called Zaha's name, brought her back to the physical world around her. After that she looked down at the screen and refused to raise her eyes as they moved across the rest of the lobby.

The elevator was waiting for them. The same round golden teardrop as before. They rode up quickly and the doors opened to reveal the same meeting room that they had once used to negotiate with Byron.

Tassi and Yonas were seated around the table, along with everyone else, which made Erik raise his eyebrows in question. He approached the empty seat between his mother and grandmother and stood behind it.

"What are you two doing here?" He asked the two Suits.

They looked at one another, and Tassi, her long braid wrapped around her head like a crown, finally spoke.

"We're going with you," she explained.

"As spies? Doesn't seem like the Agency trusts me at all," Erik said with a smirk.

"We are going to protect you and also as extra firepower in case you need it. You don't know what you'll face on the other side," Tassi said with no facial expression.

Erik nodded, but he did notice they hadn't addressed the whole spy or lack of trust accusations.

Yonas spoke up. "You don't like us. That's clear. So just think of us as another tool to get the people you do care about home safe."

Erik narrowed his eyes in response. It sounded like they were basically volunteering to be cannon fodder. Erik felt a nauseous roll of disgust in his belly because he knew he would agree because he wanted everyone else safe. He swallowed and carefully did not look at Matthias. Whatever the Suits had planned he could handle. They would all be watchful.

Finally, Erik nodded at them and turned to face the rest of the table.

"There are some new developments that you need to know about." Erik gestured to his grandma. "Gram, you wanna fill them in on New York, and earlier today?"

"Yes." She stood, her white shirt bright against the dark blue jeans she wore. Her dark brown skin practically glowed. She filled them in on New York, with Matthias and Erik chiming in with what little they knew. Then she spoke of the daylight attack in San Francisco. Dayida added nothing. She simply stared forward, not reacting to anyone's looks, as her part in the fight was described.

"Well, we can't go now," Daya stated.

All of them noticed the look Erik and Matthias shared.

"We can't go now! This is probably all a trap!" Elana practically yelled. Erik was surprised. He had only known her a few weeks, but he had never seen Elana so volatile before. From the looks Matthias and Patrah wore, neither had they. Daya looked at her girlfriend sympathetically.

"That's exactly why you have to go," Hettie answered.

"Why? To die?" Elana asked.

Erik held back the sarcasm of asking what in the hell she had to lose. He looked over at Daya. He knew what she had to lose.

"No. Because it's our only chance to get any information from the source. We're flying blind. We don't know what they intend with New York. Is it a full-scale invasion? Is it a small rogue cell? Are there cracks in their plan that we could exploit? The only way to get that information is in Zebub," Erik answered.

Everyone was silent and watching. A flash of orange and brown in the corner let him know where Daniel was, but he did not focus on the ghost as he continued.

"I won't say that things haven't changed. We have an assurance of safe travel, but the Angelics only respect strength. We may have to be ready to defend ourselves at any time. I don't know what we'll face, but I know we have a better chance if we're all together," Erik finished.

Tae was nodding. Elliot was looking at his aspirant thoughtfully. Even Elana seemed to be wavering. Daya's face remained as hard as ever.

"I don't like it," she stated calmly.

"Neither do I. I just think that we have to go. So we can maybe prevent something worse," Erik answered.

"Do you know what it's like to lose someone you love? To find out the horrible things they did with her body? To find out—" Daya's voice choked off and Elana had long since turned her back to them and was facing the wall.

Erik tilted his head at her.

"Are you serious? You think I don't understand the danger we're in? The things . . . the *people* that we could lose? The ways we could lose them?" He was quiet, as he thought of Daniel. It wasn't quite the same thing. He was asking her to visit the world of the Angelics, who had desecrated Elana's body. On the other hand, Daniel had been a non-Blooded. Someone who had been pulled in just to be used against Erik, and then thrown away like so much trash. They both had their pain.

He looked up and saw the apology written across Daya's face. He waved it away and rose from his chair, moving around the table until he stood in the space between Daya and Elana. He turned to face Daya and crouched so he wasn't looming over her.

"I know it's a much more dangerous thing I'm asking you to do. Even on top of the massive danger that's already part of your day-to-day life. I won't presume to understand what you're feeling. But whatever it is? It's valid, and if you don't want to do this anymore? If you want to pull out? I won't think less of you."

Daya looked over her shoulder at Elana, who had turned back to face them.

"We'll need to talk about it," she said quietly.

"I understand," Erik said as he returned to his seat.

The rest of the meeting was ironing out other details, such as what to take and when they would meet. Afterwards everyone else took the elevator down, and Melinda was sent up to join him in the meeting room. She looked oddly shy and he realized they had not spoken, only the two of them, since their time in the Brisbane training facility.

He looked down at her and smiled conspiratorially. "You want to see my office?"

She returned the smile. "Totally."

They made their way to the elevator and stepped inside. Instead of going down, the elevator rose up through the glass roof, as if it didn't even exist. They were shrouded in complete darkness but Melinda made no sound. She just gripped his hand tighter. Then they were through and the glare of light was all around them. The very top floor was small. A simple dome on the roof. There was only one room, the office of the head of the San Francisco branch. His office.

The walls were lined with TV screens, all of them muted. His predecessor had kept them loud and blaring, which made sense, as he'd been a loud, blaring sort of man. Especially when he was informed that he was no longer in charge. There had been much yelling and flying spit.

As they stepped out, Melinda looked all around in wonder. Erik didn't blame her. The office still struck him as well. He'd only been up here a handful of times. The dome above them was clear glass. The room was dominated by a circular desk of faceted crystal that reflected soft rainbows from the right angle, with gold edging, and supports. The desk was covered with computers and monitors smaller than the ones that lined the walls.

There were a couple of stuffed chairs between the elevator and the desk and Erik turned them so they were facing each other. He fell into one and gestured for Melinda to take the other.

"What's going on?"

She looked up at him and smirked. "I thought you said we were going to go get ice cream."

He saw the spark of mischief and smiled as he stood. "I did say that, didn't I?"

He squeezed through the gap left in the circle of desk and reached underneath it. Though he hadn't spent much time in the office, he had made sure the mini-fridge was stocked. It had been filled with nothing but bottles of liquor before. Given the things that the former head of the Agency had been complicit in, Erik could almost understand. He pulled half a gallon of vanilla-caramel-swirl from the small freezer compartment and two spoons out of the drawer above the fridge.

He maneuvered back to Melinda and cracked the lid on the ice cream. Scooting his chair closer to hers, he handed her a spoon and dug in as she did the same. After a few bites each, he looked to her.

"Why don't you tell me what's going on?"

The floodgates opened and while they ate she talked about her training and the small city she had made. Her voice got quiet as she described how Patrah had reacted, and what had been said.

Erik sat with it for a moment, sucking down another spoonful of sweet ice cream. Then he spoke.

"She most likely is trying to protect you. I don't know much about your power but it sounds like you did something really extraordinarily special and amazing."

Melinda looked up with a soft smile. "Really?"

"Of course."

"She didn't act like it was a good thing," Melinda practically growled.

"I know she didn't," Erik sighed. "Sometimes when people are surprised they don't see the joy in something. They just see the dangers, and what could go wrong."

Melinda nodded. "So what should I do?"

"Listen to what Patrah says but also listen to your instincts. While I'm gone if you need to talk with anyone you can talk to my Grandma. She's been doing this a long time and she'll take care of you."

Melinda smiled at that. "Really?"

"I promise."

Melinda smiled wider. All hints of her previous worry and sadness melted away like the ice cream was starting to.

One of the two phones on his desk began to ring. He picked up the old-fashioned black rotary phone.

"Hello?"

"Erik, it's Patrah. Are you done spending time with Melinda yet? If not, I can always come back later."

"Hold on." Erik held his hand over the mouthpiece and moved the headset away from his face. "Melinda, are you ready to go home or do you want to hang out a little more?"

Her face screwed up, then she sighed. "I want to hang out more, but my mothers are expecting me home to help pack up."

Erik nodded at that. He knew that Melinda and her family would be staying here at the Agency building with Patrah while they were gone. He'd been against the idea initially, but with all the new things going on, the attacks in New York and on his mother and grandma, Erik had changed his mind. This would likely be the safest place for her. He went back to the phone.

"She'll be down in a minute, Patrah."

"Okay, thanks."

He hung up and looked back to where Melinda was scraping the carton clean with her spoon.

"Okay, well I don't think your moms or Patrah are gonna be real happy with the sugar rush they're gonna have to deal with, but it should be fun for you."

They shared a conspiratorial smile as she rose and they headed for the elevator. Daniel floated through the floor directly in front of them and Erik jerked to a stop gripping Melinda's shoulder.

"What is it?" Melinda asked her voice wavering a little.

Erik shook himself and loosened his grip on her shoulder. Daniel was staring at him, arms crossed, just waiting.

"Sweetie, why don't you take this elevator down by yourself? I need to stay here and talk to someone."

Melinda looked around in confusion for a second before shrugging her shoulders and getting in the elevator. He kept waving at Melinda as the golden drop squeezed through the floor until he couldn't see her anymore.

Then he whirled on Daniel.

"What is it?"

"What do you mean?" Daniel smirked.

"Don't give me that. You know something. It's something you want to share, too. Otherwise you wouldn't have that smug look on your face." Erik knew this man; had loved him, no matter how long they had been separated before his death.

"You know this is even more of a mistake than what's happening in New York," Daniel said.

"And what exactly do you know about New York?" Erik wasn't up for another fight about traveling to Zebub.

"I was there. Trying to get some information."

"In the space between the meeting and now?"

"No, it's where I was earlier."

"Why?" Erik asked

"I had questions of my own I needed answered. But that's not the point. The point is what I found out."

"What did you learn?" Erik asked.

"You're in trouble." Daniel drew out the last word in a sing-song taunt.

"Really, Daniel? That's not attractive," he snapped.

Daniel smirked and gestured to his ruined chest. "But this is just sexy as hell."

"What did you learn?" Erik asked again, refusing to rise to the bait.

"The Angelics are up to some dark stuff. Like really dark. I didn't get to see too much because I think one of them spotted me."

Erik jolted at that. "Saw you?"

"It reacted to me, at least. I figured it wasn't best to stick around and see if they could somehow do something to me in this form. They had humans on meat hooks in a warehouse. Some were clearly Suits and others were Blooded. But there were plenty of non-blooded."

"Do you know the location of the warehouse?"

Daniel smirked. "Of course."

Erik turned to the second phone on his desk—a contraption of white crystal that sat among the computers, room controls, and other more advanced technology. The description he'd gotten was similar to the b'casters Matthias spoke of, in that they ran on their own locked-down network. They just didn't have the weird tentacle on the interface, which made them one hundred percent better than the b'casters, as far as Erik was concerned. They also didn't have a name, as far as he could figure out; they were just "Agency phones." It was a coin toss as to whether that was a stupider name than "b'caster."

Erik's bracelets slipped down his wrists and clacked against the crystal when he placed both hands on top of it. It recognized him almost immediately and began to glow. After the glow became steady and solid Erik removed his hands. The desk and phone in front of his eyes were replaced by a blank white screen. The most disconcerting thing was that it only changed what he saw directly in front of him; out of the corners of his eyes he could still see the room he was in. It made his eyes water if he concentrated on those borders.

"New York Offices," he said.

Immediately an Asian woman in a dark gray business suit appeared in front of him. Her hair was cut short and swept to the right.

"Agent-in-Charge Yoon here."

"Agent-in-Charge Allan speaking."

One side of her mouth turned down but she managed to cover it quickly. It was no news to Erik that the other Agents-in-Charge must have mixed feelings about him, to say the least.

"I'll get straight to the point. One of my sources has informed me that a warehouse in your jurisdiction is under the control of Angelics and full of perhaps still-living citizens."

By the way her stance got stiffer and her spine straighter he guessed she had known something about it. Or it could have been a response to his use of the term Angelic. The Agents didn't like it. That was why he used it often.

"Do you have a location?" She asked

Erik looked over to his left. Of course, the vision moved with him but he knew he was facing Daniel from the way his face felt chilled, as if a shadow had fallen over it.

Daniel whispered the location.

Erik repeated it and heard the sound of someone writing it down, right before she cut the communication dead. He blinked as his eyes adjusted to the dimness of the room.

"You're welcome," he sighed and tried to let go of the annoyance. He wasn't telling her for praise. He was telling her because some of those people could still be saved. He leaned back and turned on the computer that lived in a small cubby under the desk. Three of the screens on the desk came to life.

He sat back, ignoring the ghostly presence floating next to him, and watched the world flow by.

MANHATTAN

# MARIAN

She sat up and turned to the woman by her bed.

"Where are my clothes?"

"Marian, you should stay in bed," the woman replied.

The woman called her Marian. Was that her name? Did the woman know her? Did she know the woman? Her mind was full of holes but she knew there was something she had to do.

The woman stood up. She was . . . tall. At least seven feet. The crown of her head was covered in a short gray bob that brushed the ceiling. Her face was unlined despite the gray hair but it had the same gray tint to it. She had no heels on. Just sensible boots that her dark green pants were tucked into. Her shirt was the same green, with darker green trim around the neck and arms. Marian struggled to remember what this meant.

Finally it came to her—healer.

"No, I can't rest. I have to warn someone. I have to tell them about the warehouse."

The woman put her hand—the fingers just a bit too long and the palm a bit too narrow—on her chest and pushed her back with ease.

"You passed the message on already. You arrived and immediately let the Agent-in-Charge know what you saw."

Marion tried to lift her arm but it felt so heavy. She had to turn her head to look at it. She had lost one of her eyes. The memories came—transforming her true eye at puberty, crafting her Odin-eye from metal and knowledge and her own flesh, blessing it with ritual and hammer. She believed she could craft a new one but it would take time and she had to go somewhere else; somewhere special. A nest? She couldn't remember.

"What's wrong with me?" She finally asked.

The woman looked away from her, out the window on the right.

"You took your flock form. Do you remember?"

Her thoughts were hard to put in order but as she concentrated, she remembered the pain of splitting herself among many smaller forms, the fear that pounded through each of them as they fled. The harrowed night flight. The pain of death, as pieces of her fell prey to owls and other predators, or simply to the darkness that fooled their senses and confused their flight.

She had lost too many pieces of herself.

"We're pumping your body with what it needs to build itself back up physically. Your mind . . ." She shrugged. "We don't know."

She nodded. Marian remembered that she was rare. Her people didn't usually leave their home nests. She did, though. Why? She went back to the memory of her people and their nests. She held onto that thought and slowly clawed her way to a related memory, and so on. She gathered more knowledge of her line and her people, until she reached the knowledge she wanted.

Most of her memories would return, slowly. Details may not return but the general shape would fill in. It would simply take longer for her brain to recover than her body.

"Attack?"

The healer looked at her again. "They believe that something has happened to Anoan, by the way that the portals closed. Perhaps the darkness itself. For now, they are classifying it as a city gone rogue. None of the other Ante cities will even speak of Anoan. They say they are shunning it. The other Headquarters are placing themselves in defensive modes as much as they can without raising too much suspicion. They're pulling back from meeting with Antes; fewer missions, while fortifying and arming themselves."

She nodded. Only bits and pieces of what the woman said made sense to her, but she tried to remember every word so she could decipher them later, as she healed.

The healer was leaning over her, ready to say more, when she heard the door open. Five people strode in. Four of them obviously surrounding the woman in the center. The four outside were dressed in black suits while the woman in the center wore a dark gray one. The two in the rear stopped at the door, stationing themselves on either side of it. The tall one with the same gray, stretched-out features as the healer stayed on the outside of the open door. The second, no less tall but less angular, with a copper tint to her dark skin and a shaved head, stopped right inside the door.

The other two guards gave her pause. She wondered if she would be used to them when her mind recovered but something in her said no. These two would always startle her. Their eyes, noses, and mouths were identical and everything, from eyelashes to irises to teeth, was colored the same: a red-brown like rich clay. She thought they were wearing masks but then the eyes blinked in unison. Other than the small ovals of their faces, the rest of their visible skin was covered or made up of patchwork fabric. Their fingers ended in tiny knots, loose fabric hanging from the tips.

She tore her gaze away from them as the woman in gray stepped directly in front of her and spoke.

"I would like to thank you for bringing us such important information at dear cost to yourself."

Marian studied the woman. Average height with dark hair that had some white strands that she made no effort to hide. Her eyes were drawn to the tension at the corner of the woman's lush lips. She wanted to reach up and smooth it away. She remembered being allowed to do so but something niggling in the blank holes of her mind told her that was no longer the case.

After some effort she remembered the woman's name:

Agent-in-Charge Hilarie Yoon.

Hilarie cleared her throat and said, "If you could remember the actual address, that would be even more helpful."

Marian searched her memory and struggled to recall the moments right before she had broken apart. She remembered flashes; people hanging on hooks, the Ante crushing her Odin-eye, the Antes coming, the boy not listening to her. No matter how she strained, though, the address was part of the knowledge that she had lost. She knew what but not where. It could come back in time, but they could also be moving their operations right now.

She focused on the boy next. She remembered what he looked like, olive skin and long dark fringe that fell into his face. But she couldn't remember his name. Suddenly her weak body began to shake and sweat burst onto her skin.

What was his name?

He had been important and she had promised she would remember and already she had broken it.

What was his name?

She needed to remember!

She felt a large hand on her forehead, too large to be Hilarie's.

"Agent-in-Charge? I'm sorry but I told you she wouldn't be ready for this so soon."

"You did." There was a pause. "I apologize."

She heard the sound of retreating footsteps and she let the mental exhaustion of struggling to remember drag her down into fractured landscapes halfway between dreams and memory.

Marian was released from bed rest a couple of days later, though she was still confined to a wheelchair and to the building. More of her memory had returned, and that morning she had remembered something about the warehouse's location. She made her way to the Agent-in-Charge's office, refusing a number of offers from people wanting to push her chair and one rude man who just did so without asking. She had made him stumble by braking the chair completely and then glared silently until he left.

The gray and bald bodyguards were outside the AIC's office and waved her through. The office was dim. The only light came from the setting sun outside the windows. The two ragdoll bodyguards were in the corners. Their cloth looked darker somehow. Their clay mask-faces were now a dark twilight-gray, the lips frozen into comically-extreme sad faces.

Hilarie looked up from her desk and spotted her.

"Did you remember something?" She asked immediately.

She nodded and wheeled closer. "Not an address, but I believe it was in the Meatpacking District."

The Agent-in-Charge was already reaching for the more mundane-looking phone on her desk. She lifted up the handset and began speaking as soon as the mouthpiece was against her face.

"Concentrate searches in the Meatpacking District. Check former, unconverted slaughterhouses and packing plants especially. Double up the teams, but reiterate it is only find and report. No heroics until we have a definite location."

Hilarie hung up and looked at her closely.

"How are you recovering?" She asked.

Marian cleared the lump in her throat. She could still not clearly remember what had broken them apart but she was feeling more and more like it had been her fault. "My memories are returning. Slowly, but they are returning."

Hilarie nodded. "Good, if any other—"

The crystal on her desk exploded into a rainbow that bathed the whole room until Hilarie put both her hands on it and it settled into a more subdued white glow. When she removed her hands two beams of white light shot from the crystal and focused on her eyes.

"Agent-in-Charge Yoon here," she said.

She cursed the loss of her Odin-eye. If she'd had it she could have used it to see through Hilarie's eye. She still would not have been able to hear the voice of whoever was calling Hilarie but she was a fair lip-reader. All of it was moot, though. Her Odin-eye had been crushed and all she could do was listen to Hilarie's side of it, which only consisted of one other sentence.

"Do you have a location?"

Hilarie scribbled something down and then broke the line of light with her hands, shutting off the call. She picked up her other phone again.

"I have a lead, but it's not in the Meatpacking District. I suspect a second location. Split off half the teams and have them check out Inwood. Remind them to be careful."

Hilarie hung up and let her head hang down. A memory surfaced—of her standing behind Hilarie, rubbing her shoulders and leaning over to—Marian quickly turned her mind to something else. She looked up and saw the ragdoll bodyguards looking at her, their frozen faces studying her.

She turned to leave.

"Stay," Hilarie said quietly.

Marian maneuvered the chair around again and looked up at Hilarie, who looked just as calm and collected as ever, but she saw the way Hilarie concentrated her eyes on Marian's forehead instead of meeting her gaze.

"Sure."

Hilarie went back to work, acting as if Marian was not there at all. looking through reports and making the occasional short phone call.

Marian dozed in her chair until a book appeared in front of her, held by the patchwork fabric hand of one of the ragdoll guards. She took the book and tried not to look too hard at the hand. It was brown and red, and up close it looked as if it was covered in fresh blood.

They seemed more Ante than Agent, but she did not question her superior, let alone her ex. She turned to the book. It was a compendium of lesser-known bloodlines of the British Isles. She began to flip through and came to a portrait that looked like one of the two ragdolls. It was posed in front of a mantel. Its clothing looked like Elizabethan-era garb, with bright-yellow pants and suit jacket in yellow and brown motley. Its mask/face was porcelain and heavily painted in blues and pinks; a caricature of an angelic baby face. It stood with sword raised, staring straight off the page.

*Called the Jester bloodline, they are believed to originate only on the British Isles. In truth, no one knows much of these descendants. The need to cover themselves with fabric and masks comes to the bloodline later in life; a psychological need that seems universal. They have the ability to create masterpieces of costuming and makeup that can make them look like anyone, but they prefer their obvious masks and motley. Older members are rarely if ever seen uncovered. People that have caught glimpse of them unclothed tell tales of skin actually turned to fabric, and of faces that look like masks already. They can speak but rarely feel the need to. Their powers lie in the direction of misdirection, the stage, and costuming. Many go into theater work, either as stage managers, stuntmen, costumers, or makeup artists. There are a small but noticeable minority of jesters that uses their talents towards darker ends, becoming some of the most dangerous assassins in the known world. Their masks and motley change colors and designs without discernible pattern. No one knows if this is an aspect of their power or simply a matter of quick-change. Some have suggested the masks and motley serve as communications to others of their blood.*

The phone rang and Marian jumped.

"Agent-in-Charge," Hilarie answered.

She watched Hilarie's face spasm for a moment before it settled.

"I want to send as many as we can spare. Arm them with everything we've got. If we let this continue without reprisal this will be the beachhead to something much larger."

Hilarie spoke of logistics for a while longer but Marian stopped paying attention to her ex-girlfriend's words.

Marian wanted to go. She wanted to fight alongside her brothers and sisters and protect the nest she had made for herself. She owed them for her own pain and for the boy who had died to buy her time. She remembered more of his death now, but still not his name. She began to wonder if that were not a form of punishment in and of itself. Marian opened her mouth to say something, though she knew the answer would have to be no in her still weakened state.

She froze as the shadow of the raven rose in the back of her mind, the brief, intense moments of wisdom her people sometimes experienced.

She was needed here. She closed her mouth.

So Marian stayed with Hilarie as she worked to distract herself and they waited for news. As time dragged on, she stared at the hands of the ragdoll bodyguards—assassins really—and felt terrified, because she knew that much more blood would stain their hands before this was all done.

# SAN FRANCISCO & ZEBUB

# MATTHIAS

Matthias spent the days between the meeting at the Agency building and their departure introducing more independents to Erik. When he came to pick up Erik on the day of their departure, he was surprised to find his former aspirant dressed up. He had shaved the sides of his head, leaving a little of the stubble while the hair on top was still curled into a tight afro. He wore a suit of dark red with a black button down and black belt. He didn't go as far as to wear a tie, and his shoes were Doc Martens, but it was still a very different look for Erik. It made him look older, and more mature. Matthias looked away as Erik opened the door. Erik threw his duffel bag in the back alongside Matthias's own and slid into the passenger seat.

"Where are Dayida and Ms. Jayl?" Matthias asked, smiling at the glimpse of the bracelets he had gifted Erik under the dark red cuffs.

"They went in earlier. They want to spend most of each day at the building. I told them they could just work off-site most of the time, but they insisted," Erik answered.

Matthias nodded and pulled the car out of the driveway.

"Are you ready for this?" He asked as he steered toward downtown.

Erik laughed, a little too wildly. "No. Not at all, but I don't see that we have a choice."

They spent the rest of the drive in companionable silence, only occasionally speaking to confirm this or that final thing.

"Tae knows his part, right?" Matthias asked.

"Yeah, I talked to him about it, made sure Daniel was nowhere around," Erik confirmed.

Erik had decided he wanted Tae and Elana on information duty, gleaning whatever they could about who on the other side might be turned to their way of thinking. Tae could use his vision and Elana's intangibility would be useful. He had also tasked them with watching Tassi and Yonas.

When they arrived downtown, Matthias parked in one of the long-term lots, not knowing how long they would be gone. Time seemed to move a little faster there, but still there was no telling what would happen on the other side. He could have returned the car to the Organization, but they hadn't asked for it.

They walked into the lobby and saw Dayida and Ms. Jayl waiting for them at the counter. They all greeted each other and Erik turned to the young woman behind the counter.

"Hello, Zaha."

The woman smiled at them all and asked. "Is it time?"

Erik nodded and Zaha took a deep breath.

Ms. Jayl stepped up to the young woman and laid her hand on Zaha's shoulder. "You need not worry. We will not let anything harm you while the portal is open, or afterward," she said.

Her soothing voice was the same one he remembered from his younger days. He watched as the stiffness left Zaha's body so fast that he worried she would slump out of her chair.

"Are the others here?" Matthias asked her.

"We are." Tae came around from one of the nooks behind the desk. Elliot was right behind his aspirant, wearing a pair of black jeans with a black leather jacket that made his skin glow and his dark hair and eyes more mysterious. Tae had opted for blue jeans and a gold shirt with a pattern that looked like thousands of tiny crowns traced across it. He also wore a black leather jacket.

"Are we just waiting on Elana and Daya?" Matthias asked.

Everyone nodded and Erik looked down for a moment before asking. "Has anyone seen or heard from them lately?"

Everyone shook their head except for Elliot, who shrugged. They waited as the minutes ticked away. Matthias opened his phone and texted a few of his connections some last-minute information. Tae was chatting with Zaha while Elliot shifted uncomfortably from foot to foot, not meeting anyone's eyes. Then Elana floated in, followed by a scowling Daya, who nonetheless had her luggage slung over one shoulder.

"We're here." Elana did not sound pleased.

"Thank you both for coming," Erik said.

They both frowned at him and Matthias spoke up to break the tension. "Everyone ready?"

"No, but let's do this," Tae answered, and they all grabbed up their bags. Out of the corner of his eye, Matthias saw Zaha roll her chair back and shock flash across her face before she could stop herself.

Matthias knew Daniel had arrived. He did not turn and neither did Erik, though the young man had to be aware of the presence. They moved toward the golden elevators, where Erik gestured them all into one. The golden drop expanded further and further, becoming fatter to accommodate them all.

Elana hovered outside.

Erik looked at her and then to the left at something Matthias could not see and spoke. "Everyone inside. The elevator is the only way."

Matthias remembered this from his research. The way to the portal was sealed by a bloodline called The Winding Path of the Left Hand. They were never that numerous, and of the handful that remained, a few could create paths and doors through pain and blood. The Agency didn't keep any records of what they paid for the creator's service.

The silence became tense as the doors closed.

"This will be . . . uncomfortable," Erik warned as he touched the wall.

Matthias watched him make a complicated gesture with his thumb and pointer finger, drawing them together and apart at odd angles. Finally, he stopped, and the elevator began to rumble and the floor began to dip in the center.

They all slid toward this center, and scrabbled to keep their footing. The walls were pushing them closer together as well. It wasn't just the floor that was stretching. They were being pulled from either end, becoming taller and thinner. They were crushed together; pressed body to body. Crushed further, and deeper to the point where they should have been flattened. All groans and cries and yells were gone. The air itself was forced silent by the pressure.

The feeling was not pain exactly. But it *was* on the verge of pain—the edge of it—that level of discomfort that threatens to turn into pain with one wrong move. Matthias could not tell whom he was pushed up against, but there was not an inch of his body that was not pressed against someone else.

All of a sudden, right before it became unbearable, when Matthias started to think something had gone wrong and they would simply be stuck like this forever, it stopped. The golden bubble came to a stop and burst around them, showering the room with golden light that faded slowly. They were released and there was space and breath and air.

Without thinking, Matthias reached forward and punched Erik on the arm, fairly hard. The man turned to him.

"You could have warned us," Matthias said.

Erik shrugged. "It was better to do it without warning; less chance for anxiety to build up."

"More chance of a panic attack," Tae said, voice higher and tight.

Erik frowned but then nodded looking chagrined. "You're right. It wasn't for me to decide how you would all react. I apologize." Most of the anger left their faces at his apology, but there was still some anxiousness. If the pathway to the portal was that traumatic, what kind of transition would the actual portal entail?

Matthias turned to look around the room that held the portal. It made him think of a cell. There were no doors or windows, and no way in or out. The walls were plain gray stone but they had symbols scrawled all over them in gold and red: precise circles and stars. Symbols and letters he hadn't bothered to learn. Erik moved forward and held his hands over the wall. Matthias turned toward the portal, which lay in the middle of the room in the center of four connected arches of black stone.

Erik's Agency liaisons, Tassi and Yonas, were waiting for them with bags over their shoulders. As per usual, they were wearing black suits.

"They should be expecting us," Erik said with a smirk. "Who wants to go first?"

They all looked at each other. With a loud swallow, Elliot strode forward, turned to smile back at all of them, and stepped through the portal. Elana floated through right after. Then Daya crossed, with her powers turned on: her skin grey and rough and her face nearly featureless. Tae followed next, his eyes blazing brightly with power.

Somewhere along the line, without discussing it, they had all decided to go through with their powers running on high, ready to defend themselves.

Matthias looked at Erik who forced a smile onto his face and nodded at Tassi. She stepped through, her braid flashing around her in an invisible wind and a peaceful look on her face. Her bloodline was rare to the point of unknown. All Matthias had been able to dig up were a few sentences about mountains and being married to a wind god. Yonas followed right afterward with her face turning transparent, skin and muscles invisible, so that only her skull showed through. She was a daughter of death, the child of one of the Psychopomps, though Matthias couldn't tell which. As they each passed into the portal they simply disappeared as if they had never been there at all.

Matthias smiled as he looked back at Dayida and Ms. Jayl.

"Take care Yida, Ms. Jayl. We'll be back soon."

They both returned his smile and came forward to hug him. As Ms. Jayl embraced him she squeezed tight and whispered in his ear.

"What did I tell you about calling me Hettie?"

It wasn't funny but still the laughter ripped out of him, a nervous release he'd needed. He called on the power in him and watched as the world turned to gray scale, heat glowing in his vision. He could almost see the portal itself.

He dove forward and his body exploded. Everything about him that was physical, the material of his body, dissolved and he was just consciousness. He threatened to break apart as he was swept through space, tendrils of his self thinning and spreading. He struggled to keep them together. He traveled like this for days or weeks or months, spread out among the stars where time had no meaning and space was the dimension that he had somehow become.

Finally he saw the end of the road. It was a bright, shining crack in the unremarkable space around him. He hit the crack and it held him like a web. Its sticky arms gathered all of him together, even the tiny bits he had lost and not noticed. He was spit out and landed in a crouch. His power was no longer surrounding and shielding him. It curled in his chest, pulsing, and waiting as it always was. He looked up to find the rest of his allies arranged in a semicircle in front of him, facing a group of monsters and humans.

Like him, all their powers were inactive. They had been unable to maintain them during the journey.

The portal behind him made a crackling sound and he moved out of the way. Erik landed fine, but then fell to the ground and began to convulse. His scream cut through the air. Matthias watched as Erik raised his hands, which were curled like claws, and began to rip at his own face. Matthias immediately reached for his wrists, pulling Erik's hands away before he could do more than mar his cheeks with a few scratches.

"Erik, what is it?" Matthias asked.

But Erik just kept screaming; long drawn-out painful howls. His body wasn't convulsing any longer, but Matthias could feel the strain as it tensed. Pink-tinted tears ran down his face and mucus ran from his nose and mouth. His lips bled from multiple bites.

"What is wrong with him?"

The voice was oddly accented; a mix of London and Surfer Boy that clashed and sounded a mess. Matthias knew it was no one they had brought with them. Whatever it was that was happening to Erik, the effect seemed to be lessening. His cries were softer now and he moved slowly, pushing himself off the ground. Matthias tried to help him but the other man shrugged off his hands. Matthias became aware that Tae was also crouched nearby.

Erik rose to his feet, and Matthias could see the way he locked his knees to stay upright. They faced the assortment of Antes and humans, though he remembered they called humans 'dants here.

"I thought we were granted safe passage." Erik's voice was a growl and little drops of blood flew from his lips.

There was a series of sounds, growls and screeches, along with bright flashes of light and scents that exploded and faded with unnatural speed. Matthias did not close his eyes, cover his ears, and pinch his nose, though he dearly wanted to. He focused on the monstrous shapes of the Angelics—no, the *Antes* that were all around him.

"They have no idea what has happened. No one else has reacted this way."

Matthias looked at the man who had spoken, one of four humans he could spot in the crowd. The man looked like a middle-aged college professor in some Midwestern town, if the professor were wearing pristine white robes and clearly believed he was in charge. A middle-aged Midwestern college professor going to a frat's toga party, and thinking he was still cool. Matthias hated him instantly.

"You are?" Matthias asked.

The man was about to respond when one of the Angelics came up and pushed the man back. It moved forward on multiple spindly legs. It had a pencil-thin torso with multiple arms sprouting from its shoulders. "I am Chayyliel, a Queen of the Ruling Courts and Head of the

House of the Long Arm. Be welcome in Zebub." Mouths on its shoulders opened and closed, echoing every word it said.

"We don't care—"

A hand on his shoulder stopped what Matthias was about say. He turned to Erik, who shook his head.

"And who are your companions?" Erik asked.

Chayyliel gestured and another Angelic came forward. This one had legs that bent the opposite way and its entire body was covered in coarse black hair, with the exception of its neck and face, which were covered in tight skin so pale it had a yellow tint. It had no mouth or nose that he could discern. Instead there were at least a dozen haphazardly placed eyes that seemed to focus on them all at once.

"May I present Bethadi, Head of the House of the Darkening Sun."

The Angelic did not speak. Matthias did not think it could. At least not verbally. He saw nothing resembling a mouth. Then he remembered the burst of smells and lights as they had landed. Was that how this bloodline communicated? To their surprise the Agency hadn't had much information on Zebub or the other side of the portal. Just vague things they'd made assumptions about.

It continued like that, Chayyliel introducing monster after monster, giving Erik their name and title. Matthias missed a lot because he was focused on Erik, watching to make sure the man did not collapse again. Thankfully he seemed to be getting stronger not weaker as more time passed. One thing that Matthias *did* notice is that none of the other Angelics were introduced as Queens the way that Chayyliel had introduced itself. One of the facts the Agency was fairly certain about was that there were numerous Queens for each city. Was that wrong? Or did Chayyliel simply not invite any of the others?

Finally, Chayyliel gestured and the four humans stepped forward. Along with the older man from before there was a younger man and two women. The two women both wore white and silver bodysuits that shone against their dark brown skin. The younger woman had one arm that was an intricate skeletal creation of silver and red. The younger man was in a shirt and pants that seemed to have a lot of unnecessary ruffles and whose stance was angled wrongly, as if his body had some injuries or stiffness that forced him into uncomfortable positions.

Chayyliel chorus-voice-pointed at each as he introduced them.

The older robed man. "Holder Mayer of Kandake Athenaeum."

The older woman. "Holder Riana of Hypatia Athenaeum."

The younger woman with the silver arm. "Holder-Apprentice Razel, also of Hypatia Athenaeum."

The younger ruffled man. "And lastly Holder-Apprentice Haydn of Enheduanna Athenaeum."

Each bowed their head in turn but none said anything. There had been some mention of the Athenaeums in the Agency's files. Places of learning and power. The only places the humans—*'dants* of this world—could find sanctuary and power of their own. Matthias wondered at them working alongside The Ruling Courts. but one thing he knew crossed all planes of existence: those in power will betray those they are supposed to serve for more power. That was a universal truth.

Erik stepped forward, his stance now steady and solid. When he spoke his voice was still rougher than its usual tone. "I am Errikos Sabastian Allan, Primo of the Organization of Drum and Fire, Head of the San Francisco Offices for the Agency of Interdimensional Travel and Cooperation. These are my companions:

"Bloodeds Daya, Elana, Elliot, and Tae. Independent Matthias, and Agents Tassi and Yonas."

"And him?" Chayyliel gestured behind them and they turned. Matthias finally got his first glimpse of Daniel and it was not a good one. The boy looked sick but then Matthias waved that thought away; after all he was already dead. However, Elana looked like herself *before* her death while Daniel seemed frozen at the moment of death and unable to change beyond that. The gasps from his companions let Matthias know that they could all see him. Even Daniel looked confused looking down at his floating body.

Eventually he settled into crossing his arms over the hole in his chest and staring them all down.

Erik cleared his throat. "That is my companion, Daniel."

Matthias frowned at the term companion but then what was Erik going to call him? There was no official designation for Daniel and none of them had prepared for this eventuality. After an awkward silence the older man, Mayer, stepped forward and spoke.

"We know you must want to rest after your journey, but the Courts wished to have you for dinner first."

"That's some disturbing phrasing," Matthias muttered. He knew Erik had heard him from the flash of a smile that had appeared on his face.

"How is it that we speak the same language?" Erik asked Mayer.

Mayer looked at Chayyliel first and waited for the Angelic to nod before he answered the question.

"Our city and yours are linked. Though our city is older than the modern incarnation of yours, there have been older cities there through the turning of the ages. Since we are linked, there is an echo; effects are transferred from one to another. You will find odd coincidences like this. The places where the Hives are located here are most likely where your center of government is located. Things like that."

Matthias was surprised to see the other Holder and the two Holder-Apprentices listening as closely to this explanation as the people in his own party were. He would have assumed that they would all know this.

"Let us all adjourn to the courtyard for dinner. I am sure the other Courts will be anxious to meet our guests."

Erik raised an eyebrow but only said, "What about our bags?"

Chayyliel waved one of its appendages, pincers cutting through the air with an audible sound. Smaller things appeared around their feet. They looked like crosses between crabs and slugs, bulbous bodies covered in chitinous armor with two large appendages up front. Except in this case the appendages ended in very human-looking hands. All of their bags were taken—in Matthias's case yanked from his hands—and the things sped off.

Chayyliel turned and began to walk away, the other Angelics falling in behind him. The rest of them followed. Matthias hurried to walk beside Erik. He wanted to ask him what had happened, but not when they were surrounded by so many enemies. The young Holder-Apprentice Haydn came up on their side.

"We do hope you'll be able to help us with the darkness." He said, sidling in between the two of them and placing a hand on Erik's arm, turning his back to Matthias. Matthias bared his teeth at the man's back but said nothing.

He watched Erik shrug off the hand. "We'll do our best. Where is *your* Holder?"

The young man's face darkened, turning a purple-red, but what was interesting were the erratic patches of skin that stayed pale.

"How do you know I have one?"

Erik raised an eyebrow and Matthias took the opportunity to interject himself into the conversation.

"Because we're not dumb?"

The boy turned back to Matthias with an ugly snarl, which Matthias met with a small smile and continued to speak.

"We were actually listening to the introductions and your titles. We noticed that Riana and Razel matched up—Holder and Apprentice. But neither you nor Mayer seem to have the same." Matthias kept his voice sweet and curious, and the boy scowled at him for a moment before moving off without another word.

"We are not to speak of those who are missing."

The voice was quiet and too close. Matthias started, having not sensed the younger woman coming up behind them. She was stunning up close, her deep brown skin marked with healed scars. Her silver and red hand was a work of gorgeous intricacy. Her eyes were a brown so dark they were almost black.

Erik and Matthias shared a look.

"Why are we not allowed to know?" Erik asked, just as softly.

"It's not just to you. We are not to speak of it to anyone. Which reminds me. You are not to speak of your world to any 'dants but us four."

Matthias looked around at the odd black walls in the hallway they were moving down. The surfaces were not smooth but covered in jagged outcroppings. From some angles the outcroppings looked like pieces of bones, with a partial skull here, and the rounded end of a tibia there. The old fairytale of Jack and the Beanstalk came to mind. "I'll grind your bones to make my bread," the giant had said, but here it seemed they had ground bones to make a wall. How many people had been used to make this long hallway?

"None of the humans here know about other worlds, do they?"

He asked it quietly as he stared at a spot on the wall where the light reflected on an almost whole skull, sheared from the eyes up but mouth open, screaming out. He looked back at Razel.

"Humans?" Razel asked.

Matthias glanced toward the front of their group where Elliot and Tae were having a conversation with the Holder Mayer, who kept glancing back at them. No. Not at *them*. At Erik.

"Humans are what we call ourselves in our . . . world." He heard Erik explain but Matthias kept his eyes on Holder Mayer. There was something off about that man.

The man turned back to Tae, who shot Matthias a look over his shoulder, letting him know that he had noticed Holder Mayer's oddness.

He turned back to Razel in time to see her glance at her master, Riana, as she answered.

"Most of those who live here know nothing of other worlds or other ways to live."

Matthias guessed that she herself had not known until recently.

"They most likely do not want to instigate any kind of panic." Erik's voice was neutral as he spoke what they all understood to be a lie.

Razel frowned at him. "Their city is being devoured and they do not have the freedom to run or any knowledge of how to defend themselves. I would say that the 'dants are already panicking."

Erik inclined his head, acknowledging the point.

Riana moved through the group toward them and gestured for Razel to join her. Razel inclined her head at them both.

"Be careful."

It was said so softly that he thought he might have imagined the words as she walked away.

# LIL

Lil woke up in the clearing, still bleeding and in pain. She was unsteady, as she always was in these moments between dream and reality, when she thought her body still whole. The pain and trauma of her new body hit her fresh every time.

She groaned and lifted her head from the ground, finding Kima and Uchel talking off to the side and Assan crouched over her.

"Good you're awake. Get up," he grumbled.

Lil snorted and flapped her hand in his face.

Assan grabbed her wrist and Lil struck out with her other hand, catching him in the side, causing him to lose his balance and fall into the dirt.

The sound of his indignant yell drew Kima and Uchel's attention to them and the two women hurried over. Kima's tan skin was covered in cuts of varying depths but none of them were bleeding anymore. It probably had a lot to do with the green paste that was smeared all over Uchel's small and knotted hands.

"You're awake. Good." Kima offered.

Kima knelt beside her and held her arm out to help Lil to her feet. Lil stood shakily and faced Uchel.

"Are you hurt?" The older woman asked.

Lil gestured to her side.

"You reopened your wounds?" Uchel interpreted.

Lil nodded.

"Do I need to look at them now?"

Lil shook her head and endured the concentrated stare of the woman as she did her best to see if Lil was lying. Finally, Uchel nodded and spoke.

"Okay, then we need to figure out what we can and leave."

Lil nodded and turned looked at the tree that now stood in the middle of the clearing. The bark covering it was an abstract mix of dark and light. In small places, where the bark was thin, Lil saw hints of glittering black skin shining through.

"What was that thing?" Assan asked, looking directly at her.

Lil rolled her eyes and shrugged her shoulders exaggeratedly. She had never seen or heard of anything like it in all her time in Kandake. She reached for her pocket where her stylus and pad of paper were still secure. Before she could write anything down, though, a voice spoke from behind them.

"A monster."

Lil turned and saw the merchant from earlier, the one who had given her the knot of wood. They still wore their mask and full-body robe and moved across the ground in odd jerky movements. When she saw the symbol on their gloves again it knocked loose the memory she had been reaching for before. It had been worn by some of the refugees from The Out when they'd come to Kandake. She had asked Mayer about it and he had told her a little about the cult of the 'dant beneath our feet. Most 'dants did not cling to anything resembling religion. The 'dant beneath our feet believers were one of the exceptions.

"An abomination called Maasu," the merchant continued.

Assan raised his gun and aimed it at the stranger.

"Peace. I mean you no harm. In fact, it was I who gave your companion what she needed to defeat this menace," the merchant explained and kept moving forward.

Lil wrote:

*How did you know I would need it? Did you know it would attack?*

The stranger read the note and let out a laugh, an odd echoing titter reminding her of the animal noises in the dark forest beyond the clearing.

"We knew that something would be sent after you and that you would need help. Something to show you some of the power you carry so carelessly."

Lil clutched at her pocket that held the root.

The merchant nodded. "Yes, they are very powerful. Even we do not know all the things they can do."

Kima stepped between the merchant and Lil.

"Who is we?"

The masked person tilted their head to the side and studied Kima.

"You are trying to change this world. A noble pursuit. But it is too late. This world had some potential once. No matter how it began, there was hope once. But that was long ago."

Assan had come up on Kima's side and looked angry. His light brown skin was flushed with red, and his lips were twisted so that his teeth were showing.

Her pad was already out in her hand and she scribbled quickly and held the paper up. Lil ignored Kima's arm and moved out from behind them before this could devolve into a fight.

*Why do you care?*

"If any of us are to survive what is coming? You will need to complete what you started in the Ruling Courts. You must discover the truth."

*Why can't you do it?*

"We were cursed long ago, child. We were the hope that was killed; shattered, divided, and spread to the wind. We can no longer do what needs to be done. But you can." There was a soft wistfulness to the voice but it quickly became blank once again.

"How do we know that this isn't trap?" Kima asked moving to stand beside Lil.

"You don't." The figure made a gesture that looked like an odd, uneven shrug. "We can only say that we harbor no ill will toward any of you and hope that our actions will prove this."

*They did give me the wood that stopped the thing.* Lil wrote and showed to Kima.

"And if I wanted to betray you, I would just go to the Ruling Courts and tell them about your little band of revolutionaries," the merchant said.

Assan and Kima both stiffened and Lil cursed inside her head. It might have been true, but it wasn't exactly the most innocent thing to say.

"I have no interest in either you or anyone in your little movement. I am here to help the Holder do what must be done. And so I have two gifts for her."

Lil had turned back to the stranger. They moved closer with an odd jerky glide, as if they barely touched the ground but when they did touch it they stumbled.

"We cannot restore your tongue. That is gone forever. However, your voice is not gone with it."

They reached into their robe and Lil watched the ways in which the robe shifted and moved as they rummaged beneath it. Finally, they pulled out a knot of wood, larger than any that had been on their table. The branches that tangled together were almost as thick as her wrists and large thorns sprouted from from every angle; wicked, curved things whose tips sparkled. The wood itself was pale gray with an underlying shininess.

"We provide you with this gift."

They stepped forward and Lil's hands automatically rose to catch the tangle of wood as they let go. The thorns pierced her palms deeply. She let out a choked sound and tried to drop it but the thorns were embedded in her hands, the thing writhing in her grip, the branches looping around both of her wrists and latching on. She hissed through her teeth at the pain.

"What have you done?" She recognized Kima's voice but did not look up from the wood. She was pushed back and found Uchel in front of her studying the knot of wood attached to her hands. Uchel did not touch it.

"It will finish in a moment. And I would put away the weapon. It will not harm me but it will insult me and will simply rob you of a valuable resource."

The bark of the knot slowly turned from pale gray to a light pink and then a bright red. It was the dark red of old blood when it finally dropped to the ground. No one made a move to touch it. Lil looked down at the wounds it had left behind. She could see inside them as they gaped open, looking drained and sickly white. As she watched, each wound closed, leaving only thin silver lines all over her hands and wrists.

She looked up to see Kima and Assan pressed against the stranger. Assan's gun pressed into their belly and Kima held a knife up to the mask. Lil felt a warm lick of comfort in her stomach. They both had stepped in to defend her, even if it was only because she could be of use to them. It helped her feel less alone.

They both backed away slowly and the merchant followed step by step until he was in front of Lil again and Assan and Kima were on either side of her. Uchel had moved off to the side, watching the merchant warily.

"And for our second and final gift we grant you information. The Ossuary in the Courts is not the only repository of knowledge in Zebub. There is another, built by the same ones who built that Ossuary: those who survived the purge of the Ruling Courts. The ones who stayed as they were for a while longer."

Lil was reaching for her pad when the knot of wood rose from the ground where she had dropped it. She jerked back in surprise but watched it as it floated up. When it reached eye level, the branches began to squirm and slither around each other. They lengthened and stretched in an arc above her head.

They formed the words she'd been prepared to write down.

**DoYouMeanTheTraitorCourt?**

She stared in wonder at the words floating there. The others watched as she held out her hand toward them and the words untwisted, reaching down to snake across her palm like a pet showing affection.

The merchant broke the silence. "That is what they are called now, yes, but in the days when Corpiliu was built they were known as The Court of Swift Deliverance. They were honored for many years until their deception was discovered and then they were punished without mercy."

**WhatWasDoneWithThem?** Lil had barely thought the words before the wood snapped back into the air and they formed for every one to see.

"That is not as important as what they left behind and how it can help you," the merchant answered.

**HowCanIFindThisPlaceOfKnowledge?** Lil could not stop herself from smiling as she looked at the branch. It immediately squirmed and became other words.

**HowAmIDoingThis?**

"There are many secrets that have been lost or deliberately discarded. There are wonders that grow all over Corpiliu that are forgotten by almost all. This land and all that once grew upon it now dies along with that knowledge. The branch you hold belongs to a special tree that links this world with others and serves to link mind and land."

Lil did not truly understand *all* of what was said, but she understood enough.

The merchant seemed to think their explanation satisfactory and moved on. "To find this place of knowledge you need only ask the allies you trust above all others, the ones who have stood by you and rescued you again and again."

**WhoIsThat?**

"We have no doubt that you can figure it out, child."

Lil nearly growled in frustration as the branch twisted into another question.

**WillYouAnswerKimasQuestionNow?**

Lil realized that the branch could only write so much, stretch so far, because it unwrapped and reformed to spell out her next question.

**WhoIsWe?**

The mask did not move, of course, and yet Lil could feel the arrogance and quiet amusement that shone from the figure.

"You ask the wrong question, my child. *Now* we are no one. The question is who *were* we."

Lil noticed that the figure had been moving back slowly and they as a group had been following unconsciously, keeping the distance between them the same.

"We have much to think on. We should go," Uchel finally spoke. Lil turned to find Uchel staring intently at the merchant, but when Lil turned back to the merchant, he was gone. The slightest noise in the woods behind where he had been was the only sign of where he might have gone. Lil turned back and Uchel was searching the woods with her shrewd gaze, as were Kima and Assan. Lil joined them in searching but could see nothing at all.

"Kima, gather the herbs that you can," Uchel said, breaking the quiet.

Kima immediately headed back to the table and began to pick up spilled piles of colorful leaves and put them back into the bags and baskets they had carried here. Every once in awhile Lil would see her toss something to the side rather than save it.

Uchel stepped in front of Lil, reaching for the branch that still hovered in the air, but the thing flung itself back against Lil. It curled itself around her right forearm but did not cut her skin with any of its thorns. Uchel stared at the place where it pulsed slightly against the black fabric of Lil's sleeve.

Uchel frowned at the branch, and Lil raised one eyebrow at the older woman, who held up her hands and silently backed away with an exaggerated smile on her face. The expression did nothing to hide the worry and fear in her eyes.

They walked back to the house silently. All the small animals they had heard before were silent now. When they arrived at the house Lil said nothing to them and ignored the soft call of Kima as she continued to her room. Lil knew it was rude, doubly so because she was a guest here, but she did not want to talk right now.

She wanted to think.

As soon as she entered the room, the Nif who had formed her shoes and endured throughout the night slithered off. They collapsed in a pile in the corner and a number of the ones who had stayed behind hurried over and petted their exhausted relations.

Lil sat on the bed and thought of what the strange merchant had said about allies. Arel and Jagi were the obvious choice—ones who had stood by her side and never left and never given her reason to doubt. Except she could not find them or her sibs.

Lil sat on the bed and pulled out the root. She opened the bag and let the small bones fall into her palm. One of them bounced out of her hand and fell to the floor. Before she could get off the bed, there was the small sound of chittering and one of the Nif hurried over and raised it toward her with its starfish like arms.

She reached for it and froze staring at the Nif as it cooed at her.

The Nif. Allies she had made before all of this, who had been there for her all along.

She had never been sure how smart they were. Were they sentient beings who understood what she said, as they sometimes seemed? Were they animals who had learned to imitate 'dants behavior? Or maybe neither of these things? Maybe comparing the Nif to anything she knew was a mistake.

With a single thought the wood slithered off of her arm and floated in the air before the Nif.

**DoYouKnowOfKnowledge**

**HiddenInTheseWoods?**

And suddenly she was facing more than one Nif as all of those who had been scattered about her room rushed forward at once making affirmative noises at the same time.

**CanYouLeadMeThere?**

They were already rushing toward the door of her bedroom and looked back at her impatiently. She had not removed the jumpsuit yet, so she put on the boots she'd found in her room before the Nif formed into shoes again. She looked out the window and realized that Yanwan was not that far from rising. Already a false dawn lit up the sky. If she was going to do this tonight she should leave now.

She placed her finger over her lips and the Nif immediately quieted down. She cracked open the door to her room and looked out into the dark of the main room. She quieted her own breathing and tried to listen for any sounds. There was nothing, so she slipped through the door. The Nif tumbled over each other to get in front of her and lead the way. She moved silently through the house, creeping down the stairs and through the small living room into the foyer. They were almost at the front door when the voice stopped them.

"You trust that merchant?"

Lil turned and peered into the dark. There was the rough sound of a match being struck and the glow of light came from the dark corner she had just passed. Uchel was sitting cross-legged on the floor, in the shadow of the stairs. The light came from a candle in the woman's lap which lit up the wrinkles of her face, turning them into folds that made her look older, wiser, more dangerous.

Lil watched her. The branch that was now wrapped around her waist like a belt slithered its way free. The words formed between them.

**ITrustTheNif.**

Uchel looked down at the small creatures of shadow. Some gathered around her feet and others in a line straight to the front door.

"Well I guess I can't fault you on that. Since they did save your life."

Lil looked at the woman for a long moment before the branch reformed.

**HowExactlyDidYouFindMe?**

Uchel looked at her for a long moment before she rose from the floor smoothly, her age not at all evident in her movements. She moved toward Lil.

"It was in the woods a ways from here. Quinn and Assan found you as they were scouring the forest for herbs. You were wrapped in a cocoon of darkness. When Assan . . . disturbed them, they reformed into Nif and surrounded you. Quinn convinced them—"

**Quinn?**

"She has had some past experience with them."

Lil only raised her eyebrow at that but Uchel shook her head.

"It is not my story to tell."

Lil nodded, accepting that.

"Go. I will be here when you return," Uchel said.

Lil turned to go but stopped only a step from the door and turned back to the older 'dant who stood in the same spot watching her.

**KimaIsNotTheLeader**

**IsShe?ItsYou.**

Lil was sure of it. All the little things that didn't add up, the way Kima would defer to Uchel. The way that none would dare to cross the older 'dant. Lil had thought it was simply respect but there was more to it. This was the leader of the resistance.

Uchel's expression did not change.

"And now that you know, will you tell someone? The Ruling Courts perhaps?" It was said calmly, with no fear or caution.

Lil rolled her eyes before the branch reformed.

**WhyWouldIDoThat?**

**IHaveNoQuarrelWithYou.**

Uchel nodded, staring at her for a bit longer.

"Will you actually return?"

**YesButWhoKnowsWhatI**

**WillLearn?WhatWillChange?**

With that, Lil finally exited the house and moved with the Nif into the forest surrounding the house. Some of the foliage had recovered well from the burning. New growth was peeking through, though it sprouted from burnt stumps and branches. At one point, as they moved, Lil became aware of other buildings—small things of scavenged wood and metal she could see in the pre-dawn light. She saw no one as she moved through the outskirts of the small, scattered community.

As she followed the Nif deeper into the woods the foliage got denser. There was less evidence of burning, and less evidence of any 'dants. It grew dimmer as the canopy overhead blocked most of the light. Lil occasionally heard the calls of birds or the hunting yowls of small akoshes. If the sound was close then a group of the Nif would split away and run off. Sounds of squabbling and fighting would grow distant and the group would rejoin them later.

After what felt like hours she stopped, shocked by the total stillness around her.

The sounds of animals had been left far behind. The eerie silence almost qualified as a sound on its own, like a ringing in the air, or a resonance on the edge of hearing. The bushes around her grew taller as she continued to move, reaching past her hips. Their resistance and strength grew as well, so that she started to sweat as she pushed through. The Nif made their way one of two ways; either on the ground, moving through and around the roots that Lil kept tripping on, or the more adventurous ones skated across the tops of the plants, the fronds bending under their small weight.

Suddenly all the foliage was gone and Lil was stumbling and falling to her hands and knees. The pain of it reverberated through her elbows and legs and she bit through her lip. She stayed there, palms skinned raw, knees aching.

Lil looked up. The foliage around the clearing was too thick to see beyond. She looked behind her. The place she had fallen through had bent and broken plants that were slowly repairing themselves and returning to their former glory.

In some ways, it reminded her of the clearing that the night market had taken place in, but more powerful. Energy faintly pulsed, tinting the air with a rainbow sheen but this clearing was much smaller and completely bare. Also the ground here was nothing like the dirt-packed ground of the forest. It was stone; hard and rough.

Lil felt exhausted and achy—the effects of her fall into the clearing and the earlier fight combined to make her muscles scream in protest. She struggled to her knees and looked around at the large circle of black stone she rested on.

*Why do you come?*

The voice came from all around her. It was thick and liquid, like something you could sink and drown in. Lil understood the words even though she had no familiarity with the language. It was unlike any of the 'dant languages she knew; a steady pulse of sounds with no pauses or hesitation. The words flowed into one another like they were one word and she heard the translation in her head.

The branch moved from her arm and spelled out words in the air, anxious to answer the presence.

**IAmLilianaBlackthornJohns.**

**IComeForKnowledge.**

The ground began to shake and the tension that had been in the air took on heat and fire. It was a force of displeasure that Lil could feel.

*Speak.*

The branches moved again. The same message again, with the same two lines. First higher in the air and then against the surface of the stone. There was no reaction from the power around them. The branches began to shake and the letters of the words became loose and fell out of shape as the heat grew and she panicked.

The voice was like thunder when it spoke again. Sweat burst out all over her body and her eyes felt dry and sticky.

*Speak or be destroyed.*

Lil could no longer control the branch at all. It flopped and twisted next to her, writhing against the increased pressure and power just as she did. In desperation she grabbed the branch and did what she had been doing so much of lately. She bled. She dragged one of the sharpest thorns across her palm and let her blood spill onto the stone.

The blood bubbled and steamed where it landed. The steam filled her nostrils with the smell of burning meat.

Then everything stopped: the pressure, the shaking, all of it. Lil could breathe the air without heat searing the moisture from her mouth.

*I see.*

The ground had stopped moving underneath her and Lil lay flat, her cheek against the warm rough stone. It was no longer hot as fire, but a low, comforting heat that soaked into her abused body.

The voice echoed around her and this time purred in her mind as well.

*Yes. Blood is better than words. Blood speaks. Mine to yours. Yours to mine.*

Lil barely heard. She was too busy panting against the warmed stone, focused on the aches and pains in her body. She did not notice the softening of the ground, or the way that her body began to sink, until the moment her face was being pulled under. Lil tried to push herself upwards and while her upper half managed to rise a bit, it just made her hands and other parts sink faster. She tried to scream but the softened ground was already in her mouth, blocking off what was left of her voice. She waited to run out of air but it did not happen. She could breathe normally, though the air that filled her lungs was stale and old with musk and rot. But it *was* breathable.

When her face was completely submerged, all she could see was black. She could hear nothing, and feel nothing, but the ground that was slowly sucking her down. It was this sense of movement that kept her sane. As long as she was moving there was a purpose and she could believe she would not be trapped forever in the unending dark.

After only a few breaths Lil was spat out and down to the ground.

The fall was not far, but it still awakened the aches in her body. All the pain she had been put through over the last few days came rushing back. Still, Lil pushed herself to her knees and looked around. She was in a round cavern with no way in or out. The ground was surprisingly smooth, though the ceiling was littered with outcroppings of rock. The edges of the cavern had a circular river that rushed around and around. Swarms of insects congregated, with some floating on the surface and others flying in the constant mist that the rushing water threw up. The insects were the things illuminating the space. Their bodies flickered with every movement, a soft orange glow that set shadows to dancing.

The clatter of wood drew her attention to where her speaking-branch was clattering on the ground. Lil held out her hand and it slithered through the air, wrapping around her forearm. She'd had it for only a little while, but already found the weight of it comforting. There was the sound of more falling and a soft chittering as a mountain of Nif fell into a squirming, arguing pile before her.

She looked up in time to see the ceiling releasing the last of them slowly, bulging with its passengers. The bulge slowly moving down to one of the outcroppings, where it gathered like a drop of water at the tip. There was a tiny popping sound as it split and the last Nif fell to the ground.

Lil looked around, searching for why she had been led here. The air in the place felt old and stale with power in a way that reminded her of the Ossuary. The power here, however, was not tainted the way the space around the Ossuary had been. Lil took a deep breath through her mouth, savoring the flavor of it. She was busy taking in great lungfuls of the air so she did not notice the movement at first, but one of the Nif tripped over her foot and her attention was diverted back to them.

The Nif were gathering in two concentric circles. As she watched they completed the outer circle and all went still. She felt tickles across her skin and realized that the insects from the water were making their way to the center of the circle of Nif. A number of them landed briefly on her shoulders and scalp before taking off again.

Slowly, the insects gathered. They hovered and shivered and glowed brighter, and died by the dozen, falling to the ground in a constant rain. The insects fell but their light stayed in place, floating in the air, gathering more and more to itself. It grew so bright that Lil had to look away.

There was a scream that reminded her of the sounds she had heard 'dants make as they birthed children. It sounded like pain and tearing flesh and ecstatic relief all linked with one another. There was a final flash of light and when she could see again there was a 'dant before her lined with the aftereffects of the bright light. Looking closer Lil realized it was no aftereffect. This ‘dant glowed. She was now the source of light.

The ‘dant was like no one Lil had ever seen. She was a bit taller than Lil's own frame. Her skin was of a lighter shade than Lil's but not by much. But it held a glow of sunlight. Her hair was gathered into three thick braids, two on each side of her skull and one falling down her back. She wore a loose wrapping of sky-blue fabric that showed off her skin. Her arms and her legs from the knee down were completely bare. She smiled at Lil, her full lips quirking farther up on one side.

"I have not had a visitor in—" She paused and her head tilted to the side. "In fact, I do not think I have ever had a visitor who was not of my line. This is an occasion for celebration."

She tilted her head to the side farther and flashed a wide smile at Lil. It did not make her look friendlier. It made her looked amused at Lil's expense.

The branch floated into the air toward the ‘dant, and her attention went from Lil to the branch.

"Interesting."

**WhoAreYou?WhatAreYou?**

"I am all," she answered.

Lil struggled to interpret that and decided a different line of questioning might be better.

**HowDidYouComeToBeHere?**

"I am everything. In all places, but especially here, where they hid the last piece of me. Those that live here are me as well."

She gestured down at the corpses of thousands of small insects and as Lil watched they sank into the ground, disappearing, becoming a part of it.

"They live, they die, they live again."

**IMeantHowDidYouCome**
**HereInTheFirstPlace?**

The ‘dant took a step forward. Her hair and clothes moved in a wind Lil did not feel. The ‘dant's back was unbowed and so was her spirit. She was defiant and angry and her rage made her beautiful. She spoke as she got closer.

"There was war. A conflict that nearly ripped the world apart. Our children rose up against us and we lost. They took my body—those you call Antes—they took my form and all the power in it and they ripped it apart and shaped it to their ends. I was one of the last to fall and they took my body and used it to craft this world for them. This whole land would not exist without me. My bones became the rocks of the earth and the mountains and my flesh the ground. My blood and tears became the oceans and my hair the vegetation. I am this world and it is me but it was done by force, not choice. And so this world has been slowly falling apart ever since its beginning."

"I would have been dispersed, and become lone thoughts and feelings drifting in nothing until they met each other. But they spirited away my heart. A heart is no more important than any other organ, but it was whole and my essence remained whole within it."

She took another step forward and knelt before the first line of Nif, reaching out to touch them, caress them as they preened beneath her attention.

"My children," she sighed, glowing brighter. She lit up the whole space, as if Yanwan was at its brightest. In her light, the Nif cast giant shadows, shadows the size of Lil whose shape morphed back and forth from Nif to 'dant-like-figures. "Not all of our children turned against us, but they struck suddenly and viciously, wiping out many of the descendants that were loyal. My children were some of the few who stayed loyal, and survived in numbers. They joined the other side at my behest. I would have still lost, even if they fought for me, and they would have been destroyed."

"They came here with those who took my body. As I was being savaged they took my heart; smuggled it away before it could be transmuted to the core of this world. They did what they could."

"What is left of my children led you here."

Lil felt her eyes go wide with shock as she looked down at the Nif that surrounded the other 'dant. She met Lil's gaze for a moment and the sadness in her gaze was so deep that it broke Lil's heart to see it.

"These ones are the ones who stayed behind in the Hive, who held them off after the others took the heart. This is the punishment they received because none would speak. They became nothing more than servants for the Ruling Courts, forgetting who they used to be."

**WhatHappenedToTheOthers?**

**TheOnesThatRan?**

The 'dant rose to her feet and the Nif did not move, but craned their heads to keep her in view.

"They survived for a time. I gave them permission to carve my heart."

**TheyBrokeYouMore?**

"The important part is not the breaking but the asking. There are many who would choose to be broken to protect others. It is the consent that gives it sustainability, and that keeps me whole."

**WhatDidTheyDoWithThePieces?**

"Do you know what makes the Athenaeums refuges? What makes them fairly untouchable to the Ruling Courts?"

The woman was angry. Her rage was palpable in the heat in the air, and in the low groan that the earth made all around them. Lil suspected she knew the answer but wisely kept the branch still.

"Me! Pieces of my heart, freely given. They connect the Athenaeums, and give the Holders their connection. I am there in their minds and hearts. I'm their WiFi."

Lil frowned at the unfamiliar world, but before she could form a question the 'dant was waving her hand.

"Never mind. You'll learn that word eventually. No need to start now."

The Nif had gotten up from their still positions and were inching their way toward the other 'dant. She pretended not to notice but Lil saw the smile that lifted one corner of her mouth as her eyes flicked downward.

"They hid the last part of my heart here. When they linked it to this place, the power that protected them faded, and I saw the curse catch up with them. Change them. I don't know if they were better or worse off from my other shadow children. Their forms were changed but not their minds, and not their memories or knowledge or awareness."

The Nif had reached her feet and seemed to be urging one another on by their movements. Finally one was bold enough to reach out and touch her leg and find it solid. In a blink they were swarming up her form and she giggled, like a young child.

"Do they suffer more or less?" She seemed to be talking to herself.

Then she was looking back at Lil, meeting her gaze. "And then there are these Nif. The ones who found their ways from the Courts to the Athenaeums and in the presence of a piece of my heart began to recover some part of themselves."

Lil stared in shock for a moment. She had not realized that any Nif had followed her from the Athenaeum in the first place. She had not been able to tell them apart; those from the Athenaeum and those from the Courts; those that chose to come with her and those that stayed behind.

"I blather on so, don't I? No. Don't answer." She smiled and it was sharp and dangerous. "You had a question, that's why you came. Ask it."

Lil blinked, once, twice before she was able to shape the question.

**WhatIsIt?WhatComesForUs?**

"Worse than death. Worse than nothing. It is the space before creation; the demiurge that created all time and space, and all beings. My progenitor."

**WhatAreYou?**

The 'dant smirked again and Lil wanted to get mad but the barely concealed violence in the smile kept the words polite.

"You would call me a god. Many did. That is not the line of questions you wish to go down though, is it?"

**HowDoISaveCorpiliu?**

For the first time the other 'dant looked sad and Lil's stomach twisted around itself. She wrapped her arms around her middle.

"Corpiliu will fall. I will be free of this false bondage."

**IsThereAWay?AreYouLying?**

Lil noticed that the branches that spelled out the words were sharp and angular, bristling with long thorns.

The sadness did not leave her face and Lil's small flare of hope died quickly.

"I do not lie. A world made through force does not have strength enough to survive. At least not as you know it. Do not worry though. You will survive. I will tell you how. But you must do something for me first.

Lil blinked wide shocked eyes. Her mind was whirled in confusion. Her world was doomed. There was still the possibility that the other 'dant was lying, but something in what she said rang true. It was a fundamental rule of power—what was freely given was infinitely stronger than what was stolen. Intention had many effects on power and could make the very laws of the world to change with enough power.

The 'dant kept on as if she had not just told Lil that everything she had ever known would end.

"Mayer holds the piece of my heart in a tight grip. Otherwise the mantle would have already passed. He holds tight to my heart and uses it to keep himself alive long past when he should have passed on. He twists the intentions of the Athenaeum."

She looked at the Nif that clung to her form, and crawled over her shoulders.

"They all do, really, but he twists my heart's power far outside of its intention. The Athenaeums scattered across Corpiliu were to be sanctuaries and places of learning for those who wished to resist the monsters that ruled here. Most have kept at least some part of this, true, but Mayer and the others of Zebub? They work great evil with the Courts."

"A cleansing must come. It shall start with you and Kandake."

She stared deep into Lil's eyes. The wisdom there, combined with the age and pain, shocked Lil out of her own pain.

**HowDoIBreakSuchABond?**

"It is no bond he has to me but a chain. You must delve deep into the heart of Kandake. You must touch my heart. With a bond between *us,* the chain *he* keeps will break. But beware. There will be traps and defenders. Prepare yourself."

Tears came to Lil's eyes and the branch whipped through the air forming her words.

**WhatIsThePointOfItIfAllOfCorpiliu WillDieKandakeWillGoWithIt?**

The other 'dant sighed and rolled her eyes, tearing them away from a Nif curled on her shoulder that she was poking at, to its ecstatic delight.

"And what of your siblings? What of the two Antes that you care for? Will you condemn them to death when there is another way?"

The words stopped Lil's tears immediately. The guilt built inside of her like a wave. She had forgotten about Min and Davi, in the moment of grief.

"Guilt will do nothing for you. You must decide what you will do."

**YouWillShowMeHowToSaveMySiblings?**

"And all you hold dear. Yes. First you must reach Kandake's heart, though."

**IWill.**

She smiled at Lil and for the first time she sensed not violence lurking behind that smile but approval.

"Before you go, a lesson about history, Liliana Blackthorn Johns. Do you know why Babel is banned from use in the Ruling Courts or against its members, when no other power is?"

Lil shook her head.

"Babel was the first language, before all language. It existed when the world was not yet a thought. It is the language of the demiurge; the language used to create the spirit of all that is. Form follows thought. Material follows spirit and leads to becoming. It is what holds them together. With Babel strong enough you can pick them apart at the seams. That is why they fear it."

**WhatDoesThisMatter?**

**ICannotSpeakAnyLonger.**

"Babel is like any language, you need not speak it to use it effectively. Remember that."

With that final admonishment, Lil was back in the clearing, with a whole load of unhappy Nif chirping and wailing around her feet. She knelt down and petted them, and tried to soothe them through her touch the way the other 'dant had. It was odd, knowing that these beings had once been something else. Had once been the traitor court, if she was guessing correctly.

Finally, the Nif calmed down and slowly led her back to the house. Her body felt better, as if her time in the cavern had at least partially healed many of her hurts. She was sore where she should be pained, tender where she should be cut, and bruised where she should be broken.

Yanwan was already high in the sky and the land around her felt too bright. Every step felt heavy and purposeful with knowledge she had gained. When she arrived at the house the Nif had recovered some of their good humor and were gamboling about her feet as she opened the door and found the whole household waiting for her.

Staring at her.

"What did you learn?" Kima asked.

Lil slowly looked at each of them. How much should she tell them? She would most likely need them all in the coming fight. She answered as simply as possible.

**WeGoToCollectMySibs**

**ThenWeAssaultKandake.**

# RAZEL

Razel studied these 'dant who were not 'dants. These . . . *humans,* as they moved through the halls of one of the oldest hives, which belonged to the Court of Broken Angles and Choices. The nerves that welled up in Razel reminded her very much of her first dinner in the Ruling Courts. This time, however, there was no Lil to make an entrance. No Lil to steal everyone's attention. Razel found herself missing Lil, and wondering where she was. She had done her best to help her fellow Apprentice by giving the left-behind pouch to the Nif. She hoped it had done some good.

Riana walked beside her, mumbling to Razel but really to herself. She wanted no response.

"We cannot trust these 'dants. Who knows who they serve or what they want? They will most likely turn on us and we must be prepared. I do not understand why the Courts had the need to call these strangers. Our problems are our own and we can take care of them just fine. . . ."

The muttering kept on. She had very little to say to Riana lately. The revelation of additional worlds, and the scant information Riana had been willing to divulge, did not sit well with Razel. She wondered how much of her Holder's withholding information was reluctance and how much was simply ignorance. Of all the Holders, Mayer seemed to have the deepest knowledge of these alternate worlds, but he had been Holder of Kandake as far back as any 'dant could remember. So that made sense.

They entered the courtyard and Razel saw the visitors stop at the spread before them. Tables were scattered all over the courtyard, with more Antes than Razel had ever seen in one place seated all around. The air was thick with flying Antes. They swept through the air, barely avoiding collisions while their attention was directed downward.

"Holy fuck." This from the younger 'dant who had been introduced as Tae. As Razel turned to him she saw his eyes starting to burn a bright silver. It started in the center and then expanded outward until his whole eye looked like a vortex.

"Whoa." He staggered and immediately one of his compatriots was there to settle him.

"You OK, Tae?"

"Yeah, it's just . . ." Tae noticed Razel watching and from the expression on his face realized that he was not in a place to share things. ". . . a lot." He finished.

His eyes reverted from the silver whirlpools to a light brown. His dizziness seemed to leave him and he moved through the crowd of them toward the 'dants she had spoken to earlier—Erik and Matthias. He leaned forward into each of their personal space, his mouth moving close to their ears and sharing whatever Tae had realized. They both looked at him and nodded.

Erik leaned forward to reply but because of the angle she could read the words on his lips.

*Tell the others.*

As they got closer to the tables she watched Tae move from companion to companion and speak with each, always with his mouth close to their ear. Always the same hesitation in their response, and the reluctant nod of agreement.

Chayyliel and the other Antes wandered off to their own tables without a word. Erik made as if to follow them, but Mayer reached out and grabbed Erik's arm. He froze and the hint of violence grew thick in the air. He stared down Mayer, and for the first time since Razel had met the Holder, she saw him actually wither under another 'dants gaze. He let go of Erik's arm, trying to make the action seem less rushed and nervous than it was.

"Our seats are over here," Mayer said with a slight waver to his voice.

Erik stared hard before nodding and gesturing for Holder Mayer to lead the way. They moved through the tables, and Razel could see the visitors struggling not to indulge their curiosity and look around. They stared straight ahead until Mayer led them to an empty table. It was far closer to the center of the action than Razel had ever been seated before.

"Talk to him. They seemed to like you," Riana whispered directly to her apprentice.

Razel was surprised at the direct communication. Riana had been spending more time muttering or paranoid than communicating. Razel believed that actually seeing how little their power and influence meant here in the heart of the Ruling Courts had shaken, and perhaps broken, her Holder.

"Of course, Holder," Razel replied and moved from Riana's side. She made sure to place herself between the oddly translucent 'dant called Elana and Tae as they took their seats. Mayer tried to insert himself between the two called Erik and Matthias but both simply stared at him until he contented himself with sitting on the other side of Erik.

"So you are Apprentice to Riana?" The 'dant, Tae, asked with a small smile.

Razel took her eyes off Mayer's humiliation and returned the expression. "Yes, for almost ten cycles now."

Tae nodded and poked at the food on his plate. Razel looked down at her own plate, at a huge, seared chunk of botil meat with a spread of raccet leaves next to it. It looked normal to her, but she had no idea what these 'dants ate. She carefully cut off a chunk of the botil and speared it along with a few leaves of the raccet on her knife and ate it. She chewed carefully and swallowed before going back for more.

Razel waited until the others had started to eat before slowing down and turning to the woman on her other side, who had yet to eat anything on her plate.

"Do you really think you can help us with the darkness?" Razel asked. It was why they had come; a safe question. Razel longed to ask why she could see through the 'dant to her other side, but she doubted the question would get an answer.

"We hope so, but it will depend on how badly the darkness has invaded here and whether we can expect cooperation from everyone." Elana gave her a pointed look at the end of this speech.

Razel kept her face neutral. Yes, if everyone helped it would most likely be easier, but even now, as the darkness took whole pieces out of Corpiliu itself, she did not expect that cooperation to happen.

"I can only speak for myself. I will provide whatever help necessary to save my world."

The 'dant studied her for a moment longer before nodding. Razel wondered if she had gone to far. Technically she could not promise her help because it was not hers to give but her Holder's. Riana had said to get closer, though, and this seemed one way to do it.

Dinner conversation was awkward as both sides avoided speaking on things they didn't trust their new "allies" with. Razel was doing her best to figure out a new opening question when she heard the wave of noise moving through the crowd. Razel looked up from the translucent 'dant. It was June. Rumors had spread through the Courts like wildfire on what the White Snake had done to anger Queen Chayyliel so much. No one knew anything close to the truth. Because of this lack of knowledge and the silence on both their parts, June occupied an odd space in the Courts' hierarchy. Some refused to speak with them at all; mostly those who were strong allies of Chayyliel or those who *wished* to be allies of its Court. Other Courts that viewed Chayyliel as an upstart or that were already locked in enmity with its court treated June as they'd always been treated, a valuable ally and reliable source.

The division between the factions was obvious, as some Antes refused to even look at June as they passed, while others made a point of acknowledging them. They moved languidly through the crowd, the lights under their skin especially bright tonight and shaded with blues and yellows.

June came straight to their table with no hesitation. They did not look at any of the Holders or Holder-Apprentices, avoiding their gazes as if they were poison. Instead they met Erik's gaze directly and moved in on him. June crouched in the small space between Mayer and Erik, their back to the Holder, and held a hushed conversation. Razel kept her eyes on Erik but he said very little she could discern.

After a long time, Erik nodded and turned away. June stood and walked away without a glance at any of them.

Razel stared after them until a voice brought her attention back the table.

"What do you know of him?" The speaker, Tae, nodded toward June.

Razel smiled at him. "They, actually. I have had some dealings with them as of late. They have their own agenda, to be sure, but they have been . . . helpful in the past."

Tae nodded and turned back to his food. She ate and watched the table. The one called Erik had wrinkles in the skin of his face. Strain, if these other-wordly 'dants were as similar as her people as they seemed on the outside.

Mayer struck up a conversation with Erik, loud enough that he winced openly.

"We heard that you have been successful against the darkness in your home?"

She watched Erik turn his wince into a nod. "Yes, the encounter did end with the darkness leaving. It took all of us, really." He nodded at the rest of his people.

"We hope you can do the same for us."

Erik opened his mouth when a screech interrupted the conversation. Mayer's head whipped around and his eyes went wide at whatever the Ante approaching was saying. It was beautiful. No matter how she felt about most Antes, some of them still struck her with their beauty. This Ante was made of wings; hundreds of tiny incandescent blue-green-purple wings that glittered in the light. They moved in fractal patterns that made Razel want to reach out and touch.

Mayer looked back and forth once, before he translated the Ante's words. "You killed my broodmate."

Erik did not look frightened or impressed. He raised an eyebrow at Mayer. "You mean that ugly thing made of wings?"

The screeching came again, ragged and so piercing that Razel wanted to cover her ears, but she knew better than to show such weakness.

Mayer swallowed. "Chilidae of the House of Broken Barriers, member of The Court of the Neverending Wound, demands recompense for its lost family."

Erik rose to his feet and somehow in that moment he seemed much taller than his body; his presence filled the air around him and his very stance hinted at a willingness to kill. "You will get nothing from me. If your worthless broodmate had not tried to harm me it would not have had to die. It died because of its own stupidity. I was simply the tool that delivered the final blow. So, if you're feeling froggy? Leap." Razel did not understand the exact meaning of the expression but she recognized an invitation to battle when she heard one.

The air around them crackled with the potential of a fight. Razel reached under her jumpsuit without conscious thought, her metal fingers clicking against the handle of the weapon she always had there.

Finally, the Ante backed away slowly and Erik sat down, but the tension in his shoulders and arms did not go away. Dinner was silent after that. No one was ignorant of the scrutiny they were all under.

As always, they only knew the dinner was over when Antes slowly began to move away. Razel rose and Riana was instantly at her side.

"They will be staying in Chayyliel's Hive. None of the others would host them. Show them the way. Learn what you can. I will distract Mayer."

There was no pause for an answer before Riana moved off, and why would there be one? It was not a question or a request. It was an order.

# ERIK

Erik hated this world. He felt wrong. Every step was too heavy, and every breath fire. He felt stretched thin and at the same time in touch with every part of himself as he'd never been before. The Apprentice Razel had volunteered to show them to their rooms and was up front chatting with Elliot, who looked around with excited, wide eyes.

When Erik had first arrived via portal it had felt like he was physically being ripped apart. He wondered how they had gotten the drop on him, and how he had been so easily fooled. Slowly he was able to see and hear through the pain. He was unsure if it was lessened at all or if his body had simply gotten used to it.

He faked his way through dinner but his temper was a large angry animal being held in check by the thinnest ropes. Once he let a little of it show to confront the Ante, he found it impossible to pull it all the way back in. Erik knew that his body was sending out every single signal possible that he was ready for a fight. He did his best to try and mask it, while a not-so-quiet part of his mind wished that one of the Antes would take him up on it.

Daniel was floating around Daya and Elana, and probably bothering them. Normally Erik would do his best to distract his ex, but the throbbing behind his eyes kept him fully focused on making sure his eyeballs didn't pop out of his skull.

Matthias moved up on his side and leaned in to whisper in his ear.

"What the hell happened when you came through?"

Erik shook his head and stopped immediately, as that only made the pain worse.

"I don't know. It was like my body was bursting apart; like I was ripping at the seams and coming apart. It's still like that. You don't feel it?"

Matthias shook his head. "Something is different. I feel different, but it's not a pain or an ache. It's more like . . . like my connection to Artemis is stronger?"

Erik looked at Matthias for a long moment but then looked back at the tall black tower they were approaching. He looked at some of the other living spaces around him. Some looked like towers of light or plants or things he would struggle to describe. There was the one tower that looked like raw, pink flesh. He could not have been paid enough to approach that one.

"Welcome to Hive Chayyliel," Razel said. There was no inflection in her voice; no welcome or warning.

"You okay now?" Matthias asked.

"Still in a lot of pain," Erik answered.

Matthias studied his face closer. "It's not getting any better?"

"No."

"The problem with your healing hasn't cleared itself up yet, has it?"

Erik shook his head and cursed. Though his healing was still working on those around him, it had become start/stop with Erik himself. When he'd sliced his hand open last week, the wound had sealed almost immediately, but the pain had lingered, as had the scar. It had taken a week to fade completely. It struck Erik as a "First-World" Blooded problem—"I'm not healing fast enough"—but considering where they were, such a skill would be important in the coming days.

"It's not back to where it was, but it's not *not* working."

They entered the archway of black stone and were led to a staircase. Erik glanced into the rooms they passed, since most had open archways instead doors. Many were empty of anything but in others he caught glimpses of dark things living under floors and broken things that looked to be in pain, and that were too human to make him comfortable with it. They passed one corridor that made Razel freeze for a moment and then hurry past. Erik made special note of it.

She turned down the next hall and stopped to turn and face them, four doorways behind her.

"You will be staying here. Is there is anything more I can do for you?"

"No, I think we're good." Matthias stepped in front of him and gestured for the woman to be on her way.

There was no offense in her face as she swept past them all and hurried from the tower. Erik felt some of the tension leave his body now that he was around those that he could call ally. He glanced at Tassi and Yonas. For now, at least.

Erik waited until the sound of her footsteps had completely faded before he turned to the first door and gestured everyone inside. They all hurried through the door. Inside was a room with a central table and various sizes of what Erik assumed to be seats around it. He gestured for everyone to take a seat on the pods and sank into one himself. It was comfortable; somewhat firmer than a beanbag, and it molded to his body before firming up.

He looked around. Daya had Elana hovering behind her while Elliot stood to her side. Tae had parked himself in the seat opposite Erik but his eyes were boring holes in Daniel, who was hovering in the corner watching them all. Matthias hovered behind Erik's shoulder, not sitting at all. Erik's eyes lit on Tassi and Yonas standing to the side. They had been quiet and unobtrusive, which was great, but also worried him.

He turned to Elliot.

"Can you do something about us being seen or overheard?" Erik asked.

The man smiled and nodded before holding out his hands. The air shifted and then popped in rapid succession, a sense of deafening silence spread from Elliot. Since Erik was seated farther away from him, he experienced the outside of it first. He noticed the disappearance of all the small sounds that people use unconsciously to keep track of others. Their breath, and the tiny hints of movement were gone. They even disappeared from his sight, which Erik had not been expecting. For a moment, Matthias and himself felt like the only people in the room; the only people in the world, even. Then the power swept over them and they were reunited.

"That was different." Elliot looked down at his hands, eyes a bit wide.

Erik nodded and drew everyone's attention back to him. "Which brings me to the first point. Our powers are different here. Everyone needs to be careful. Use your powers cautiously at first. We don't know how exactly they've changed."

Everyone nodded as they glanced around. Before there'd been no visual sign of Elliot's power, but now everything outside of the bubble of silence was in shades of gray and blurred.

Erik tore his gaze away from the outside and back to Elliot.

"What did you talk to Razel about?"

Elliot shrugged. "Nothing much. She asked some questions. I asked some questions. Neither one of us gave anything away. Something about this floor specifically made her nervous though; her conversation got more stilted."

"I saw her flinch," Erik added. He looked over at Tae.

"What do you think?"

Tae did not respond, scowling at Daniel, eyes narrowed with a fierce silver glow coming from deep within them.

"Tae!"

Tae startled and looked at Erik in the eyes. He let out a little grunt of pain and shut his eyes tight.

Daniel huffed from the corner. "That's what you get."

Tae shook his head and when he opened his eyes they streamed with tears that he hurried to wipe away. He blinked at Erik, and Erik hesitated before glancing over at Daniel and deciding to ask later.

"What are your thoughts?"

"Razel's our way in," Tae said with certainty. "The others are in too deep, their ties to each other and this place are tangled and knotted together. Something has changed in her lately, given us an opening." Tae shrugged and fell silent.

"Are we sure we can trust what he sees?" Tassi's voice was without an edge, but Erik still felt himself riled by the questioning of his friend. She must have seen it on his face, because she hurried to continue. "I only ask because Seers are not always accurate when they have a goal. They often see what they want to see."

Erik looked at Tae with his eyebrows raised and Tae rolled his eyes in return.

Erik turned back to Tassi. "I trust him."

"The problem will be getting to Razel without her Master around," Yonas stated evenly.

"What do you make of Mayer having no assistant and that other one, that creepy boy not having a Master?" Matthias asked.

"There's something wrong with that boy," Daniel said, floating into the circle.

Erik sucked in a breath. Daniel was no longer wearing an orange jumpsuit with a ragged hole in his chest. Instead he wore a plain black t-shirt and a pair of blue jeans so worn in parts they were white. Erik knew those jeans. He had rested his head against the knee of them while he cried and Daniel ran his hand through Erik's hair.

"You've changed," Erik whispered.

Daniel smiled at him. "Yeah, something about this place I guess. It was actually pretty easy."

Elana frowned and closed her eyes and suddenly she was in a tailored black suit, with no shirt underneath, her cleavage highlighted by the rubies that lined the collar of the suit jacket. Daya let out a low whistle and Elana swatted at her before settling in close to her lover once again.

"The spiritual is more powerful here than in our plane," Tae stated. "I would guess that's why our powers are working differently; they're drawing from a different spectrum of power."

"Any ideas on how to get Razel alone?" Matthias asked, bringing everyone's attention back to the problem at hand, a deep frown etched in his face.

"I don't think it'll be a problem," Elliot said, also frowning and looking anywhere but at his sister. "Razel sort of implied that her Master wanted her to spy on us."

He shrugged when everyone looked at him.

"Their Masters—" Matthias started.

"Can we please stop calling them that?" Erik exploded. He did not appreciate the way master consistently sounded like Massa in his head.

Matthias flinched at Erik's voice and offered a small smile of apology.

"Their Holders—" Matthias looked at Erik in question.

Erik frowned, it was better than master but still uncomfortable. He finally just nodded. He was in pain and wanted to crawl into bed. He had no energy for the longer discussion.

"—might have a way to see through them or read their minds. We don't know anything about the powers that call this place home or how it all works," Matthias finished.

"True, but I don't know if we have any other choice," Erik countered quietly.

"What did that Angelic say to you?" Daya asked.

Erik shrugged. "Not to trust anyone around us. That he—"

"They," Tae corrected.

Erik paused and nodded. "That they could be an ally to us. That they knew of others that the Courts feared. That they would contact us when it was time."

"Pretty vague," Elana commented.

"Pretty dangerous," Daya countered. "They have no reason to trust us. We could easily turn them in."

"If they know enough to approach Erik then they know something of our world. Which means they know that their rulers have been stealing us." Elana cut her eyes to Yonas and Tassi, who both steadfastly ignored her. Elana continued, "Easy enough to assume we wouldn't exactly be friends with their rulers. Even if some of us have been selling the rest of us off."

Tassi and Yonas both at least had the decency to flinch at that.

"Pretty stupid to approach us so openly though," Matthias commented.

"Or it was a challenge?" Erik asked.

The room went quiet.

"I don't think we're going to get much else done tonight. Let's all split up and get some rest," Erik said, finally letting his exhaustion show in his voice.

"We'll room together," Tassi said, gesturing at Yonas and hurrying out of the room.

Daya and Elana just looked at him expectantly and walked out. He smiled until he realized that left him, Matthias, Elliot, and Tae. Elliot should room with Tae, whom he was still technically mentoring, and Matthias would stay with Erik since they had had a similar relationship. Except Erik did not want to stay in the same room as Matthias. He did not want to deal with Daniel floating in and out, or the tension between those two and the awkward silences he would suffer through.

"I'll stay with Erik," Tae spoke up.

Elliot and Matthias nodded and left the room, though Matthias left slowly and kept looking back at Erik.

When they were alone, Erik smiled at his friend.

"Thank you."

They both looked at Daniel, who smiled at them. Even without the obvious wound and in different clothing, the smile still made Erik squirm.

"I'll go exploring while you two sleep," he said and floated through the wall and out of the room.

"There's something about him, Erik. Now that we're here and my powers are different, it's like I can almost see it," Tae whispered.

Erik stood and walked over to Tae, placing a hand on the other boy's shoulder.

"Keep trying." He squeezed and then stumbled over to one of the doors. He did not remember falling onto the mattress as sleep rushed up to claim him.

Erik's dreams were filled with mad things, bodies being ripped apart and devoured. People living in giant bird's mouths. Cities that ran on the pain of one child. Angelics devouring each other as they made love. They were twisted things similar to a Bosch or Dali painting, if they had an orgy with *Paradise Lost*. Even when Erik was aware within them that they were dreams, they still felt too real for the fear to ever truly leave him.

He woke up in the dark. Though even as he sat up, light began to slowly fill the room. Before he had adjusted he could feel someone else in the room with him.

"Who's there?" He growled out. His power came rushing forth and with it a headache that ripped through his brain like a freight train.

"It's only me," Daniel said from the corner.

Erik forced the power back, and though the headache lessened, it did not go away.

"What are you doing, Daniel?"

"I came to warn you. The Angelics are coming. The darkness has shown up and they want to see what you can do."

Erik groaned and forced himself to his feet. He looked around the room. In addition to the bed he was laying in, there was a dresser with his bag pushed up against it. There was an open door that led to what he assumed was a restroom. He approached, but before going inside he saw something from the corner of his eye: a skinless man, screaming, reaching for him. Erik whirled around, hands raised and metal bracelets curving over his knuckles. He looked around the room but all he saw was Daniel in the corner staring with a furrowed brow.

He hurried into the bathroom and pulled off his wrinkled suit, lowering himself into the warm pool of water in the floor. A small crystal bowl sat on the edge of the tub, filled with fragrant sand that turned out to be soap. He scrubbed his skin and hair, and rinsed himself by dunking down. He could not figure out how to drain it so he simply climbed out of the tub and returned to the bedroom. Daniel was nowhere to be seen. Lacking anything resembling a towel, Erik dried his body with his dirty clothes before throwing them on the bed and pulling new ones from his bag. A soft long-sleeved black shirt designed with randomly-placed silver threads that caught the light, paired with teal slacks, and the same trusty black Doc Martens.

When he exited his room, the lounge was empty and Tae's room door was open. He stepped out in the hall to find the rest of his people. All were dressed, but exhaustion was still heavy on their faces.

A small Angelic was waiting off to the side. It had a pinhole mouth and red-and-white skin. It gestured and they followed it out of the tower. They exited quickly and crossed the courtyard, craning their necks to see the unusual towers in the light of the sun.

Erik stopped at the monster he saw before him. So much like the thing that had murdered most of the Suits in San Francisco, but without the added metal spikes and other accoutrements. Also it was much, much larger, so it did not look like it needed the metal additions to rip them apart. Its legs were easily twice as tall as Erik and its mouth could bite someone in half.

The Holder Mayer was at its front, petting the closest leg, running his hand up and down the sparse, thick white hairs.

"What the hell?" Erik stopped moving, as did everyone else.

The small Angelic in front of them stomped, looked back expectantly and stomped his foot again when they still did not move.

"I don't know if you can understand me, but no way are any of us getting any closer to that thing," Erik said, leaning down to look at the Angelic's face, though there were no eyes he could discern.

The Angelic peered at Erik for a moment and then hurried off toward Mayer. Seconds later the Holder was walking toward them.

"Is there a problem?" He asked in his oddly accented English.

"Yes. We've seen those things in action. We want to go no closer."

Mayer looked back in puzzlement. "The crikes are our main mode of transportation. They are not beasts of war."

"Whatever you use them for, they are capable of violence. We've seen it," Elana spoke up.

Mayer snorted. "Of course they are capable of violence. Aren't we all? If a crike is so terrifying to you, I cannot imagine what the darkness will be."

Erik cocked his head at the man. He was smarter than Erik had first assumed, because it was the kind of challenge that Erik would not let lay there. In fact, Erik could not ignore it. He was aware how dangerous their situation was. They had no escape and no allies, and for the hundredth time he wondered if coming had been a mistake. The Angelics respected strength; they could not afford to look weak.

Erik stepped forward and followed Mayer back to the crike, climbing up its leg hair like Mayer did. Though he could sense the dissatisfaction and anger behind him, none said anything as they followed his example.

The ride was swift and uncomfortably tense, but it was forgotten when they came into view of the darkness. This was no small fountain of darkness spreading its evil through a shopping mall block. This was a towering spire of darkness; nothing but a devouring hunger given form and power. It reared into the sky, its tendrils snatching at flying figures so far above them that Erik could not see many details.

"Holy shit."

Erik couldn't figure out how many of them said it at once.

# TAE

The world was ablaze with information. Everywhere Tae looked, secrets fairly twisted themselves in knots trying to get his attention. Of course, just because they wanted to expose themselves didn't mean he understood them. Some appeared as mathematical equations he had no ability to solve; some in languages he didn't even recognize, and some played out like memories from which he only got the faintest impressions. The things he did understand were magnificent.

Nothing very strong came off the darkness though, as if it devoured even its own secrets. If he strained, he could pick up something like cold indifference. Tae got the feeling that it did not do this out because it had to. It had other options but just liked this one; hunger and casual cruelty in equal measures, and Tae was terrified.

He turned back to the others in the carapace of their unholy transportation. There was an aura of still blue around Erik's head as he looked up at the huge manifestation. Slowly the blue began to move and then was shot through with flashes of yellow as Erik snapped out of the shock that had held him.

"We need to find its anchor to this world and sever it. Daya." She looked over at him. "Power up and get in there. Elana, cover her and see how far you guys can go without being noticed. Tassi and Elliot, you are on distraction. Stay fast and free. Tag out if you get tired."

Daya nodded and her power flared to life but unlike on earth her skin did not get gray and rough but black, smooth, and luminous. Her features were striking and clear. She looked down at herself for a moment before Elana floated over, embracing her from behind and disappearing both from view. Tassi took off her shoes and stepped over the edge of the crike and into the open air. The wind burst into existence, lifting her high into the sky. Elliot stepped over the edge and climbed down the leg.

"Tae, I need you to come with me and look for any weak spots on the creature. Yonas, you'll come with us and see if being a daughter of death is any good when it comes to this thing. Matthias, you're watching our backs," Erik finished.

They all nodded and climbed out of the crike. Those they had ridden with said nothing and Tae knew they had no intention of fighting. The Holders, their apprentices, and the few Antes were here to observe only.

Once on the ground Tae did a quick scan of the parts of the darkness emerging from the crumbling building. Tae could see nothing of value and followed Erik as he ran into the building next to the pink, living monstrosity that was being eaten. The building they entered was of the same material, and as they hurried inside they found the stairs were oddly hollow white lengths that Tae's sight told him were bone. After two flights Tae was breathing harder. After five they were all panting, and then sudden relief came from behind him. Tae was still tired but he also felt like he could run forever; his limbs loose and ready. He barely touched the stairs as he sped up them. He could see the forest-green energy playing over his body. He identified it as Matthias sharing his ancestor's blessings. Tae could not have been more grateful as they reached the final landing and burst out onto the roof.

"Now is the moment of truth, I guess," he heard Erik mutter.

Tae started scanning the building and the darkness, but he was still getting nothing. His eyes burned as he concentrated harder, and noticed a flash of color and power in the corner of his gaze that he could not ignore. He looked over and saw Erik burning as if he were on fire. His face was remote and too perfect. His features did not change but grew sharper and more pointed as if another face were pushing out from behind his.

Erik's power flared around him and Tae could swear the sky itself began to pulse in time with the bright red flush that suffused his skin. Erik grunted in pain and Tae saw him grasp at his head for a moment, before running for the edge of the roof. Matthias gasped and then let his own power flare to life. For a moment Tae could have sworn the other man had horns, and was dressed in a loose toga with the blood of his latest kill still staining his skin. He reached into his ever-present cargo pants, pulling out two small sticks that expanded into long silver fighting batons. Matthias chased Erik, with Yonas following up in the rear, looking like nothing but a skull surrounded by purple darkness in a vaguely human shape.

Tae watched them launch themselves into the sky. For a second they floated on air and then they fell, landing in perfect time on the adjacent, crumbling roof. Tae could hear the sound of their landing from where he was.

He glanced overhead, where Tassi was flying around, avoiding the tentacles that reached for her, and batting others away with powerful winds that came to her aid. Elliot was on the ground, using his power to hide those still running from the building at random intervals, confusing the pseudo-pods' grasping, hungry mouths that sought them. Tae easily saw through Elliot's power, his eyes watering constantly now.

The limbs reaching for Tassi jerked and whirled in the air madly.

Tae searched and saw Yonas's skull wildly biting chunks from the darkness at the place they had broken through the roof. Erik was ripping into the darkness with his bare hands while Matthias whirled to and fro, keeping the smaller limbs that bent toward them occupied.

Why did everything seem easier than it had in the mall? They were faster, stronger, and more coordinated here; more in touch with their power. But if they were more dangerous, then the same could be said of the darkness. Tae still gleaned nothing from it with his sight. He should be calling out attack places and tips but there was nothing to provide, no weaknesses to be pointed out.

A whole tentacle was ripped off, pulled apart by empty air. Tae concentrated and saw Daya and Elana. Daya was tearing into the tentacles as her girlfriend clung to her back and made them invisible and intangible to the searching tentacles. Still, it was only a minor inconvenience to the darkness, as a new appendage sprouted almost immediately, this one with heavy spikes that lined it root-to-tip.

Just as Erik was about to be skewered by the new appendage, Daniel flew out of nowhere and the tentacle went for him instead, ripping through him. Daniel reformed quickly but in that moment of dissolution, and with his powers jacked up to eleven, Tae saw something—a hint of what Daniel really was.

"What are you doing here?" Erik's voice asked so loudly Tae had no problem hearing.

Whatever Daniel's answer, if he did have an answer, it did not carry over to Tae. Daniel continued to flit this way and that, joining Matthias in keeping the smaller limbs busy, while Erik and Yonas attacked the bases of the larger limbs. Tae watched, seeing Erik and Yonas gouging chunks out of the darkness, but his main concentration was on Daniel.

When another of the limbs of the darkness swept through Daniel, Tae was ready and he saw it—the moment of hesitation before Daniel's body broke apart. Tae's power broke through and he saw a part of what Daniel was hiding.

He must have made some sort of sound because Daniel looked at him and Tae saw it in Daniel's face. He somehow knew that Tae had figured part of it out.

"Tae!"

Erik's scream was the only warning he had. He saw the look of absolute horror on his friend's face. Erik's eyes were entirely swallowed by red. Tae turned and saw a piece of darkness that had snuck behind them and started devouring the building he was standing on. There was nowhere for him to go as the piercing darkness sent a sharp limb right toward his heart. He was to die with the same wound as Daniel. This was the ghost's revenge. The roof collapsed under him and he saw nothing more.

# ELANA

Elana heard Erik's cry of despair, but did not see what caused it. She and Daya were currently moving deeper into the building, hopefully closer to whatever was keeping the darkness anchored here. Elana had learned that not only was she able to shield the senses, as she and her brother had always been able to do, but her intangibility was transferable here as well.

Somewhat.

She clung to Daya's back and did her best to forget any separation between them. When she merged with Elliot they were one being, as were their powers. This was more difficult. They could push through matter but it was thick, like pushing through molasses, rather than the way Elana floated cleanly through walls.

Elana let Daya carry her piggyback. Daya used her arms and legs of rock to navigate through a world turned to pudding. They moved in silence, Elana concentrating on keeping her powers working through both of them and Daya focused on moving through the floors of the building.

Every once in awhile they would find a safe, protected area and Elana would leave Daya hidden there while she scouted ahead. Elana always came back to find Daya fighting off tendrils of darkness that had found her in the meantime.

This way they moved deeper and deeper into the building, where the walls were no longer pink, but a sickly brown with veins of black pulsing through them. Elana simply led them toward areas where the darkness was more dense, and more deeply rooted, hoping that it would take them to whatever this manifestation's anchor was, this thing's version of the tree at the mall.

Soon everything they passed was completely subsumed by the darkness. There was nothing but never-ending blackness so uniform they could barely discern distances. Daya moved forward slowly through the wall in front of them. When they emerged from the other side they were confronted by more of the same: endless darkness, except for the small bodies crumpled on the ground.

They had seen no other signs of death on their trek through the building. Those who were caught or left behind had been devoured completely. These children, and they were children, too small to even be teenagers, were the first bodies they saw. Daya tensed under her arms and Elana realized her girlfriend had deduced the truth as well.

It was rooted in the children.

They moved closer and saw the way the darkness was sprouting from the mouths of the three children, their bodies contorted so that together they formed a triangle, their limbs twisted to form lines and circles within the triangle.

"What do we do?" Daya asked, frozen where she stood.

Elana let go of Daya, slowly pulling her hands free and waiting beside her to see if any attack would come. She counted to twenty and then fifty and then one hundred and still no attack came. Elana took a step away from Daya, and then another one and another one, until she stood over the children.

They were breathing. Their small chests rising and falling. Elana felt as if her heart were in her throat because she knew what they had to do. She knew what they had had to do with the tree.

She turned back to Daya and could see by the way Daya had closed her eyes, by the tremble in her bow lips, that her girlfriend already knew the answer. Daya said nothing, though, and Elana knew this was on her. As strong as Daya was, she would need someone else to suggest this, someone else to voice the horrible thing that she would have to do. That way Daya could shove some of the guilt onto Elana. She took this burden for the woman she loved. Gladly.

"They have to die," Elana whispered, but it was a shout in the silence around them.

"What! No!" Daya shouted, but it was too slow, too stiff, rehearsed.

"It is the only way!" If she could cry, Elana had no doubt she would be doing so now. She acted in this play for Daya, but the emotions were still too real. "I would, but you are stronger. You can make it quick. Painless. Give them the peace they have been robbed of."

She offered the last as a balm on Daya's spirit.

Daya said nothing but took a step forward and there was a moan from behind Elana. Daya froze in place, her mouth dropping open. Elana turned, already scared of what she would find.

The three children's mouths had opened wider around the darkness that spewed from their orifices; another shudder and moan, and their mouths opened wider yet.

*Why do you come here?*

The voice came from all three mouths; heads twisted at unnatural angles, faces pointed unseeing at the ceiling. All the more disturbing because none of the heads turned to look at them. A chorus of innocent voices forced to speak for the thing that used them as if they were nothing.

"We come to st—"

Daya waved her hand, silencing Elana for a moment. Daya stepped in front of her and faced the triangle of bodies.

"We come to ask you to stop your actions. To come to an accord, an end to hostilities."

*Hostilities? We know of no hostilities. We know of hunger.*

"What did you eat before you came here?" Daya questioned.

*We ate what we wanted, as we always have.*

"There are other living things here. People who have to—"

*And do you not devour other living beings to satisfy your hunger?*

"That is different," Daya explained.

*How?*

Elana held her breath as she watched Daya try to negotiate with the horrifying darkness.

"We do not harm other sentient beings."

*There are those who argue that the animals you eat are living, feeling, loving beings. What does your assumption of sentience have to do with anything? Even leaving that aside, did the beings of this place not steal those of your plane?*

The silence was long and Elana felt the same shock and terror that was coming off of Daya. The darkness was too knowledgeable, too well-versed.

*Did you think us stupid? We are older than both this world and yours. Even leaving that aside, we devour all that exists within a being—their body, their knowledge, their soul. They no longer exist outside of us.*

Daya at last spoke again, her voice strong. "No matter the mistakes that some of us make, there are always those of us who try to do right."

*Do not mistake us. We do not judge you for devouring others to satisfy your hunger. We understand each other.*

"You will leave this place and ours alone or we will destroy you." Daya stated coldly.

Eerie laughter exploded from the children's mouths. What should be cackles turned to giggles and made it sound all the creepier.

*This is ours. All of it. We shall devour what we want and none shall stop us.*

Daya's black stone face shifted into a look of determination and she crossed the final distance between herself and the children. Elana turned away, unable to look, but she heard the three cracks, one after the other. She looked nowhere but at the ground until she felt her girlfriend's hand in her own. She turned and embraced Daya, arms wrapped around her neck while Daya's stone arms wrapped around her waist.

The building exploded around them.

Elana clung to her girlfriend desperately, wrapped them in her power as they were blown through the air. She felt debris moving through their bodies. Elana opened her eyes and they were crashing toward the ground, straight for one of several piles of rubble that now littered the street. She could most likely phase them through it, but one slip of concentration, one small distraction, might mean Daya's death as she materialized with something in her body. Elana did not want to risk it.

She held tighter to Daya and pulled with all her might. It was not a smooth flight at all but as they skidded to a halt they managed to avoid all of the larger, more dangerous shards of what had been the building. She looked down at Daya and their gazes met. All was right for a moment.

Elana heard a scream and looked up in time to see Tassi catch both Erik and Matthias as their limp bodies hurtled toward the ground. Yonas, the one who had been screaming, seemed to take control of herself, and the speed of her descent slowed and she landed lightly on feet that looked more skeleton than flesh.

They all arrived on the ground and as they waited for Erik and Matthias to stir they watched what was left of the two buildings slowly sink in on themselves. At least there was no hint of the darkness.

"We did it," Daya said quietly.

"No, you didn't." They turned to find Matthias stirring and sitting up from where they had laid him in a relatively debris-free area. He reached over and grasped Erik's hand as the other man began to wake as well. "It is not destroyed or even hurt. It is only biding its time."

"Matthias, we were there. We destroyed its anchor." Elana made sure she did not look at her girlfriend as she said this.

Matthias looked up at her. "You may very well have done, but it either has another or it doesn't matter as much here."

She looked at Daya, who was giving Matthias a suspicious and disbelieving look.

Matthias threw his free hand into the air. "Trust me! The Huntress is the head of my bloodline. I know when a hunt has gone awry. It gathers under us all and we need to get the hell out of here before it comes back."

Tassi spoke up from where she was supporting her exhausted partner with her shoulder. "Where is the crike?"

Elana looked around and realized that their transport was gone, and with it anyone who knew the area.

Daya nodded and looked around at the rest of them.

"Where's Tae?" Daya asked.

The way that everyone looked away except for Erik; the way Erik's face broke as he looked at them and refused to look away; the way tears began to slip down his cheeks, making trails in the dust that covered them from the destruction of the two buildings, told her all she needed to know.

"No," Elana whispered, but Daya said nothing, her stone form slipping away to reveal the flesh-and-blood woman who was close to breaking.

Finally, Erik looked away, and Elana was glad, because the blank sadness in his eyes was too much to take along with her own sharp grief.

There was a rumble behind them.

"We need to get going, now," Matthias said quietly from where he still sat on the ground, and pushed himself to his feet. Even though he wobbled, he stayed standing.

They had only staggered a few feet, no direction in mind but away, when a large crack echoed through the air, and Elana turned to see the darkness exploding from the ground behind them and rising high into the sky.

This was no pool of darkness, no puddle of nothing coming for them. It was also no tower of darkness devouring a building. This was a wave, an unending tsunami of nothing raising up to meet them. It seemed to pause and slowly Elana felt it, this darkness's cold disregard. It knew they were here. It knew what they were here for. Elana did not know how she knew, but she did. Even as she opened her mouth to suggest a fast retreat, it came toward them, cresting like a wave too far above their heads, and then crashing down.

Elliot ran for her and she rushed to touch his hand.

# MATTHIAS

Matthias held Erik up. The younger man had been blank and staring since they lost Tae. Daniel had not helped with the sad and quiet, "I told you not to come," before he simply disappeared as the darkness expanded.

At the last moment, as the darkness crashed down at them, Elana and Elliot had joined bodies and powers, taking on their merged form. Matthias still felt awe whenever he saw them do so. As far as he knew it was a power unique to them. They had held out their four hands and formed a barrier against the darkness. It had allowed them to run and get some distance.

Once they'd had breathing room Matthias had tracked their way back to the Ruling Courts. They walked unmolested, except for some strange looks from others moving through the street, dirty and injured. Most were too invested in their own pain and loss to pay much attention to the oddly dressed people in their midst.

The flood of people thinned the closer they got to the Ruling Courts. No one was running to the Courts, which said enough about how the people felt about those "ruling" them.

Matthias had not seen Daniel since the battle, and he wondered where he might be. They entered the courtyard of the Ruling Courts to deafening silence. Even the sound of movement was cut off as they moved toward the tower. Most of them were bloodied with ripped clothing. Matthias was aware that they were being watched and that most of those watching were not friendly. He moved steadily, refusing to give any more signs of weakness. They had almost reached the tower when Razel emerged from the pulsing pink tower. She looked around the courtyard until she spotted them and hurried over.

""I heard what happened. Are you all alright?" She asked.

Matthias felt Erik tense under his arm and squeezed as tightly as he dared trying to communicate calmness and support and most of all patience. Erik slowly released the tension but would not look in Razel's direction.

"No, we are not." Elana's voice was flat and dead.

No one else spoke as they entered Chayyliel's Hive and made their way to their rooms and no one told Razel to stop accompanying them. As they reached the corridor Matthias began to escort Erik to his room when the man stopped and would not be moved. Mathias remembered that Tae and Erik had been sharing a room and shifted direction, escorting the young man easily to the room he had shared with Elliot.

"Thank you," Erik whispered. His first words since he had screamed at Tae's loss. The skin of his face was drawn and tightened with pain at the corners of his mouth and eyes. "Bring her."

Matthias did not have to ask who he meant. He gestured for all of them to follow him without looking over his shoulder. "Bring Razel."

He settled Erik in one of the seats and only then did he turn and see everyone inside the room including Razel. It was quiet for a long moment and then Erik looked up at them. Razel flinched away from his gaze.

"Elliot."

The man nodded and the silence enveloped them in seconds. Razel looked around in curiosity but no fear showed in her eyes.

"You will tell us the truth of what is going on." Erik's voice was quiet but it still filled the space.

"What do you mean?" Razel moved forward and slowly lowered herself into one of the other seats. She met his gaze, and then asked. "Where is Tae?"

Erik blazed back to life, like a fire going from kindling to six-foot flames in a second. He was up and moving through the room. He was in Razel's face before anyone even thought of trying to stop him. Erik did not touch her but stopped only a foot from her face.

"Tae is dead and some of that fault is mine. Some of it I will live with forever, but the fact of the matter is that you gave us absolutely no information and I smell something fishy. I will lose no one else, do you hear me? No. One." Erik practically growled it.

Razel nodded but also brought her silver arm into the space between them, clacking the fingers together before his face.

"I understand your pain and your need, but you will not threaten me."

Matthias saw Erik's eyes narrow further before he backed up a little, resting his ass on his heels.

"I did not threaten you. Your point is taken, in any case. Now, tell us about Holder Mayer and Holder-Apprentice Haydn."

Razel straightened and seemed to weigh her options before she started to speak. She told them of a brave young woman who had tried to save her world and gotten nothing but pain in return.

"I don't know where she is now, but neither does anyone else in the Courts, if the rumors are correct. Or her sibs or the Antes that fled. So far, everyone seems to believe the rumor of June and Lil having an affair. Krezida is also missing but no one seems concerned with that."

"What did you tell Holder Riana about us?" Matthias asked.

Razel met his gaze without any hesitation, her features blank.

"Nothing. I did not know anything after all. She asked me but I gave her nothing but inconsequential information. She could not tell the difference." The contempt in her voice was clear to all of them but the question was whether it was real or feigned. If it was real, would it be enough for her to turn against the Ruling Courts?

"How loyal are you to her?" Matthias asked.

"When I had just crossed the threshold to five, I created a mechanique that could clean the foul water in our area in the city. News got to Hypatia and Riana. She came and used her own mechaniques to tear mine apart and kill everyone I had ever known. She took me back to Hypatia and taught me what she knew. I learned to hate early. I also learned to hide my emotions. I learned to do what is necessary."

She fell into silence and Matthias looked around at the contemplative looks on all their faces. No one seemed overtly hostile anymore and Elliot looked like he was five seconds from trying to wrap the girl in a bear hug, which would likely get his arm torn off.

"How do we know that any of this is true?" Matthias asked, leaning down to help Erik stand and move back to his seat. The younger man offered no resistance.

Riana shrugged at them. "You may ask around for my history. It is a well-known incident. The Ruling Courts do not like anyone killing their subjects but them. As long as they are alive, no matter the condition, there is the chance that they can be used."

"There is something else you are not telling us, though. Why does so much death cling to you?" Yonas spoke up for the first time. When Matthias looked over, her eyes and the flesh around them had completely disappeared, revealing large sockets of bleached white of bone.

Razel showed a small bit of surprise at the pronouncement but her face closed off again.

"I have not killed," she said.

"But you've done something far worse. The pain of loss and death of hope clings to you like a second skin," Yonas stated.

Razel's skin had greyed as Yonas kept speaking, but her expression remained the same.

"What do you do with the people you steal from our world?" Erik asked out of nowhere and everyone's attention was laser-focused on Razel.

Razel sported a small wrinkle of confusion between her brows before the expression cleared. Her lips thinned out and almost disappeared completely as she pressed them together.

"I thought they were criminals; those the Ruling Courts had decided deserved punishment." She looked down at her hands.

"Does that make it any better?" Tae muttered.

Erik shushed him and gestured for the woman to go on.

"No. I don't suppose it does." This was said almost to herself but Erik heard it and noted it.

"They are changed," she said.

"Changed how?" Erik asked.

Razel swallowed and for the first time Matthias saw her as something less than perfectly composed.

"I do not know all of it. I am only given pieces. Our main job, Holder Riana and I, is to take the skins—"

"Skins?" Elana interjected.

Matthias saw the way she clung to Daya's hand and wished they did not have to hear about it this way.

"Yes. We use the recreated or retained thought processes and new mechanique internals to craft a being that looks exactly like the 'dant on the outside but on the inside is something else. Stronger. Faster. Smarter. But no longer independent, no longer who they were."

"Oh god."

Matthias could not tell which of them whispered it. It might have been all of them. The abductees who reappeared, the ones who everyone described as "wrong." This was what was wrong. How many of these—people—were back on Earth, in San Francisco? Did they even know what they were or were they just living their lives until some switch was flipped?

"That is the most common but occasionally we are asked to do something else. Something special." The hesitation let them know she did not relish talking about what came next.

Matthias imagined none of them wanted to know more but Erik bit the bullet and asked.

"What other things?"

"Sometimes—" Razel coughed and stopped talking for at least a full minute. They all let the silence stretch on until she was ready. "Sometimes it was the opposite. We took what was inside someone. We took their meat and their soul and themselves and bound them into new bodies. Bodies that were each unique and powerful, built on a base of power, alchemy, and mechanique on a grand scale."

"You mean like that black glass monster I fought on my first night awakened? That was a person twisted and tortured?" Erik looked sick even as he said it.

"Not just a person. A Blooded," Matthias whispered. "Think about it. If you can copy the mind and everything it knows? Why keep the . . . meat of some specimens and not others?" When he said meat he grabbed at his own chest squeezed until it hurt. "Because this is where our powers lie, not in how we think or in our skins but in the meat of us. Think of it, a monstrous body with the powers of one of the Blooded on the inside."

There was no real evidence, but Matthias felt sure he was right. They knew non-Blooded were abducted more often than Blooded and no Blooded were ever returned. He looked around and could see that others believed him. They were all looking at him, even Tassi and Yonas, with horror written over their faces. The anger rose up in Matthias at that. How dare they look horrified? They had been doing this, subjecting stolen children and others to this. They would have made Melinda into one of these things. He didn't think Erik had made that connection yet because of the shock. If he did make it they would likely have to stop him from killing Razel.

"You did this to people?" Erik's whisper. "You took them and tortured them and twisted them on orders from the one who killed your family?"

"You would dare to judge me? I do not know how it works in your world, but here the people in power grind those below them to dust slowly everyday and few escape. If, to escape, you must turn on others, what is the other choice?" Razel asked. Her voice filled the space between them but barely rose.

"You can justify it all you want, but the fact is that you decided your life was worth more than all of the others you were destroying. I'm not ignorant of that thought process. I've been victim to it more than once." Erik's voice was quiet and held no emotion.

"The Athenaeum does good. It is a sanctuary and helps those—" Razel started.

"It's supposed to, but from what you've said, only Lil acted as if she wanted to help others," Erik interrupted.

Razel was silent. There was no response she could give.

"Do you want out?" Erik asked.

Matthias hoped the answer was yes because they had already shared too much to trust her fully. He dreaded what Erik might do.

"Out to where?" Razel asked.

"We will take you with us, if you want," Erik said.

Razel was silent for a long moment before replying.

"Yes. What do you need?"

"Nothing for now," Erik answered. "After today's failu—" His voice cracked and he cleared it twice before he continued. "After today's failure, we can't stay much longer. I think we've shown that we aren't going to be of much use against the darkness. Either they'll send us through or we'll have to find our own way. Be prepared."

"And when I'm called on by Holder Riana to do my duty?"

"Then I am sure you will do it to the best of your ability. It is only that your main duty is to us now."

"I see."

Something was communicated between them in their locked gazes, something Matthias did not understand. All at once Razel rose and headed for the door. Tassi and Yonas went to stop her but they hesitated at a shake of the head from Erik and moved out of her way. As soon as the door was shut behind her.

"Why did you just let her go?" Tassi asked.

Erik looked at her. "What was the other option available to us?"

"We don't know if we can trust her."

Erik nodded in agreement. "You're right, but what can she tell them really? That we are useless against the darkness? I think they saw that. She has no real information on us but we gained much knowledge from her."

Tassi stayed silent at that but she did not look much happier.

"We have to trust her." Erik sighed and leaned back in his seat, the back of it molding itself to his preferred angle. Matthias watched him and floundered at what to do. He could see the cracks beneath Erik's mask; the way that he held himself, as if he might shake apart at any moment.

"What do you mean by offering her sanctuary on Earth?" This time it was Yonas.

"She's already given us good intel. We know what attacked me when I awoke, what attacked my mother and grandmother. We know that they have been planning this for a long time. Which makes me think at least some knew that something like this might happen to their world and were planning ahead. They might even know what this darkness actually is. She will also be a good source of information once we get back."

"So that's it? Were just heading back to wait for all of this to come to us? And what about coming here to help all these people?" Daya asked. Her voice was dry and sarcastic.

"We tried to help them and we lost. What more can we do? Lose more of our people?" Erik asked, the hurt plain in his voice for them all to hear.

Matthias could see what was happening. Erik was still young; only eighteen and this was his first command; his first time losing someone under his leadership and one of his first friends in the new world he had been thrust into. Maybe even his first friend in a long while. Now he wanted to give up. Matthias imagined that everyone who had led people into battle had felt the same thing. He saw Daya's face and knew she could see it too. She had seen this before, and had experienced it herself. She was making the effort to remind Erik of all the reasons this mission mattered more than one life, without saying it out loud.

Daya took a deep breath. "There's something we need to tell you." Matthias watched her grip her girlfriend's translucent hand even tighter. Daya haltingly told them of what they had found in the building, what the darkness had said to them.

"We've already seen that it can cross over into our world. If we leave now we simply wait to be attacked. How many more lives will we then have on our conscience?" Daya finished.

"What would you have me do?"

"I don't know, but we can't just let this happen. You're the one leading us. Don't let Tae's death be in vain."

Matthias tensed. It was a risky move. Calling on Tae's death could motivate Erik or it could ignite his temper. Matthias held his breath until Erik sighed and the exhaustion seemed to etch itself deeper into his face. Erik closed his eyes for a moment, but his lips moved silently. Matthias tried to read the words but they were moving too fast. His hands were raised and rubbing at his temples. Finally he stopped and opened his eyes again. Matthias stifled a gasp at the burning red that flared in his eyes. The others were not quiet about their surprise, but Erik did not seem not to notice.

"Lil. We need to find her. She was the only one invested in saving this world. Someone with that drive, and with that need did not just stop because she no longer had official backing. We've been going about this the wrong way—I've been going about this the wrong way. They said fight, and we didn't question it. We need information and since the Ruling Courts don't seem to be willing to give it, we'll get it another way."

"Tae said that Razel was our way in and—" Erik broke and looked down at the floor for a moment before looking up at them all again, steel and fire in his gaze, "—since we no longer have Tae's visions to help us we'll have to feel our way through. Tomorrow I will talk to Chayyliel about more freedom to explore this city. I doubt he will let us out without guards, but I want to get us familiar with the city."

He turned to look at Matthias. "Would you be able to track her if you had something of hers?"

Matthias started to shake his head but then thought better of it. "At home, I would say no, but here I don't know. I also don't know if her magic would be able to block my power."

"It's still worth a try. I'll speak with Razel and see what we can do," Elliot said.

Erik nodded. He stood and swayed. Matthias was there immediately, hands on Erik's hips to steady him. Erik smiled in gratitude but it was muted and small. It was likely all he could muster right now.

"Elana, I have a request," Erik said

Elana looked up from where she and her girlfriend had been curled into each other.

"Yes."

"Reconnaissance. Of all of us, you are the one who can get around the most easily. Can you get the lay of the land tonight?" He asked.

Elana was quiet but nodded and Matthias looked at the two of them. They were still in shell shock over the skin revelation. Why had they not taken Elana's meat and made it into a monster? Or had they? If the questions were at the edge of Matthias's mind they must be front and center in Elana and Daya's.

"Are you two alright?" Matthias asked.

Elana looked at him and shrugged before tugging on Daya's hand and leading her from the room.

The others followed, with Elliot saying he was going to sleep in Erik's room tonight. Matthias waited until the door closed before he began to guide Erik to one of the bedrooms.

"Don't want to go to sleep," Erik mumbled even as he lay down and Matthias stripped him of his shoes, leaving the rest of his clothing alone. "Nightmares."

Matthias frowned and went to leave when Erik's voice came back to him.

"Don't go. Sleep with me?"

Matthias hesitated.

"Please."

He stripped off his own shoes and climbed on the bed behind Erik, curling around him and not commenting on the way that Erik's hand gripped his own so tight, the way Erik's body shook, the way wetness slowly soaked the pillow they both shared.

# MAYER

Mayer was running out of time and choices. The loss of his apprentice and the subsequent knowledge that the Courts had shared with him had narrowed his goal down to survival. Their world was doomed, crumbling around the edges, missing the essentials to rebuild. It would have been falling apart anyway but now with the darkness its destruction was expedited. Those that they had summoned had failed and now their own plans had to move forward. There was no going back. Not if they wanted to live.

He entered the workspaces below the Hive of Sorrows and Riches. Now that the plan was moving ahead quickly he had access to all of the workrooms, and not just his own. Mayer bypassed his personal work space to go to the main collection warehouse. The room was large and divided into two halves. On one side were the cages with the specimens pre-change. They were guarded by numerous Antes chosen for their imaginative way of disciplining 'dants. The Antes sneered at him as he moved toward the other side of the room. He ignored the cries of the 'dants in the cages, begging for freedom or death.

He looked at the post-experiment soldiers—the Maasu. They were arranged in unmoving ranks, no hint of breath or life at all until needed. The perfect soldiers. The Courts had been the ones to present him with the old recipe for Maasu but it had been he, Krezida, and Razel that had refined and improved the process. This side of the room only had one Ante.

"Hello."

There was no response. There never was. The Ante was a Turms, and they never spoke to anyone but their own kind.

"Do you have any news of the Hunter I sent after my missing Apprentice?"

The Turms looked up at him. Well, he assumed it was looking at him. There were no eyes on its face to speak of. Nothing but the small black pinhole of a mouth. It shook its head slowly from side to side and Mayer bit his lips to keep from cursing.

Liliana was more formidable than he had thought. Even without her tongue she had managed to defeat the creature he'd sent after her. He could send another. No one would miss two of these monstrosities among the hundreds that he had helped make.

Yes. Mayer would choose another; a more deadly type. But he would not send it alone and he would not send it after Liliana. He needed to draw her out. For that Mayer would need information and he might have an idea of where to get it. He left the Hive and retired to his room to rest until later in the night.

None of the moons were showing their faces and the night was nearly pitch-black when Mayer left. He had known this would be the case when he'd arranged the meeting days ago. He donned a black cloak with power woven into the fabric. Power that would make him harder to spot. Underneath he had removed his traditional clothing; the less chance of anyone recognizing him, the better. He headed directly into the Drowned.

They met at the wall of the water that always threatened to reclaim the Drowned, where it lapped and rose and constantly threatened to break free. No one came by the water if they could help it, fearful that anything near it could break the power holding the water back.

Three figures emerged from the shadows. The one in the center he knew, but the others were surprises.

"Who are they?" Mayer asked.

"My bodyguards, of course. There are many dangerous things out on these streets," the 'dant said as he came close enough that they could recognize each other's faces.

Mayer nodded in acknowledgment. "It is good to see you face to face."

Byron smiled at him. "You as well."

Mayer had been surprised when, over four cycles ago, one of the mirrors in his office had lit up with this young 'dant's face, but he had been intrigued by knowledge from this other world. Byron had proven an invaluable resource, granting access to the power-wielders of Earth. Everything he had told Mayer, Mayer had passed along to the Ruling Courts. It was information that had helped them form a plan and would certainly help them in the future.

"I hear that you have visitors right now? My old friends Matthias and Erik and the rest of their group. A Piece of advice for you; keep an eye on them. They are more dangerous than you assume." Byron said.

Mayer raised his eyebrows. "I know danger when I see it. They have failed. It won't be long until they are no longer an issue. They will be no obstacle in the coming invasion."

Byron smiled again and Mayer could easily read the contempt lurking at the corners of his mouth.

"I have a favor to ask," Mayer stated, swallowing his disgust at having to ask this 'dant, or anyone, for anything.

Byron nodded for him to go on.

"My apprentice has been on the run. I need to lure her into a trap. That means I have to find bait. I want you to find her two siblings and the Antes that ran with them. I was hoping you could use your persuasion to ferret them out."

"Don't you already have hunters out looking for them?" Byron asked.

"And now I would like you to join them," Mayer replied, sidestepping the implied question.

Byron looked at him in silence then smiled a dark smile, one that made Mayer's spine stiffen. "I can definitely help you with that, but first and foremost, let's talk about the payment."

Mayer raised his eyebrow. "You can have whatever gold—"

"Gold?" Byron's voice was cold. "I have no need of shiny metal. I know what is coming, and what I *need* is knowledge. I want access to your Athenaeum."

Mayer frowned. "Of course. It is open to all. Once I have done my duty here—"

"No. No delay. I want access to it, whether you are there or not."

Mayer rose to his full height and pushed back his hood. The rage he felt made him feel something he hadn't for centuries. Young. This human dared to ask for unfettered and unsupervised access to Kandake? Mayer could crush him right now with the smallest flex of his power.

"Uh, uh. Sit down," Byron tutted.

Mayer found his legs bending against his will, his ass planting itself in the damp sand. He gritted his teeth before opening his mouth.

"And no talking," Byron ordered.

Mayer's mouth slammed shut, teeth slicing off a piece of his tongue. He swallowed the blood that filled his mouth.

"I think it's clear that I could take what I wanted but I am offering you a trade," Byron said.

Mayer narrowed his eyes at Byron and began to hum so quietly none of them noticed. The Lullaby of Alu was meant for use in dreams, against those spirits who attacked while sleeping. Easy enough to alter it. The bodyguards had slumped to the ground before Byron realized what was happening.

"Stop—"

Byron did not finish the order before Mayer was humming louder, letting the melody wrap itself around the human's mind until he also slumped into sleep. As he lost consciousness, his power loosened, and Mayer stood and opened his mouth to spit blood into the churning water.

Mayer walked over to Byron and woke him with a swift kick to the stomach. When Byron was done coughing and gasping, the Holder leaned down until his face was only a foot from Byron's.

"Do not try that again," Mayer spat into the boy's face. "I am older than you by centuries. I have survived challenges you could not even dream up. I can make you suffer in ways that you can't dream."

Byron smiled up at him from his place lying in the damp sand.

"The offer is still on the table. One location for access to Kandake at all times," Byron offered.

Mayer found himself smiling against his will. The boy's audacity reminded him of himself in his youth. It was also why this ally was such a danger. Mayer closed his eyes and sought out his mental connection with Kandake. His mind skirted down the links that joined them and felt the pulse of Kandake respond. It was his place of power, and always would be. There was really nothing this weak 'dant could do to it. Finding Liliana was a priority. No one in the Ruling Courts liked loose ends, and they tended to blame those closest to the problem rather than those responsible.

He projected the image of the 'dants in front of him at Kandake. The Athenaeum reflected the image back at him and whispered the word in Babel: *Enemies.*

He repeated it over and over until the pulsing around the image of the three in his mind's eye went from a calming midnight blue to a bright searing yellow.

"Fine. Bring me the location of Liliana's siblings and the Antes protecting them and I shall give you access to Kandake. This I swear on my bond with my Athenaeum." He said it quietly and watched the triumph flare in the child's eyes. Yes, he would give them access. They would simply not live that long once they entered. Kandake now would view them as intruders and deal with them as such.

Byron pushed himself to a sitting position and held out his hand. "Agreed."

Mayer moved forward and they shook on it, once, twice, three times, before Mayer pulled his hand back and walked away. He left the waterside to the sound of Byron kicking his companions to wake them as he had done to the boy. Wrapping his cloak tighter about himself Mayer immediately circled back through the dark of the night. Near silently he chanted the poem-spell "My Love Is a Shadowed Soul," which wrapped him even more deeply in darkness, rendering him nearly invisible. He crouched behind one of the tall sand dunes that superstitious 'dants had built as symbolic magic to hold back the water.

"What game are you playing, Byron?" The 'dant did not sound pleased.

The other one spoke up as well. "Yeah, you never said anything about an invasion!"

"I am not required to tell you any of my plans. You agreed to follow me for power. Do not try and pretend that you care about anyone but yourselves at this point. Do you think I betray my world without a thought? I have plans upon plans, as I'm sure our friend Mayer does. The earth needs to be woken up and it needs to change, but it doesn't need a new overlord or new monsters. The ones it already breeds are quite enough."

"You don't even know where the children are." The 'dant's voice was soft and derisive.

"Yes, well, I know who will know where they went, and that's really all I need."

Byron stared at the water for a long moment and said nothing else. Mayer eventually left, walking through the darkened streets back to the Ruling Courts. Now it was just a matter of waiting, and he had many things to keep him occupied in the meantime.

# LIL

Lil sat on the bare floor of the room. The bed and dresser had been pushed farther into the corner and she had sketched out a crude map of Zebub on the uneven wood floor. Over that she had traced the circle and cross, one of the oldest symbols of power that she knew. She took the root out of her pocket and opened the pouch. Carefully she placed one of the small bones on each of the points where the edges of the city intersected with the circumference of the circle. After this, she reached for her knife and sliced into the meat of her forearm so that the blood would run down her hand and drip from her middle finger. She moved quickly around the circle, dabbing each of the roots with a drop of her blood.

As she did so, energy filled the room. It linked her to the points of the city. A buzz started in her belly and she prepared for a burp that never came. When she was done, she used a cloth in her pocket to wipe up the blood and bind the cut so it would not drip indiscriminately. She looked up at the Nlf, who were all gathered on the bed, watching. She sat in the area meant to represent The Out, careful not to smudge any of the lines.

Lil swallowed and closed her eyes. She took a deep breath, felt the chill of the air in her throat. She shivered and took another breath. She opened her eyes and found the map had opened up all around her. The rough chalk drawings had reached out of the floor, anchored by her drops of blood. The city became a vision of chalk and air.

Min, Davi, Arel, Jagi, Min, Davi, Arel, Jagi, Min, Davi, Arel, Jagi . . .

She chanted their names over and over in her mind, and each repetition of the names gained a beat, a gong that she felt throughout her body. The city around her moved, swirling around her, her view moving from the Out to the center of the city. There, in a building not too far from the Ruling Courts, she could see four pulses of light, two with the blood red of family and two with the silver glow of something she didn't examine too closely.

She let the names reverberate again in her mind and tried to connect with them, to feel what they were feeling. They were close to the Ruling Courts and she wanted to make sure they had not been captured. Not that it would stop her. She would come for them no matter what awaited her.

For a second she connected with Min and felt her sister's fear and longing, and her need to show strength for their brother and her worry for Lil. She felt no danger or pain. She did not feel the nervousness of impending doom. Lil let the connection fade.

She memorized the location of the building and slowly let the power go. The energy left the air, though she could still feel the buzz of power in her bones. She owed that merchant a lot, including for the idea of combining her blood with the root to break through whatever had been blocking her from finding her sibs. Her blood and this knotted wood had been so much stonger when used together. She rose and collected the root carefully, rubbing them clean of her tacky blood and lessening the connection. Once Lil had finished she could barely feel them any longer. She wiped the map and symbols from the floor.

The branch that rested on the bed rose into the air with her thought, and floated forward.

**IGoToFindMySibs.**

The Nif at her feet chattered and made sounds of comfort, support, and affirmation. She smiled down at them, ignoring the way the expression pulled on the wounds around her lips.

She exited the room and found Kima, Assan, Quinn, Hlani, and Uchel all sitting around talking in the main room of the house. They stopped and looked at her. She smiled at them, ignoring the pain.

**IKnowWhereMySibsAre.**

**IGoToRetrieveThem.**

Kima stood up. "We will go with you."

Lil tiled her head to the side.

**Why?YouKnowIWillNot**

**HelpWithThisRevolution.**

**IHaveToFocusOnOtherThings.**

Lil had not told them everything she had learned, especially that their world was doomed. She would tell them eventually, but right now, she could not deal with the fallout of panic and nervous questions. Kima nodded but so did the others in the room, which let Lil know that her short and vague conversation with Uchel and Kima had been shared. Lil had told part of the truth: that she had spoken to the being that made their world; that she must claim Kandake for all of them, for a way out.

"Yes, and we have spoken. Our world is more important and so we will help you complete your quest, so perhaps you can help us in return," Kima said.

Lil frowned but said nothing. She would not turn away help that could be critical in reuniting with her sibs, but they would get nothing in return. There was no point in a revolution. Lil needed to focus on how to survive the coming dissolution of everything she had ever known. She promised nothing. She owed them nothing.

**ThenComeAlongWeGoTo**
**CollectMySibsAndTwoAntes**
**WhoAreAlliesOfMineIKnow**
**WhereToFindThemButItIsVery**
**NearTheRulingCourtsSoWe**
**MustTravelInDisguise.**

Kima looked over at Quinn who smiled and nodded.

"I know just the thing."

Quinn hurried upstairs to the room she shared with Hlani and quickly returned with a roll of paper in her hands.

She unrolled it and Lil realized it was a map of Zebub painstakingly rendered down to streets and buildings, many tagged with notes. There were scatterings of colored dots here and there.

"Can you point out where they were?"

Lil nodded and looked down to study the map. She found the Ruling Courts on the map, a mass of black dots on the them. Perhaps black meant Antes? She used her finger and traced the street to the building she remembered. She let her finger rest on it for a moment before pulling away.

Quinn leaned over to look at the place her finger had marked, then looked up with a large smile.

"They're at a House of the Madame." She said.

Lil rocked back at that news. June's house. She hoped June had survived whatever Mayer had planned for them and whatever Chayyliel tried to pull. She tightened her hands to fists at the thought of that monster, and the way he had betrayed her. Lil paused, if she meant Mayer or Chayyliel.

Quinn looked up at Uchel and waited for a nod before continuing.

"We have used the Houses of the Madame as sanctuaries and meeting places before. They are sympathetic."

**AreThey?**

She had no way to communicate her suspicion and disdain for their naïveté with the branch, but her face must have said it.

"They have never betrayed us and have submitted to every security measure we have ever requested," Uchel said firmly.

Lil nodded.

"I have the perfect outfits for us." Quinn quickly rolled up the map and disappeared back into her room. When she returned she had an armful of fabric. "The Houses of the Madame cater to an . . . unusual clientele, and 'dants and Antes mingle freely in their Houses. This is to our advantage. One of the problems with disguises is that when you try to blend in and hide, you look suspicious. If you distract with your clothes then 'dants will remember that and not your face."

Quinn shook out a purple dress which turned out to be a long, layered robe. Separate thin gauze layers of different shades of purple that blended into a darker royal shade when they lay against each other.

"Hold out your arms, Lil."

Lil eyed the 'dant suspiciously but did as she asked.

The robe fell around her body like chill wind, not fabric. She turned to face Quinn and the woman belted up the front with a thick piece of silver twine that crossed back and forth from her chest down to the floor. She pulled out a dozen ribbons of silver. She approached Lil and gestured for her to lean down. When Lil did the 'dant attached the ribbons to the little hair Lil had left.

"Now just a little of this." Quinn pulled a small bottle of powder from her pile and uncorked it with her teeth. Placing a finger over the opening, Quinn upended the bottle, shaking it. Putting the bottle right side up she took her finger coated in the brown powder and patted it around Lil's mouth. "This will hide the visible scars."

"And as for the fingers, well, gloves. She looked at Lil's damaged hands and took tissues, stuffing the two fingers of the one glove and the one finger on the opposite glove. When Lil glanced in the mirror she saw someone bright and busy. The face was boring; the body and the ribbons that fell like silver hair were what caught the eye.

In moments Quinn had the rest of them dressed similarly: Assan was draped in red and orange that made him look like living, moving fire. Kima wore black, but her face was painted a bright silver with crystals across her eyelids and down the right side of her jaw. Hlani's pale skin and red, fiery hair were accented by a blue robe similar to Lil's own purple one. The exposed skin of her arms had been painted the same shade as her hair and she wore a half-mask of pure white.

Quinn herself had on white that made the golden tones in her skin more prominent. She took her dark hair and bathed it in a solution that studded it with gold dust. She painted her eyes wider in the mirror herself, accenting them with gold and black until they seemed to take up half her face.

Uchel had not changed anything about her appearance. When Lil looked at her questioningly the old woman laughed a bitter chuckle.

"I do not need a disguise. I am old, that is enough to make me invisible to most." They all donned large black robes with hoods to keep their brightness hidden until they were closer to their destination. They moved through the forest quickly and emerged behind a large, crumbling building of dark blue stone.

Kima leaned back from where she was leading the way. "This is the best approach to the city. Few people are ever here."

Lil nodded and they turned, emerging into an abandoned, quiet street. Most of the buildings looked abandoned, but Lil caught hints of habitation. Food and human waste was carefully corralled and placed far away from the living spaces. Squatters. They moved through the neighborhood with no problem. As they crossed another street Lil realized they were close to the place where her parents' home had stood. She refused to look in that direction as they passed by.

They arrived in the center district of the city. It was known by no ownership title because, unlike the rest of the city, no particular Hive claimed it. It belonged to all of the Ruling Courts and none at the same time. Antes who were not part of any Court or did not rank highly in their Houses lived in this district.

"We may remove the robes now," Kima said. They all did and, following their example, Lil tossed the robe into a convenient alley. "Keep your heads up, remember—pride and arrogance."

They moved through the streets, illuminated by light vines whose bulbs had been coaxed to grow along doorways and windowsills. There were some Antes and 'dants out and about; more of the former. Most of the 'dants were accompanied by an Ante or dressed elaborately like they were and heading in the same direction.

They arrived at The House of the Madame just in time to see 'dants and Antes alike fleeing the house. There was a great commotion inside and Lil heard screams. Screams she recognized.

The branch that had been wrapped around her waist underneath her robes whipped out and straightened into a staff before landing in her palm. Lil stared at it in wonder; she had no idea it could become a weapon as well. The thorns under her palms turned soft and the others longer and sharper. She spun it in her hands.

She looked at the others. Both Kima and Assan had their guns out. Quinn was whirling a pair of swords around in her hands, each one longer than her torso. Lil had no idea where she had hidden such weapons, but was glad that she seemed to be an expert in their use, from how she wielded them. Hlani reached down to her boots and pulled two short hammers from them. The heads looked heavy and dangerous enough, but the opposite sides had been sharpened into spikes.

Uchel was palming something in her hands and Lil looked at them no more as another scream sounded. That was Min. Lil moved toward the door before anyone could think to stop her and ready to kill anyone who tried.

# AREL & JAGI

Arel and Jagi did their best to entertain the pups. They had been in the new House of the Madame for two days and still had not left the room they had arrived in. They were cramped and bored. Unlike their first hiding spot, this House of the Madame was in the city center, too close to the Ruling Courts. It had already been searched so they need not worry about that, but it was much busier than the other House had been. And most of the visitors were Antes, coming under cloaks of magic or darkness—whatever was convenient to hiding their patronage of such a house.

The Door who had greeted them on the other side of the tunnel was completely different from the one they had just left. This Door was all angles, not the lush welcoming fullness they had left behind. Their skin was a pale white with blue undertones that made them look on the edge of freezing. They had no smile lines about their mouth; in fact, their face was totally smooth, absent of any lines.

Still, The Door had welcomed them and not been stingy on what they could provide—clothing, food, and even books to entertain them. They could not leave the room, however, and that had started to wear on Min and Davi after the first few hours. Now two days in, even Arel and Jagi found themselves short on patience with one another. They stayed awake as the pups dozed between them, wrapped in the interweaving cocoon of their extra appendages. What had started as a comfort for the two Antes, knowing their charges were safe, had turned into something the two 'dants seemed unwilling to sleep without.

"What is our—" Jagi started. *plan/next move/goal?* his tentacles finished for him.

Arel was silent at first. He could feel the fear and nerves in his companion, in the shaking at the places they touched.

"We must—" *find/locate/reunite/join with Lil.*

A knock at their door interrupted their conversation and they untangled themselves and hurried to answer before whoever it was woke the pups.

"There is a new guest," The Door spoke.

Arel and Jagi looked at one another.

"Is there something unusual about this guest?" Arel asked.

The Door nodded. "A 'dant. Not one I know."

Arel and Jagi understood immediately. This House of the Madame was centrally located, more expensive. Most 'dants would not be able to afford the services of the House or any of its companions. And any that could? The Door should know immediately on sight.

"Describe him."

They talked about his light brown skin, red hair, and the spots across his face and finally his two companions. Arel and Jagi realized it was Byron. The boy whose idiot friends they had wanted so badly to kill. Arel and Jagi shared a look acknowledging that they should have eliminated the threat when it first presented itself. They would not make that mistake again.

"Did he ask about anyone?" Arel asked.

The Door shook their head, "No."

"Be careful of him," Jagi replied. "We will prepare should we need to run again. Let us know if anything bothers you about him. No matter how small."

The Door nodded and left. Arel and Jagi returned to their previous position, but, too nervous to speak, they simply stayed awake late into the night watching Min and Davi.

They'd fallen into a fitful sleep at some point when a sound startled them all awake. Arel and Jagi froze in the darkness waiting for it again and when it came they realized it was not a noise so much as a vibration. Slowly Arel and Jagi withdrew back into themselves and stood. They were on either side of their still-sleeping pups, trying to pinpoint from which direction the feeling was coming from. The door to their room flung open; the Door of the House stood there, obviously woken in the middle of sleep. There was a frown on their face.

"Come. Quickly."

Arel and Jagi did not hesitate, each one scooping up one of their charges and hurrying to follow.

"I was asleep and the House contacted me and showed me that that 'dant somehow was able to use power on me. Here! In my own House!" The anger in The Door's voice turned it into a growl. "The 'dant questioned me about you, when you had arrived, and how. I told him everything. I apologize."

Arel and Jagi ignored the apology and hurried along. Min was stirring at the rapidness of their movement though Davi still hung limp in Jagi's arms.

"I went to confront them and confine them to their room until I could speak with you but they were gone. The House does not have much concept of time so I do not know how long ago they left."

They were hurrying through the main room, following The Door somewhere, when they were all thrown off their feet. They looked to the front door, but it was the floor that was bucking and bursting. It came from beneath them in a shower of dirt and it was all that Arel and Jagi could do to leap out of the way and shield their charges. They saw The Door churned under the ground in the explosion from beneath. Arel reached for their hand but they fell beneath the loose dirt before the two could connect.

What came out of the ground was huge; larger than Arel and Jagi combined. Its body was squat and thick, close to the ground, moving on dozens of articulated limbs that ended in what looked like 'dant feet, if the toes were three times as long as they should have been. Its neck was long and curled to and fro. Swiveling on the end of the long neck was a 'dant face: a young girl screaming and screeching, no intelligence in her eyes. The lower part of her jaw stretched away from her face, showing row after row of sharp teeth. The teeth glittered, as black as the rest of it.

For Arel and Jagi it did not matter that they had never seen anything like this before, they recognized it from the whispered stories they had been told as pups themselves.

"Maasu," they whispered in unison underneath the wailing of both Min and Davi.

The legendary animals of war. The created monsters that the Ruling Courts had been so free and loose with early in Corpiliu's development.

The secrets of creating Maasu had been lost and none had been seen since the beginning times. It should not have existed. The depictions of Maasu in the old texts and stories was often of wanton murder and destruction. They were made of pieces of living beings, enhanced with mechaniques and power, with instinct and knowledge from the component pieces. They were horrific tools of murder.

And here one was in front of them.

Arel passed Min over to Jagi's other arm.

"Go."

Jagi hesitated for a second but nodded and moved to the right while Arel stood taller. His apertures opened and he let his other appendages slip out and spread around him. He whipped them at the creature's head, narrowly avoiding the thing's fanged jaws. Arel used his tentacles to spin himself across the room. It bit into one of them and he growled and used his momentum to rip it from the Maasu's mouth. What gushed out of his injured appendage was the black sludge, the trash and darkness that was his power. He watched Jagi run as quickly as possibly with the pups in his arms.

The Maasu spun and lifted the massive trunk of a tail that swayed behind it. It crashed down in front of Jagi, who barely avoided slamming into it. Jagi spun back, but the only other way from the room led upstairs: a dead-end.

He put Min and Davi on the first step.

"Min, protect your brother," Jagi said.

The little girl nodded, even as her lip trembled and tears slipped down her face.

"When you see a chance to get out of here, you take it. Okay?" He had both of his hands on her shoulders.

The girl nodded and Jagi smiled, leaning forward to kiss her on the forehead.

"It will all be alright, Min. You shall survive this," Jagi whispered.

Then he did the same for Davi, gave him the same benediction and hoped he was not lying to them. Jagi turned to where Arel was fighting the thing and losing slowly. He growled low in his throat, his apertures snapped open, and his own extra appendages slid out. Jagi whipped one across the room, catching the Maasu in the face so that it turned its rage toward him.

It roared and charged, and Jagi let out a battle cry of his own running to meet it.

# LIL

Lil was through the door. The first thing she saw was Min, standing at the far end of the room. She had pushed Davi behind her and was holding him there with one arm. The arm they had taken, the one that Lil had replaced, was held in front of her, fingers splayed, drifts of frost floating before it. Lil looked at the creature that filled most of the room and the two Antes fighting it. Arel and Jagi were quite the sight. They distracted the creature, ran around its attacks, and used their tentacles to hurt it from all sides. Every time they got close enough to lay a hand on it, a part of its black carapace dissolved under the touch.

Lil's entire body lit up with triumph. She had found them and they were unharmed, except that she had to act fast if she wanted things to remain that way. Lil picked up a rock and threw it so it landed at Min's feet. Her sib looked up at her and opened her mouth.

Lil quickly held up her finger to her lips and Min contained her noise to a small yelp.

Davi looked in her direction and started smiling through his tears. The thing's tail was still draped between her and them but that was up to her to change. Lil pulled her dagger free and sliced a finger through the glove. She painted the symbols on the blade that had made it strong enough to penetrate the armor of the creature that had hunted her before. Lil slammed the knife down into the tail just as the rest of those who'd accompanied her came through the door.

The thing roared but moved its tail from the spot, and Lil quickly gestured for her sibs to run to her. They did and she hugged them before passing them over to Quinn.

The branch flew from her hand to hover between them.

**TakeThemOutsideProtectThem.**

**IWillComeAfterThisCreatureIsDead.**

Quinn nodded and gathered the children to her. Min started to struggle but Lil placed her hand on her head and she stopped. She leaned over and kissed her on the cheek, doing the same to Davi and tasting the salt of tears that still flavored their skin.

Then she shoved them towards Quinn who ran out the door with them. Lil turned to the monster, which was whirling in pain and confusion. She grabbed for the branch and it became a staff again. Lil waited for the right moment then struck, pushing the thorned tip through one of the holes that Arel or Jagi had burned in its hide.

The thing screeched and shook, ripping the branch from its side, causing more damage. Its face swung toward her and Kima and Assan began to fire their guns. One of them caught it in the right eye and the orb shattered and leaked milky white down the thing's face. The other bullets ricocheted off its armor and she heard Arel yelp as one caught him in the leg. Lil turned and gestured for Kima and Assan to stop. They lowered their weapons and she gestured them outside.

That left herself and Hlani and Uchel along with Jagi, and Arel, who was stumbling back to his feet ignoring the blood slicking down his calf. One of the things' legs came within range and Hlani slammed one of her hammers down on it. The crack resonated through the building. Lil looked at the metal of the hammers and their odd blue shimmer. She wondered at their origins.

Lil could see other dents in its skin from where Hlani had struck. Lil continued to use the holes Jagi and Arel burned into it as bullseyes. The creature was bleeding and roaring and twirling, injured but not slowing down. They needed to hurt it worse in order to kill it.

Lil thought of the magic at her fingertips and the things she could summon with will alone, but none seemed strong enough. Babel had always been her strongest weapon. She felt in her pocket under the purple robe. The root had allowed the tree to grow and for her to find her sibs. What would it do if she placed it in her own mouth against the stump of her tongue? The thing roared again and Lil did not hesitate any longer. She placed one of the roots in her mouth.

Her tongue did not grow back and she ignored the surge of disappoitment. But it felt as if the root had attached itself to the stump. As if a phantom tongue now occupied her mouth. Lil tried to form a word of Babel and before she finished thinking the word she felt it grow to life in her mouth. It passed from her stump to the root itself, she felt it as it rattled in her mouth. She spat the word out along with the bone. It struck the creature and the word flared to life in the air.

Written Babel.

Lil memorized the curve of it, the way that the word rotated around itself. The word faded and the world exploded with noise. The thing screamed as its back half was blown apart. Hlani ducked behind a wall and Arel and Jagi were facing the thing head on but a large splash of its innards fell onto Lil. She wished she could speak if only so she could curse. Lil noticed the branch now floating next to her again spelling out the foulest words she knew. She did not stop it.

Arel and Jagi came forward.

"Lil."

They stopped a foot away and held their hands out, waiting for her to make the move that would put them in contact. She took the step forward and they folded her into her embrace. She felt their fingers on her face. They both found the scars around her mouth at the same time and seemed to understand what they meant.

Their faces went dark with anger, their pale white skin shading further into gray, their normally light gray markings turning black.

Arel and Jagi cautiously allowed one tentacle each to emerge from themselves and placed the tips gently on each of her temples. Lil was flooded with the warmth of caring and the relief of having located each other. Their voices were twined around each other into one and sounded in her mind.

*We are glad you are safe.*

Lil tried to communicate back at them the same way. She heard a voice but was unsure if it was her own. It sounded familiar but she worried it was wrong somehow.

*None of us are safe. Corpiliu falls apart.*

She waited for the shock to reverberate through them but it never came and she realized.

*You knew?* The voice is incredulous and sounds sharper and she shudders again, not liking it.

*We suspected. There is a prophecy passed down in our House. It speaks of a world before. That we were led here but it was always meant to be a temporary haven, not a new home. It speaks of someone who will lead us back.*

Lil shivered at the insinuation in their voice; the blind faith and belief. She did not like it but had she not already accepted as much from the being whose bones made this world?

*Come, we should go before any more of these creatures—*

*Maasu.*

Lil stopped to ask them what they knew and they flooded her mind with all the information they had. Created creatures, horrible, tortured mish-mashes of former beings. As soon as Lil saw the rumor in their minds that both alchemy and mechaniques were used in its construction she knew who had sent it after her. Now that she knew, she doubted it was over. Her Holder had always been a planner.

*We have to go. Now.*

Lil pulled away from them and reached for their wrists, dragging them out the door. Hlani and Uchel were already reacting to her panicked movement and were disappearing through the door. The street was still deserted when they emerged but Lil could see the flicker of movement in other buildings' windows. The screams had stopped and so curiosity had taken hold. They had moments before others showed up to investigate.

Min and Davi ran to her as soon as Lil was free of the building and she could not resist leaning down to hold them tightly. The branch floated behind her and twisted on her mental command.

**WeNeedToGoNow.**

**MayerIsBehindThis.**

**ThereWillBeMoreComing.**

That was when Lil heard the rumbling and turned to see three other Maasu come careening around the corner. One looked like the thing that had attacked them at the open market, but with even more appendages sprouting from its body. Another flew through the air on numerous fast wings that sliced through the air and gave the impression they could cut through flesh just as easily. Its body was long and divided into segments that spun independent of one another. The final one bringing up the rear was huge, the size of a small building, and its body was low to the ground with a curved back. The back unfolded, only instead of wings emerging, what came out were dozens of tiny black monsters, flying and zeroing in on them.

# SAN FRANCISCO

# ZAHA

Zaha screamed as a yawning pit of blackness opened in front of her. The others in the lobby hurried over, drawing weapons from coats, powering up. She saw people's clothes shred as their arms melted into their torsos or shifted into claws. Before anyone reached her a body came hurtling out of the darkness and slammed into her. Zaha fell to the ground and looked up in time to see the portal disappear as quickly as it had appeared.

"Ma'am, please disentangle yourself from the unknown entity."

Zaha rolled her eyes. She was about to snap back at the man when the body on top of hers groaned and she recognized the voice.

"Tae?"

Zaha turned and slowly slid out from underneath him, trying to move him as little as possible. Hands grasped her own and helped her free. As soon as she could, Zaha scrambled around to see the face of the body. It was Tae. Bruises littered his jaw and cheeks and from the way they disappeared into his collar she assumed he was completely covered in them. His eyes fluttered opened and his mouth opened but nothing came out.

She looked up at one of the Agents around, all trying to convince her to step away from Tae.

"Where is Acting Agent-in-Charge Jayl? Get her here immediately. It's Tae. One of the people who accompanied Agent-in-Charge Allan to Zebub."

Someone ran off and Zaha looked down, wary of touching Tae, scared she would injure him more. In minutes Jayl and her mother came into view.

"Here, let me see to him." The older Jayl came forward, her hands already reaching for the bruises on his face. When her fingers touched them, they started to fade from vivid blue-black, to purple, to yellow-green. And then she pulled her hands away and gently tapped his face.

"Why can't you heal him fully?" Zaha had not meant to ask the question. She had spent most of her time at the Agency doing her best to keep her head down and listen. To learn. She didn't want to draw any more attention than what she already had, as the woman who had survived contact with the darkness.

"I could, but a sudden healing can be as shocking as a sudden injury. I don't know if his system can take that shock."

Zaha nodded and said nothing else.

Tae's eyes fluttered opened and then shot open as he tried to scramble to his feet.

"Tae. Tae. Calm down." The older Jayl kept a soothing hand on him until awareness flooded back into his gaze.

"I'm back but . . . how?" Tae stuttered.

"We were hoping you could tell us?" The younger Jayl asked.

Tae shook his head at them and put one of his hands to his forehead. "No. I wish I could. The last thing I remember—" Suddenly he went quiet and stiff. "Daniel."

"Daniel?" The younger Jayl asked, stiffening and standing up.

"Yes, we were—"

Tae stopped as the younger Jayl put her hand on his shoulder. "Not here. Let's go to my office."

Zaha watched them stand, and then, to her surprise Tae reached out and took her hand. Zaha felt his hand shake. He was not taking liberties. He was terrified. She squeezed his palm and followed him across the room to the odd elevators she hated so much.

One uncomfortable ride later, the four of them were piling into Dayida's office; not the large one of the top that Zaha knew Erik had used, but a larger, more mundane one a floor below.

Neither Jayl protested Zaha's coming along, so she slowly relaxed as they sat across from each other on the two sofas tucked into a nook by the window.

"What were you going to say about Daniel?" Dayida asked, the anxiety in her voice easy to read. Zaha felt her own hand tremble at the thought of the horrible specter that only she could see.

"He's a traitor."

"What?" The older Jayl asked.

"I don't know a lot of details yet. I got shunted here before I could see a lot, and I'm still sorting through what I did see . . . but I'm absolutely sure he's working against us. Although . . ." Tae trailed off.

"What, Tae?" The younger Jayl prompted.

Tae continued. "I don't understand how I'm still alive. How I got here. I should be dead. The darkness and the building collapsing had me dead." He tilted his head back and closed his eyes but they popped open a second later. "Erik!"

"What about Erik?" The younger Jayl asked, leaning forward.

"He must have done something. I saw his eyes flash red right before I fell," Tae said.

"Red?" The younger Jayl questioned.

Tae looked at her. "Yes. Our powers were different there. Abilities enhanced; changed. Erik was in constant pain when he used his powers. I think he might have done something."

"How are things going over there?" The older Jayl asked.

Tae winced. "Not good. This isn't the little thing that we had here, it's a full-blown invasion and the darkness is straight up swallowing buildings and people. I don't know if there is a thing any small group of people could do about it, no matter how powerful."

Zaha saw Mrs. Jayl and Ms. Jayl share a look and then nod. They both went silent and finally Tae asked them a question.

"How are things going here?"

The continued silence was answer enough but Tae waited and looked at each of them waiting for one of them to answer him.

Finally, the younger Jayl sighed and leaned forward.

"Everything is going to come out. No one can keep it secret for much longer, even the government."

Tae's looked at all of them in shock. The older Jayl nodded in confirmation.

"I've been watching the news and reading the blogs and there are more and more reports of disappearances. More reports of weird monsters on the prowl, and not just from the magazines that no one really believes anymore. There are too many eyewitnesses for people to ignore it much longer." Zaha said.

"Eventually something too big is going to happen and the rest of the world is going to sit up and take notice. The governments of most countries have to have done so already," the younger Jayl said.

"It's a good thing you're back, actually. Your sight might come in handy as we try to figure out how to deal with coming out to the world." The older Jayl looked at him speculatively.

"Still, they probably could use my help more in Zebub. I should go back," Tae said slowly.

"No, you shouldn't," Zaha said before anyone else could.

They all looked at her and she shrunk in on herself before straightening her spine.

"I've been studying files on dealing with the—the Angelics. I don't think it would be a good idea," she revealed.

They all looked at her curiously but none of them looked angry and so she continued.

"They can be very strict to agreements when it suits them. It would be very easy for them to hurt you and claim you had only been granted safe passage for your first visit and had no such protection this time," Zaha explained.

The young Jayl nodded. "We'll try to find a way to send Erik a message, at least, and let him know that you aren't dead. Zaha, why don't you show him to one of the rooms here to rest."

"Actually, I just want to get home," Tae spoke up.

The younger Jayl hesitated but nodded and Zaha helped Tae out of the room. She looked at him, the purple under his eyes, the way his cheek looked sharp enough to cut glass.

"Come, I will drive you home," she offered.

"You don't have to. I can call a cab," Tae demurred.

"Don't be silly. I'm off in a few minutes anyway. Think of it as a first date," Zaha said, linking her arm in his and smiling at his shocked expression.

# DAYIDA

They saw Tae off, promising to look into some way to contact Erik and others, as if she had not been looking for one all along. Dayida closed her eyes. She ignored the presence of her mother. She rubbed at her eyes and the bridge of her nose, wishing the constant ache would go away. She twisted her upper body back and forth trying to loosen the tension in her back.

Dayida had already gone through the files the Agency had on Zebub, and it was depressingly sparse. From population numbers to points of possible entry—all of it conjecture at best, but mostly blank. Dayida had also been re-reading the files as an excuse to avoid her mother. Hettie cleared her throat and Dayida opened her eyes and looked up.

Hettie Jayl stood over her, framed in the light. Hettie was what some people would call an Amazon: tall, thick, and muscled—she stood 6'5" in her bare feet, with dark brown skin that looked smooth as silk. Her hair was down, dreadlocks that started black and then got lighter and lighter until the tips that brushed the backs of her knees were a golden brown.

"Dayida, you've been avoiding me," she said.

Dayida sighed and met her mother's eyes. They had once been the same hazel-flecked brown as her own all the time but nowadays they were more likely to be a mix of the black and dark blue of the deepest oceans.

"Yes."

Hettie's head tilted to the side. It reminded Dayida of a scientist studying a suddenly interesting specimen. "At least you admit it. Yet we must work together. More than ever. The Angelics mean war."

"I know." Dayida went back to rubbing her face where it ached.

Hettie sighed. "Perhaps it's my fault. You were always shy and fearful as a child—"

"Cautious! Not fearful. I was *cautious*," Dayida snapped. "And how would you know in any case?"

Hettie paused and nodded, just once, acknowledging the point.

"Still, we don't have time for caution. We agreed to work together and that is what we must do. Do you believe that the Angelics only intend to attack New York? They will hit us before long."

"I know, Hettie. I want to understand why they are attacking."

Hettie sighed and lowered herself back into one of the chairs that faced Dayida's desk.

"The why is important but not nearly as important as making sure that we live until we get the answers. My guess is that they have no faith in their ability to defeat the darkness and intend to take our world, to buy themselves time. We need to start preparing for that."

"Matthias gave us the list of independents in the area for a reason. We will contact them tomorrow."

Dayida took a breath to interrupt but Hettie hurried on.

"We will ask those who are willing to patrol in groups, to pay special attention to any areas people have recently gone missing. I think at this point we can both agree that the Agency and perhaps the government itself is proving less than useful. They must be aware that New York is only the beachhead of a much larger invasion. Yet they have not chosen to contact us. So, either they are telling *none* of the other offices or they are simply not telling *us*. Which means we are effectively cut off."

Dayida rested her head in her hands and watched Hettie with a bitter twist to her lips. She could feel the tightening in her shoulders that came along with accessing her powers and she took a deep breath to sooth it away. Hettie trailed off and Dayida did not know if it was because she had finally cataloged the look on her daughter's face or if she had sensed the brief flare of her power.

"I wish you would not assume I was stupid," Dayida said slowly.

Hettie's eyes widened.

"I have, in fact, already called the independents. I am also about to call the Organization and see what resources they would be willing to share. I also thought that this could be a land grab, but the way they are going about it makes no sense. They have the power to attack in multiple places, with powers and appearances that would cause immediate panic. I'm assuming they had a better plan, and were pushed to do this early. Which I'm guessing is thanks to the darkness. But all of this is conjecture and until we know their plans and reasons, we are fighting blind. I do not like being uninformed," Dayida said. She longed for the solitude of her studio and the ability to shut out the world but those days seemed like they would be a long time in returning.

Hettie said nothing, simply sitting back and staring for a moment. When she finally spoke her voice was soft.

"I do not think you're stupid. I never thought that about you, my child."

Dayida stiffened at the term of endearment.

"We simply do not know each other. I do not know your capabilities and you do not know mine. We are like strangers," Hettie continued.

"And whose fault is that? As for you I know—" Dayida stopped. What was she going to finish the sentence with?

- enough

- that I don't care

- you killed my father

All of them were true in some sense. And applicable to her as well. She had decided to reveal her complicity in Daniel's fate as soon as Erik returned. She couldn't have that secret between her and Erik any longer and how could she ever expect Erik to forgive *her,* if she could not find it in herself to try and forgive her own mother?

Dayida swallowed and spoke. "You are right. Even if we do not ever become close like family, we have to know each other to work together."

Hettie's eyes widened again and Dayida smiled. The second time in as many minutes that she had shocked her unflappable mother. She could admit some joy at that.

"I have Agents out watching all the known portals between Zebub and here. I am contemplating simply shutting them down but—"

"If they're active you know the points of entry they are going to use," Hettie finished.

Dayida nodded. "At least the most likely ones. I've also been diving into the files that were left here to see if there is anything that could help us. Any observations they made in their dealings with Zebub that could help us out."

Hettie nodded and the silence between them stretched.

Dayida took a huge breath and closed the file under her hand, lifting it and handing it across the desk. "Did you want to help?"

Hettie smiled and nodded before taking the file and cracking it open. Dayida watched her for a moment before reaching for the next one in her stack. They sat in silence for well over an hour reading file after file. Then Hettie made a small inquisitive noise and Dayida's head came up.

"What is it?" Dayida asked, leaning over her desk.

"Maybe nothing, but there's a note in here of several attempts on an older Blooded seer known as Fallon. Agents were sent to acquire him multiple times but every time he was already gone."

Dayida snorted. "Well, he wouldn't be much of a seer if he couldn't see them coming."

Hettie leaned over to the stack of discarded files by her chair and flipped through them, lying one after another on the desk between them.

"Well, yes, and that wouldn't be that interesting, but the thing is, there's a file here for every year going back twenty-five years. Each one contains a request for a seer. The name and reasoning given changes but the details of their powers, their protections, and physical details are identical. It's slipped in among vague requests for specific bloodlines. Though his bloodline is never mentioned," Hettie pointed out.

"That's . . . odd. Why try to hide that they wanted this one particular Blooded? And how did no one notice?" Dayida asked rubbing her chin.

"Each of these was a personal request from an Angelic who crossed over to the Agent-in-Charge. I wouldn't be surprised if he knew, but no one else did. He probably only gave his Suits minimal details," Hettie theorized, snorting and leaning back in the chair.

Dayida nodded. "If this is the same person over and over, someone in Zebub wanted him pretty badly and for a very long time. The question is why."

Hettie shrugged. "I don't know, but look at this." She reached for another file. This folder was bright red and stuffed so full that it looked fit to burst at any moment. Dayida shuddered at the sight of it. She'd skimmed it but had deliberately done her best to not look at details.

It was one of several bright red folders that chronicled those taken and sold to the Angelics. This one was just list after list of bare details—

name, age, description, cost, cover-ups enacted. The others had more details about each but Dayida did not really want to know.

Hettie reached across and put her hand on Dayida's.

"I know. It's the numbers, though, the number of acquisitions stays pretty low and steady way back to the 1800s. A couple of people a year—nationally. Then twenty-five years ago the numbers start to increase spectacularly to two-a-city and then begin to climb every other year after that. By the time we get to 2010 it's over one hundred requests per city."

"Impossible. It was high but there's no way the Organization could miss it rising that high." Dayida pulled the file from Hettie's hand and flipped through it. Hettie was right. They had been pulling a hundred people from San Francisco and the surrounding cities every year. She noticed the circled R next to most of the names. She leaned over to show it to Hettie. "Do you think this means returned?"

Hettie looked up with dark, worried eyes. "That would be my guess. We always knew some of the abducted came back, we just had no idea it was so many."

"Me either," Dayida answered. "So what, you think all these people were Seers?"

"No." Hettie shook her head. "We know that a lot of those they took were not Blooded at all. But this seer is obviously someone they're desperate to recapture. And both started twenty-five years ago. They must be linked. Want to bet this Seer knows something about this?"

"We need to find this person and ask them some questions," Dayida said.

"Yes," Hettie agreed.

"Finding them could be difficult."

Hettie shook her head. "Not that hard. If there's one thing I know about Seers? Most can't help but interfere in the lives of those around them. Contact all the independents again and ask if they know of anyone who helps the neighborhood they live in but shuns praise and attention. People like that garner attention no matter what they do."

Dayida nodded and picked up the phone on her desk to start dialing, while Hettie dived back into the files. She saw the small smile on Hettie's face and could not help but echo it. Their first attempt at working together had gone well. She hoped the trend continued.

# MELINDA

Patrah and Melinda were out in the panhandle park when the attack happened. One moment the park was peaceful and the next an older woman who had been sitting feeding the pigeons grabbed a jogger and launched him through the air. Patrah told Melinda to stay back and then moved toward the lady. Melinda leaned around the tree that she had scrambled behind, to get a look at what was happening. The woman was busy slamming the man's head into the ground as he tried feebly to push her off.

Patrah kicked the old woman in the side with no warning, knocking her off the man. The jogger groaned and tried to push himself to his feet but fell back down again. Patrah grabbed him by the armpits and began to drag him away, but the older woman had already recovered and dove for them.

Melinda could see something was wrong about the woman: her eyes were too wide, and she opened her mouth and spit and hissed, but said nothing. The woman hit Patrah in the middle and the two of them rolled away across the grassy knoll. Patrah was up in seconds, on the woman's back, trying to hold her down and clamp her wrists together.

Even from the distance Melinda could hear her Counselor's voice trying to convince the woman to calm down and stop fighting. The old woman wasn't listening and slammed her head, too far back for normal, into Patrah's face.

She needed to help. Melinda sat, leaning back against the bark of the tree. She tried to drift off quickly the way that Patrah had taught her but she couldn't stop wincing with every blow she heard land, wondering if Patrah or the old woman was winning. She looked around the trunk again and watched them trade blows. The old lady was vicious. Clawed hands swiped at Patrah's eyes, while also trying to catch themselves in her short hair.

Melinda turned away again, pressed her back hard into the rough bark, concentrating on that. She took a deep breath, and let go. She let go of the feeling of the bark against her back and the grass under her bare legs. The sounds of the fight were the last to go, but she was able to let those drift away as well.

The land of the dreaming exploded around her, reflecting the living world in odd shapes and angles. The tree she had been leaning against was very ordered in the dreaming, the bark a repetitive diamond pattern, the branches spreading above her perfectly even, like the spokes in a wheel. Melinda loved the weird ways that things looked in the dreaming but she had no time for that now. She looked over to where Patrah and the old woman were wrestling. In the dreaming, they were represented by the way they saw themselves. Patrah was a fighter, marred and bruised and bleeding but covered in a patchwork of gleaming armor, with a determined set to her face. The old lady was no lady at all. Here in the dreaming, Melinda could see what was wrong with her. Her dream self was twisted in a way that looked very painful. Patrah had explained that there were things that could do that: tear someone up inside so bad that people started to tear *themselves* up. This was different, though; something inside of the woman was trying to shed her skin, and force its way out.

Melinda cast her hands out and the stuff of the dreaming came willingly to her palms.

Quickly.

Quickly.

No time for finesse now. She just needed effective soldiers.

She made them only half as tall as her; smaller and easier to make. She gave them wicked claws on their feet and hands and made them muscled. She gave them vicious teeth and smooth heads with nothing to grab onto. They flowed quickly from her palms, a dozen creatures coming to life under her direction. Melinda sent them after the older woman's dreamself.

Patrah had been careful to explain to her that any damage she did to people in their dreams would manifest in the real world in odd ways. You were tearing at their psyche. You could accidentally do a lot of bad things to someone.

This wasn't an accident, though. This was on purpose and as much as she wanted to look away Melinda didn't. She needed to see what she had done. Her dream creatures ripped into the old lady with teeth and claws. They ripped at her odd angles and tore at the skin of her dreamself.

Melinda's vision went double and she could see it wasn't working. In the real world, the old lady was still trying kill Patrah. Her creations were tearing at the old lady's dreamself, but she wasn't reacting. It wasn't enough. Melinda could tell by the way the wounds and blood on Patrah's dream self were multiplying that her Counselor was losing the fight.

Melinda panicked and broke through into the real world. The midnight blue of the dreamworld tore around her, a large hole right between her and Patrah and through that hole she could see the real woman on Patrah's back trying to get leverage to knock Patrah unconscious.

Her creatures marched through the hole with no hesitation. In the sunlight of the park they practically glowed, their midnight-blue skin showing up brightly against the grass as they scampered in a line toward Patrah.

The old lady felt them this time. She screeched and flung them about but they took no damage. They were made of dreamstuff; there was little in this world that could harm them. She could hear other people screaming but all her attention was on keeping the dream creatures in this world and on target. The old lady was completely preoccupied with them and Melinda saw Patrah rear back and kick with both her legs. The woman flew through the air and slammed into a tree.

Melinda lost control over the creatures in surprise and they popped out of existence as she fell to the ground, exhausted. Patrah looked around and Melinda followed her gaze taking in the many phones pointed in both of their directions.

Patrah rose to her feet and Melinda could see all the scratches on her face sluggishly bleeding. Melinda could see the way she was frowning as she got closer. Patrah picked Melinda up into her arms.

"Did I mess up?"

Patrah looked at her and said. "No, you didn't, sweetie, but we need to get off the street." But it was in that tone that meant even if Melinda hadn't messed up, Patrah was afraid of something. Melinda looked over to where other park attendees were approaching the unconscious old woman, and Patrah moved them both in the opposite direction.

# PATRAH

She hurried through the park, Melinda in her arms. The girl was too tired to complain about being picked up. The creatures that Melinda had created had disappeared but there were too many people who had seen; too many people who had their cell phones out and recording. There was no way to keep this quiet and Patrah needed to get them away before she could focus on damage control. She wanted to bring the old woman with them but it would have only draw more attention. Patrah would have to locate her later. Someone was surely calling her an ambulance right now.

The sun was beginning to set and Patrah wanted to get Melinda to the safety of the downtown building before full night. By the time they reached the car Patrah had shaken off those who had tried to follow them. Melinda was lightly drowsing as she placed her in the seat and buckled her in. They made the trip to the Financial District in excellent time.

Patrah wondered at getting a space right in front again. There always seemed to be parking in front of this building even when there was none for blocks in either direction. Some application of the Agency's might, either through godspower or simple bureaucracy? Either way, Patrah was extremely grateful for it as she moved around the car and pulled Melinda back into her arms.

She hurried up the steps and through the lobby. The sun was mostly down so the person behind the front desk was no longer Zaha but the night receptionist, a very friendly young man who went by the name Ford. She nodded at him and hurried past to the corner of the building where a folding of the walls, a small twist in design, hid the stairway from anyone who did not know it was there. Patrah had gone looking for them on her first day in this place. She did not enjoy the odd elevators with their liquid malleability.

After climbing three flights she turned another hidden corner and was faced with a balcony of sorts; one that used to look over the atrium. Doors peppered the wall opposite the balcony. Most had been offices but in the last few days they had been converted into small suites for Suits and visitors. Even at its height the Agency had not had enough people for all the offices they had. Bureaucracy was the mother of useless redundancy but in this case, it had worked out.

Mere seconds after she knocked, the door was opened by both of Melinda's mothers, who looked at her in question.

"What's wrong?" Elise asked as she took her daughter's sleeping form from Patrah.

"She overextended herself too quickly without using the exercises I taught her."

"Why would she do that?" Elise asked.

"There was an emergency." She kept on before they could ask any questions. "She will simply need to sleep and rest. She'll be fine in the morning."

The woman nodded and took her child into the room, presumably to lay her in bed. Jeni stayed in the doorway studying Patrah with a critical eye.

"Is everything okay?" Jeni loved her daughter very much but never really asked anything about the girl's training. She did not want to know about it, really.

"I don't know. People got video of Melinda using her power," Patrah admitted.

Jeni's mouth dropped open and she stepped into the hallway, closing the door behind her so that neither Melinda or Elise could hear what they were saying. "What now?"

"I am going to talk with Dayida about that. In the past, the Organization would send people to pay off those who had evidence."

Jeni looked at her. "And those who would not be bought?"

Patrah winced. "They had their reputations ruined, their credibility destroyed beyond repair so that no one would believe anything they had to say."

"What's going to happen to Melinda?"

"You don't need to worry. She is my aspirant and I will do all in my power to keep her safe."

Jeni nodded, clearly wanting to say more but unsure of what it was she wanted to say.

"I have to go meet with Dayida now," Patrah said.

Jeni opened her mouth but closed it again just as quickly and with a simple nod slipped back into her room; back to her wife and daughter.

Patrah went off to Dayida's office and found her seated behind her desk, her mother Hettie sitting in one of the two chairs that faced it. Both had been looking through folders until Patrah had knocked and let herself in without waiting for an answer.

"Patrah, how can I—" Dayida broke off as she took in the expression on Patrah's face. "What has happened now?"

Patrah hesitated and finally asked a question of her own.

"What happened here?" She gestured at the folders haphazardly stacked all over the place.

"Tae has returned," Dayida revealed.

Patrah froze at the shiver of fear that wracked her frame. Why would Tae be the only person to return? Unless the others were—she stopped the thought before it could fully form.

"The others?" Patrah asked.

"Fine as far as he knows, though he was sent back in the midst of battle," Dayida answered.

"Sent back by whom?" Patrah asked.

"He doesn't really know, but his guess is Erik."

Patrah sat in the free chair next to Hettie. "But his powers have nothing to do with travel. It's one of the rarest abilities among the Blooded and not at all connected to berserkers."

Hettie and Dayida were nodding through her talking, well aware of these facts.

"Tae said that all of their powers were affected, and that they worked differently in Zebub. It's possible it has something to do with that. The more disturbing part is that Daniel is a traitor in some way. It was the last thing Tae saw before he was swept back here," Hettie stated grimly.

"So maybe Daniel did it to get him out of the way?" Patrah offered.

"Tae doesn't think so. He's fairly sure that Daniel wanted him dead, and not somewhere he could spread the information to others," Hettie replied.

Patrah nodded, digesting all this. "Where is Tae now?"

'He went home to his parents' house to rest."

"Is it safe for him to be out there?" Patrah asked.

"What do you mean?" Dayida replied.

Patrah took a deep breath and relayed her own story while Hettie and Dayida listened silently. After she finished she watched Dayida and Hettie worriedly.

"The woman who attacked you. Could she have been another Blooded?" Hettie asked.

"She could have been, but I do not think so. The glimpses I got of her dreamself as we fought were like nothing I've ever seen," Patrah explained. "Then of course there are the continued actions of my aspirant, who can do impossible things like they are nothing."

"This isn't the first time that footage of a Blooded has been captured," Dayida stated after a second of thinking.

"Except that now we have all these other stories and videos cropping up. This is no longer about one photo or video, one eye witness report. This is about a critical mass of information being spread to the general populace so that even those who would usually scoff at the stories will have no choice but to take them seriously," Hettie stated. "We are on the verge of exposure and there's nothing we can really do but prepare for it."

Dayida nodded reluctantly. "You're right. Things are changing and we need to be prepared, but we also have to focus on how to keep those with power safe. I think we have to work under the assumption that the Angelics do not want our help for a problem in their world. They want our world for their own."

Hettie nodded, as did Patrah after a moment.

"We need to bring everyone in. I don't just mean warn them, but protect them. When this gets out there and people believe? It isn't going to be just Antes that are hunting us. Humans are going to start hunting us too. A panicked populace under attack by monsters suddenly learns that people with supernatural powers have lived among them the whole time?" Patrah finished and watched both nod in recognition.

"We can't pull everyone in. Who would be out there patrolling for the Antes and making sure they don't get the drop on us?" Hettie asked.

Patrah admitted it was a fair question, but they had to do something.

"Then we bring in the non-combatants. The infirm. The young ones, and anyone with a power that leaves them vulnerable," Patrah amended.

"And where do we keep them all?" Dayida asked. "Gathering them together might only provide a larger target and we'll end up having our most vulnerable members taken out at the same time. There are no safe places anymore."

There were almost two hundred Blooded in San Francisco, and that was just those who belonged to the Organization. It did not include the hundred that belonged to the Agency or the estimated hundred-to-two-hundred independents and their families scattered all over the San Francisco side of the bay. Oakland had an almost-equal number of Blooded but fewer people that claimed membership in either group.

Patrah was wondering about the feasibility of contacting just a fraction of those people when her b'caster began to vibrate in her pocket. She pulled it out and let its protuberances slink along her skin. The image of Maestra Luka flared to life in front of her right eye.

"Maestra Luka?"

"Blooded Patrah. I would like you to set up a meeting for myself with Agent Dayida. For tonight, if possible." Maestra Luka was posed in a chair, still, with a very serious expression.

"Hold on Maestra." Patrah put her hand over the receiver and turned to Dayida.

"Maestra Luka requests a meeting."

Dayida's eyebrows rose.

"Tonight, if possible," Patrah continued.

Dayida nodded. "Tell her to come over in an hour."

Patrah relayed this through the b'caster and came back.

"Ninety minutes OK?"

Dayida nodded.

After Patrah hung up, Dayida spoke. "I think we should table this until we hear what Luka wants. It will give us insight on what the Organization is doing, at least."

The others nodded.

"If you'll excuse me, then, I need to go work out some of this tension. I will be in gym if you need me," Patrah said as she walked out.

"I wasn't aware that this building had a gym," Patrah heard as the door closed behind her and she went to beat the hell out of a sandbag.

# MAESTRA LUKA

Maestra Luka paced back in forth in her home. The Organization was in shambles. Many of their Maestres and Blooded had disappeared, including Hu. It wasn't clear yet how many had dropped off the radar of their own volition and how many might have been taken. They were all arguing too much; their conference calls a chorus of raised voices trying to drown one another out. They could not agree on a plan of action and new factions were forming. She had fielded five calls from fellow Maestres subtly feeling out her position; three of those had ended with a concealed offer of support, should she choose to form her own block of power.

Luka had never been overly concerned with power. Luka liked where she was. She did not want to take on more, but the more frustrated she became, the more she thought that if taking more power was what she had to do to bring these headless chickens to heel, then she would. She picked up her phone and dialed.

After hanging up with Patrah, Luka called Maestra Hertin. She answered after only one ring.

"Luka."

"I am moving forward. I am going to form an alliance with the San Francisco office of the Agency, currently under the regency of Dayida Jayl. We are headed for war and Primo Erik is one of our best hopes of coming out of it alive."

There was a stretch of silence and then a husky, musical laugh that Luka remembered from their time as Blooded together. A tangle of missions and bed sheets and Hertin's throaty voice. They had both moved on. Hertin was married now and had children, but the memory hit Luka sharply, and she could not help the shivers that went down her spine.

"Bold. I approve. I will support you."

"Good." Luka cleared her throat to clear out the hoarse purr that had seeped in without her knowledge.

Maestres Dahlia and Fortuni were harder sells, but both signed on in the end. Luka left her apartment and was about to get into her car when she felt it. The shift in light and shadows. She turned toward the disturbance.

"Who's there?" It was across the street, in the dark between two cars.

There was no answer but she still could feel it watching her.

"I'll ask one last time. Who's there?"

There was no answer and she turned up the ambient light all around her, feeding it with the power in her body. Before she got a good look, something struck her shoulder and spun her around. Her whole side went numb.

"I'll tell you one thing. You are fucking with the wrong one tonight." It came out slurred. She let off a bright blast of light from her left hand and heard the thing howl. It also gave her her first real look at what she was facing. An Ante of the Phian bloodline. Telepathic, which was not that great for her. They resembled hairless monkeys but with putrid yellow skin. It had no mouth to speak of, but extremely large eyes that took up over half its face. Its fingers were tipped in razor-sharp claws that it tapped on the cars on either side of it, leaving behind green smears. She had been struck by its poisoned claws. If she could keep it too distracted to use its powers of hypnotism, and keep out of its claws, she had a chance. Luka quickly sent a flare of light through her body, burning the poison from her system. She felt the paralysis drop away.

She flashed an extremely bright flare of light at it, lighting up the night sky. Luka knew that neighbors must be seeing something but she had no choice right now. She reached for her b'caster but made the mistake of catching its gaze. A bolt of pain lanced through her body and the b'caster dropped to the pavement. The light dimmed and she fought to breathe as the feeling that every muscle in her body was cramping at the same time wracked her body.

Fighting only made her body spasm worse, so Luka stopped resisting, and let the pain and cramping force her to the ground and into a ball. Not fighting back lessened the pain just enough that she was able to think around it for a moment and call all of her power, but not to her body. Instead she channeled it through the body of the other being with her.

Luka had never tried to do something like this before—funnel her power through another living being. There were some Blooded who used bonded beings as conduits for works of power that would normally kill them but that was more as a way to pull more power into yourself, and not to push it into someone else. Luka could think of nothing else to try, though. She did not think her flashes were going to do much damage, and she couldn't concentrate hard enough to do anything more complex.

Luka pulled all the power that she could through the Angelic and heard something pop, then a high wail of pain. Her own pain lessened. She concentrated harder, feeling the presence of the Angelic and latching on with her senses, pulling more of her power through it. It was an odd sensation. Luka believed that she pulled her power directly from her link with her dead ancestor. Putting something else in that link felt wrong. Unholy.

At the same time, the power that filled her felt sharper than ever before. Filtered. She felt she could use it with more delicately than ever before.

The popping sounds continued, and she finally had enough control over her body to flop over and look at her attacker. It was deflating on the ground like a sad balloon. The ground around it was covered in a mess of liquid as parts of its body exploded, burned, and liquefied.

"This is my world you piece of shit. You don't know who you are messing with."

Luka looked down at the burnt husk of the Angelic. This was why beings that usually did this were bonded. It allowed the other being to handle power not native to their body. She took some of the power that had filled her body and turned it back into the Angelic, who had died filtering it for her. Luka burned what little was left of it to ash.

No evidence was left behind as she climbed into her car and headed for the financial district. She needed to speak with Dayida immediately.

She arrived at the building and was immediately escorted to the odd elevators by the young man behind the desk. She had read descriptions of the liquid elevators but it was very different to actually experience it. She did not enjoy it. The boy led her out and gestured at a door.

Luka knocked.

"Enter."

Luka pushed open the door and took in the woman behind the chair. She had seen pictures of Dayida Jayl before but never met her in person. Something radiated from her that Luka felt from across the room. Something that made her want to stretch in it and luxuriate like a cat in patch of sunlight. She turned to the other woman and recognized her immediately. Hettie Jayl had left before Luka had come to the Bay Area, but the stories about her were still told.

Luka inclined her head to both and sat in the empty chair. Luka saw no need to beat around the bush. "I want to offer you an alliance. The Organization has splintered, and if I am to bring any order to it, then I need clout. An alliance of mutual assistance between us would be exactly what I need. We can all see the writing on the wall. Angelics are coming, but so is the darkness. If any of us are to survive, we must work together."

Dayida nodded. "I can see the intelligence in what you say. What do you have to offer this alliance?"

"Trained operatives with intimate knowledge of the bay. We here in the Bay Area will have to rely on ourselves. Those in other cities will be looking to their own defenses. That may actually work in our favor, or at least not be a liability. This will be a nationwide attack, but not coordinated; the Angelics won't be able to work that way. Each city will be facing its own force."

Dayida nodded. "We've been talking about guarding the non-combatants but were trying to figure out a way to do with without making them bigger targets."

Luka hummed to herself and thought about it for a moment. "The Organization has several safe houses that might do, but I'm not sure I trust any of the things in our files to be secure anymore."

"What do you mean?" Dayida asked.

"For them to have taken so many of our own? I can't imagine they didn't have some inside information. And some of the Maestres that disappeared, like Hu? They don't fit the pattern. With most there's evidence of a struggle, but others? Like Hu? We think they left voluntarily. I'm not sure what they are planning but—"

She stopped.

"Go on," Hettie encouraged.

"Many were from our retraining department."

"Re-education," Hettie spat. The contempt in the air was thick, but Luka refused to lower her gaze. The Organization had been using the tactic long before she had come into any position of real power.

"The point is that many of them had access to very high-level records. There may be few secrets that the Organization has left," Luka replied.

They spent the rest of the night throwing ideas back and forth. Tomorrow Luka would gather more allies and use some of the money in the Organization's coffers to purchase more safe houses only known to the three of them. Dayida would do the same with the Agency money. They would spread them out as much as possible and assign guards with weapons taken from both of their armories and pray for the best while preparing for the worst.

# ZEBUB

# RAZEL

Razel made her way out of Hive Chayyliel to her room in the Hive of Sorrow & Riches. She could not stop thinking about her confrontation with the humans from the other world. She contemplated telling Riana everything but decided quickly against it.

Razel petted the light bulb vine by the door until it woke up and began to glow with a soft pink light. She stripped herself naked and lay on the pallet of blankets she was using as a bed. She allowed her flesh hand to trail across her body, cataloging the scars on her skin. There under her right breast was the cut from a mechanique that Riana had thought would aid in helping those with a stooped back walk upright again. There was much demand for such a device from the miners in the north of the city. Of course, Razel had been the guinea pig. Most of her injuries were from being forced to test out her Holder's crude creations. She had only escaped more serious injury by fixing many of them when Riana was not looking.

Razel looked down at her arm, the one that she had crafted from her torque of office when she was halfway between thirteen and fourteen cycles. The arm she now had because Riana had been so sure that she was right. Razel had known the mechanique was not stable enough but she had been ignored and the result had been the toppling of metal, the pain as her arm was sheared, flesh, muscle, and bone cut through so easily. Riana had not let her change anything of the original design and had only seemed annoyed that Razel was right as she lay on the floor bleeding out.

Riana had eventually staunched the blood and helped Razel to her room. She had offered to call Enheduanna and have the Holder come over and grow her a new arm. Razel refused. She knew as well as Riana did that trusting those vipers to any bodywork was just as good as handing yourself over as a zombie.

Razel had crafted the hand in three days. She knew that Riana's sympathy was non-existent for anyone but herself. She had only a few more before Riana would have summoned her back to her duty and not long after that Riana would start to view her as slow and damaged, even though Razel could never be anything of the kind. So she had crafted it quickly.

Still, the arm was dexterous, and the look on Riana's face whenever she caught sight of it; when the knowledge that it would take her far longer than three days to craft even a rough version of it flashed across her face? That envy was one of Razel's petty forms of revenge.

Why had she even thought of telling Riana of the human's . . . of *Erik's* offer? Razel closed her eyes and imagined the tall, gray walls of Hypatia, the stiff lines and the reams of paper and models inside. Hypatia was her home. It was where she felt safe. The idea of abandoning it for the rest of her life? It terrified her. Who would Razel be if not Holder-Apprentice of Hypatia?

She was still wondering when she heard Riana arrive. Even had Razel been asleep, the bellowing of her name would have woken her. Razel rose from her pallet and pulled a robe over her body before she exited into the main room. Riana was pacing back and forth, her teeth worrying her bottom lip bloody. She opened her mouth to bellow again as she turned, and caught sight of Razel.

"And where were you?" she asked.

"Resting. Did you require me for anything?" Razel calmly responded.

Riana did not respond at first and simply paced back and forth. Razel knew from experience not to disturb her when she was in this mood, lest she become the target of her Holder's ire. Riana finally spoke. "They have failed."

"Why did you expect them to succeed when entire groups of Antes, all bending their power to the same cause, failed?" Razel asked.

Riana turned to look at her with a raised eyebrow, but it was a valid question and Razel refused to take it back. She normally knew better than to question her Holder, but something inside of Razel, some remnant of the woman she had wanted to be, had begun to rear its head after the conversation with Erik. That was what they were offering. The chance to be who she wanted to be, even if she left everything she had ever known behind.

"They were not meant to succeed." Riana said.

"What do you mean, Holder?" Razel asked, shock going through her system.

"The darkness cannot be defeated. This world if doomed." She said it calmly and clearly but Razel could not understand the words.

"What do you mean?" Razel was taken aback. "Of course we can defeat it. Why else have we been creating all these Maasu, if not to fight when we are threatened?" One thing she had not told the humans was that it was Riana's predecessor who had found the blueprints to create the Maasu war mechaniques again. She did not know if they would hold this association against her.

"Do not be foolish!" Riana snapped. "We will all be leaving this world far behind and claiming another. That is what the Maasu are for."

"What world?" Razel asked, but she already knew.

"Their city of San Francisco, of course. The resources of that world are deeper than our own. Once we arrive there we will be in a better position to fight the darkness, but first we must subdue the 'dants that occupy that place."

Razel kept any expression of horror from her face, instead allowing a small smile to creep onto it. She ignored the nausea that rose up in her at the thought the Antes having a fresh world to devour. Riana seemed satisfied by her expression and began to pace again.

"Why was I not told?" Razel asked.

Riana did not even glance at her. "Krezida was not told either. She was beyond useless. She was told the story that you were; that the creatures were for defense. You were only told what you needed to know."

The bitterness in Riana's voice hinted that she herself had not known the whole time; the stiffness in the words hinting at the repetition of an excuse that had been given to her.

"That is why they were brought here. Not to defeat the darkness but to give us an idea of what we will be facing. Anoan was forced to begin early by the devouring of their city, but we shall plan this and San Francisco will not stand a chance."

"How much time do we have?" Razel asked.

"Months, weeks, maybe only days. We do not know for sure. Linnea was devoured as well."

Razel swallowed the sour taste that rose up into her mouth. She had no time to be sick.

"What about Hypatia? We will just leave all of that behind to be devoured?" Razel asked. She thought of all the reams of knowledge she had yet to go through; the mechaniques she still wanted to build.

"Of course not." Riana replied. "Even Anoan was able to save many of its buildings with little to no warning. They have been preparing for this. We will pull Hypatia through the rift into the new world. There is already a building set up to house it over there. Why do you think I agreed to work with them? Useless girl."

Razel noted that she said *I,* and not *we,* but she did not interrupt. She narrowed her eyes at being called useless. It was far from the first time that Riana had insulted her and it would most definitely not be the last. She believed what her Holder was saying. The facts felt true, but her Holder was not that good of an actress. However, Razel did not believe Riana had known any of this for that long. She could not have kept from lording it over Razel for so long.

"They have shown themselves to be formidable fighters. It is why we cannot allow them to return. They will sound the alarm and delay the takeover," Riana said this and went silent again, pacing back and forth.

"I am going back to bed," Razel said.

Riana stopped and finally asked, "I called you to ask if you learned anything from them after their defeat?"

"No, nothing. They were in shock from the loss of one of their own. They should be simple to contain. They are scattered and broken."

"Good." Riana smiled and Razel took that as her permission to return to her bed, such as it was.

Razel lay down and wondered what to do. She could try to warn them but she could not chance leaving now. She decided she would wait. If she were to ally herself with someone they would need to prove themselves worthy. She would wait for a message; wait to see what they would do. Either way she would be going to a new world, although doing so not under the control of the Antes sounded much better. She dreamed of flying above a world much like her own, but one where 'dants were in charge. When she woke in the morning, the 'dant Elana was drifting into her room, telling her it was time. They were preparing to fight their way out.

Razel remembered her dreams of flying and smiled. "I have a better plan."

# ERIK

Erik drifted in and out of troubled sleep all night long. Visions of destruction and death crept through his mind and startled him awake more often than not. He watched people torn apart while he did nothing. In other dreams, he died over and over. He would let monsters rip away his body so others could run. He saw his children devoured as he himself died. One thing kept reappearing: the image of a particular woman; tall, her skin the same Mediterranean brown as Matthias's. She watched him at all times; sometimes from behind something, sometimes from a distance, but always there. When he lay awake he found himself haunted by whispers where he could hear no detail but his name. Ghostly figures blinked in and out of existence in the darkness of the room, holding their hands out beseechingly. He closed his eyes to them and slipped back into disturbing dreams. When morning came he was not rested.

He slithered out from underneath Matthias's arm and made his way to the bathroom. He figured out how to fill the bowl on the stand by fumbling with the crystals along the edge. He washed in cold water that helped to focus him. When he entered the bedroom again, Matthias was still sleeping.

Erik decided to check on everyone else. Everyone but Tae. Tae, who he had lost. He froze, lost in the dread of losing another one of them; even Daniel. He took a deep breath and remembered there was no choice but to go forward. Daya had done an excellent job of making that clear last night.

Erik opened the door to find a tangle of vines pretending at being human. It was a blue, flowering vine that had folded and twisted itself into a vaguely human shape. Where the eyes would have been, two bright blooms were open, the petals a startling mix of neon pink and yellow. It held up its "hand" to stop him from going forward.

"What is going on?" Erik asked.

He could see other Antes in front of the other rooms. One was the ball of feathers and rage that had confronted him at dinner the night before. Another looked like a miniature storm cloud swirling around itself. The final Ante was a lump of translucent, milky-gray goo expanding and contracting rhythmically.

A buzzing started, and Erik watched as more and more of the buds on the vine Ante's body opened and flowered. The source of the sound became apparent as the first of the bugs emerged from within the tangle of its body. They were small and their wings moved too fast to get a good count. More and more flew from inside the thing's body and surrounded it, attracted to the flowers, and as they fed Erik noticed that their buzzing was taking on a rhythm. It rose and fell more distinctly and resolved into words.

*There has been an attack in the city. We are here for your protection. You are to stay in your rooms.*

Erik did not believe it at all and he certainly did not like it.

"If the danger is outside the Hive, then there should be no problem with me going to speak to my companions." He went to move around the Ante and the bugs flew from its surface to form a moving wall before him. Erik was close enough to see the details of their horrifying forms: they were long and thin, with both ends brandishing mouths filled with serrated teeth. The grinding of these twin jaws was what made the buzzing sound. They had four limbs that hung down from their bodies, all of which ended in wicked, sharp-looking hooks.

"What is the meaning of this?" Erik asked impatiently.

The buzzing answered him. *Our orders were to confine you to your rooms.*

"I see."

Erik could feel his power rising in him, and along with it rose the pain in his head, but it was easier to deal with today. There was also a shiver of pleasure that accompanied the pain this time; the relief of stretching a muscle that had been cramped and still for too long.

He was ready to reach forward and see how this Ante did when its vine was in pieces when he thought of Tae.

Erik had lost people before. He knew that thoughts of them could hit at any time for any reason. There was very little rhyme or reason to how the mind dealt with grief, but he could not help but think that this was a sign. Should he have ordered a retreat as soon as he saw how big the darkness was? What would defeating a single manifestation of it even solve? There was something about this world that made the temptation to sink into the easy trade-off of action and reaction very strong.

He let the power fade from his body.

"You will bring me Chayyliel immediately or I will not be responsible for my actions."

*Lord Chayyliel will arrive as soon as able.* It was hard to read emotion into the buzzing of hideous insects but Erik did not think he was imagining the contempt and dark humor in the words.

He pulled back. "I see."

Then he closed the door in the Ante's "face." Erik went to the bedroom and shook Matthias awake.

"They have posted guards at the doors. We have to move, now."

Matthias blinked at him owlishly, face soft and sweet, but Erik refused to be charmed by it. All too soon, Erik's words sank in, and world-weariness seeped back into Matthias eyes and face.

"What should we do?" He asked.

"Can you think of a way to call Elana in here?" Erik inquired.

Matthias smiled. "I sure can."

He stood and Erik followed him back into the living room. He was not expecting Matthias to simply tilt his head back and scream.

"Elana! Yo, Elana! Elaaaaaanaaaa!" In a matter of seconds, she had floated in through the ceiling with a sharp smile on her face.

"I could have done that." Erik said with a reluctant smile.

"But you didn't, so I solved the problem." Matthias smiled back.

Erik shook his head and turned back to Elana.

"Did you find anything last night?" He asked her.

"Not really. I stayed out until the sun almost rose and I didn't notice anything happening in the immediate vicinity."

"Okay. I need you to go to all the others, don't let anyone see you. Let them know to be ready. We're getting the fuck out of here ASAP.

"Then, I want you to find Razel. Tell her we need to get out of here and she needs to be ready to go."

Elana nodded and sank through the floor, off to do all that he had asked.

Erik looked at Matthias. "We should get ready."

They washed up and Erik pulled his red suit back on. It was a little worse for the wear but better off than the clothes he had peeled off yesterday. Barely an hour later, by Erik's estimation, Elana reentered the room.

"Okay, here's the plan." She said.

Erik raised an eyebrow at her declaration, but kept his mouth shut and listened.

"I am going to phase all of you out of here and into an adjacent room upstairs where no one is watching. Razel is waiting for us there. She says she has a way for us to get out of The Courts."

"Um, any details on this daring escape?" Matthias asked.

Elana looked faintly embarrassed. "She said something about dragons and I didn't ask any more questions."

"Dragons?" Erik questioned skeptically.

Matthias turned to him. "Oh, so after everything you've seen, dragons are where you are going to draw the line?"

Erik shrugged. "Fair point." He turned back to Elana. "Go get the others first; come for us last. Make sure you aren't seen."

Elana nodded and drifted out the way she had come, through the ceiling.

They waited silently until she returned.

She reached for Erik. "It'll feel weird. At least that's what everyone says."

"Get Matthias out first. Come back for me."

"No—" Matthias started.

Erik turned to face him and smiled. "Shut up."

He did, and allowed Elana to wrap her arms around him. "So, here's the thing; you're the propellant here. Bend your knees and jump up."

Matthias crouched quickly.

"Not that hard!"

She cautioned him a little too late and they shot through the ceiling. Erik heard a thump and yelp from above him and held his breath waiting for the guard outside the door to make itself known, but there was nothing.

"So, this is what's happening." The voice came from behind him.

Erik almost wished he would never hear the voice again, but he also felt that same sick happiness that it was still around. He knew by this point that Daniel was not just going to disappear.

"Yes, we have to make a break for it." He replied.

"Don't want anymore blood on your hands?" Daniel asked.

The hands in question clenched and Erik said nothing.

"First me and then Tae. It seems like young men are just destined to die around you. I wouldn't be that shocked if Matthias was next."

"Shut. Up," Erik ground out.

"Oh, did I strike a nerve? You know it's true. Tragedy and death follow you. Always have."

Erik did his best to ignore what Daniel was saying while wondering what was taking Elana so long to come back for him.

"I'm sorry. You know I don't mean to be mean. I'm just being honest," Daniel said.

Erik could hear the pout in his voice.

"Sometimes people use the idea of honesty as a reason to be mean. I'm wondering if that was something you always did or something that's happened since you died," Erik replied as he made the mistake of looking at Daniel. His ex's clothing had changed again. The jeans were the same ones he remembered from their time together but the shirt was now an old, ratty black t-shirt. The word Dolly was emblazoned across it in bright pink. Little spots of lighter pink on the word showed where rhinestones had long since fallen off and been lost.

It was one of the shirts that Erik had raided from his mother's closet as a teen. He'd used it as a lounging-around shirt, but after he and Daniel started dating, they had taken to wearing each other's clothes. A silent declaration of their relationship, since they weren't allowed to make a verbal one.

Daniel was looking down at the ground, the expression on his face hurt. Erik steeled himself against the sympathy that rose up in him. Daniel had always been blunt to the point of insulting. So was Erik just being more sensitive? Even if that was the case, he had just lost a friend. Surely he was entitled to be sensitive about it.

"What do you want out of this, Daniel?" Erik finally asked.

"Just for you to admit I was right. That coming here was a mistake," Daniel said brightly.

Erik felt his lips thin as he frowned. He had lost Tae, that was true enough, and he would mourn that long and hard, but they had gained information they could use. The stubborn part of his nature reared up in him.

"No. I'm tired of this, Daniel. I am sorry you died. You'll never know how much, but I'm done with allowing you to talk to me any kind of way you want."

Daniel stared for a moment and seemed about to respond when Elana drifted back down into the room. She looked at both of them and spoke. "Am I interrupting something?"

"No."

"Yes."

They glared at each other and Erik turned to her. "I'm ready, let's go."

The sensation was odd; as if he had stayed the same, and the gravity around him decreased. The air turned thicker, like soup. He bent his knees and pushed off. They glided slowly up through the ceiling. As soon as his feet cleared the floor everything went normal again and he landed lightly, bending his knees to absorb the shock.

He looked around, seeing everyone accounted for, Yonas and Tassi next to each other as always, silently waiting. Daya and Elliot were talking in the corner, and Matthias was rubbing at his head and frowning at Erik. "Show off."

They heard a commotion from below them. Razel, who stood near the door, turned to them.

"They've found out you're missing. We need to move. They will think you have gone down." Razel opened the door and squeezed out into the hall. Erik and the rest followed close behind. She led them to a stairwell and they moved up two flights. The sounds from below faded away.

Razel whispered back to them. "These floors are empty and abandoned, so we should not run into anyone—"

"Where do you think you are all off to?" The voice interrupted from the landing they had just passed. Erik looked back down to find the creepy, Holder-Apprentice boy looking at them.

Razel spoke from the step above him. "We are leaving, Haydn, and there's nothing to do about it."

He frowned at her and took a step closer to the stairs.

"You don't know who you are messing with here. I am something beyond what you understand—"

Erik was tired of this speech before it begun. He had heard little men try to make themselves feel important and big all his life, and they had no time. "Daya?" Erik asked since she was closest.

"Gladly," she answered.

She stepped forward, her hand already flying into a punch, her skin rippling as they watched, going from flesh to gray to strong black obsidian by the time it connected with Haydn's face and sent him into the wall. He fell to the ground and did not move. They were about to continue up the stairs when Erik heard it, muffled though it was. Someone was screaming. Erik looked around to make sure everyone else heard it. They all shared a glance.

Erik stalked back down to the landing, tracking the sound to a door down the hall. He pulled it open. The woman who was facing him was unbowed, despite the bruises marring her face. Her hair held every different shade of color and she started to struggle against her ties when she saw their faces.

"Holder Krezida?" Razel's voice asked from behind him.

# KREZIDA

The door opened, and Krezida straightened her spine as much as her tied position would allow her. She waited for her erstwhile apprentice to walk through the door, but instead she was confronted by Riana's apprentice Razel and a large group of 'dants she had never seen. From their clothing, they were not from Zebub or its environs. One of them, a tall 'dant with long curly hair, hurried over and untied the ropes that bound her feet. He was about to free her hands when Razel told him to stop.

Krezida looked at the girl furiously, but Razel only met her eyes with a cool expression before pulling the gag from Krezida's mouth. The apprentice was careful not to let any of her skin get too close to Krezida's teeth.

"This is not some simple innocent. This is Holder Krezida; she is poisonous. In spirit and in body."

"I thank you for the compliment, Holder-Apprentice Razel. Now untie me."

Razel ignored her and continued to talk to the other 'dants.

"I do not know that she would aid in our escape in any way, and she might deliberately hinder us.

Krezida hissed at the girl. "You mean to escape? Take me with you."

The girl finally turned to face her. "Was that a question or an order?"

Krezida gritted her teeth. "Take me with you, please? If you will deliver me to my Athenaeum, I will reward you all handsomely."

If she could get to Enheduanna she could lock the doors and windows and wait out whatever was happening, surrounded by the things that she loved. The Antes would take care of the darkness with the Maasu. She would hunker down until the danger passed, and then reemerge.

"Will you swear not to injure any of us or betray us in any way?" This was from the man who had been about to untie her.

She leaned close to whisper exactly that, hoping some of the scent she had applied to her hair days ago before Hadyn had stuck her here still lingered. Before she could test the theory, Razel put her hand on the man's shoulder and pulled him back.

"Be careful, Matthias. When I said that she was poisonous in body, I meant it. She is an alchemist. She is practically made of potions and formulas that could harm you in seconds."

"You're not wrong, girl, but it would be foolish of me to kill any of you. There are enough of you to overwhelm me easily and it would not endear any of you to take me with you."

"True enough." The girl agreed, then she smiled. "Swear on your bond with Enheduanna."

Krezida balked at that. She had meant everything she said but she always cherished her right to break her word if a better opportunity presented itself. If she made such a vow and then broke it? Her bond with Enheduanna would wither, if not break entirely. Razel was too smart.

"I swear on my bond with Enheduanna Athenaeum that none of you will come to harm through my actions," Krezida vowed.

Razel nodded in approval to the crouching 'dant, and she was free.

"Come," Razel said and walked out with all of them following.

Krezida stopped at the sight of her unconscious apprentice. She remembered all the pain he had put her through. All the questions, and all the attempts to have her pass her bond to him. She knelt by Haydn's unconscious form and felt around the scar at his neck. She had studied the recreations of the dark dungeons before and she knew there was always a safeguard so that those who owned them could reduce them to pieces easily. From there it was a simple thing to return them and have them reconstituted with the quality you felt was lacking. Krezida wanted none of that this time. She found the loose flap of skin and pulled with all her strength. There was a loud tearing sound and a thin rope of flesh ripped its way from Hadyn's throat, sending his head spinning across the hall. She stood and walked over and crushed the head under her boots until the brains were smeared across the floor.

When Krezida looked up, both Razel and the dark-skinned 'dant were watching her, while the rest of them all averted their eyes.

She rose and composed herself, smoothing out her hopelessly wrinkled robes. They hurried up the remaining stairs and emerged onto the roof. Razel immediately hurried over to the pen where the dragons buzzed lazily in the sun.

"What the hell are those?" One of the other 'dants asked. The one that Krezida could see through.

"The dragons of Hive Chayyliel," Razel stated. "I have not taken any for a ride yet but they are tame. The more vicious breeds are kept on the borders, where they can be unleashed on invaders or raiders. These are also the smaller personal-use ones, which is helpful."

"They look like giant dragonflies." The 'dant who spoke was standing next to the other 'dant who Krezida could see all the way through.

Razel stared blankly for a moment before saying slowly. "Well, they are dragons, and they do fly. These will take us to safety."

The translucent 'dant and the one with long black braids shared a look. The one with the long hair spoke up. "I think that I will fly under my own power, thank you."

She floated a couple of feet of the roof, her hair whipping about in the sudden wind.

"Me as well," the translucent 'dant said.

"Well, dragons for the rest of us, then. I will show you how to get a ride. I must go first so the lead dragon chooses me. The others will follow." Razel moved to the pen, which was in the shape of a dome, giving the dragons room to fly but no route of escape, not that they would attempt it. They were much too lazy and well-trained for that.

On one side of the pen was a pump and a stack of buckets. Razel picked up a bucket and placed it under the spout and pumped twice. A large gout of thick red sagua came from the spout and filled the bucket.

"What is that?" One of the 'dants asked. The one Razel had called Matthias.

"A mixture of things," Razel answered. "Watch me."

Razel stood under a small, oddly folded section of the pen and placed the bucket in a hook on the outside, and the dragons fought each other to get into the little nook, which was the only area where their probosci could reach it. Razel pulled on a thin silver chain and a small gate came down inside the pen, separating the first dragon from the others.

The dragon did not panic. It crept forward and dipped its proboscis into the bucket. As soon as it had drained the bucket, Razel pulled the thin silver rope by her again and the section of gate directly between her back and the dragon lowered. From their position in front of her, they could see the four long and thinly jointed legs wrap around her torso. Two came from under her arms and crossed themselves over her chest. The other two came low on the hip and wrapped themselves around each thigh. Then Razel was airborne, circling above them.

"Next," she called down.

The dark-skinned 'dant in red stepped forward immediately and followed what Razel had done perfectly. It took a while to get them all attached, but it was as Razel said: the dragons attached to them were simply content to follow the lead of Razel's dragon. Once the last of them, Krezida herself, was up in the air, Razel directed her dragon to fly away from the Ruling Courts. They were moving across the center district and toward the Drowned. That was fine with Krezida. Enheduanna was not that far from the Drowned and she could walk from there if necessary.

As they neared the far edge of the center district, plumes of smoke and the sounds of battle became more distinct. Things were flying all about, and they got close enough to see they were not dragons, but something else.

Razel looked over to where the commotion was happening. She lifted the hand that was metal to her face and circled two fingers into a ring. As she watched, Krezida could have sworn she saw the glint of yellow light appear in her circled fingers.

"It's Lil." The excitement was clear in her voice.

"Then that's where we need to go," Erik stated.

Razel nodded, and Krezida saw her reach up to manipulate the legs that held her aloft in some abstract pattern. Krezida could not see exactly what she did since she was so far away, but Razel's dragon turned toward the fight and began to accelerate. All the others followed. Krezida began to panic. She knew nothing of how to steer a dragon, and she had requested escape, not death in battle. As they neared she saw the things that they were fighting. Razel should recognize those monstrosities as easily as Krezida did, but still she did not turn the dragons away. Razel was leading them straight back into the jaws of the Ruling Courts.

Krezida would not do it. She would not go. She reached up to the legs that were holding her and felt around, trying to figure out what Razel had done. There were little crevices at the places where the legs joined the body. She slipped her fingers into one experimentally and tugged. Her dragon tilted wildly, and she screamed and let go. The dragon righted itself but did not correct its direction. Now it was headed even closer to the fight at a faster rate.

Krezida reached up again and slipped both hands into the spaces and tugging both at the same time. The dragon swung her around and she felt the lower pair of legs start to release her. She screamed and reached up, grasping at anything and everything as she slipped from the dragon's grip. Krezida felt the legs release her completely and screamed as she tried to hold on, but there was nothing to grasp. She fell faster, the breath being stolen from her lungs. Spots appeared in her vision. Blackness. Pain. Nothing.

# KIMA

Kima had been ready to die for quite a while. You don't join a revolution against those who wiped out whole neighborhoods without realizing that your choice could easily lead to your death. When you pretend to be the leader, you surely know you will not live to see the new world that you are fighting for. Still, never had she thought it would end like this.

Kima fired on the smaller baby things that had sprouted from the back of the parent monster. They did not seem as tough as the others and her shots did some damage, knocking them from the sky. A blast of cold froze her back, and she turned to see one of the smaller baby-creatures she had missed flash frozen. Without thought she flipped the gun in her hand and brought the butt down on the ice as hard as she could. The thing shattered and she turned back to the fight.

Assan was aiming at the smaller flying ones like she was, and bringing many of them down before they could attack the companions. Quinn and Hlani were facing the monster similar to the one that had attacked in the clearing. Limbs sprouted from its back, each ending in new and horrifying-looking tools of pain and torture. They were not injuring it greatly, but neither were they hurt too badly. Kima was satisfied enough with their lack of death at this point.

Uchel was huddled in the back with the children. They stood protected behind a large sheet of ice that Lil's sib had created. They would lean around the sides and Uchel would let loose with some of her poultices, which burned the smaller ones, but had little effect on the larger monsters. Lil and the Antes split their attention between the giant one tearing up the street and the long flying one, which would dive in quick to take swipes at them before shooting out of range once again.

Kima did not even notice the dragons swooping in until she heard the scream. The sound of the 'dant slamming into the ground cut through the din of battle and Kima looked up to see other dragons approaching in a ragged line. She looked closer and saw 'dants clasped in their legs, but could not see much through the dozens of flying small monsters. A swarm of them was blasted apart by a fierce wind and suddenly a woman was in their midst, her dark hair whipping about her as she tossed the creatures back and forth. She cleared a path for the dragons and as they got closer Kima recognized the young woman being carried by the lead dragon as Holder-Apprentice Razel. She had never seen the woman in person but Kima had memorized her description, as she had all Holders and their apprentices.

Two of the dragons behind Razel were starting to droop, as if their passengers were getting heavier. Kima looked and saw that one was carrying a 'dant with dark skin and a stocky build. His eyes were shining red and the anxiousness for a fight was written clearly across his face. The other held what looked like a living statue. They became too much for their dragons and the poor beasts simply let them go.

They fell directly onto the back of the large monster with a resounding crack. For the first time in this encounter, the monster squealed in pain. The cracks continued attacking from there and the thing began to move desperately, trying to reach the 'dants on its back.

All of its children immediately pulled back their attacks on anyone else and headed to their parent. These 'dants were powerful. Suddenly one of the 'dants on the ground leapt into the air. Her body dissolved into only bones as she moved. She flew directly into the swarm and any of the creatures she touched fell down dead.

Glancing over at Hlani and Quinn, Kima realized that Lil had moved over to help them, leaving the larger creature to their new allies. Lil placed something in her mouth, and Kima was hypnotized as she spit out something glowing that hit the creature. The blackness shattered and what was left lay convulsing in the street, a raw pink bundle of flesh that seemed pained by everything. Kima put it out of its misery with one shot that shattered its raw face and ended it still.

Lil ran up and gathered back the thing she had spit.

The other dragons landed.

Kima saw the moment when Lil saw the other Holder-Apprentice. The smile on her face went tight but she did nothing else. Razel, for her part, had no expression on her face, but she nodded at Lil in recognition.

The 'dant with the long braid who seemed to control the wind was concentrating on the many-winged monster still circling above. She buffeted it from all sides and forced it lower and lower to the ground. Once it was within reach of the two Antes, they wasted no time in grabbing each of the wings at the joints until they rotted off in their hands. The thing squealed and fought back, but they were too fast for either of its mouths.

The largest monster finally let out a shrieking cry and collapsed to the ground, unmoving. Any of its lingering children immediately wheeled away from the battle and scattered in all directions. The two 'dants that had been on its back leapt to the ground. The one that looked like a moving statue approached the last large creature that the Antes were focused on. She punched through its carapace with no effort and pulled out a handful of meat mixed with metal. She did this repeatedly until the creature simply shuddered and stopped moving.

The others gathered, and Kima noticed Lil's branch hovering over her shoulder. Kima's eyes were drawn to Lil's sibs to make sure they were alright, and then to the two Antes. Only after that did she start to look at their new companions. She holstered her gun and gestured for Assan to do the same. These new allies were powerful. There was no need to threaten them. They had all moved into two groups, one around the dark skinned 'dant in red and the other around Lil. Razel stood halfway between the two groups, facing Lil.

Finally, Lil stepped toward her fellow Apprentice, the branch shifting to spell out her message.

**RazelWhatAreYouDoingAndWho**
**AreYourCompanions?**

Razel stepped forward, uncaring about the pieces of monster that clung to her otherwise-pristine white boots.

"I have left the service of Riana. I am here to help."

**YourHelpWouldHaveBeenMoreUseful**
**AnotherTime.**

Razel seemed to understand what Lil was saying even if Kima did not.

"I did what I could. I hid The Root and provided it to your Nif companions."

Lil's eyes widened thoughtfully and her face lost some of its severity, although much of it had to do with the scars that covered her lower face and gave her a perpetual frown.

**WhoAreYourCompanions?**

The branch wove the question in the air again.

Razel glanced back at them and hesitated.

"I believe it better if they tell you themselves. And not on the streets." The dragons that had carried them here were still circling overhead, waiting for more orders. "We have just escaped from the Ruling Courts, and they will be looking for us."

**ThatSoundsAwfullyFamiliar.**

Lil's lips turned up in a bitter smile that Razel returned.

**LetUsGatherYourCompanions.**

As a group, they approached the others, who were near the head of the large monstrosity. They had their heads bowed, as if in prayer, but they were only whispering to each other.

"We gave them peace. That is what matters," one was saying.

Kima looked at the young man. "What do you mean?"

All of the newcomers looked very uncomfortable all of a sudden, and before Kima could press, Uchel came forward, Lil's two sibs following her reluctantly. Lil immediately knelt and both children ran into her arms. She hugged them tightly and Kima could have sworn she saw tears glisten in the corners of her eyes before Lil took a deep breath and rose to her feet. Her younger sib, the boy, had his arms around her neck and she was holding him to her chest. The older girl had stayed standing but her hand was gripping Lil's free one so tight that Kima could see the strain of pressure where her small fingers pressed down.

"We should leave these streets now," Uchel said. "We will go back to the house, there we can get acquainted with our new friends."

The ground shook beneath their feet and Lil looked down at it in worry. She looked down to her sibs and then over to Arel and Jagi. She needed to tell them now but she did not want her sibs to hear the news. They had been through enough. They did not need to be scared again so soon after finding her. The Antes stepped forward and pried her sibs from her. They protested but Arel and Jagi soothed them and made sure to keep Lil where the two could see her while moving far enough away that no part of the conversation would reach them. She nodded her thanks to them and turned back to the group, which was now watchng her curiously.

**NoWeWillGoToKandakeThereIsStillMuch ToDoAndLittleTimeToDoItYouMust SendSomeOfYourPeopleToWarnTheOthers.**

"Warn them of what?" Kima stepped forward. She knew that Lil had been keeping something from them this whole time. She had not risen to be Uchel's second-in-command without knowing when someone was lying.

Lil looked at her blankly for a moment.

**AllMustSeekShelterAtKandake.**

Lil paused again, and even as the words formed by the branch, they moved slowly, as if they were full of reluctance, and when Kima could read the words she knew why.

**ThisWorldWillDieSoon.**

The clamor around her grew as the others read the words and exploded in questions.

"That is a lie!" Assan was the loudest in his denials, but Kima could see the way the truth sunk into him by the despair slowly creeping across his face.

He shoved his way forward and Lil did not shrink under his closeness; instead, she looked him straight in his eye.

**IfYouThinkMeALiarThatIsFineButWarnThemStill DoNotLetOthersDieFromYourStubbornRefusal.**

"Why did you not tell us before?" This was from Hlani, always ready to believe the worst, and this time it was proven true.

**BecauseWeDidNotHaveTimeForThisWe DoNotHaveItNowButHereWeAre.**

They all straightened at that, the rebuke clear in the contempt on Lil's face. They had all had a shock, but there was no time to sink into it. If she said to gather at Kandake then there was probably something there to save them. She had to focus on that. There was some way to save them, if not their world.

**TheDarknessEatsAtTheWholeOfOurWorld AndItCannotTakeMuchMoreBeforeItCrumbles.**

"Then how will being in Kandake save us at all?" Hlani asked in the same defeated tone.

**IDoNotKnowButTheSpiritPromisedAWay AndBetterToHopeThanToGiveInToDespair.**

Kima looked at Uchel, any lies seeming useless now. Uchel met her gaze and for the first time she looked truly old to Kima. She had always been old physically, but inside she had the fire of a young revolutionary. Uchel took risks and led them with courage, and now Kima could read that she was lost. She couldn't be. Uchel was not allowed to be lost. That was one of the costs of leadership. She had to lead regardless, and Kima saw Uchel read the expectation in Kima's expression and shake her silence off as they looked to her.

"Assan and Kima. You will go to spread the word. Your weapons will be dangerous to all of us in an enclosed space like Kandake, so of less use."

Kima looked over at one of the Antes guiltily. It was no longer bleeding from the leg, but she was fairly sure it had been her ricochet that had caught it.

"You will tell all of our contacts within Zebub, and have them spread the word to all that they can. Then you will send messages to all of our contacts in other cities." Uchel paused and looked over at Lil. "Will the other Athenaeums protect them?"

Lil looked unsure, but eventually her branch spelled out:

**TheyWillDoTheirBest**

Uchel nodded. "It is their best hope."

Lil's branch floated betwixt them.

**TellThemThatWhenTheyArriveAtKandakeToStay**
**InTheFirstFloorLobbyMayerIsNotThereSoAll**
**OtherLevelsWillBeDangerous.**

"Will you not be there when we arrive?" Kima asked suspiciously.

**IWillBeThereButInNoConditionToHelp**
**IWillBeInTheDepthsOfTheAthenaeum**
**ClaimingItsHeart.**

There was no response to that except to nod. Kima and Assan looked at one another. With a deep breath, they took off toward the depths of the city, ready to convince everyone they had ever known that the world and everything in it was going to come apart.

# MANHATTAN

# MARIAN

Hilarie had not left her office for four days. As a consequence, neither had Marian. Some of her memories had wandered back into place but there were still many holes in her mind. She still did not remember the boy's name and the shame that rose in her every time she thought of his lost face was deep and cutting.

The raid on the location had not been a total success. They had lost a number of Agents but they had been able to free most of the people trapped in the facility. They killed those they had to leave behind. She had heard Hilarie give the order over the phone. She had heard the steel in her voice. Marian had watched her put the receiver down with shaking hands and bury her face in her hands for twenty minutes before she'd lifted it once again, to go back to work.

The phone rang, and Hilarie looked up from her work and Marian from her book. She was getting used to hearing only one side of the conversation.

"Speak."

Hilarie cocked her head to the side.

"Have you managed to capture any?" She asked.

She signed at the answer. NO, her sigh said.

"Kill any?"

That sigh again. NO, again.

"How many of our own have we lost?" This time Hilarie stayed silent but her lips tightened and her face went pale.

TOO MANY, in the paleness of her face.

"Okay, regroup. I want no one in teams of less than ten. Do you understand?"

She must be talking to one of the Agents who took the lead hunting down the Antes who had escaped from the warehouse. They had managed to kill a few there by working in concert. No Antes had been captured for questioning and they were stretched thin. Guarding all known portals from Anoan was taking up enough of their agents without those patrolling the streets.

One of the bodyguards, his motley in yellow and green today and his mask one of white studded with citrine, stepped forward and turned on the television. Marian saw Hilarie turn to snap at him, but stopped, considering. She looked at the television and her mouth dropped open. Marian followed her gaze and felt her own eyes bulging. Live on the television and muted was an Ante big as life. One there was no way to explain away as a human in a costume.

It was perched on the apex of a building's roof, two legs on each side clamped down. The legs looked human except that they ended in golden hooves. The upper thighs were furred with white and gold fur that, thank goodness, also covered the crotch. The stomach was human enough except for the three vertical slits that gaped open, showing small teeth, clenching and gnawing on empty air. Its shoulders were broad and furred in gold. Its arms were human enough, except that they were not physically attached to the body. They floated at the Ante's side, dripping blood and raw meat in the gap that separated them from the shoulders. The head was unattached as well and also dripping, but the head also had four faces that kept rotating so a different one was facing front.

Man. Goat. Serpent. Lion.

"What the hell type of Ante is that?" Marian whispered.

"A type we've never seen before. A type they've never let over. Now it's here and big as life." Hilarie shouted, already picking up the phone and dialing.

The shot pulled back so they could see more of the location. It was on the steeple of a church and as she watched, the head spun once again so the lion face was front and center. It opened its mouth and let out a roar.

Hilarie was shouting into the phone but Marian could not look away. Then, as she watched, something flared behind the bloody gaps of the creature's shoulders and she saw them: great big white and gold wings.

"Oh, hell no," she whispered.

She looked back at Hilarie, who had hung up the phone and was now turning toward the glowing crystal that was calling for her attention.

"Hilarie. They're going to use religion."

On the screen, a priest was leading a few people toward the church instead of away.

"The hell they are," Hilarie whispered.

Hilarie slammed her hands down on the crystal that had been glowing brightly.

"Yes, I see it, sir. I am currently trying to deal with it. When might we expect backup?"

Hilarie frowned. Backup wasn't coming anytime soon, Marion guessed.

"Understood." She took her hands off the crystal and the glow stopped and from the way Hilarie looked at it Marian could see she wanted to hurl it across the room.

She looked up and met Marian's gaze, giving her a grimace.

"All major cities are preparing for their own potential invasion. There are no Agents to spare right now but they still expect me to do something about that." She flapped her hand at the television without looking at the picture still splashed across the screen.

"I'll go," Marian said. The raven wisdom rising up in her again. This was why she had stayed behind and healed longer. They were stretched too thin to send anyone else.

"Don't be a fool. You can't even stand for long periods yet."

She knew that Hilarie did not mean it the way it sounded but still she flinched. It hardened her spine, her resolve.

"What is our other choice? You pull someone off an important duty? Send in a green recruit to die? I may not have all my faculties back yet but I know how to be an Agent."

"Still doesn't get around the whole walking thing," Hilarie said, but Marian could see her faltering.

"Well I wasn't planning on going in this form," Marian offered.

Hilarie's voice went high in surprise. "Are you kidding me? After what happened the last time you split into the murder?"

"Yes. It did not go well last time," Marian acknowledged. "But that was at night and an emergency. Right now, it's daylight, and we can plan. All I need is some of our big artillery. I break apart, reform behind that thing, take the shot, break apart again and fly back here."

"You know it's not going to be that simple. It's never that simple." Hilarie was sitting back in her chair, and Marian knew she needed to convince Hilarie of this.

One of the jesters behind her, the same one who had turned on the television, was gesturing behind her back, pointing first at themselves and then at their partner in motley. She looked over to the other one; their colors today were orange and sky blue, their mask a shiny silver one in the shape of an older man's face, with a large beard. They nodded their head.

"Then send two of your bodyguards with me. Surely you can spare two of four as you sit here in your protected building?" Marian asked.

Hilarie scowled then nodded slowly. "Fine. If you're sure."

Marian nodded and gestured for one of the jesters to proceed her, pushing her chair out of the room before Hilarie changed her mind. The other joined them as they exited.

"Let's head to the armory and see what's left."

As she had assumed, many of the weapons that had been specially designed to take out Antes were out on loan to various hunting parties. There were always at least a couple specials kept back just in case.

Of the smaller, easier to conceal and carry options, there were two handguns. One of them she recognized fired a bullet loaded with acid that could eat away at even the toughest Ante but also anything else in the way. She thought of the crowds around the church and picked the other one.

"What does this one do?" She asked.

The quartermaster was a young man with beautiful dark eyes and pale brown skin who said to call him Van. He answered, "It works on beings that have spent a large amount of time in other dimensions. Every world moves at a different vibration, and the longer you've been in another dimension, the longer it takes for your body to adjust to a new frequency. This gun takes advantage of that difference in vibration and moves their body a half step out of phase with our world but in a different direction."

Marian looked at him blankly and gestured for him to go on.

"Basically, it turns them to stone." He shortened.

"Why wouldn't it just move them to the dimension of that particular frequency?" Marian asked.

"It would if there were a dimension on that frequency." He smiled at her. "Best of all, it has very little collateral damage; it won't do anything to anyone whose body is vibrating at our world's frequency, because it can't detect or change anything."

The jester signed at Van and the man smiled and nodded in return.

"You understood that?"

Van looked at her oddly. "Yes, it's only standard ASL. I know and speak most languages." He bent below the counter and came back with a small round bit of metal in his hands.

"What's that?" Marian asked.

"What they asked for: an EMP. It'll take out any cell phones, cameras, anything electronic in the area."

Marian looked at the jester and nodded.

"I'll fly in. You follow and hit everyone with the EMP. Also, a distraction would not go amiss. We don't need any more eyewitnesses."

They nodded and she pushed her chair into the elevator that took her to the roof.

Marian sat there in the afternoon sun, and sank into the awareness of her body. To her surprise the splitting was less painful than she remembered. The gaps where her body was still not whole made it easier to break apart. The ravens rose from the roof, not all of them the same size any longer. Now there were smaller ravens among them, the pieces of her growing back.

The flight itself was not difficult. They kept focused on the goal and allowed instinct to guide them. Thanks to the daylight they spotted predators and other potential dangers far ahead and avoided any losses.

The murder of ravens approached the church. The Ante had not moved from its perch at all. Not even to acknowledge the dozen people that were crouched behind the police barrier on their knees praying toward it.

They wheeled through the sky and circled twice before the whole murder landed on the steeple behind the Ante. The serpent visage was facing the flock but it did not react. She waited for the distraction that the jesters were supposed to provide, and watched the head continue to rotate. There was a high-pitched whine followed by a muffled whump and then many voices raised in dismay. The EMP. Then there was the sound of an explosion very close by, and the grumblings of frustration turned to screams of fear. A sure sign they were distracted.

Marian brought her body back together slowly, making sure it came together balanced on the roof. She raised the gun and took aim. The shot was loud and the head spun around, the lion facing her and roaring and catching the blast directly in its mouth. She saw the transition happen, all movement stopping and the color leaching from its skin.

The head and arms fell with loud thumps to the ground below. Whatever had been holding them in connection with the body obviously gone now. The jesters were there suddenly, holding a bag between them that they quickly pulled over the statue on the steeple. It disappeared and the bag shrunk so one of them could hold it in one hand. They bowed in her direction and then they were gone. Marian knew she was a kick-ass Agent. She smirked. *Lester would have been proud,* she thought, as she broke apart into the murder again and started the journey back.

# ROBERT

Robert woke up in an odd infirmary. At least he assumed that's what it was, with the rows upon rows of white beds, all of which were occupied by people with bandages on their wrists and mouths. He tried to lift his arm to look at it, and the weakness of his muscles confused him. He floated in a fog, trying to recall what happened.

He remembered leaving San Francisco and making the decision to talk to his parents about the secrets they had kept from him all his life.

It had not been hard to make the decision to go home, but once he had arrived on the East Coast he had wandered a bit. He kept his cell phone charged and with him, but answered none of the calls. It was more for comfort; the knowledge that he could talk to someone if he wanted. It reminded him of the real world; that everything wasn't powers and monsters all the time. He'd landed in New York and taken time to tour the city of his youth and take in the former sites of places he remembered fondly that had since been torn down to make way for coffeehouses that served drinks in mason jars.

Robert had moved through the city of his memories balanced on the edge of joy and sadness. He tried his best not to think about Erik or Dayida and what they must think of him. It didn't work, but he still tried. Could they truly think any worse of him than they already did? He had been a horrible husband and father and could no longer pretend it had been for anyone's benefit but his own.

By the time he made it to his old neighborhood, he was almost ready for the confrontation he knew was coming. His parents were still in the same small apartment that he had been raised in alongside his two brothers. He did not know where Nicholas and Alexander had been for the last fifteen years. Robert had never felt like part of his family. He didn't remember the exact moment when he'd realized he was different, but he had been young, and he'd never been able to shake the feeling that they all knew something that was barred to him. That they were in touch with each other on a level that he never could reach.

It was that feeling that fostered the longing and resentment in him, and helped him decide to leave his family as soon as he turned eighteen.

He let out a bitter laugh as he thought of the parallels. Leaving his family without a word when he was eighteen, and leaving his family without a word when he was thirty-eight. It was a horrible symmetry. Robert opened the front door to his parent's building with the same jiggle and hip slam he'd done when he'd forgotten his keys as a child. Twenty years had passed since he'd been here and no one had fixed it; an appropriate metaphor for their family.

He took the flight of stairs, deliberately not looking to see if the carvings that he and his brothers had done in the elevator were still there. He was already filled with nostalgia. Any more and he was frightened it would be too much and he'd spontaneously burst into song like some weird musical. He climbed two additional flights and arrived at apartment 323; the second three on the door was still crooked. He knocked and listened for voices beyond the door.

Robert braced for his father or mother to answer, so the face of his older brother was a shock to the system. Alexander had grown older. His thick black hair was now laced with gray. He had facial hair; a full mustache and beard. When Robert had left his facial hair had been scruffy and barely visible.

"Romanos?" His brother's expression was odd, as if moving back and forth between annoyance and excitement. It had been a long time since anyone had called him by his birth name. Finally, his brother reached out to pull Robert in for a hug. Robert went stiff but eventually folded his arms over his brother's back, patting Alex's shoulders just to make it end.

"Alex, what are you doing here?" He finally pushed the words out.

His brother pulled back and looked him the face before laughter with a bitter edge burst out of him. "Family dinner," Alex answered when he stopped.

"Ah," Robert replied.

Alex took him by the hand and led him into the dining room, just as their mother's voice called out, asking who it was. When Alex pulled him through the door Robert's eyes immediately found her, sitting at the head of the table, spoon half-raised to bring soup to her lips. She saw him and dropped the spoon, rising from the table. Robert could see the tears gathering in her eyes and he felt his own breath stuttering, though he tried to force it still.

"Romanos, my child." She was around the table in a flash, his face in her hands as she kissed him on both cheeks. Then she pulled back and slapped him across the face. "That is for never contacting us. The only way I know of my grandchild is on the internet. Whatever problem you had with us, that was not right."

Robert swallowed but could not respond. He shrugged and she rolled her eyes before pulling him into another hug. He looked over her shoulder. His father was still seated to the right of the place his mother had been. Across from him was another empty chair that Alexander stood behind. Next to his father sat his younger brother Nicholas, head shaved, his ears adorned with large black plugs. He smiled at Robert and it was as slimy as he remembered. Nicholas' bare arms were covered in tattoos and Robert recognized some Greek letters before he looked at the man seated to his younger brothers right. He wore a stylish red sweater and horn-rimmed glasses that accentuated his large black eyes, which were glancing around the room uncomfortably. His skin was a rich brown and his awkward smile revealed slightly crooked but perfectly white teeth.

Next to his older brother's empty chair sat a woman with pale white skin and dark brown hair that curled wild and loose around her round face. She was staring at Robert directly, assessing him with cool indifference. He riled under the feeling of being judged unworthy. All the reasons he had left came rushing back and the guilt he had started to feel receded.

His mother pulled back and turned to look behind herself.

"Oh, of course. This is Yohanna, Alexander's girlfriend."

The woman nodded and stayed silent. Robert returned the gesture and did not offer his hand.

"And Nicholas's husband Demetri."

The man in the red sweater rose, half leaning over the table to reach out and shake Robert's hand.

"Pleased to meet you," he said with a nervous smile.

"Same."

Robert let go and pulled back but Demetri stayed nervously standing until Nicholas pulled him back down.

"You're about to get your pants in the food, dear," he chided.

"What? Oh, sorry." Demetri sat down quickly and shared a quiet smile with Nicholas. It made something clench in Robert's belly and he had to look away.

"Join us for dinner? We can start to catch up," his mother offered.

Robert was surprised at how much he wanted to say yes; to get caught up in the same old dinner antics that they used to when they were younger. But he couldn't do it. He had come here for some answers and he needed them now. If he stayed here and fell back into the patterns of his childhood he'd never ask. He'd just let their stronger personalities push him around.

"I'm sure they all know, don't they?" Robert said it lowly but they all heard him. He knew it since they all turned to look at him.

"Romanos, what are you talking about?" His father's voice was sharp and Robert remembered his lack of patience; his lack of caring for the child that had no power. He had not known that was the reason then, but he certainly knew it now.

"The fact that you're all Blooded."

His mother's face went sallow and even Nicholas looked at him with his mouth tight and expressionless.

"Are they?" Robert nodded to Yohanna and Demetri.

"I am," Yohanna answered, head tilted to the side, her hand in Alexander's as he stood by her chair.

"Um, I'm not awakened," Demetri stammered out.

"But you still know? Funny how you were told and I was not." Robert stared at his mother's face and could practically see her anger rise.

"His own family told him. Not us," she said tightly.

Robert let out a bitter laugh. "Of course not. Talking was never this family's greatest strength, was it? But let's get some answers now. When did you awaken, Alex?"

His older brother met his gaze calmly. "Eleven."

"Nicholas?"

Nicholas smirked; the smug look his younger brother had perfected in the crib. "Five."

Robert nodded. "No one thought to tell me?"

"It's not our way," his mother said. "Our family has always only told the awakened and let the others of our family lead normal lives."

Robert couldn't help but laugh again. "Normal? Did any of you ask me if I wanted a normal life? And if that was your intention, then good job at such a spectacular failure. My wife has been using me to keep herself from awakening. My son is some sort of foot soldier in a war and I am—well, who the fuck even knows?"

"Look, Romanos. We are sorry you never showed signs of being special—" his father started.

"Why don't you just shut the hell up, father?" Robert yelled and saw the blankness spread across his father's face. "You weren't there for me when I was a child, and you think you get to have an opinion now?" His voice rose to an unattractive shriek at the end, but he could not help it. He watched his father until he was sure of the man's continued silence. Then he turned to the rest of his family. "I wasn't an idiot! I knew there was something going on!"

"We didn't know how to tell you, and we worried that if we did anything it would affect your awakening even more," Alexander said.

"So instead I just got to feel excluded, like I didn't even belong in my own family?" he shouted.

None of them had a response and Robert felt a moment of triumph; one that had been coming for a long time. Then Yohanna's voice cut through the silence.

"What exactly are you looking for here, Romanos? What do you want?"

Robert stopped, both at the audacity of this stranger daring to address him by a name he had thrown off two decades ago and at the realization that he had no answer for that question.

"I want—" He didn't know how to finish, and as Yohanna opened her own mouth to say something else, the ground between them exploded. Monstrous things that he could only assume were the Angelics that Dayida had told him about came through. Three of them. The first simply looked like a giant black serpent with no face or features at all, terrifying but at least identifiable and comparable to something Robert had seen before. The second two he had no idea what to compare to. The second one through the hole was a rounded ball of flesh; pink with veins of blue and red rising to its surface before they disappeared again. It rolled along the ground but Robert saw little things pushing at the flesh from the inside, propelling it forward. It disturbingly reminded him of when Dayida had been pregnant and Erik had pushed his little foot or hand so hard against his home that they had seen the imprint from the outside. The third was burning. Robert had no other way to describe it. He could see the warping in the air, could sense the heat radiating from it. The floor sizzled and blackened underneath it, but there was no flame. The second and third had no eyes but they did not seem to need them as they headed for his family.

Alexander went for the serpent, dived upon its back and pulled it back from where it had been about to strike at Demetri. He locked his arms around the serpent's body and pulled back.

Nicholas had pulled a sword from somewhere and leapt forward, bringing it through the ball of flesh, carving it in half. Robert caught a glimpse of blood and organs before they reformed as two balls. One bounced up and melted across Nicholas's face. He dropped his sword and began to grope at his face. Demetri screamed and rushed forward, pulling at the pink putty that was blocking his husband's airways.

His father was now on the table trying to direct the action, but no one was listening to him. The serpent had gotten free of Alex and had him wrapped in its coils. Yohanna screamed and shifted into another form. Her hands and feet were now clawed and wickedly sharp. Her mouth full of sharp teeth. She'd dived at the serpent and begun to tear at it's skin. His mother was on her feet facing the warp in the air.

Somehow as he stared at his mother she seemed to get bigger, sharper, and longer. Her fingers grew unnaturally long and her face did as well, becoming a thing of nightmares. He felt the fear well up in his stomach and it froze his body motionless. He managed to shift his eyes over to the warp and saw that it was slowly backing back toward the hole in the ground, away from his mother. As soon as his eyes were not directly on her, the fear drained from his body. If he glanced at her from the corner of his eye, quickly, she looked the same as she ever did. If he looked too long though she started to stretch out again, turning into a monster.

Robert saw his father and Demetri had managed to the get the thing off of Nicholas' face and it was now pinned to the floor with the sword. The second half of the creature was wrapped around his father's hands trying to reach his face. Demetri was busy trying to revive Nicholas by breathing in his mouth and pumping his chest. He watched his father for a moment; saw the pink slip up his wrists, and to his elbows. He thought about helping but was still undecided when it reached his father's neck and he cried out, causing his mother to look over. As soon as his mother took her attention off the warp in the air a flash of unbearable heat had swept over them all and everything went dark.

He'd woken chained and speared to the wall, with his family on either side of him. He did not know how long they had been on the wall but he had woken up a few times to the same sight. None of the others were ever awake when he was and even if they were it was not like they could speak. His lips were gone, his tongue and teeth still there but behind a wall of flesh with no orifice. He'd passed out from panic the first three time he'd awoken because of that simple fact.

Now Robert lay in the bed, panting as if in remembering his body had gone through it all again. His hands slammed up to his lips; they felt cut and raw, jagged and uneven. He licked out and felt scars and ridges. He tried to push himself up.

"Rest. You need it."

Robert's head snapped around but he could see no one in the room with him that was not on a table and unconscious.

"Remember me, Robert?" Daniel appeared floating above him and smirking. Robert let out a yelp and, had he been stronger, would have rolled off the table completely.

"Daniel?" He was shaking. "What are you doing here? Are you one of them, like Erik?"

Daniel smiled and it was not nice. "No, Robert. I'm dead. Thanks to you."

Robert moaned low in his throat. "Are you here to haunt me?"

Daniel smirked. "You wish. I have much more important things to deal with than you."

"Then why are you here?"

"Change is coming, Robert. I'm offering you a chance to not only be a part of that change, but to have a position of power within that change."

Robert was tempted by power, as he always was, but Yohanna's voice echoed in his head. *What do you want?* What did he want?

"What are you asking me to do?"

"So here's the thing. This world is going to be under siege soon." Daniel looked down at Robert's bandaged wrists. "You've already experienced the first wave. There are many more to come. There is no way to stop it. So you must decide which side you want to be on—winning? Or losing?"

Robert stared at the boy who had every cause to hate him.

"And which side is the rest of my family on?" Robert finally asked.

"I think you know that," Daniel smiled, moving to Robert's side. "But you've always been more practical than the rest of your family, right?" He saw the hand reaching for his face but could do nothing to stop it. He felt the touch, like feather-light electricity down his jaw and under his chin. "You help me out and I promise not to kill any of your family, on purpose. As well as giving you a place of power in the new order. What more could you ask for?"

Robert thought about the offer and looked at those around him. His eyes landed on his mother's form. Her usually stocky body looked somehow bird thin against the white sheet. Her steel gray hair spread out around her head. As if seeing her had started a chain reaction, his gaze landed on his father and then on Alexander, then Nicholas, then Alexander's girlfriend Yohanna and Nicholas's husband Demetri and he felt something stir inside of him.

They were good. They would fight to the last. Robert was not good. He wasn't evil either. At least he didn't think so. But he knew a good deal when he saw it. Maybe they'd defeat whatever was coming, in which case great, but, in the more likely event that they lost, at least they wouldn't die.

He had always assumed that his family kept things from him out of indifference, if not straight-up malice. But maybe they actually were trying to protect him? After the attack, he could almost believe it. This was an opportunity to prove to himself and to his families that he was worth more. That he could care about them in that same way. He would do this thing for them.

"Yes. I will help you."

He looked back to Daniel but the ghost was gone. Exhausted, he lay his head down and sank into sleep.

# ZEBUB

# BYRON

He had delivered on his part of the bargain in the middle of the night. Calling on Mayer, they had met again by the water, and he had received the key to the door of Kandake and told the older man where to find those he was looking for. It had been a simple thing to return to the House of the Madame he was staying in and question the proprietor as to where the two Antes with the two 'dant children had fled to.

His ambient powers did not seem to work here—no one just liked him from being in close proximity to him—but when he focused, his powers were stronger than ever. He had cut through whatever defenses The Door had and gotten the information easily. The same with The Door at the second House of the Madame.

He wondered if he could go further, and maybe push his powers into telepathy? It was terribly tempting to try.

The sun was rising in the sky as they arrived at Kandake. The huge doors were closed and no lights burned in the windows at all. It felt abandoned.

He smiled as he approached and pulled the small fold of cloth that he carried in his pocket. He unfolded it carefully, revealing the three drops of blood, not soaked into the fabric but resting on it, whole and round. He located the first place that the Holder had mentioned; a small depression where the door met the floor. He picked up the first drop carefully and let it fall in the depression. The second drop went in a small recess on the inside of the door handle, easy to mistake for just regular pitting. The final drop he balanced on his thumb as he reached for the handle. Right were his thumb would land, a thorn jutted out. He let the tip of it pierce the drop of blood and sucked it in.

The door unlocked under his hand and he pushed it open. The lighting was dim, barely bright enough to see anything. He gestured for Bastion to go first, and followed with Melisande bringing up the rear. From whatever direction an attack might come, it would hit one of them first, giving him a chance to fight back.

"What are we looking for?" Bastion asked belligerently.

Byron smiled. He supposed it was no longer necessary to keep it from them. He doubted they would be useful for that much longer.

"I awakened at a very young age. Most charmers do. They find themselves in some situation where they are desperate enough, where they need someone to like them so much that their power comes online. When you charm others, you start to see the dark side of people liking you. Wanting you."

"Okay, what does this have to do with anything?" Melisande asked.

Byron simply ignored the question. "Right up here, Bastion."

He did not know for sure that they should turn right, but it felt like a good choice, and they just needed to get deeper, closer to the living portion of the building. He felt the air pressure change and the temperature skyrocket beside him and quickly leapt forward as a funnel of fire blasted out from the side of the wall.

Melisande cursed loudly behind him, but it was frustration, not pain.

"Still alive back there?" Byron laughed at his own joke, ignoring the look Bastion threw at him. He continued his explanation. "There's a chance, you see. To not only save our world, but to change it too. But I need more power. I need to be able to tame what is coming and make it do what it should have done the first time."

"What do you mean, 'first time?'" Bastion asked. His voice was quieter, and more cautious. They had arrived in a cramped portion of the library. Books curved overhead on rickety wood shelves. There was barely any space for them to move.

"The world has been made and destroyed so many times now. It is a process of expanding and shrinking. Each time we are created anew; a little different perhaps, but the same basic plan. Always with the same problems: the same hunger and pain; the same bitterness and oppression. It's a flaw in the design. I plan to fix it."

The walls around them had widened up and they were approaching a rough staircase. As they climbed Byron continued. "Those with other powers—more explosive or obvious powers—tend to overlook charmers. Most don't even bother to learn what bloodlines we descend from. But it's important. Charming is manipulation. It's forcing your way into someone's mind and making a place for yourself. It is anything but harmless."

They reached the top of the stairs and stood in a hall of statues; some made out of ivory, some out of gold, and some seemingly carved of water or fire or other non-solid-materials somehow made firm. As Bastion passed the first one, a metal woman, nude, holding a man's head in one hand and a knife in the other, it turned to face him and spoke.

"You come to the hall of memories. What is it that you seek?"

Bastion yelled and jumped at the first word.

"Passage?" Byron answered.

"Passage is free. Go as thou wilt, but have you no questions for us?" The statue answered.

"No." Byron did not need anyone to tell him that any questions in here would have a catch attached. The statues had Catch-22 written all over them.

"I have a question," Melisande said.

Byron swung around to silence the little idiot but it was too late. The statue who answered Melisande looked to be the nude form of a man made of white marble veined in pink. He had wide hips and shoulders and held a whip in one hand and in the other a jug against his hip. His head was that of a cheetah and the look in the statue's eyes was pure predator.

"Ask your question, child." The voice was a purr more than anything else. It invited confidence and seduction.

Byron eyed it suspiciously.

"When will Bastion and I get the payout that we deserve?" Melisande asked, looking at Byron with a smug look.

It took everything in him not to kill her then and there.

"Your reward is at hand," the statue answered.

Byron smirked as they cheered. He understood the answer, even if they did not. He pulled on the power that he was loaning them to get moving again.

He began to speak again as they walked.

"Ruth understood what was wrong about the world. Together we tried to find a way to fix it. It's well known that all the gods are dead, but death is not the same for gods. It's also known that when one uses their powers too often, riding on that thin line of exhaustion, sometimes you can make contact with your god. We found a way to make that contact more long-term and useful. Communication could happen, but it took a sacrifice of one of us to act as conduit. Ruth volunteered, and gave up her form."

"I took her power and some of her essence inside of me and had a direct line to our ancestor. Then I joined the Agency. Do you have any idea the kind of information a government can gather when they have little to no moral compass? It's amazingly vast. They have the answers to eternal mysteries hiding in their files and records, but they haven't put the details together yet."

The hallway they walked down got more and more narrow until Byron's shoulders were brushing the walls. The hall widened into a circular room that had only one exit opposite the entrance.

"It wouldn't have worked if Ruth and I didn't have the same fount of the bloodline, as we suspected. It was only later, with the information I finally put together, that I learned who the fount of it was." Byron looked around the room. "Irony or destiny? It's so hard to tell the difference sometimes." Just as Bastion was heading out of the other end of the room, Byron deliberately kicked a small outcropping of different-colored stone. Spikes flew at them from the ceiling and he pushed Bastion forward, saving both of them any injury. He heard a cry of pain behind them.

When he turned to look, Melisande was holding a hand over her upper arm, where a spike had scored a line in her clothing and skin.

"It's just a flesh wound. Walk it off."

He rose and turned back to Bastion who was looking at him in anger. Byron prodded at Bastion until the boy started walking forward again. It felt good to let all of this out into the air. He had held it inside for so long, and now it felt like not only was he telling Bastion and Melisande, but he was speaking to the universe as well. Wherever what was left of Ruth rested, he hoped that she could hear him, and was proud of him. He would take this world and remake it; without the prejudice and without the anger and without the things that separated people.

They moved through a hall that was obviously older than anything else they had been through; the stones of the walls were crumbling but covered with faint traces of paint, images of small figures that looked like humans fighting off monstrous beings. Didn't take a genius to work out the symbolism. Byron stopped moving as soon as they exited the hall spotting the many small spouts in the roof that lined the hall on either side. He looked all around him, searching for a hidden lever and spotted a few of them.

"You'll love the new world. There will be no reason for the anger you carry inside you all the time," he said as he triggered the lever closest to him. What came out of the spouts was not fire, as he had expected, but something black and viscous that fell over the boy's head and silenced any sound he was going to make before it was formed.

He stepped back into the previous room to avoid the sloshing liquid. He watched as it drained away, sinking directly into the stone. He looked behind him and saw Melisande crumpled on the ground. He had wondered why she had said nothing through the process. The wound in her shoulder was now a putrid yellow and dripping onto the ground.

"Huh. Guess it was more than a flesh wound." He moved on and kicked the still-decaying corpse of Bastion out of his way.

The next doorway opened onto a stairway heading down. It crossed a number of other stairways, like an Escher painting, but as far as he could see, everything was right side up. He breathed deep, finally feeling whole again. His power rushed back to him with every breath; the deaths of his two companions having released it from their bodies. He had felt hollow without it. Their attempt to charm the Antes had proved that the little bit of power he was able to grant them was truly useless here, and having Ruth's power back, layering over his own, made him feel that much more powerful. So powerful that he could feel the presence of the Athenaeum itself. Watching. Waiting. Not happy.

Byron tried to speak to it, leeching as much charm into his voice as possible. "Hello, I am not here to hurt you, Kandake."

In response the stairway he was on began to shake and rotate, moving on a direct collision course with another. Byron ran down the steps to the landing and leaped onto one of the stairways below him. He landed, and crouched down, covering his head as the stairwells above him collided and rained down chunks of stone.

"Okay, so lying to you isn't gonna work? Fuck."

Byron hurried down the stairway he had landed on and through a hallway that looked vaguely familiar. He turned the corner and skidded to a stop in front of three people, all of whom looked pissed. He cursed at Kandake. The thing had only pretended to be open to them. It had pretended to let them in and had instead moved him around so that he was back near the entrance. He zeroed in on the figure of Matthias, who looked quite murderous.

"Well, fuck me."

He did not waste any more time and turned, taking off down the same hall he had been down before. He heard the footsteps behind him and cursed. He had never wanted to hurt Matthias, but now he might have to kill him. It did not sit as well with him as he had thought it would.

# LIL

They moved quickly after Kima and Assan left. Lil knew where Kandake was in relation to the Ruling Courts and led them through the streets. She spent much time glancing around. Having spent so long inside the Courts and then in the Out, she had not realized how badly the darkness was ripping Zebub apart. Everywhere she looked, there were barren patches where ruins testified to buildings that had recently stood there. 'Dants stayed in their homes, peaking out through curtains. It was not safe, but where could they go? The Athenaeums were all closed because their Holders were absent. They could brave the wild ways between cities but they must have heard that other cities were affected as well. They could attempt to find one of the 'dant-only enclaves that littered the wastes, but those 'dants had generations of experience hiding.

They could do nothing but pretend that the walls would protect them and be ready to flee when they proved ineffective.

Davi was dozing in her arms and Min was clearly exhausted as well, stumbling along with them and refusing to be carried. They had taken her lack of tongue and inability to talk in stride. Neither of them could read so Arel or Jagi read them what she spelled with the branch. Now that they were with her, and Arel and Jagi were at her back, she felt settled. The trembling in her stomach, a worry that had pushed at her since she had been separated from her sibs, was finally gone.

Razel moved up alongside her.

Lil nodded in acknowledgment.

Razel cut her eyes at the other 'dants walking with them. "They are from a different world. One that touches our own."

Lil was no stranger to the idea of other worlds. She had read of such things, but the fact that such people had appeared just as she was told there was a way out of her dying world could be no coincidence.

**WhyDidTheyCome?**

"They believed it was so they could help us to try and fight the darkness, but the Courts never intended to fight it," Razel explained.

**DoTheyKnowWhatItIs?**

"If they do, they have not told me."

Lil nodded. She would not mention the demiurge. She did not know how the others would react, knowing that the horror that devoured them had created them as well. It was something she was still wrapping her mind around. Something she did not understand yet.

**WhatDoTheCourtsPlan?**

"They plan an invasion of the other world. They plan to fight the darkness from there," Razel said.

**ItIsFoolishToFightAWarOnTwoFronts.**

"They believe they will need the resources," Razel replied.

Lil's only reply was a shrug. It made no sense to her. Had they wanted to use the other world's resources, it would have been much better to strike some sort of bargain. Except that this would mean the Ruling Courts would have to share something, give something up. None of them dealt with that particularly well. Especially if these 'dants were the entire population of the other world. Most of the Antes and all of the Courts would balk at treating with anything like 'dants as equals. Better to conquer them and rule, rather than get their cooperation.

None of the outsiders had reacted to overhearing what Razel said. Was it because she had already told them or had they suspected as much?

Lil turned down the street that would lead to Kandake. One of the others angled toward her as they moved. She shifted Davi so he was in the arm away from the approaching stranger. Simply because they acted as allies was no reason to trust them. The continuing ache in her body was proof enough of that.

"I am Erik."

**Lil.**

"I would like to ask you a few questions."

Lil was not surprised. She had some questions herself.

**AQuestionForAQuestionAnAnswerForAnAnswer.**

Erik smiled at her. "Agreed. What are your plans when we reach this Kandake place?"

**IWillEnterTheDepthsIWillFreeTheHeartOf ItFromMayersControlOnceSheIsFreeSheWill ShowMeWhatToDoNext.**

Erik nodded. "Okay."

**WhatIsYourGoalNow?**

"To help the people of this world and to get back to our world to help our people."

Lil snuck another look at the young man. He was not much older than her. He wore matching red pants and jacket that were stained and ripped in various places. The shirt under the jacket was black and relatively clean. His eyes looked tired but honest. She had been fooled before, but she believed that the young man believed what he was saying at that moment. Perhaps that is why she ended up volunteering information.

**ThisWorldIsDoomedOurOnlyHopeIsHerPromise.**

"Who is she?" Erik asked, watching her. She had no idea if it was the question he intended, but he was not taking it back and so she answered.

**SheNeverToldMeHerNameSheWasAnOldOne HerBodyUsedToBuildThisPlaceSheSaid SheWasOneOfTheLastToFallInTheWar.**

Erik looked lost in thought at that. They turned and Kandake was visible in the distance. The place was dark in a way that Lil had never seen, and it saddened her. Many 'dants resented the Athenaeums. But that resentment lived alongside an odd hope. The hope that if you were in big enough trouble, the Athenaeums would help you. To see it dark made her feel as if she and Mayer had taken the hope out of this part of the city when they went to the Ruling Courts.

**AreTheirAntesInYourWorld?**

"No. The only ones that appear are those that come from here. Perhaps in some of the darker forests and swamps or in the caves yet unexplored there are some hiding but I do not believe so."

Lil nodded and she wondered at such a life: one without the fear of Antes always hanging over your shoulder. She had no doubt that their world had its own problems. She had lived too long to believe in any world that was perfect. However, the idea of the weight of Antes being off her back was like being promised something wondrous in the distance. If she could take Davi and Min there, they could be raised in a place free of Antes. A hand landed on her shoulder and she took in the pale, chalk-white skin.

She looked back at Arel and Jagi. And then thought of June. Could she leave them behind? Could she take them with her? They were not horrible. Was it possible there were other Antes in this city who were like them? Antes not inherently vicious?

She was pulled from her wondering by Erik's voice asking his next question.

"You believe this 'old one' though? What evidence did she provide?"

She shook her head as she remembered.

**NoEvidenceWasNecessaryICould**

**FeelCorpiliuThroughHerTouchThe**

**PlacesIHadNeverBeenThePlacesThatHadDiedLongAgoI FeltThemAll**

**AndForABriefMomentIKnew**

**EverythingAboutThem**

"Sounds like some pretty good evidence to me," Erik said, almost to himself.

It made Lil smile.

**IWouldAskYouToTakeCareOfMySibs**

**InCaseIDoNotSurviveThis.**

The man was silent for long enough that she worried that she had asked for entirely too much. They did not know each other at all but, something in her body recognized him as a kindred spirit. He had been through pain, though his scars were not as visible as her own. She could see the determination in the folds of his face. The attempt to do his best and protect those that he loved. She knew the promise of someone like that was something she could trust.

Or she hoped it was.

She had no intention of leaving her sibs after having just found them, but if she had to give all of herself to wrest control from Mayer, then she would do so. She trusted Arel and Jagi to protect them, but they would know nothing of the new world. Min and Davi would need someone to teach them. When he spoke it was quiet.

"I will do my best. You have my word."

She believed him. As they neared the doors Lil saw that one of them was hanging open just a little bit.

**ThisShouldNotBeOpenEveryoneBeOnYourGuard.**

She handed Davi's still-sleeping form off to Arel and made sure Jagi had Min well in hand before pushing her way inside the place she had known for so long as her home. The light bulbs had been dim but as she entered they lit up to their full brightness. Some dust had settled in the time since they had left for the Ruling Courts and Lil could see the footsteps that had disturbed it. It led down the central hall, and directly into the depths of the building.

She turned to look at her many companions.

**SomeoneMustStayHereTheyMustHelpCorral**
**ThoseWhoWillCome.**

None of them said anything and so Lil looked at all of them and decided.

**ArelAndJagiIDoNotThinkTheSpiritOfThe**
**AthenaeumHasAnyLoveForAntesSoItMayBe**
**BestThatYouStayHere**
**AlsoITrustYouWithMySibs.**

They had seemed about to argue until she added that last part and they nodded frowning. She turned to the others.

**QuinnAndHlaniIWouldLikeYouToStayHereAsWellMany**
**OfTheDantsWhoComeWillNotFeelSafeAroundTwoAntes.**

Finally, she turned to Razel, but before she could say anything the other woman spoke.

"I will stay here as well. For now, I still have a bond with Hypatia. Kandake may not take kindly to that, no matter how small it is."

Lil nodded and smiled. She turned to the others.

**IThinkASmallGroupWouldBeBestThreeOfUsNoMore.**

"I will go." Erik stepped forward, as she expected him too. He was the leader. He would not be much of one if he asked his people to do something he would not.

"Me as well." The other young man with the tan skin and loose black curls stepped forward as well.

Erik turned to the rest of their group. "Stay here, help if you can. Matthias and I shall return soon."

Lil turned and started down the hall, confident that the two would follow. Lil could feel the heart of Kandake calling to her; the strength of it. The part that surprised her was that Erik seemed to have a sense of it as well. He turned sometimes at the same time as her though he never got ahead of her, which was a good thing for his health, since there were traps along the way that she disarmed as she came into range. These were to keep those who did not belong out, and Kandake felt Lil was still allowed entrance.

They found the first body around a corner and Erik hissed as he saw it.

He knelt down and felt the neck and then the wrist. "Melisande. What is she doing here?"

The other 'dant near them, the one with the curlier hair and the big sad eyes, growled.

"If she's here, then Byron probably is too."

Lil did not know who they were speaking of, but it was obvious that they believed this Byron was the man who had infiltrated Kandake.

The next body was not that much farther on, though in much worse shape, falling apart and crumbling into decay.

Erik knelt down next to it, leaning in close. "I can't tell if it's Bastion or Byron. Probably Bastion. I doubt that Byron would be killed that easily."

Just then they heard the sound of footsteps in front of them. Lil looked up to see a 'dant in a black suit, similar to the red one that Erik wore. His hair was curly and dark red; his skin a very pale brown covered in freckles, especially his face. His eyes widened at the sight of them.

They all stood frozen for a moment and then the 'dant turned and ran off and the curly haired 'dant took off after him.

# SAN FRANCISCO

# TAE

Tae was accompanied by Patrah and Hettie as they approached the small house in east Oakland. They had insisted on bringing him, so he could speak "seer to seer," they said. It didn't make much sense to him but they had both insisted. So here they were walking toward the last known address of a man who was known to stick his nose in others' business and help them without request. He sounded like an asshole to Tae.

The afternoon sun was high in the sky and people were walking about. There was nothing to say this was dangerous, but Tae felt a familiar lurch in his belly as they turned up the walk.

He had called on his powers after getting home the night before, expecting the limitations that his powers had had before traveling to Zebub. Instead he had been slammed with so much information he had been knocked unconscious. He awoke to his mother and father leaning over him, his mother lightly smacking his cheeks while his father flicked water on his face. Apparently, he had screamed as well. The neighbors on both sides of them had come over to check that everything was alright. It must have been quite a scream, to shock city dwellers into actually exposing themselves to potential embarrassment and pretending to care about someone they did not know.

The continuous lurch in his stomach worried him too much and so this time he was cautious. He brought his power up slowly. Feeling it in his legs first, his knees locked and allowed him to go no further, his hands snapped out to stop both Patrah and Hettie.

"What is it?" Patrah asked

"I don't know yet." He brought his power up to his neck and into his eyes. Slowly and gently he looked nowhere but at the ground. He ignored the information his powers shouted at him about when the foundation had been laid and the names of the men who had built it. Instead he looked only at the surface and saw it. A thin metal wire the same discolored gray as the concrete it lay upon it. He followed the wire with his sight off into the lawn and then into the house.

"Trip wire of some kind." He narrowed his eyes at the house and again, and had to push through a multitude of useless information that tried to reveal itself to him. He focused on what the wire would do. "An alarm. There's one person inside." The person's outline became clear but his eyes glowed so brightly with a prism of light that any facial features were washed out.

Tae came out of it and allowed the power to ebb from his body. He stepped over the wire and made sure Patrah and Hettie did the same. When they were at the front door he turned to them.

"So, do we knock or just try to go on in?"

"Knock, of course. You should always begin as you mean to continue and we don't want him to think we're here to trap him against his will or capture him," Hettie answered as she lifted her hand and rapped on the door three times in quick succession.

They waited outside for a long time, so long that Tae wondered if the man had left through some other way. Just as he was about to chance bringing his powers up again to check, the door swung open. The man on the other side was pale, with a waxy look to his skin. His hair was thin but long; a deep brown that curled across his shoulders. He leaned on a cane and stared at them with bulging eyes that lingered in the border between brown and yellow.

"Can I help you?"

"Yes, are you Fallon?" Hettie asked, smiling in a way that relaxed Tae, and it wasn't even aimed at him. The man instead seemed to tense up.

"No one by that name has ever lived here."

He went to close the door on them.

"But was that your name once, before you lived here?" Tae asked.

The man froze and looked at him through narrowed eyes. He rustled through all of the small pockets on his vest before coming up with a dirty green-and-silver monocle. He looked them up and down and Tae felt the shiver of being seen. Truly seen.

"You're not Maasu at least. That's good." Still he looked them up and down for another moment before he opened the door wide and invited them in. He did not take them far, directing them to a living room directly off to the right from the front door. "Have a seat."

They all did and he took them each in in turn before turning to Hettie.

"You're the one in charge here. Let me know what you want with me. I know you can't be here to capture me because my warning would have gone off. Yes, young man, even the one you thought you avoided."

Tae looked at the man in surprise.

"I learned long ago not to rely on power or mechaniques only. While you stepped over the wire infused with a little power, you missed the mechanique sensors. They would have picked up Maasu from miles away. I was just making extra sure at the door. Oh, and the doorway itself? If you had bad intentions when you entered, it would have exiled the three of you to a small pocket dimension. You'd be frozen in time for about an hour and would emerge thinking no time had passed, but I would be long gone."

Tae looked at him wide-eyed, surprised that he had not picked up on any of this. But perhaps it had been dormant because none of it applied to him?

"I've been running for a long time now, boy. I have a lot of tricks perfected and I'm always making new ones."

Tae nodded.

"Now what can I help you folks with?" The man asked, sitting down as well.

Hettie spoke up. "First, you can tell us what Maasu are."

"Maasu are . . . they are creatures of war. Monsters that are hard to kill because they are already dead; things stitched together to specification. They are not mindless so much as single minded. They are given a target or a mission and pursue it relentlessly."

"So are they those things made of blackness? Or the people that have been going crazy and attacking others?"

"The Maasu are both. They are the instruments of war. Traditionally they are armored in blackness because they are used at night more often than not. Traditionally they are made of mechanique mixed with alchemy and power and pieces of living beings. When the Ruling Courts of Zebub got their hands on the plans again, they had the idea to do the reverse as well. A human on the outside but a monster on the inside. They are still creatures built for war."

"Why do the Ruling Courts want you back so badly? What have you seen?" Tae asked.

The man stared at them for a moment before throwing his head back and laughing until he started coughing. Once he recovered, he explained. "I'm no seer, boy. I'm a Holder."

Tae gasped and the man chuckled.

"Well, former Holder. My apprentice took over long ago."

"So you're from Zebub?" Tae asked.

"You bet your ass I am. Born and raised until I jumped portals a couple of decades ago. Wasn't that hard. They had just started sending the Maasu back through and I just loaded myself in with the ones that looked human. Those were the only ones they were sending through at the time."

"Why?"

The man sighed and closed his eyes again.

"Because they think they can make a better stand against the darkness from your world than their own and they are not wrong."

"Why is our world better?" Tae asked.

"It's older. More stable. The roots of Corpiliu are rotten and they will fall all too easily."

"How do you know all of this?" Hettie asked

The man sighed. "Because I worked with them. I was the one who rediscovered the blueprints for the Maasu, and the one who designed the reverse Maasu."

"Why?" Hettie asked, her tone sounding surprisingly neutral to Tae's ears.

"Because I knew the darkness was going to return. All of the mechaniques I built to calculate its return told me it would happen in my lifetime. I took the information to the Ruling Courts because I was a fool and they convinced me to look for weapons; anything we could use against the darkness. I helped them because I thought I was helping my people and then when I found out the truth I ran." The man put his face in his hands.

"Why didn't you try to help anyone? Tell anyone?" Tae asked.

The man was silent and Tae felt his face harden as he continued. "The darkness is coming; has already made inroads into this world. You can't run anywhere else now, so what are you going to do? Sit in your little house until the darkness swallows you whole or wait for your former masters to come find you?"

Tae saw both scenarios playing out in front of his eyes as he described them and he also felt how likely they were. The darkness was the more likely of the two.

The man closed his eyes and rubbed at them through the lids. When he opened them he met all of their gazes one at a time. "What do you need?"

"We would ask that you come with us. That you help us fight what you found and what you built," Tae said.

The man was silent for a long time but then he nodded and stood, leaning on his cane for balance. "Let's go."

They walked from the house and Tae felt Hettie put her arm around his shoulder. "Told you we would need a seer to talk with him."

# DAYIDA

Dayida pressed the gas down as hard as she could and swung around the corner. Her power flared in her shoulders and she maneuvered the car fantastically. The other two in the car were quiet at least. One was an independent from Oakland—Citrine, a lovely dark-skinned young woman who calmly sat with her hands in her lap and swayed with the movement of the car. In the back, a nervous Suit from the Agency sat. His pale fingers twisted in the "oh shit" bar, making them even paler. His name was Uwe and he looked ready to scream at any moment. The team had been working together for a couple nights so far.

When Luka got something in her head, she did not play. They had talked and organized and negotiated long into that first night. When the next day had dawned, they were still in her office, but they had a plan to try and protect the area.

One of the things they had to worry about was mass hysteria. The photos and videos had thankfully been few and far between and most were still being written off as hoaxes. They had managed to gather all the corpses of the dead black armored things and the Antes that had died so no one was selling any "alien" or "cryptid" autopsy videos yet, but it was only a matter of time. The black Maasu were hard to kill but not impossible. It was the human-looking monsters that worried her far more. There were more and more reports coming through of normal humans suddenly turning vicious and violent. Some of them just seemed to hulk the fuck out at whatever was in range but others had been slyer. One man in London had gotten way too close to planting a bomb close to Buckingham Palace.

A Blooded in London had managed to stop that through blind luck, though it had cost her her life.

They weren't winning by any means. They lost more people than they saved. More people on their side were dying than those on the other side. They were fighting a war of attrition, but it wasn't a massacre yet, and they were getting better. They were figuring it out. There were seven different cars patrolling San Francisco, each one with three Blooded. Others were taking care of Oakland and the Peninsula, all the way down to San Jose.

They used a police scanner plus the Alarmers of the Organization to try and find the attacks as they started. This call had come in only moments ago across the police scanner. A woman and a monster in the park. Dayida yanked the wheel and cut across three lanes of traffic to skid her car onto the grass of the park.

The woman was sprawled on the ground unconscious, her child crying, still protected in the circle of her body. Dayida sped up and then slammed on the brakes as she yanked the wheel to the right. The car slid perfectly between the mother and the monster. The driver's side slammed into the creature's side and in that moment Dayida shoved her palm against its hard shell through her open window and summoned the burning metal that was her birthright. The sword sprang into being. The point easily pierced its side, going deeper as it grew. She whipped the car the other way, letting the creature's own momentum pull it off the sword and away from the car.

She stopped it on a dime and turned to the others.

"You." She pointed at the Suit. "Get the baby. I'll get the mother." She looked at Citrine. "Keep that thing away from us until we can get her in the car and don't get hurt."

Citrine smirked. "Done and done."

Dayida had found a purpose in these rescue attempts. Her power lent itself to leading people into battle. Though she was careful not to dive too deeply into her power. Her worries about her mother held her back at all times. Still she was growing used to using it in these runs, simply enjoying the rush of joy that came with helping others. She hurried over to the woman and found the Suit hovering over them both, hemming and hawing. He looked at the baby, then back at her, and then back at the baby.

"Oh, are you fucking serious right now?" She asked.

She reached down and snatched up the baby. "Grab her now, and you better not drop her."

He leaned down and picked the mother up in a fireman's carry. He staggered but didn't fall. Dayida cradled the still-crying child against her chest and ran back to the car. They settled the mother in the backseat. The Suit buckled her in and then settled back himself. Dayida unceremoniously plopped the now-sniffling infant into his startled arms.

"Don't drop the baby either," she ordered.

He nodded shakily and she closed his door and slid into the driver's seat. Citrine was facing off against the beast, which kept reaching for her, but the power she generated around her was keeping it at bay and even hurting it.

*It's like having a semi-sentient force field, that's also a big cat who likes to claw people*, Citrine had explained when they first met.

Dayida had nodded as if she had understood. She definitely did now.

The creature looked like a rat and a crab had mated and then their baby killed them and added pieces of their bodies to its own. It was batted back from Citrine, and Dayida saw four parallel lines appear, splitting its armor.

"Get in the car!" Dayida yelled.

"You're the boss," Citrine shouted and hopped into the passenger seat but not before taking one more chance to throw the creature into a convenient tree.

Dayida slammed the car into reverse and sped back into the street. She narrowly missed being squished between two SUVs. They honked and the drivers leaned out of their windows to curse at her but she was already gone, waving out the window at them. They were doing better than most of the other teams and Dayida knew that was because of her driving skills. Her instincts, while meant for battle, were quite useful when it came to dealing with the roads of San Francisco.

She also liked taking the hills at fifty miles per hour. The liftoff was pretty damn awesome and it made Uwe squeak. She didn't do it now, in deference to the baby, but she was tempted. Speaking of the baby; she glanced at him in the backseat and saw Uwe's green face as he did his best to hold the baby securely but not too tightly. He was mumbling under his breath, but his smile as he looked down at the baby was surprisingly sweet. Perhaps he wasn't so bad after all.

"Tell the others we've got two more," Dayida said. They needed to drop off the rescues and then go out on patrol for another call in.

Citrine reached for the old-school CB radio on the dashboard. They were the best that Dayida, Hettie, and Luka could do on such short notice, but they worked surprisingly well.

"Cars for Caring, this is Car One. Reporting two more captured strays for the group home, where should we deliver? Over."

"Well done, Car One. Take them to the honorable place. Over."

Dayida nodded to show she heard and understood, and turned the car toward the Legion of Honor.

# HU

Hu was tired of running. He'd been doing it for over two weeks now, moving around so no one could find him, relying on cash reserves he had hidden around San Francisco. He had been trying to think of a plan, something that would get him out of the mess he was in. He was in the jaws of a trap. He had not been high enough up in the conspiracy to know who they were actually working for. And didn't that just piss him off. But he'd also been high enough up that no one on the other side was likely to believe him. He was now staying in places that he had always been too proud to even look at straight on. The SRO in the Mission was the closest to hell he ever wanted to go, but it was heaven, given the refuge it allowed him.

That is until the door shook. Not a knock. Rather the door shook. Hu did not wait for another sign. He pushed open the window by his bed and slid out onto the fire escape with his small bag of belongings. He scurried down the fire escape and leapt down from the lowest landing, ignoring the locked ladder. Hu looked up to see two people looking out of the window. First, he had them pegged as Suits but then they stepped out onto the fire escape and they were not in the traditional suits. They watched as he jaywalked across the street with his head turned, staring at them the whole time.

They both crouched and leapt from the balcony.

Hu moved swiftly, pushing through the crowds on the sidewalk and eventually just moving into the street itself and running in that narrow gutter between sidewalk and lane.

There was a crash behind him and he turned to see they had landed in the middle of the street. Broken asphalt rose up all around them.

They ignored the chaos around them, the cars skidding past and stopping just short of hitting them. They were definitely not the Organization either. They were causing too much ruckus in public. He ran faster and then said fuck it. If they were willing to be this open, they wanted him bad. And it most likely was not to talk.

Hu's body bent as he called on his power. He stumbled but recovered his balance as he transitioned from two feet to four. He swept between pedestrians who screeched and jumped at the sudden cheetah in their midst. Hu glanced back and saw that his stalkers were somehow keeping pace with him. Hu reached an intersection and braced himself to make a break for it when he recognized one of the people in the stopped car to his right: Blooded Haru from the Organization. He looked back to the two things that looked human but were most assuredly not, and decided he would take his chance with those he could have an actual conversation with. Seeing someone in danger usually meant the person got a chance to explain things.

Hu kept running as he returned to bipedal form, this time stumbling horribly and slamming into the side of the car with his whole body.

The people inside startled and they all raised hands to ward him off before one of them, Blooded Haru, who had begun her training just as he ended his, recognized him.

"It's Maestro Hu," she said, her voice hard to read.

The other two in the car raised their eyebrows, which Hu did not think was a good sign.

"Yes, it's me! And I'm being followed by two things that look human but are definitely not."

They looked behind him and their faces got grim.

"Get in the car," the man in the passenger seat said.

"Thank you."

"Now," he said, and Hu hurried into the backseat next to a teenager. "I'm Longworth."

Hu nodded and concentrated on putting on his seat belt while Blooded Haru gunned it through a red light.

"Wow, they just are really not giving a fuck right now, are they?" The younger girl said, sitting up in the backseat and turning around. He glanced back as well.

“I don’t think we’ve been introduced, but perhaps that language isn’t appropriate right now,” Hu reprimanded.

The girl turned to look Hu in the face.

“Oh, are you trying to play that? Right now? My name is Reina FOYPOS. It stands for fuck off, you piece of shit.” Reina smiled at him.

“We good?” She asked, gesturing at him. He said nothing, mouth falling open. She smiled wider. “Yeah, we’re good.” And turned back to look behind them.

He glanced to see the two figures finally falling behind the speeding car. Blooded Haru began to slow down and the Reina girl sat back properly in her seat though she made no move to put on the seat belt.

“Suit Longworth, can you call it in?” Blooded Haru asked.

The Suit in the passenger seat was a tall and thick man. His blonde hair was long and braided along his nape and down the back of his shirt. He picked up the CB radio and pressed the handset.

“This is Car 6 reporting in. We’ve found Mr. Hu. He was almost picked up by another company, but we got to him in time. Over.”

“Is the other company still following you? Over.”

“No, we lost them.”

“Okay, then bring him in.” The words crackled over the radio and Hu breathed a huge sigh of relief. “We’ll need bait for the hook.” Hu caught his breath.

# MAESTRA LUKA

Luka walked into the large building with no fear. She was dealing with politicians, and that meant that she could show no weakness. She already had two strikes against her when it came to dealing with the government—she was a woman and she was Latina. At the same time, these "disadvantages" had trained her well not to give a flying fuck what most of these men stuffed on their own importance thought of her.

The woman at the front desk asked for her name and directed her to the third floor while looking her up and down. Luka had not come in her most professional dress because she was tired and could not be bothered to give that much of a shit about living up to their expectations. Her slacks were clean, if a bit threadbare, and her button-down shirt was untucked but it was otherwise in place. Of course, it could have been the Converses on her feet that the receptionist was gawking at. Luka had been running and fighting too much lately to consider wearing heels.

This being the Bay Area, it was somewhat better than other cities she had lived in. Meaning she was not the only brown person roaming the halls of government, though gentrification and tech bros had whitened it up considerably. The office she wanted was right off the elevator. It wasn't the office she had told the woman in front she was going to. Luka did not have time for red tape.

The Mayor's office was not easy to get into for most people, but Luka was not most people. She ducked into the woman's washroom and took a deep breath, playing with the light streaming in through the small, sealed window. Luka brightened it and dimmed it and made it run around the room. The simple exercises calmed her. The next step involved her least-used power, because it was the one she had the most problem with, so her nerves were uncharacteristically raw.

Luka gathered the light around the room and slowly bent it around her body. She looked in the mirror and saw nothing.

All of Luka's senses were working except her ability to feel light. As long as her power bent to making light avoid her body she could feel nothing of her sense of light. The world felt different, wrong. She hurried from the bathroom, opening the door as little as possible, leaving so anyone who saw to convince themselves it was the wind. She did the same as she slipped inside the Mayor's office. In the outer office people were working and chatting. She was careful to disturb and touch nothing as she moved toward the private office behind everyone.

Luka felt the panic welling up in her stomach as her body reached out for the light that she was keeping out of its reach. She cracked the Mayor's door very carefully and slid inside.

He looked up as the door closed behind her and Luka let the light come rushing back.

He jumped and his mouth fell open.

"Hello, Mr. Mayor. We have to talk."

"Do we have an appointment?" The man looked flustered and uncomfortable.

She did not sit, enjoying looking down on him.

"What I am about to tell you is not usually revealed to politicians so low on the totem pole of power." Luka knew she was antagonizing the man but she could not seem to help herself. "Simply put, this world is not what you thought it was." Best to get the shock out of the way quickly. "This is not the only plane of existence and we are facing an invasion."

He smiled at her in that way that people did when they thought someone barking mad. She saw his hand move under the desk and sighed.

"So, I'm going to assume you just hit the silent alarm. We'll talk more when you're alone."

Luka spied the window behind the man. She could turn invisible again but was glad she didn't have to. Instead she changed her body to bright golden light. It felt amazing. The anxiety that had pierced her when she was invisible was completely absent. Unlike the dim, artificially lit outer office she could hide her own brightness in the light of the window, and did so. When the security guards came running in, the patch of sunlight behind the Mayor was maybe a little brighter than it should have been, but who would notice that?

Luka was confident that even should they check the security feed they would see nothing. Even if they had people watching live they would have not seen her. The Agency had people whose power lent itself to interfacing with technology and they were running interference. She had never heard of such a bloodline and was going to request their files from Dayida as soon as she saw the other woman again. They were still wary of one another but they had found common ground and were slowly becoming something like friends.

Hettie was much more terrifying. The woman looked at Luka as if she were someone that Hettie had not yet decided should be allowed to live. Luka was over forty years old and had been through her own travels and tight scrapes. She did not fear much but Hettie Jayl was no one to play with. Hettie was convinced that the Organization had betrayed her and though Luka had not been with them at the time she could see that Hettie painted them all with the same brush. The things Hettie had done while part of the Organization had been legendary, and the rumors of what she'd been up to over the last two decades? If even half of them were true, she was an extraordinary Blooded and a vicious enemy.

Once security had searched the office, and the Mayor was getting sidelong looks he definitely did not enjoy, he dismissed them. Luka waited another few minutes before she floated out of the patch of sun behind the Mayor. His eyes went wide as her bright form moved in front of his eyes. She made herself flesh again.

"Can we not do that again, Mr. Mayor? It will just be more annoying and your staff will start to think that you've lost it. Can't afford that rumor in an election year, can you?"

She watched him move his hand away from the security alert button.

"Thank you."

"How did you do that?" He asked shakily.

"As I was saying, there is another world that is invading." She gave him the general spiel, people descended with powers and enemies in the other world. She refused to get into a philosophical discussion with the man.

It took Luka over an hour to talk the Mayor down from his panic attack and another hour to get him to stop asking inane questions and focus on the matter at hand. Once he was finally working with her, she had to admit he was not completely inadequate. If . . . no, *when* she survived this, she would force the Organization to revamp its rules for contact and cooperation at the local-government level.

They sat and worked out the details of an alliance to keep their small section of this world safe.

# ZAHA

Zaha felt guilty, but it swiftly passed. They had all promised that they would help her find Carlie, but so far there had been nothing. So she was borrowing some things to see if she could find out on her own. She had listened to all the office talk. She knew that most of the Suits were born with powers. Zaha also knew that wasn't the only power there was. Some of the Suits weren't born special at all, which had surprised both the younger and older Jayls, as much as herself.

One of the Suits, his surname was Botha, though she forgot his given name, had explained that he was of no bloodline whatsoever.

When the older Jayl had incredulously inquired as to what he did for the Agency, he had explained that he was an excellent scrier. Hettie had seemed to understand, though she still watched him with surprise on her face. The younger Jayl, however, asked for an explanation and Zaha got one as well. There were rituals that many could tap into with the right equations, will, and perseverance. Her plan had started to form then.

Finding the Agency library had been easy and sneaking a book out hadn't been as difficult as she imagined. Zaha was fairly sure they would have just let her borrow it but she didn't want to have to explain. She understood that her friend was not a priority for them because of everything going on. They were mourning those they lost, but they also moved on quickly, refilling teams and partnerships immediately. Zaha felt like she was seeing what war did to people emotionally and she was more scared of that than the war itself.

Zaha's intentions were pure and she would be forgiven, of that she had no doubt. So why was she breathing so fast? She did her best to calm her mind and look down at the book. The title, *Of Things Forgotten, People Lost and Names Remembered,* seemed very promising. She flipped through until she found a page titled "To Call a Missing Loved One".

She read the description and then the method. It was supposed to reach out and connect you with someone that you hadn't seen or heard from in a while. It was perfect. According to the book it would compel the person to contact Zaha as soon as possible through the most direct means available.

The math was not simple but once she pulled a piece of chalk from her art kit and began to mark the equations onto the hardwood floor she flew through them. Her focus in college was cultural history but she was no slouch in math. When she had the final equation, she chalked it out in a circle, placed a candle in the exact center and lit it. The candle flame went yellow and then black and then disappeared.

She waited. When half an hour had passed she went to recheck her math. Then she recast it and waited another half hour. The changing of the flame color meant Carlie was alive but it refused to trace her location and Zaha could not figure out why. Zaha took a deep breath to hold back the scream she wanted to unleash. She refused to give up. She decided to try another of the rituals; equations; spells—whatever they were called.

She found one called "To Find a Thing Hidden", and the calculations weren't nearly as difficult, which gave her some hope. She had to give a time for the moment she had first "gained" the item, and she hesitated. When had they had first met? The first day of third grade. Or should she use the first time she had considered Carlie her friend? End of third grade, when Carlie beat up Joanna MacNair for starting rumors about Zaha. She chose the first time she laid eyes on Carlie. The other requested information was simple. How old was the object? Twenty years and one months. Where was the item last seen? The Embarcadero mall. What was the location to search? She figured Carlie was most likely still in San Francisco proper but she still expanded the radius of the search to include Oakland and some of the peninsula and north bay. Just in case.

She lit the candle one more time. Carlie's name was still visible written along the edge. The flame burned with the same golden hue as before. As she held the final equation, written on a small square of cloth, directly above the flame, its color shifted from golden to something brighter: a silver. The flame detached from the wick and floated up to her fingers, consuming the cloth without burning her. It then flared to white and floated over to the map that Zaha had laid on the floor. Slowly it circled until it landed and burned a tiny pinprick hole in the map before disappearing.

Zaha hurried over to the map and looked at the location burned into it. The house was only a mile or so away; walkable, but Zaha was in no mood to deal with the catcalls and yells about her headscarf that would plague her. She took her car.

She pulled into the driveway of an ordinary-looking house and stepped out of the car, after double-checking she had the right address. Zaha should really be calling this in, telling someone like Tae or one of the Jayls. They would probably be mad about the things she had done, yeah. But they wouldn't just leave Carlie in there. She didn't think.

But then what if she had already tipped off whoever had Carlie? What if right now they were planning to move her somewhere completely different? Somewhere more protected? Somewhere Zaha would never find her again?

Zaha was still biting her lips in indecision when she felt the shiver of someone watching her run up her back. She turned slowly and saw someone peeking from behind one of the trees in the yard. Once the person saw Zaha looking in their direction they moved out of the shadows. Zaha caught her breath, getting ready to run if necessary.

It was the young girl, Melinda.

"Melinda, what are you doing here?" Zaha asked.

"I'm not really here." The look in her eyes was detached, spaced out.

"What do you mean?" Zaha took a step back toward her car.

"You should leave this place." Melinda looked around. "I wanted to help but Patrah says I'm too young. So I went to bed. I dreamed. I asked the dreaming if anyone needed help and it brought me here. But we should leave."

Zaha got the gist of what she was saying. Zaha knew that Melinda and Patrah's abilities centered on sleep and dreaming. She was still trying to reconcile these people with her faith. She was not devout, had not been to a mosque since she was fifteen, but she did believe. Tae was easiest to deal with. Most holy work featured seers of some kind. He had suggested talking to Patrah about it but the others disturbed her more; even the child currently looking at her expectantly. Zaha answered her. "I can't leave. I'm looking for someone."

"Are you?" Melinda looked at her. "Who?"

"A friend who disappeared."

The young girl looked at her for a long moment and then seemed to come to a decision. She nodded and strode up to Zaha, looking at the building.

"Let's go then."

"You're coming with me?" Zaha asked, surprised and nervous.

"Yes. We don't leave friends behind. Ever," Melinda answered, some of the soft blankness leaving her face.

"That is very sweet of you, but you're young and I don't want to endanger you."

Melinda's eyes flashed and suddenly they were the eyes of an old woman, not a young girl. "Do not patronize me. You are much more likely to die here tonight than I am."

Zaha swallowed at that. She felt the truth in what the girl said. She was more likely to die tonight than the girl who wielded powers she didn't understand.

Melinda knocked on the door. "Hello. Anyone home?"

Zaha caught her breath and grabbed the little girl's arm. "What are you doing?"

The girl looked at her serenely. "Seeing if anybody will come open the door. Unless you had another plan."

"Well I didn't think announcing our presence to them would be the smartest plan," Zaha hissed.

"They already know we're here." The matter of fact tone sent chills down Zaha's spine. "If they haven't come out to greet us yet it's because they want us inside. If that's the case they might as well polite about it and unlock the door."

They waited but there was no answer from inside.

Melinda shrugged her shoulders and stepped through the door.

"What in the hell?" Zaha did not curse often, but this felt more than deserving of the opportunity. The door then unlocked and swung open. Melinda smiled at her from the other side.

"It doesn't look like anyone lives here."

Zaha took a step inside and had to agree. The rooms were empty and covered in dust as if no one had ever walked across the floor.

"There's someone nearby though. They're dreaming dark futures. I can feel it."

Zaha stared at the girl but decided not to question the pronouncement.

"Anyone awake?" She asked instead.

Melinda shrugged and pointed at a door in the wall. "The dreamer is down there, though."

Zaha crept forward, alert for any sounds, and opened the door, revealing a set of dark wooden stairs leading down.

"Of course it's a creepy basement. What other choice would there be?" Zaha said out loud. She could hear the hint of hysteria in her own voice. She stood on the top step gathering her courage.

*Zaha*

The voice drifted up from the darkness and immediately scattered all her courage to the wind. She stood frozen as the voice called again.

*Zaha*

It sounded like Carlie.

"That's not creepy at all," Zaha finally whispered.

*Help*

Zaha finally understood the actions of so many of those stupid people in horror movies, because, even though she was ninety-five percent sure it was a trap, there was that five percent doubt that squirmed around in her brain. She could not turn away if Carlie needed her.

"What do you think?" She turned to ask the suddenly silent little girl, but Melinda had disappeared.

Zaha reached for her phone. She would call Tae and tell him, but when she pulled out her phone, it remained dark, no matter how hard she tapped at the screen or its buttons.

*Please*

The voice drifted up again and Zaha swallowed her fear and put her foot on the next step. She descended slowly, ready to run back up the stairs if something came at her. When she turned the bend in the stairs she saw the dim basement laid out in front of her. It was as bare as the rest of the house, with no furniture or sign of habitation. There was a water heater in the corner covered in cobwebs, and a washer and dryer that looked like they belonged in the 1980s.

And Carlie lying statue-still on the floor, wrapped in a thin, gossamer layer of darkness.

"Carlie," Zaha whispered softly, hurrying down the final steps.

Carlie's mouth opened and closed as Zaha stepped closer. Carlie was struggling for breath, trying to speak, and the darkness that covered her body writhed and swirled like a living thing. Finally, Carlie's eyes shot open and her head turned to look at Zaha. Tears gathered in her eyes and her lips parted. The darkness exploded from Carlie's mouth in ropes thick as Zaha's wrist, forcing the mouth so wide it looked like it might split at the corners. Zaha tried to flee up the stairs but it was too late. She felt the darkness wrap around her ankle. The same aching cold she remembered from the mall shocked through her body.

She fell to the ground, hitting her chin on the last step. There was nothing to hold onto and her nails scratched furrows in the floor as she was pulled closer to the darkness. She screamed and heard the thunder of footsteps on the stairs above. She looked up and saw Patrah and Tae come running through the door above her armed with large knives.

"Help!" She reached out for them.

They hurried down the stairs and Patrah immediately struck out, her knife cutting through the tendril holding Zaha. Zaha was able to scrambled to her feet and rush over to the stairs, where she turned and watched as they sliced through the tendrils, one after another.

She knew what was coming. She knew it. Still, she watched as the knife severed Carlie's neck. Zaha's breath was caught in her chest and it felt like everything was going black around her, but she was denied the comfort of unconsciousness. Like the reports she had read of the mall, without the anchor, the darkness faded away. Patrah and Tae turned to look at Zaha. Tae moved to block her direct line-of-sight to the body. It did nothing to help, but she appreciated the gesture.

"Go upstairs. Wait for us. We'll be there soon," Tae said.

She stumbled up the stairs and out the door, where Melinda restlessly moved from foot to foot. When she saw Zaha she walked forward and threw her small arms around Zaha.

"I'm sorry. I left to go get them and then I had to bring us all through the dreaming and it took longer than I thought. I'm sorry."

Zaha finally embraced her back.

"It's not your fault. Thank you for bringing help," Zaha said, looking around. Except it now seemed she could not stop seeing the now headless corpse of her Carlie no matter where she looked.

Yes. Help.

# ZEBUB

# MATTHIAS

Matthias took off after Byron, ignoring the yells behind him. This had been a long time in coming and he could not wait—not when his prey was in sight. Perhaps later he would blame it on the way the power had started burning and bubbling in his blood as soon as he'd caught a glimpse of Byron: the thrill of the hunt.

Matthias pushed himself faster and skidded around a corner. A sword swung out at neck height and Matthias bent backward just in time to go under the blade. He saw the room he had entered was filled with weaponry that was randomly shooting between the shelves, rearranging itself and causing a danger for anyone who wanted to cross. Byron was bending and twisting his way through the room. Matthias watched closely. He was sure that the weapons were somehow slowing as they got closer to the other man's body.

Matthias pulled more power through his body and world around him snapped into black and white, all the movement in the room immediately known to him. He moved quickly, darting and dodging, and reached the end not that far behind his quarry. The next hall was a straightaway and he pushed himself, getting closer to Byron as he turned another corner, around which was another door. Matthias went through it, and saw Byron moving towards an exit on the far side of the room. Even as Matthias took a step forward he knew he had made an error. He could feel the stone sinking underneath his feet.

"Great. Now I'm in Indiana Jones," Matthias muttered as stones fell from the walls and the room began to fill with sand. He slowed his forward progress and looked back at the door behind him. It was closing slow enough that he could make it, but Byron would also make it through the far door. Who knew how long it would be until they found him in this labyrinth?

"The hell you say!" Matthias yelled, making a decision, then reaching into the front pocket of his cargo pants and pulling out a small ball of twine. He threw it at Byron and watched it expand into a full net that took Byron across the legs and dropped him to the floor.

"You piece of shit!" Byron yelled, twisting to tear at the net on his legs. He got free just as Matthias came into range.

"Believe it or not, Matthias, I am sorry for all I put you through. But it was necessary," Byron explained as he circled.

Matthias was silent, taking in his opponent's body language.

"We had to be here right now. At this time. It was meant to be."

"Stop spewing bullshit. You're no Seer," Matthias growled out and struck, catching Byron with a glancing blow to his cheek.

The serious expression dropped from Byron's face as he dodged and came up sporting a wicked smile. "It was worth a try, right?"

Matthias just sprang at him. Byron tried to come under him but Matthias was a hunter and he would not be tricked by his prey. He came down on Byron with his full body, slamming him into the ground with all his weight.

Matthias straddled Bryon and pulled his head up by his collar before punching him.

"That was for Ruth," Matthias said.

Byron moved out of the way of the second punch and bucked Matthias off of him. He scrambled to his feet and spat blood into the sand.

"Now, Matthias. You know as well as I do that Ruth abhorred violence. Not a very loving tribute, eh?" Byron smirked, revealing pink, blood-stained teeth.

Matthias dove forward. His hands went for Byron's throat. "You don't get to say her name!" Before he could connect, Byron caught him with an elbow in the chest and pushed him off trajectory.

"I knew her better than you ever could," Byron hissed, moving forward.

Matthias dropped and caught Byron's legs with his own. He wrestled until he was on top and got his hands around Byron's throat. Byron looked deep into his eyes and Matthias's hands started to loosen before he could fight off the charm.

Byron slid from underneath him and stood.

"Snake." Matthias jumped to his feet.

"So, what you really thought about myself and Ruth finally comes out," Byron replied.

"Don't ever compare yourself to Ruth. She used her power to help people, not manipulate them and hurt them!" Matthias feinted left and kicked right.

"Is that what you think? That Ruth didn't reach into minds and make people love her, slowly but surely? Maybe that's why you're still mad about it. You did get attached to her awfully quick, didn't you?"

Byron laughed and turned so Matthias's kick hit his shoulder and countered with a kicked at Matthias's crotch. Matthias moved to the side easily.

"Really? You're gonna go there?" Matthias asked.

Byron smiled. "If you're not using it with me anymore, why should your new boy enjoy it?"

Matthias went to sweep Byron's legs out from underneath him and noticed that the sand was now above their ankles in some places and growing higher quickly.

"Yes. Maybe you want to pay attention to the fact that we have maybe five minutes until we both die in here," Byron said, following his gaze.

"Yeah, I noticed," Matthias growled at the man. He turned his senses to the room around him, taking in the stones that made up the walls. There was a small round one by the exit that was not the same as the others. A different composition. He moved over to it as fast as he could with sand now up to his knees and pressed it. It sunk into the wall, followed by a grinding sound as the sand slowly stopped falling from the walls to the floor. Matthias was winded by the fight and having to move through the sand. He watched Byron fall down exhausted. Byron was well-trained but his powers did nothing for him physically, unlike Matthias's own.

"So do we keep trying to kill each other right now, or wait until we're rested? Maybe wait to be rescued? How do you vote?" Byron laughed.

Matthias didn't say anything; just watched him, looking for glimpses of the boy he had once cared about in the monster he had become.

"You always were a dreamer, Matthias, dreaming of a better world. Dreaming that people were good. But you never were much for action."

Matthias looked pointedly at the bruises on Byron's face. He lowered himself against the wall and sat. "I wouldn't say that's still the case, would you?"

"I guess not," Byron said, touching his face lightly.

Matthias caught movement in the corner of his eye. Something humping its way under the sand, moving fairly fast toward them. "We're not alone." He whispered and rose to his feet.

"On your feet, unless you want to meet whatever it is in its own environment, so it can burrow into you through your ass," Matthias shouted, eyes never leaving the movement.

Byron leaped to his feet.

"What lovely imagery."

"It got your lazy ass up, didn't it?" Matthias asked.

It came straight for them and they both dived to the side, watching it disappear when it hit the wall.

"Maybe it hit the wall and died?" Byron asked.

"You are entirely too hopeful. When did that happen?" Matthias asked.

Byron went quiet and Matthias heard the sound of it behind them. He turned in time to see it rear up out of the sand. It was long and thick like an anaconda, but mottled brown, and lining each side were a hundred legs that ended in flippers that pushed it through the sand. It struck forward and Matthias moved, knocking Byron out of its way. The thing dived into the sand again but Matthias was already on his feet and jumping towards it. He landed heels down on its back and its head reared out of the sand in front of him.

He whipped his hands around the neck, avoiding the fangs that were snapping in the air.

"Look out!" He heard the warning and rolled to the side, hearing the sound of tearing flesh but not feeling the pain yet.

Warm wetness fell onto Matthias side and he pulled harder, leaning farther back until the creature's spine finally snapped under his hands. He waited even longer, until it had stopped moving before he finally let it flop from his arms. Matthias started patting down his body for a wound until he heard the stuttering of breath from Byron behind his back. He knew the sound of death. He turned and saw Byron gasping on the ground. The inside of his thigh was a mess of blood and muscle, quickly turning the sand below him into a swamp. The tail end of the creature had ripped open his thigh and his femoral artery.

Watching his first best-friend-turned-greatest-enemy bleed out in front of him was more affecting than Matthias had expected. Not enough to take Byron in his arms, but enough to sit beside him on the sand.

"Wouldn't have given you the warning if I knew it was going to lead to this," Byron frowned. Matthias could see the lie in his face.

"Why save me?" Matthias asked quietly.

Byron shrugged. "Seemed like the thing to do."

Matthias had no response.

"At least we did right by you," Byron suddenly said.

"What the hell are you talking about? This hardly makes up for all the problems you caused me. All the things you did," Matthias said with a bitter tone.

"You got out of the Organization. That was all Ruth and I really wanted for you," Byron gasped, eyes going unfocused.

"You're not making any sense, Byron," Matthias replied.

"It's a shame. It would have been so beautiful. I would have made this world so great. It would have been a golden age for us all and you stopped it before—" He stopped speaking and went still. Matthias sat there looking at the corpse of the first boy he had ever loved. There was no satisfaction in his belly. There was no feeling of completeness. Just a hollowness in his chest where he thought he might have once felt something.

# MIN

Min was not happy. She had just been reunited with her sister and now Lil was gone again. At least this time she knew Lil was somewhere close. She sat quietly with Davi while Arel and Jagi asked Razel questions about what had happened in the Rulig Courts while they were gone. It wasn't long before other 'dants started to show up. Some were carrying bags with them, but most came with nothing but the clothes on their back. A lot of them paused when they saw Arel and Jagi, but Razel and the others urged them to come inside. The older 'dant Uchel was very good at calming anyone who was panicked.

The conversation around them got much louder and Min started to pay attention to what the 'dants were talking about. She listened harder and started to shake.

Arel must have noticed because he leaned over to her. "What is wrong, pup?"

"Is this world going to end?" Arel and Jagi shared a look over their heads and then looked back at them.

Davi was staring at them all. She didn't know if he could understand the idea of their whole world ending. Min wasn't even sure it made sense to her, but it scared her.

"Lil will save us," Jagi said with confidence.

"But how?" Davi asked.

"What did your sib say to you when you first came to the Ruling Courts?" Jagi asked them.

"That she would take care of us," Min answered.

"And hasn't she done that?" Arel asked in turn.

"Yes," Davi answered.

"Then trust that she will continue to do that," Arel whispered.

They were quiet until Davi leaned his head against Min's side and looking at the two Antes asked, "Can you tell us a story?"

Min was too old for a story, but she listened anyway as Arel and Jagi took turns telling them about a young girl called Mbande of the Swamps who lived in a different world and ended up ruling it. It did a good job of taking her mind off of what she had learned.

Eventually she must have fallen asleep, because the next thing Min knew, it was only her and Davi, and Arel and Jagi were not there. They were surrounded by 'dants, with everyone jostling for space. That must have been what woke her up. She was nervous without Arel and Jagi nearby but trusted they were close.

"Hello, young one, you are Liliana's sibling." The voice was like music and she looked up at the most beautiful Ante she had ever seen. She remembered him vaguely from the fight in Lil's room. She looked at its clear skin filled with lights that moved and exploded. She heard Davi gasp next to her.

"You look all sparkly, Mister," her little brother said wonderingly.

The Ante winced.

"Please call me June, not mister. I'm a they, not a he."

Min saw Davi put his hand in his mouth. "Sorry," he mumbled.

June smiled. "It's alright. Now you know."

They both nodded.

"I remember you," Min said. "You were there when this happened." She held up her arm.

"Yes, I was. I am sorry I could not help your sib more then."

Before Min could say anything else a familiar pair of hands dropped onto her shoulders. She leaned her head back and saw Arel behind her and Jagi picking up Davi and settling him in his lap.

"June," Arel and Jagi greeted at the same time. "We are glad you got the message," Arel continued.

"Arel. Jagi." June nodded at both. "I have some contacts who passed the warning on. I passed it to every House of the Madame in Corpiliu. All the ones in Zebub at least have closed and evacuated everyone here. It is good to see you both whole and healthy."

"We have you to thank for that. The Houses of the Madame offered us shelter when we needed it. You have our thanks," Jagi said.

June shrugged and smiled sadly. "Only doing my part."

"We thank you anyway," Arel said.

"You are very welcome." June looked over their shoulders. "I believe I see some others from my House. I would like to greet them. We shall speak again."

Without waiting for a reply June began to push their way through the crowd. They all watched June go, shoulders drooped, lights dimmed.

"June looks sad," Min whispered to Arel and he nodded back at her.

"Yes. They've always wanted to change the world. To make it a better place. I think those will be the ones who take this ending the hardest. They will have to start all over again, learning a whole new way of life, and all they will have to remember of the old is that they did not change it in time to make any difference," Arel said quietly.

"That is all many of us will have to remember," Jagi added.

They watched more 'dants arrive, and eventually they started to spill onto the stairs and down the halls. Any time 'dants seemed to be getting close to breaking the boundary that Lil laid down, Arel or Jagi left Min and Davi behind and went to remind them that it was for their own safety.

Min saw a few Antes in the crowd here and there. Most were like Arel, Jagi, and June—shaped like 'dants just with different skin or faces or a few too many limbs.

She asked Jagi why this was.

"Well, you see, pup, a lot of the Antes that don't look like 'dants look down on us and think we are lesser. So you're bound to find more of our kind speaking with 'dants or listening to their warnings. Some probably belong to the revolution. Others might just have friends among the 'dants."

At one point when both Arel and Jagi were gone, a group of 'dants Min's age surrounded them. Min had not seen any other children since the night her parents had died. She looked at them and thought they looked strange. Their eyes moved to and fro quickly, following any movement. She looked over at Davi and her sib also watched them with a wary expression on his face, hand already in his mouth.

"What's with your arm?" One of them said, pointing at Min's gloved arm. Min unfolded it in front of them. It cracked, and a layer of frost fell off; a sign of how nervous she was.

"I lost mine and my sibling made this for me."

"What does it look like? Take off the glove."

A second child piped up and reached forward to do so. He pulled at the hem of her glove and his fingertip made contact with her arm. The little 'dant began to scream. He pulled his hand away but Min could feel where some of the skin was now stuck to her. He cried and ran into the crowd.

Min narrowed her eyes at the other children and they all ran off quickly.

"That was not polite, Min," Jagi said as both Antes reappeared.

"Neither was touching me without my permission," Min replied.

"She is right," Arel said.

"Will you tell us another story?" Davi asked, pulling Jagi's leg until he sat down, at which point Davi crawled back into his lap.

Arel sat down too and lifted Min to sit between them. Min leaned against him and looked down at her gloved fist, clenching and unclenching it as Jagi told them stories about the worlds that drifted too close to one another and the people who crossed over.

# ERIK

Erik started after Matthias but a hand gripped his wrist, stopping him. He turned and looked into Lil's eyes. She shook her head and pulled once hard on his wrist before letting go. The branch that spoke for her twisted in front of him.

**WeWillClaimHimOnOurWay**
**AllPathsAreOnePathHere.**

Erik grumbled but nodded. The branch settled back around Lil's wrist. Erik wanted to ask if it was spelling words in English because of him or if the written language of Zebub was English. He looked at the books they passed as they moved on. Many had titles in English but they were outnumbered by the titles in other languages. Some he recognized like Spanish, Chinese, Greek, Amharic, but there were others that looked like nothing he'd ever seen before. Were they just Earth languages he was unfamiliar with or native languages of this world?

Erik's thoughts stuttered when he realized that, for the first time since they had arrived in Zebub, he was not in pain. He lifted his hands to his temples. The low-level migraine was gone. The shadows moving in the corners of his vision, and the whispers too low for him to hear; they were all gone. Even his physical pains seemed to be healed completely. They reached a fork in the hall and, seeing footsteps in the dust headed in one direction, Erik turned to follow where Matthias had gone. Again, Lil grabbed his wrist and pulled him in the other direction.

He somehow knew that she was right; the way that Matthias

went was not the way they should go. Something called to him like magnetic north.

They walked in silence for a while, Lil disarming rooms as they moved through, pointing out the traps both physical and mystical.

**ThereWillBeThreeTests.**

"Why three?" Erik asked.

**ThreeIsAPowerfulNumberItHasBeenSo**
**InAlmostEveryCivilizationItRepresents**
**BodyMindAndSoulTheyWillTestEach.**

"Not to question this whole thing, but it feels like the sort of thing you should be doing on your own?" Erik asked.

**IfTheseWereTheTestsOf**
**TheAthenaeumYouWouldBeCorrect**
**ThereWillBeTestsFromKandakeThatIWillFaceOnMyOwn**
**TheseAreFalseTestsMeantToKeepKandakeChained**
**ThereAreNoSuchRulesWhenFightingInjustice.**

Erik was silent for a moment.

"This woman who you met. The one who said this world was made of her? Can you describe her?" He asked.

**SheWasStrengthAndPowerEvenInSpiritItWasClear**
**SheHadBeenDifficultToTakeDownAndEvenWith**
**WhatTheyDidToHerBodyTheyDidNotDefeatHer.**

"Did she tell you a name?" Erik asked.

**NoSheDidNot.**
**ButICallHerTheDantBeneathOurFeet.**

Erik nodded. Was it Bia? If they had taken her and twisted her into this world, then perhaps that somehow explained all the pain he had been experiencing since arriving? They reached a dead end. Normally Erik would suggest they backtrack, but he could feel that this was the right way. The way they were meant to go. Lil stepped forward and placed her hand on the wall and it split apart.

Sand spilled out on their feet as it opened. Lil took a step inside, struggling to climb the unstable sand. She paused just inside the door and Erik had to squeeze around her to see what she was looking at.

Matthias sat next to Byron's corpse. For a long time, Matthias did not acknowledge them, though he had to have heard the door opening and their entrance. He simply stared down at the corpse of the man next to him. They all looked at Byron's body but no one asked questions or mentioned the dried tears on Matthias's cheeks.

Lil did not try to communicate with them, and stood still until Matthias finally looked up smiling.

He stood. "It took you all long enough." The smile on his face was a broken thing, missing the joy that usually cascaded from it.

"Maybe you shouldn't just go off running when you see someone," Erik quipped, but he could muster none of his usual sarcasm.

They were interrupted by the grinding of stone and looked up to see Lil gesturing impatiently at the opposite door, which had started to close again. The three of them hurried to it and headed through. They walked in silence for a long time, though Erik did reach over and place his hand on Matthias shoulder, squeezing it once. Matthias's own hand came up and gripped his. They walked like this, hand in hand, down yet another hallway, until suddenly they crossed over . . . to someplace else.

He did not know how to explain it but Erik felt it all over his body. They were not in the building of Kandake anymore. They were elsewhere. Erik inhaled the sharp copper smell of the air. The feeling in the room was familiar; it was the same buzz and softness that overlaid his mind when Erik called his power up.

**CarefulWeAreNowNearTheHeartNothing YouSeeCanBeTrusted.**

He did not need the warning. Anyone with sense could tell that this was not an area to take lightly. He kept silent and his hand in Matthias's.

# LIL

The rooms were suddenly much plainer and the shelves on the walls held crumbling scrolls more than bound books. Dust was thick on everything, as if no one had been this way in centuries. It was larger than the other rooms. Twists and turns within its four extremely tall walls turned it into a maze. Lil had no idea what kind of tests Mayer had layered in here, so she crept forward carefully.

The only reason she knew the type of tests was because of what the 'dant beneath our feet had said. They turned to the right were immediately forced left by the curve of the wall. They found themselves in a small alcove created by the winding walls. It was lit up like it was on fire. Long vines of light bulbs blazed from every inch of the wall and curled around dozens of shelves stacked with small stone disks. What drew Lil's eyes, though, was the pile of junk pushed into an unaccountably dim corner. Lil took a small step closer, leaning in. She was able to make out certain shapes, and gasped.

"Jesus wept." Erik exclaimed.

Lil did not understand the expression, but she felt, and agreed with the sentiment behind it. Piled in the center of the room were the pieces of her body that had been removed. It made a very small pile, to be sure. A few fingers and toes and some small, indistinguishable chunks of flesh. She knew exactly where each piece was torn from, though, because every night she ran her hands over her body, relearning what was hers, and what they had taken from her.

"Jesus? Really?" Matthias asked.

The conversation faded into the background for her as she moved closer. Her hand went out, reaching for her tongue, which stood atop the pile, a foul flag pole. Before she closed her fingers around it, Lil noticed the writing around the edge of the pile.

"What does it say?" The voice startled her but Erik and Matthias had come up on either side and were looking down with her. The text was in one of the more obscure power languages, a mix of Eastern Muria and Atlani.

Her branch spelled it out for them.

**WhatYouTakeIsWhatYouLose.**

"Well, that sounds ominous as fuck," Erik stated.

Lil knew this was a test of Mayer's, but she longed for her tongue back. Once she had the piece, she was sure that she could make use of power to reattach it. She could speak again. She could cast Babel. *I could be useful again.*

That thought stopped her cold. Where had it come from? She been useful this whole time.

She had helped to defeat the first Maasu she'd encountered. She had talked to the 'dant under our feet. She had found her sibs and reclaimed them.

She would claim Kandake as well.

Her worth was not in her body alone but in the mind that drove her. Lil wished that, with that revelation, all her yearning for the pile of things they had taken would have left her, but that wasn't true. She still wanted it badly, but she could see past it now.

She still wondered if she could fight off whatever curse or spell Mayer had lain on her pieces but she knew the cost would be much too high. Even if the cost was just a delay in the time it took them to get back to the people they'd left behind. Lil closed her eyes and turned with a slow step and moved past the pile. With every step away, the desire to turn back decreased, and when she finally allowed herself to glance back, she saw the pile was now nothing but a mass of rotting offal, heaving and pulsating as if it lived and breathed.

"I'm gonna say it was a good thing that none of us tried to touch that thing," Erik stated.

Lil nodded and moved around another corner of the maze, suddenly finding herself in an apartment that was very familiar. Lil bit at her lips, feeling them bruise with the pressure. Her parents' old apartment. She could feel it coming, like a shiver up her spine.

"What are you doing here, Lil?" The voices spoke in unison and Lil saw Erik and Matthias turn to face those who had spoken. She stayed still.

"Who are they?" Erik asked.

**MyParents.**

Lil answered without looking. When she could bring herself to turn they were not dead or decaying as she had feared. They simply stood there wearing the same nightclothes they had had on when they died.

"You couldn't even save us but you think you can save this world?" They asked, their voices melding together again.

The expression on their faces was something she had gotten used to long ago: a mix of wariness and disgust. She had first seen it when she was only six cycles, but it still cut through her every time she saw it again, making her feel like a young, helpless child.

"You should've known you were never a worthy member of this family, let alone worthy of holding an Athenaeum," Lil's mother said, frowning at her.

Her father put his arm around her mother and pulled her close, looking at Lil in reproach. "We've never liked you, remember?"

Suddenly she was looking down at the scene outside of Kandake when she had been given to Mayer. Her six-cycle self clinging with stubborn determination to her father's leg and screaming as her parents pried her off.

Mayer stepped forward, touched her young self on the forehead. Lil saw her six-cycle self go slack and obedient. She remembered this, remembered screaming in her head, trying to fight off the control that snaked through her tiny body. Lil's younger self followed him into the Athenaeum. It was the last time she had seen her parents for three cycles, until Min's birth.

The vision did not follow Mayer and the little 'dant inside, though. It stayed out with her parents as smiles crept across their faces and they held each other tighter.

"We're finally free of her," her father whispered.

"Free to make children we can actually love," her mother replied.

And that was the detail that broke through the haze of pain that Lil floated in. It was what she had always imagined her parents said after she was taken away.

Exactly. Down to the intonation.

The world around her was changing again, no doubt to another scene built to convince her that her parents had never wanted her. Lil did not look. She closed her eyes and began to think it through. If the last one was body, then this one must be the test of the mind. Her parents were dead, so Mayer could not be using their memories. The trap had to be using her own mind to ensnare her. And if she was truly in her mind, then she could change it.

Lil felt the world spin again and she was in her bedroom, right before their deaths. When they had apologized and hugged her. She held on to that memory and opened her eyes to find the images of her parents smiling at her, real, genuine smiles she could barely remember. Then they were gone and she was on her hands and knees on the cold stone floor. Lil stayed there shuddering and taking in deep breaths until hands came down on her shoulders. She looked up to see Erik and Matthias looking at her in concern.

Lil had forgotten they were there but she was glad of their hands on her shoulders since it brought her back into the real world quickly. She needed to push through. She would not let others see her like this for long, even allies.

Lil rose to her feet. As soon as she gained her footing, the scene around them spun and reformed. Now they were in The Out, in the center of a small dim clearing. The grass grew to their knees and branches tangled in Matthias's hair. The dense impenetrable forest around them creaked and shuddered with wind.

"Where are we?" Matthias asked. His eyes glowed yellow in the light, the way that animal's eyes reflected light.

**TheOut.**

Except that wasn't quite right, because while The Out had some shy wildlife, this version was teeming with life. The bushes around them and the canopy above shifted with movement. Warm fur brushed past her ankles, the softness of feathers dragged across her cheeks, but she could see none of the creatures that surrounded them.

Things growled and roared and squawked all around them. Matthias's scream was more one of surprise than pain, but by the time she turned there was only rustling as he was dragged into the forest.

"What the fuck?" Erik yelled. As she turned to him she saw a blur of red and yellow shoot from the surrounding forest and tackle Erik, taking him into the trees as well. Lil ran forward hoping to catch him and bring him back, but it was too late. When she reached the place where he had disappeared, all the plants were still, as if nothing had passed through them.

Lil took a deep breath and pushed down the fear gathering in her chest. She had seen them both in action. They could take care of themselves. There was no need to worry for them. Still, she scanned the forest for any signs of them.

It was only when Lil heard the soft growl that she turned from her search. A four-legged beast was directly across from her, entering the clearing with no sound. Its fur was the yellow of aged bones. The top half of its skull was growing over its face like an obscene mask of pure, shining ivory. A bonewolf. Its eyes watched her, judged her, and found her wanting. Its head would come well above her hip and it was longer than she was tall. The fur on the body was short and she could see its muscles ripple underneath its skin.

Lil held out her hands palm-to-palm and traced them through the air, a simple Kimerical physical prayer to calm wild beasts. She finished and absolutely nothing coursed through her.

The bonewolf took another step toward her and snarled loudly. Lil swallowed and tried something else, stomping her feet in a Uka pattern that was a litany of nature's true names and that should have made anything in range accept her as kin.

Again, Lil was shocked to feel nothing, so when the bonewolf crouched and leapt for her she didn't move fast enough. The jaws closed on her shoulder and she screamed, falling backwards. Her fall pulled the bonewolf with her and its own momentum flipped it over her shoulder. She screamed again as its teeth ripped from her body.

Lil rolled and scrambled in the other direction. She got to her knees and faced the animal, which was now circling her slowly and snarling. The branch came to her hand and stiffened. She used the staff as leverage to get to her feet and waited. She did not have to wait long. The bonewolf ran across half the space between them, quick and low to the ground, and then launched itself towards her throat. She snapped the staff up between them just in time to stop the bonewolf's teeth closing on her throat but it was not strong enough to stop the creature itself. The thing clawed at her body while she struggled to push it away. One of the thorns on the staff pierced one of the bonewolf's eyes as they struggled. It yelped and backed away.

Lil knew it would attack again and she would likely die when it did. None of her power worked here. What chance did she have against this monster who wanted her dead? And it did want her dead, but not just dead; in pain. She could read the intention in the air. This was no predator hunting to feed itself or its family. This was pain and death and revenge. It would kill her and it would relish every moment of the kill.

Lil watched it circle ever closer and thought of never returning to her sibs. She thought of Min and Davi waiting for a sib who would never return. She thought of them lost as the darkness closed in. She thought of Arel and Jagi and the fierceness with which they would defend her sibs; the fierceness with which they *had* defended her sibs. She thought of the way they believed in her and the way they cared for her. Sudden rage rose up in her. Not just the need to survive but the burning desire to make the thing attacking her suffer; to teach it its mistakes through pain. Even if Lil died here she wanted the thing to suffer for the rest of its days. She wanted it to remember her. Lil stared into the beast's last remaining eye as it snarled from a distance, and recognized it.

She recognized it and struggled to her feet.

The point was not to kill the predator; not to murder all that hate and lust and anger. The point was to accept it into yourself. That hate, lust, and anger? It lived in every soul. The bonewolf growled and approached. She was leaking copious amounts of blood from her shoulder and only hoped she was right because she would only be able to try this once.

This time when it leapt she moved closer, reaching to get hands up to grasp its paws. She opened her mouth wide. As soon as she had made the decision, it became easy. A simple choice. The beast's snout came into range and she snapped forward, bit down. Bone shattered under her teeth, as skin and muscle tore and blood filled her throat. She swallowed it down and kept chewing.

The bonewolf struggled to get away but now she had its taste. She knew its flavor and would not relinquish it. She pulled it into her mouth, chewing and swallowing its anger and its pain, taking all of it into herself. When she swallowed the tip of the bonewolf's tail the forest melted around her and she found herself in another room with a single door.

Erik and Matthias were by her side, both dirty and covered with scratches but they had no open wounds that she could see. She looked down at herself, covered and sticky with blood, and saw that the wound in her shoulder had healed.

"What the hell was that?" Matthias asked.

**TheTestOfSoul.**

"Okay, so that was the last one?" Erik asked.

**TheLastofMayersTests.**

She gestured to the only door in the room, with pillars on either side and every bit of its surface covered in carvings.

**YouCannotEnterThisRoom**

**ThisIsKandakesTest**

**SheShallFindMeWorthyOrNot.**

They looked at each other and nodded. Erik spoke.

"We will be here waiting for you to return after you hold Kandake."

She did not know this man, not truly, but his faith gave her hope. She reached out a hand and he grasped it in his own. She smiled at him and turned to exchange a nod with Matthias before walking through the dark doorway.

Lil walked through the door and it was gone from behind her and in front of her—Wade and Antny were staring at her. They looked exactly as they had on the night they had helped her traverse Zebub.

"Wade. Antny." She spoke without thinking. Their names got stuck in her throat but were recognizable. She started in shock and reached into her mouth, feeling her tongue. Then she looked down at her fingers. They were all there, no gaps were someone had taken digits from her. She started to plead for their forgiveness, but they would not let her.

"You left us."

"You ran."

"We died in pain."

"We died in fear."

Every word was another split across her heart.

"What can I do? How can I make it better?" Lil asked, *screamed* into the illusion of the Athenaeum that surrounded them.

"Trade your life for our own."

The request caused Lil's breath to catch and her hands flew to her chest, as if her life would abandon her right in that moment.

"And what shall you do with this life?"

"What we should have been allowed, a full life. We shall be children, we shall run and play and jump in this new world like we never have in this one."

Some of her emotion ebbed away, and she made note of the fact that they were talking about a new world.

"And how will you help in the fight that is coming?"

They were silent.

"I have sibs . . . and others I would see survive. Will you fight for them?"

Again. Silence.

"The world is harsh. Yes, I abandoned you, but I am not responsible for all the ills that befell you during your life. I am sorry for your loss, and will likely be sorry my whole life, but trading my life for yours will do nothing but cause more suffering," Lil said sadly.

Both boys took a step towards her, but they also started to melt into the ground. Lil watched as they dissolved. She did not take her eyes away, despite the way her vision went blurry. Lil had not seen Wade and Antny's first deaths. She would not dishonor their memory by turning away again.

After they were fully gone, Lil wiped her cheeks and searched the dark around her. She expected another memory to show up, another failure, but the 'dant who appeared was not one she recognized; covered in armor of black and red that pulsed and writhed across its form. Gauntlets reached up and peeled away the face covering.

It was the 'dant under our feet.

But not. Her skin and hair were lighter than the other one she had met. Also, this version was older, numerous lines of pain in her face. This was Kandake. A representation of the Athenaeum she had grown up in. Lil was intrigued and excited, even as much of her mind still thought of Wade and Antny. The pain sat in her chest like a rock.

Kandake seemed to read this in her and spoke.

*You must make choices that hurt to Hold an Athenaeum. You will feel sadness but you must always look to the bigger picture. Kandake must be chosen above all others.*

Lil didn't like that. She would always put her sibs and the others she loved above anyone else. That was not something that would ever change.

"What if the big picture entails leaving Kandake to be destroyed or abandoned?" She asked.

Lil could feel the anger of Kandake pulse around her.

*That will never be a choice you should make.*

"So I should look at the big picture and always follow it unless it involves having to sacrifice you?"

*Yes.*

"Then you do not really want someone to help others; you want someone to protect you."

*Protecting me is helping others. The knowledge, the wisdom contained in these walls will help generations to come.*

"Only if you are dedicated to helping others, no matter the cost."

*You did not give up your life for Wade and Antny.*

"True, but that was not because I felt like I was more important than them or that I deserved to live while they do not. I did so because there is too much responsibility on me and I can help more people by keeping my life."

The smugness radiated from Kandake. *Exactly.*

"But if giving up my life for Wade or Antny would help others? If they could keep my sibs safe forever? If they could save this world? Then I would give up my life readily. Can you say the same?"

There was silence which Lil hoped meant Kandake was thinking.

*You are very different from Mayer.*

The voice was quieter.

"I am. Mayer has held you in chains for many years, making sure that he lived but not fulfilling any of his promises. He has sided with the Ruling Courts. I will never do so."

*And what would you do?*

"Be a beacon in the dark. We must help others and ask for help in return. We must stand together in this if we are to survive."

*Very few of my later Holders have ever felt thus.*

"Perhaps that has been the problem. It is long past time for something new."

Kandake spoke quickly, words tumbling over one another. *This is the way it has been done for millennia—*

"And how has that gone for you?"

There was silence.

"When you require someone to put you and their duty above everything else, then that duty becomes all that matters. It is entirely too easy for people to mistake power for duty when their duty involves taking charge of powerful things."

*And if you had to make the choice between saving all this knowledge and your sibs?*

"I would find a way to save both, but if I had to choose then I would save my sibs. I love them."

*You would allow all this knowledge, books for the ages, to be destroyed?* Kandake did not sound pleased, but neither could Lil feel anger in them.

"Yes. Those who value knowledge and power above lives are the problem. Knowledge is important but knowledge can be regained and rebuilt. The pain of losing one you truly love is never really gone. It is always there and alters your world."

*I used to love and be loved. Before I was an Athenaeum.*

"You remember that?" Lil asked startled

*At times when all of Corpiliu is sleeping, which happens too rarely, pieces of us will reach out to each other, to know each other. And then I remember clearly that I was a goddess. That I strode across the land. That I had children who loved me.*

"Yes."

*You brought one of my children with you tonight. I feel him nearby. His presence clears my mind. As if his presence allows me to think more clearly.*

Lil stayed silent, unsure what Kandake meant, but not wanting to stop the Athenaeum's train of thought. Kandake looked at Lil closely; circled her and looked her up and down. Finally, she smiled.

*You are now my Holder, Liliana Blackthorn Johns. Rise and let it be known.*

Lights blinked into existence and swirled about her body. The ripped purple robes and ragged silver ribbons she was still wearing disappeared. Clothes formed around her naked body, all white, but cut similarly to the outfit that Erik had been wearing. A loose-buttoned shirt was tucked into tighter pants. Her feet were encased in shoes that felt thick and hefty. Over her shirt she wore a jacket that hung to her waist.

She looked at Kandake, who had begun to fade away.

*You will leave this place. You will go to the place where it all began. You shall take all of the pieces of my heart with you, and all those who seek its shelter. Now go. They need you.*

With a wave of Kandake's hand, Lil found herself in the front hall, watching Arel and Jagi face off against a monster as an army waited in the background.

# ERIK

Erik looked over to Matthias after Lil had disappeared through the door. He watched Matthias lean against a pillar and close his eyes. An odd feeling of lightness rose in him. He looked down to find himself drifting out of his body. He found himself strangely calm about this. He drifted up from his body, through the roof, and through the sky. With a small kick of phantom legs, Erik's perspective flopped over and he was looking down on the Athenaeum; looking down at the many enemies suddenly gathered at its doorstep. He could see Mayer and Chayyliel and Riana in the crowd, though they disappeared as he rose higher and higher. He could see hundreds of cities and the space that separated them was small but treacherous; deserts that looked baked to glass, storms of sand and lightning, and waters teeming with so many vicious animals they looked as if they were boiling. He could see the darkness. He could see it swallowing whole chunks of the land, darkening parts of cities, making this world its wormy apple.

He rose even further, the whole world becoming clear.

It was not a full planet. It looked as if someone had tried to stretch playdough over a globe, but only had enough to cover a third it. It made Erik think of skin, stretched to its limit. In some places, the skin of the world was almost transparent, and he could see the white beneath, the preserved bone that gave it its form.

The world turned, and he was facing her unfinished part.

Her?

But he could see her clearly now, curled in a ball beneath the flesh of the planet. She was twisted in a way that a yoga instructor would envy. Her face was in profile and he could see the pieces of her that were missing. The side of the face he could see was missing most of its top half. The cheek and nose had divots in it where pieces had been dug out. Only her lips were still whole.

Erik tried to drift closer, but no matter how he moved, he stayed at a distance. Then the perfect, dark lips sighed and smiled.

She whispered.

*My child.*

Erik started, which made his perspective spin in the air.

*I have waited for one of my children for so long; one of my blood, of my line.* The affection was thick in her deep echoing voice.

He tried to speak but he had no body to speak with.

*Simply think it and we shall both hear.*

"Where am I?" His own voice echoed.

*Your physical form is where it was; your mind is with me, deep in the bones of Corpiliu. I was the last to fall. I would not give up and so they killed me and used my body, piece by piece, to form Corpiliu.*

"Bia." It was no question. Erik knew this woman, down in his marrow and blood; the blood that led all the way back to her.

*I have not seen one of my physical descendants in so long. Some of my spiritual children were here for a time, pretending to be traitors to me.*

"In the war of the descendants?" He asked. He remembered all the different histories that Matthias had run him through. There was war in all of them.

*Yes. But also among the non-blooded. They stole and brought here. A few of my physical children hid among them. The Traitor Court squirreled away my heart and my Blooded children cut it into pieces and parceled it out. Each became the heart of one of the Athenaeums across this world.*

"And now this whole world is ending. What should I do?" He felt fear and sadness. The thought of his ancestor—the image of her in pain and the thought of losing her—made his thoughts feel slow and damp with grief.

*You will do what you must, as I ever did. For now, I am a shield; I have laid myself between the darkness and your world, but it eats through me and I tire. I long to join my family in death. So I pass the burden of protection to you.*

"I'm not ready yet; there's too much I need to learn. I've lost people already."

*You will never be ready; those who earn power are never ready for the burdens as well as the joys. But all of this is yours. All that Corpiliu is, is yours, because it is me and I give it to you.*

"What do you mean?"

*Take them with you. My children who suffered so. Take them with you.*

"I don't understand."

*You will when the time is right.*

He was moving away, fading back into his body, even as he struggled against it.

*You must go. The time comes. You are needed. Remember that you are my child; this world's child.*

"Wait! Once you are gone, will the darkness come to Earth?"

*Yes. You must discover how to defeat it. Speak to those who have done so already.*

Erik could no longer see her. He had zoomed back in to see Kandake still surrounded by monsters of all shapes and sizes.

"How do we destroy the darkness?" He shouted, even as he sank completely back into his flesh.

*The demiurge cannot be destroyed. It can be weakened and it can be torn and injured but it cannot be destroyed. It is the spirit of creation itself. It cannot die. There is always a demiurge.*

# SAN FRANCISCO

# MAESTRA LUKA

Luka had managed to leverage her alliance with Dayida Jayl and the Agency into enough power that she had control of most of the Organization's operations on the West Coast. She was working on spreading her influence further. As it was, she had shared their methods with other cities. Many were reluctant to seek or offer help to their local Agency offices, though many did contact the independents in their area and offer an alliance.

She was in contact with various cities in the Midwest and East that were managing to hold their own against the increased attacks—Madison, Philadelphia, Atlanta, and Weehawken among them.

The biggest disaster was Manhattan. The island was chaos. The Angelics did not have complete control by any means, but the island was burning. Whoever won would have a pyrrhic victory. The Organization had cleared out all of its people and many non-Blooded citizens via tunnels and portals the Agency knew nothing about. Dayida had managed to get some information from the Agency; they still had agents on the island, and they were holding off the Angelics as best they could.

Manhattan was a loss. The stories of monsters had mostly been called hoaxes by the mainstream media. More and more citizens were leading credence to the stories now, though. There were dozens of theories on what was happening, from biblical to zombie apocalypse. The only firsthand information coming out of Manhattan anymore was courtesy of two blogs that remained active. One had been a cooking blog dedicated to berries called

Berry Delicious, run by someone who called themselves TheBlackest-Berry. The other was a political satire blog called Tricky Dicks, run by someone calling themselves DeeperThroat.

Both bloggers had taken to reporting on where in the city was currently safe and provided enough photos of unbelievable creatures and attacks that their stories were getting more traction. It was only a matter of time before people saw past the government excuses of flu quarantine and terrorist attacks, and the shit really hit the fan.

Rumors were growing. Pictures of Blooded and Suits were starting to appear online and Luka had decided they had to do something about it.

Her visit to the Mayor's office had managed to do more help than harm. They had a liaison in place now and communication was constant. Most of *that* communication was through Dayida. They had divided communication duties between them; Dayida took care of communications within San Francisco, Oakland, and the rest of the Bay, while Luka took care of the contact with the outside world.

She looked at Dayida across her office, which had become their shared workspace.

"You know what we have to do," Luka said without preamble.

Dayida held back a sigh. To Luka's surprise, Dayida had turned out to be a crack tactician, though she claimed not to know how she had acquired the skill. She understood fighting a war not just with weapons, but with words.

"We'll organize a press conference," Luka continued.

"And say what, exactly? Monsters are real, listen to us?" Dayida raised an eyebrow.

"We'll have to prove it."

Dayida narrowed her eyes. "How?"

Luka was sure that Dayida knew how. She just wanted to force verbal confirmation from Luka.

"We'll have to show them our powers," Luka said.

"No. Not gonna happen."

Luka knew that would be her response. Dayida used her powers quite well when necessary, and even seemed to take some joy in them, but she never spoke of them and, when asked, would only stare the asker down until they apologized and scurried away. Showing the whole world her power, and then answering questions about it, would be the last thing that Dayida would want.

But Luka knew they also needed Dayida. She had a solid name in the art community, and even if she wasn't a "celebrity," some would recognize her name. Or her son's. There were others in the Organization who had larger name recognition in their public life, but none as involved in the protection of their city.

"Two brown women telling all the scared white folk in the country that there are really monsters out there, oh, and look, we have special powers that you don't have?" Dayida looked incredulous.

"We're not just talking to white people," Luka said, exasperated.

"I know, but they're the ones whose reactions I'm worried about. There will be some who will be okay and there will be those who will be terrible and both sides are going to be scared. Fear tends to bring out our prejudices faster than any other emotion."

Luka was silent. She could refute none of what Dayida was saying.

"Still, we have a duty," Luka said.

Dayida raised an eyebrow at the other woman.

"We do. I to my oaths and you to your son. We have made our promises and we must stand by them," Luka continued. "If we allow the information to continue to trickle out we will have no control over how it looks."

Dayida nodded. "But what about protection? Whoever shows their power is going to be in danger."

'That's why we'll involve no one else but the two of us. It will be easy enough to protect the two of us."

Dayida scoffed. "No, it won't be. After this? Anyone we associate with will be assumed to be Blooded as well. They will be stalked and badgered and hunted. No one the least bit different will be safe."

"How do you know this?" Luka asked.

"History," Dayida answered.

Luka did not doubt that Dayida meant her own personal history as well as the history of the world. "Still, it is better that people be aware and prepared."

"What's to stop them from turning on us? They've done it before."

Luka lowered her head and conceded the point. "Nothing. My hope is that people will focus their fear and anger on the Angelics and darkness. And once that battle is over they will see us for the allies we can be."

"You are a fool." It was said with equal parts exasperation and fondness. "But you are determined, and perhaps you'll be right in the end."

"No matter what, it is better than it coming out by accident, and you know it will eventually," Luka countered.

"Yes. I am already stressed. This is simply another worry." Dayida said it quietly.

"I know," Luka replied. All attempts to contact Zebub had gone unanswered, and the status of their people was unknown. It was horrible for all of them, but she could not imagine how Dayida was holding it together. She rarely showed any sign that one of those missing and in danger was her own son.

Luka knew that Dayida had been regularly contacting any Blooded, Suits, or Independents that she could who had any talent connected with seeing or divining. None would speak about what happened in the meetings, but seeing how tense Dayida always was afterwards. It did not take a genius to figure out she was getting no news.

Luka left her new friend to go back to her notebook. She made notes on planning the press conference. She would run everything past Dayida once she had it sketched out, but wanted to give the woman what little quiet she could.

# HU

Hu walked into the building cautiously. He could still get out of this by turning into a rat and slinking away. Yes, it would mean fighting through the real rats that called this place home but he had done that and worse before. Here and now, though, Hu had backup, and it was better to face these things with others.

Hu was a lot of things but he had never chosen another world over his own. Hu did not feel guilty for his choices. He had made the decision he thought best at the time, and what good would regret do? He was already suffering the repercussions from those choices. This was his atonement, as far as he was concerned. There was no need for self-flagellation.

Hu cautiously climbed the stairs to the room he still had paid up until the end of the week.

He had not enjoyed his sit-down interrogation after turning himself in—especially since Hettie Jayl had kept looking at him like she wanted any excuse to smear him across the floor like a bug. Hu didn't have much to give them except the truth; he thought they had been working to save the world, not dooming it.

They had all looked at him like he was an idiot, but it was much easier to identify lies in hindsight. When someone you've known forever says there is danger, you believe them. When someone you trust says you are helping, you believe it.

Hu opened the door to the small room he had been staying in, and looked inside. It was clear, and had only one place to hide: the closet. Hu slowly approached the closet next to the window. Before he could cautiously push the closet door open, he heard the thump of heavy feet behind him in the hallway. Hu dove for the window even as his body shrunk in on itself. It was a near thing, but by the time he went through the glass, he was small enough to fit through the frame. He landed among the shards of glass; small, gray, and light. Hu could feel the cuts, but it was better than whatever the things behind him were planning.

This time, instead of going down, he went up, his tiny-yet-sure feet taking him up the stairs at a quick pace. He leapt onto the roof, already changing back to human. He turned and saw the same two attackers from before right behind him. They spread apart to split his focus. He glanced back and forth between the man and woman. Both looked human, except for the snarls across their too-wide mouths and the deadness of their eyes.

Blooded Haru jumped one of the creatures from behind. She came down on the one wearing the body of the man, and pinned him to the floor. He roared and bucked beneath her but she managed to put him into a hold. Haru's bloodline was Xochipilli, the Aztec God of Games, and any games or athletics she engaged in she won, including wrestling.

Unfortunately, it looked like she could hold it down but could not get enough leverage to knock it out. Still, neither could it gain an advantage long enough to hurt Haru in any way. Before Hu could decide if he should help, the other one came for him. Hu pulled his power into his body. The brown fur itched as it pushed its way through his skin. His new body reared up to its full height and swiped at the Maasu with a claw. The thing fell back with a hiss but then lunged for him. Hu's brown bear body was not fast, and he caught the blow in the stomach. It forced him back several feet and knocked all of the air from his lungs.

Hu went with the force of it, flipping over and changing, rising as a gorilla. He reached out with one of his large fists and slammed it into the face the Maasu, who looked like an Olsen twin but punched like a freight train. She went down but was on her feet a moment later. He tried the same tactic again, but she ducked under the arm and came up on its other side, locking his arm in a hold and pulling him off balance. He struck out with his other fist and screamed as the thing sunk its teeth into his arm.

Suit Longworth came out of nowhere with something in his hand that looked like aged and blackened metal. He ran up behind the Maasu that Hu was holding off and touched the black metal to its body. The

Maasu's stolen eyes rolled up in its head and it slumped the ground, wisps of smoke coming from its ears.

Hu shifted back to human, clamping his hand over the bite mark in his other limb, which was still bleeding freely "What is that?" He asked, gesturing to the metal in Longworth's hand.

"A tool created to incapacitate Angelics except we were never able to give it a large enough power source to knock them out. So we use it mostly as a mythical taser. But Reina here . . ." Suit Longworth gestured to his back, where Reina clung, her eyes shining pure liquid gold. ". . . reminded me that she can amp up any electrical charge without overloading the containment unit, as long as she's in contact."

"One of my many useful skills," Reina said with a smirk.

Haru still struggled with the other Maasu, flipping over and over as she tried to knock him out. Longworth put a stop to it by touching the device to the Maasu the next time it flipped her over.

Haru crawled from beneath its smoking body.

"Hey, how did you know that wouldn't go through his body and fry me too?" She asked indignantly.

"Didn't," Longworth said with a shrug.

Haru's mouth dropped open and then snapped closed. They could see her gearing up for a tirade.

"Calm down, Haru. I told him I could protect you from the current," Reina said with a light laugh as she finally dropped from Longworth's back.

Haru looked at them suspiciously for a moment before she started to smile.

Hu watched them. He had been naive and made bad choices, but even he was not dense enough to ignore this. The way the Agent, Suit, and Independent joked and laughed with one another: this was the future they needed if they were to survive what was to come.

# HETTIE

The room looked more like the press conferences she'd seen in films than she expected. The seats were packed and those armed with cameras crowded the aisles. An empty table sat in front with chairs and microphones. Hettie watched from the back of the room, dressed in a simple pantsuit, with her long dreads covered in a black head wrap. She blended into the crowd and watched. While she had not been agreeable to this decision initially, but Luka had good points and they truly could contain this no longer. Better to take control of the flow of information while they could. Dayida, Luka, and the Mayor finally walked out from a small door in the back of the room.

Dayida wore a bright yellow suit that made her brown skin and dark afro glow. She was followed by the Mayor in a plain black suit and finally Luka in a black and white houndstooth dress, her hair pulled back and white tennis shoes on her feet. The Mayor brought everyone to attention as they sat down behind the microphones.

"We have called you here for a press conference of enormous importance. As you know, the President has declared a state of emergency in Manhattan, but the answers that are forthcoming about what is actually happening on the island have been less than satisfying. I firmly believe the public has a right to know what is happening, and even more than that, a right to defend themselves."

Dayida and Luka looked at the Mayor as he gestured to each of them.

"The ladies accompanying me, Ms. Luka and Ms. Jayl, explained to me what is happening, and will now do the same for you. Ms Luka?"

Luka looked out into the crowd with a small smile. "In the beginning giants walked the earth—" She went through the gist, continuing until the murmuring and protests became loud enough to drown her out. She stopped talking and stood, slowly allowing her body to become light. The room went silent, and Luka returned to flesh and her seat to finish the story.

Hettie wished she had been allowed to help with this. Already she could feel the way the energy in the room was shifting. It had nothing to do with power and everything to do with being human. Hettie had suggested they bring in charmers to help keep the crowd calm. Dayida had seemed interested but Luka had nixed the whole idea. She didn't think manipulating those they sought to save was a good first step. Hettie could see her point, but she also knew better than to trust crowd mentality.

When Luka finished, the room was silent for a moment before it exploded into questions.

"Joseph Rapid, Buzzfeels. How long have you known about this, Mayor Li?"

The Mayor leaned forward. "Only the last couple of weeks. Ms. Luka came to me and revealed the danger that the people of The City were in. We began to work together to save lives."

"But you didn't tell the public immediately?" The man continued.

"I had hoped that the federal government would do the right thing and come clean, but the recent administration change has altered their policy of sharing information."

A young black man leapt from his seat.

"Hakeem Young, Express. Are you saying the federal government is aware of this?"

"Yes. In fact, Ms. Jayl is technically in the government's employ."

Hettie saw the way Dayida's jaw clenched as she looked at the Mayor and leaned forward.

"Yes, I am temporarily helping to run a government office in San Francisco that is part of an agency—"

A man came to his feet and interrupted her. "Yakov Milo, BartBart. What makes you think you have the right to say anything if the President has chosen not to?"

Dayida leaned back and stared at the man. The silence was only broken when Mayor Li answered the question.

"Obviously no one wants to challenge the President's authority, but neither should we leave the citizens of this nation ignorant and in danger."

"Miranda Kang, San Francisco Chronicle. What are your intentions once this menace has passed?"

"Only to live our lives as we have been this whole time," Luka answered softly, which Hettie noted was a good technique. A lot of the people looked less nervous now.

"Surely you don't expect us to believe that you don't have any motives beyond that?" A man shouted from the back.

Dayida's response was soft—not sensitive like Luka's, but rather quiet in warning. "Why?"

The man stared before responding slowly. "What do you mean?"

"I mean, why is that so hard to believe? Because if you had the power you would try to rule?"

The man went red and Dayida smiled as he sat down. Another man shot to his feet. Hettie recognized him as an art critic with whom Dayida had gotten into a screaming match. Erik had relayed the story over a year ago. Hettie had looked him up and never forgotten.

"Ms. Jayl. You are a noted artist. Does your art have anything to do with your power?"

Dayida's gaze was fierce.

"No, I have only recently come into my power."

He didn't seem to be listening. "For years, critics have been in awe of your control and color choice. This would explain it."

Hettie was in awe of the pettiness before her. This man had just gotten information that changed his whole world, and yet he was taking the time to try and drag down her daughter. The look in Dayida's face was nothing but contempt.

"Or perhaps it could be explained by talent? Perhaps I am someone who has worked at their craft for years? I very much doubt you would say any of it to a male artist, no matter what the circumstances." Her voice rose through the speech, and at the last word, metal bubbled out of her shoulders and slicked down her arms, so supple it looked like shoulder-length silver gloves. Dayida looked down in surprise and quickly pulled the metal back into her body.

The man sat down quickly and the room was silent.

The Mayor looked nervous at the display of power. "Unfortunately, we must end this press conference. There is still much work to do, but we wanted to provide the following numbers and websites for the public who wants more information: www.blooded.net can be visited for stories about the Blooded and their history. For emergency help please call 1-888-999-0099. Any official information requests should go through either my office, Ms. Luka's office at 415-555-6787, or Mrs. Jayl's office at 415-555-0982."

They all walked offstage quickly to more and more questions being shouted at them. Hettie saw the men in innocuous black suits slinking out. Government. She could also feel the fear in the room and wondered when it would break free into violence.

# MELINDA

Melinda never truly slept anymore.

Her body did, but Melinda didn't. Patrah said dreamers needed to sleep more than other people; that the time they spent walking in dreams wasn't real rest. Another thing that made Melinda different. So she didn't tell Patrah that she didn't need rest. It would make Patrah give her that look again. The one that started confused before she looked away and then only looked at Melinda out of the corner of her eye.

So as soon as she lay down to sleep the night of the press conference her dreamself rose from her body. She skimmed over her moms' dreams. Melinda didn't look in—that would be an invasion of privacy—but she felt them out. She smiled. Her moms were dreaming about each other.

Melinda stepped directly from her moms' room into the dreaming. This was another thing that she didn't tell Patrah. The woman talked about jumping into people's dreams and moving from dream to dream, but she'd said nothing about stepping into the dreaming itself; the space *around* dreams.

Melinda didn't know if that was because Patrah didn't know how to do, it or because she didn't think Melinda could do it yet.

The dreaming was always around, but it grew and shrunk around her. It shifted locations as people fell in and out of sleep. The holes in the world were ever-shifting, but Melinda did not stumble as she walked. She knelt at one point and placed her hand on the continuously shifting ground. The land was agitated tonight. People were fitful and scared, drifting in and out of sleep and nightmares. She felt it.

"You're very good."

Melinda turned around fast. Five beings were gathered watching her, where no one had been moments before. One was shrouded from head to toe in loose black. The only hint Melinda had of details was the wisps of white hair that emerged from the hood. Next to them was a young black woman. Her hair hung beaded down her back and the dress she wore was a simple white with beautiful scenes embroidered in silver at the hem, neck, and sleeves. She smiled widely at Melinda, and Melinda could not stop herself from smiling in response. The man next to her looked scary; his amber skin was studded with a lot of scars and she could see so many because all he wore was a piece of red cloth around his hips and the skull of some dead animal over his face. The person next to them was taller than the rest and entirely to thin, like they were only skin stretched over boe. Black hair covered the top half of their face, their most striking feature was the thick red lips that were quirked into a half-smile. They were wrapped in a white funerary shroud. The final figure was smaller than all the rest, Melinda's size but a fully-grown adult. her skin was clear purple gemstone and the angles of her body looked sharp enough to cut.

"I was not that good when I was still new to my power," the black woman said. No one else spoke, but the person in white continued to smile their red, red smile.

"Who are all of you?" Melinda asked, watching them. She was not afraid. They could not get to her before she woke herself up. She knew she was too quick for them, but watched warily. She had never spoken to any in the dreaming itself except Patrah.

"We are the ones who came before," the black woman answered.

Melinda looked at them, confused.

"Your teacher is one of my line," she said with a smile.

"Oh." Did that mean that these were gods? Her mothers and Patrah had explained that people with power had once roamed the world and one was her great-great-great-whole-lot-more-greats grandparent.

"I thought all of you were dead?" Melinda asked, confused.

The skull-faced man shifted with a grunt, turning his back toward her. The black woman only laughed. "We are, dear, but those of us who belong to dreams have always walked between worlds, so we have more freedom than the rest of our brethren. We can still walk this place that we once knew so well. You called to us, so we came."

"I called you?" Melinda asked.

"Your power called to us." The purple woman finally spoke. Her voice was soft and echoing. "Rolling through the whole of the dreaming."

"It has been too long since one such as us walked," the red lips whispered.

"Why do you all look so different?" Melinda asked.

"We were different people. We used our power in different ways. How we use our power and how our people look at us changes how we look," the black woman explained.

The man wearing the skull was crouched down, tracing shapes in the ground with his finger. He clucked his tongue, wiped his hand over the ground, and began again.

"You can always change. You have a choice. Remember that," the red lips stated.

Melinda had no idea what that meant, but nodded like she did, and the lips curled up into a smile. The skull-faced man stood up and turned back to face them.

"The time is now." His voice was dry and cold. "Let us hope she is ready."

"The world is changing, and tonight is one of the turning points. News is spreading through the world—news of people like you, and people like your friends. News of powers that people thought were myth and legend. Fear and panic could easily take over and lead us to disaster. Unless you stop it." The black woman looked at Melinda as she spoke.

"How?" Melinda asked, nervous.

"You must take hold of their dreaming minds and blunt the panic. Gift them with calm so they may see the bigger picture more clearly." The purple woman said. She flung her long and thick hair back. The sound was like bells chiming and Melinda saw small shards of purple fall into the blue dreaming that surrounded them.

"Isn't that wrong, though?" Melinda asked. Patrah had said it was wrong to even look in people's dreams. This was far worse.

"It is wrong for your teacher to do so. In fact, she could not do it. But you are not your teacher. This domain belongs to you as it belonged to us when we were alive. It is not simply a fun place to play. It is your responsibility. Dreams are where we shed our problems and horrors. It's where we come to terms with the waking world." The black woman stepped close, and Melinda did not move back this time.

"You only see the dreaming as this blank blueness because your teacher has told you that looking at others' dreams is wrong. But you are the Mistress of Dreams now," the purple woman said, stepping up on Melinda's other side and placing a hand on her elbow. "The ability to guide those dreaming is a powerful tool. A tool that can see truths, and wishes, and hopes. Some of us have used it to help those who have been hurt. Others have used it to hurt those who have hurt others. Most of us used some combination of these two extremes. But your main responsibility remains. To *see* and to *guide.*"

Melinda felt the rightness in what they were saying. "How do I do it?" She asked quietly.

"You only need to see this place as it really is. Then you will feel it, and instinct will take over." The red lips whispered and then they were right in front of Melinda. The body bent over. Dust exploded from the white shroud. The scent of old books wafted over Melinda as the surprisingly dry lips touched her forehead.

The world of blue around Melinda exploded and tore itself apart. Then it reformed, but this time it was full of holes. The area around Melinda was spotted with them holes floating freely in the air around her. She looked into one and realized they were not holes but portals into people's dreams. Many people were dreaming about being attacked and seeing others hurt. The ones doing the hurting had the faces of Ms. Luka and Ms. Jayl. That was a problem.

And she knew how to fix it.

She felt all the panic running through the ground beneath her. She knelt again and put both palms against the ground. Anxiety thundered through her and made her heart race and sweat break out on her brow.

Melinda called to the people dreaming. She held their dreamselves against her in their sleep until they calmed. She pulled their anxiety from them and into herself. She shook as it took over her mind for a moment. It ran from her head through her body and out of her feet, cleansed and changed. It went back into their dreams as hope. She stretched further and further. She covered the city and then the state and then the country. The dream lands grew around her as connections were made. She leapt from mind to mind and pool to pool, calming their terror and uncertainty; feeding back determination.

Finally, she could stretch no farther; she felt the minds out there, but they were too active, they buzzed and moved. They were awake. She waited and slowly her power spread. She released the minds of those who woke and pulled those newly fallen into dreams closer to her. She touched them all. Melinda felt when the others left her but did not say goodbye. She still she had more work to do.

When she was finally done, she was exhausted in a way she had never felt before. But as she let the dream world go, she woke up.

Arms pulled her close, nearly suffocating her.

"Melinda! Oh baby, thank god!"

She blinked up. Her moms were leaning over her. Melinda blinked, feeling foggy and slow. It hurt to move, and she had to squint to see clearly. She saw Patrah behind them.

"What happened?" Melinda croaked out.

"Youve been asleep for over twenty-four hours," her Mama said as she pulled Melinda into her arms. It hurt, but Melinda didn't say anything, just met Patrah's silent gaze over her Mama's shoulder.

# TAE

Speaking with Fallon had become a favorite pastime of Tae's. Especially since he had not seen Zaha in person since the death of her friend Carlie.

"This is odd," Tae said as he looked out the window. People moved in and out of the Agency building with purpose. Meetings upon meetings with groups that wanted to help; training schedules and volunteers; food storing and defenses. From what Dayida had said, it was the same in most cities around the world. Not all but enough.

"They want to save their world. Why is that odd?" Fallon asked, not rising from his seat. He took a sip of tea as Tae turned to face him.

"Come now. I doubt you've been here as long as you say without knowing that this is just not how humans roll."

They all suspected Melinda. They'd read the articles and seen the tenor of the conversation in the wake of the press conference. It hadn't been their *worst*-case scenario, but it had been much more negative than they had hoped.

Then in only a day it had flipped around. There was still fear and hatred out there, but most people had accepted it and moved on to working together. Most religions were taking a wait-and-see stance, except for a few smaller churches that had declared the Blooded children of the Gods or Satan depending on the day. No matter how great that was Tae knew they weren't normal reactions.

Patrah had laid out the wave of changed opinion; tracking how sentiment had changed with sleep. Melinda would say nothing about it, or why she had been asleep and unreachable, even by Patrah, for so long. He wished Erik were here to talk with her. Also, he simply missed his friend and hoped he was alright. He wanted to talk over the theory that had been forming in his mind because it involved Erik too. It was terrifying to keep it to himself, and while it might help, it would mean more change.

Fallon smacked his lips after another sip. "I do know that. I just think it is more useful to focus on the now instead of the how."

Tae rolled his eyes at the rhyme. "The cause is just as important as the result."

"What do you see when you look at them, young one?" Fallon asked, finally putting his teacup down and turning all his attention to Tae.

Tae looked out the window again and opened his gaze slowly. He saw skulls over some of their faces. Others had limbs that faded in and out of his sight. They would not survive or would be injured in the coming war. He also saw some of them aged, older, their families behind them. When he cast his gaze farther out, he saw buildings where there were none, Antes roaming alongside humans—devouring some, befriending others. He saw an eclipse with two moons overlapping. He saw fire and war and pain and compromise. And down the road he saw the two possible endings where every choice, big or small, inevitably led.

"What I always see. Two endings—change or death."

Tae looked down at his own body; the way it was filled with light in his vision, and the way it flared. He swallowed and shut his gaze down quickly.

# ZEBUB

# RAZEL

Razel did not know who first saw them, but it did not take long for the panic to spread through the tightly packed crowd inside Kandake. She moved against the crush of people fleeing from the door. The fact that she was recognizable helped, since some were reluctant to touch her at all. When she reached the front doors, she stared out of the frosted glass. They came in a wave. She could not pick out individuals because there were so many. It was not merely a shadow of movement but an eclipse that blotted out the street. They covered it from building to building and filled the sky.

Maasu, hundreds of them.

She looked at the others gathered by the door with her. The revolutionaries that Lil had been fighting with, along with Arel and Jagi. All looking very grim.

"Can we seal the Athenaeum?" Arel asked.

"We could if Lil were the official Holder. As it is, Mayer has control, and I'm sure he's somewhere in that crowd. As long as he holds Kandake we can do almost nothing without his permission. He can open the doors to whomever he wants," Razel said quietly, trying to keep the panicked people around her from hearing.

The force had stopped fifty feet from the front of Kandake, and there it roiled and rumbled in anger. They were close enough that Razel now spotted a few prominent individuals. She could see Riana riding on a small personal crike, and Chayyliel standing in the front line alongside Mayer, also on a crike.

"We have to give Lil more time," Razel whispered.

Jagi looked at her and nodded, opening the door and walking out. He walked down the steps of Kandake and held up his hands.

"You are not welcome here. Return to your Hives and leave us be," Jagi called out.

Mayer stepped forward from the crowd. It might have been her imagination but he looked older, his hair more lined with white, his movement more stiff and irregular.

"I am always welcome here. I am the Holder of Kandake. It is the rest of you who have broken into the Athenaeum without cause." His voice was strong, but still cracked in places.

"We broke into nothing. The door was unlocked and open when we approached. Perhaps you forgot to lock it? Or perhaps gave someone a key?" Jagi responded.

Razel could not see Jagi's face, but she clearly heard the smirk in his voice.

Mayer had no response but Razel saw the red filling his face and neck. Chayyliel stepped forward next. Its voices were low and soothing; a combination of conniving and cajoling. "If you will offer up Lilianna, Razel and the strangers from another world, we shall leave you in peace," Chayyliel stated.

Razel saw the look that Mayer shot over to the Queen and wondered how much of what was happening had been cleared with the Holder.

"A counter offer," Jagi offered. "We will offer you the chance to win those you wish to take through combat."

"And why should we agree to this?" Chayyliel asked.

"Because otherwise you'll have to storm Kandake and you know how sensitive so many of the items inside are. What if a fire were to break out?" The tone of Jagi's voice promised that something like a fire or much more devastating would definitely occur.

She saw Mayer's face tighten and he lowered himself from the crike and moved to Chayyliel's side, whispering furiously. Chayyliel nodded once and gestured for Mayer to return to his place.

"Agreed. However, when we win them, you will all empty Kandake with no damage to anything inside," Chayyliel stated.

Jagi nodded. "If you win all three fights—Liliana, Razel, and the strange 'dants. One fight for each."

Chayyliel was silent for a moment but finally lowered its head in a nod. "Agreed."

Jagi smiled. "We shall start with Razel."

It was only shock and her training that kept her from yelling at the Ante across the distance between them. She turned to look at Arel but he had eyes for no one but Jagi.

"I will go and retrieve her," Jagi said.

He walked back to the door and Razel was immediately in his face.

"What do you think you are doing?" Razel asked.

"You said we needed to buy Lil some time; that is what I've done," Jagi responded calmly.

"Yes, by throwing me to the wolves," Razel yelled at the smug Ante.

"No. You shall request that Arel and I fight for you. It is allowed to have a champion."

Razel looked back and forth between the two of them. It was true, and Riana was hardly going to fight for herself either, and they did need the time.

"Fine," she agreed. Better to pretend she had a real choice in the matter.

Arel and Jagi gestured for her to exit first. She moved slowly down the steps alone until she called for Arel and Jagi. All eyes were on her and she kept her face composed as she walked out. The sky above them seemed to literally split and suddenly Razel was in the rain, though Riana and her companions stayed completely dry. Was this one of Mayer's tricks? Or a new tactic of the darkness? Or just another sign of their world cracking apart?

She stood still in the rain facing her Holder.

"You have made a foolish choice here tonight, Apprentice," Riana yelled for all to hear.

"You have made nothing but foolish choices your whole life, and yet here you stand, powerful, despite being incompetent and useless. If you happen to win, what will you do, Riana? Turn me over to the Ruling Courts? Then who would make the mechaniques that people love so much in this new world? Not you," Razel replied, standing taller.

It felt amazing to unload on Riana, who had never said a kind word to her, who had made Razel's life a hell and forced her to pretend that she enjoyed it.

"You were nothing when I found you—" Riana blustered.

"I was already better than you at everything when you found me. I'm still better than you. No matter your emotions, that truth will not change."

Riana stared at her with an open mouth and Razel let a genuine smile stretch across her face. It felt odd, the joy and freedom. She would risk death a hundred times for this.

Riana recovered. "I will make you suffer before you die, the way I did your parents. All they asked about in the end was where you were."

"I will see you dead!" Razel snarled so vehemently that she saw the spittle fly from her mouth and shocked herself. She recognized the anger from deep within her, hiding all along in recesses she always did her best to ignore. It existed alongside the love and mourning for the parents she barely remembered.

Chayyliel interrupted them.

"Champions forward."

The Maasu that Riana had chosen came forward. It stood upright on two powerful legs like a 'dant, but that was where the resemblance ended. Its torso was too thick and long, and it broadened as it rose. Upon the shoulders, three heads rested with no necks to get in the way. Its shoulders sprouted thick tree trunks that were dozens of tentacles wrapped around each other to approximate arms. Its back sprouted wings that resembled those of a dragon.

Arel and Jagi came from behind her, and they were no longer the nice Antes that were clearly in love with her . . . acquaintance, if not friend. No, these were the warriors she had seen from the sky as the dragons had zoomed in. They both stood to their full heights. The apertures on their sides opened and closed quickly making a continuous snapping sound. They came in on either side of the Maasu, its two outer heads rotating to watch them approach.

The Maasu leapt into the air on its wings and its tentacles unfurled and whipped out at them. Just as fast, they had snapped out their tentacles and blocked the blows.

In seconds, the whole fight was just a mass of moving tentacles, whipping and ripping at each other, and the only way to tell the difference was the color of them. She watched a white-gray tentacle fly from the ring, ripped from its source. There was a cry of pain from within the mass of movement but she could not see if it was Arel or Jagi who had lost the limb. There were more cries from within the circle, including one that went rapidly high and made all the 'dants around wince and hold their ears.

Razel could see the other Maasu across the way, rearing up and watching the fight. Then the world shifted around them. Though the ground did not actually move, it felt as if the world around them had changed from one second to the next. She realized the vaguely malevolent feeling at her back from the direction of the Athenaeum had lifted and there was the feel of heat and warmth and friendship replacing it.

Lil had claimed Kandake.

Mayer cried out and fell to the ground. Razel watched as he struggled to rise to his feet again and those around him moved away rather than help.

She turned in time to see Lil come walking out of the front door. She was dressed all in white except for the thorny branch wrapped carelessly around her waist like a belt. She strode out and down the steps. Matthias walked behind her. Razel could not see Erik. Behind Liliana, the windows showed empty rooms, instead of the spaces that were packed body to body when Razel had emerged.

Lil came up on her side and paused.

"Where is Erik?" Razel asked.

The branch floated off Lil's waist and formed the words before Razel.

**StillInTheHeartOfKandake**

**WeWillRetrieveHimLater.**

"And everyone who was seeking sanctuary?" Razel asked.

**ISentThemDeeper Inside**

**TheyWillBeSaferThere.**

"Being Holder suits you," Razel said, fully taking in Liliana, her smiling face, and her confident stance. The power almost dripped from every gesture.

Lil nodded and stepped forward, raising her hands.

# LIL

Lil reached for her bond with Kandake and it flooded into her. Instead of a trickle, this was a river: wild, free, and untameable. She felt all of Kandake; the rooms hidden from view, the ones blocked off, and the ones that had to be coaxed open.

Not only did she suddenly know where these rooms were, but she knew the knowledge they contained; not intimately, but the general subjects. Lil thought of *The Lefai Compendium of Refraction and Revenge:* the first book about power she had ever read cover to cover, when she was still angry at her parents. To her surprise, when she thought of a page, it appeared in her mind's eye, stains and rips and all. Exactly as she had seen it.

She thought of other books—Ngota's *Treatise on Control*, Linche's *Poisons Both Natural and Un,* and even the small, nearly forgotten folk collection *The 'dant Under Our Feet* by Ertemisha. All of them flipped through her mind, page after remembered page. Then she thought of the pages she had sketched out of the movement of the root, so long ago. As Lil thought of them, she saw them all laid out in a pattern, and she could read it.

Her whole body froze.

She could feel the Babel blazing off the pages. The bones had been tracing out the long-lost language for her, but she had not seen it. That was what their movement had contained. The language of creation. She could have stayed forever exploring the Babel, but she felt the anger and rage and fear gathering just beyond the range of her body. Not beyond the range of the Athenaeum, though.

With a thought, Lil moved herself from the center of Kandake to the front hall. It was disorienting; like being in two places at once. At the same time that she was plucking her body from one room and putting it in another, she could feel her body being moved by an outside force. It was very confusing, and would take her a while to get used to.

She grabbed Matthias as well, pulling him along with her. When she reached for Erik, though, he slipped through her mental fingers; his body refused to be moved. It felt hollow, yet also too heavy to lift. Lil left him alone and released herself and Matthias into the front hall.

Bright white lights obscured her vision for a moment, and then cleared just as two thumps against her legs nearly threw her off balance. Lil recovered and looked down to see Min and Davi. She knelt and kissed them both soundly on the cheeks.

"I knew you would come back," Min said into her neck.

She squeezed her tighter for a second, wanting to tell Min that she would never leave her. Since neither of her sibs could read, though, Lil had no way to communicate with them without Arel and Jagi as a go between. She held them tighter and looked to Matthias.

**TellEveryoneToGoDeeperIntoKandake**

**TouchNothingTheyWillBeSafe.**

He nodded and turned to the room, speaking loudly. She stood up, releasing her sibs. She smiled at them and nodded outside. They seemed to understand and smiled at her.

"I know you'll come back," Min said as she pulled Davi to her.

Lil smiled so wide the scars around her mouth ached, but she did not care. She nodded and turned to head out. People streamed to safety behind her. Matthias walked at her back.

After a quick talk with Razel, she stepped forward and pulled the water from the air and funneled it into the Maasu facing her Antes. The rain coalesced in a funnel around the combatants and then sunk into the black-armored being. The Maasu began to swell and struggled to move. The seams of its body became visible. It screamed while Arel and Jagi hurried to her side. Once they were clear she sucked all the moisture from the thing. The Maasu became a dried husk in seconds.

Lil stepped past them and crossed halfway to where Chayyliel stood.

**YouWillLeave**

**IHoldKandakeNow.**

"You are still a child, even if you Hold Kandake. And you must learn to not speak to the Ruling Court so," Chayyliel responded.

**IAmDoneWithLessonsFromYouChayyliel.**

Lil thought of the page in *Folding Space and You*, a great primer by one of the previous Holders. The equations flashed in her mind and she put them into play, plugging numbers in. She held the resulting sigil in her mind and, pointing at Chayyliel, channeled it down her arm.

The Ante disappeared with a pop and reappeared only a few feet closer to Lil, screaming, without any of its limbs. She had adjusted the circumference of the space to only include its narrow torso and head, leaving everything else behind. The Antes in the crowd were screeching and screaming things, stinking the air with their displeasure, flashing complicated threats with patterns of light. Lil did not care. She moved forward to stand over the Ante who had thought to silence her by taking her tongue.

**YouTookFromMeLordChayyliel**

**NowYouMayConsiderUsEven.**

Chayyliel was too busy bleeding out a stream of white and screaming to see or read, but the message was not for it, but for all the other Antes in the crowd.

**GoNow.**

"No can do, princess."

The voice called through the crowd. At first Lil could not see where it came from, but then the speaker glided forward between the Maasu and Antes. The thing that came forward looked like a 'dant but it was not. She could see through it, like that one 'dant from the other world, but inside this one was darkness. The same hunger Lil had felt from the darkness in her parents' home pulsed at her from the thing. It continued to come closer to her body, to Kandake. She knew it had to be stopped.

The Antes and Maasu around it hissed and growled and snapped, they spat lightning and fire. They broke the earth beneath its feet and turned the air around it molten with heat.

None of it touched the thing.

She heard Matthias let out a long stream of what she assumed were curses.

Matthias stepped forward to flank her, as did rest from the other world. They all had anger and disgust clearly etched across their faces.

"Daniel," Matthias growled. "I knew something about you was wrong."

Daniel's smile remained the same as he looked at all of them. "And yet here we stand. I guess Erik doesn't trust—oh excuse me, I meant didn't—"

Matthias's hand shot to his pocket and came up with what looked like a small, round disk of silver. He flung it at Daniel, and as the object pierced Daniel between the eyes his whole body froze and then jerked to and fro in the air before going blurry and almost fading completely.

Daniel's body snapped back into focus. He stared at Matthias. "That actually hurt. Merging with this form must have given me some of its weaknesses. Fascinating."

"I've been stocking up on my spirit killing gear," Matthias said with a nasty smile.

Daniel frowned at him, waiting, but Matthias only watched him back. Finally, the spirit turned to face Lil again.

"I'm quite angry with you, you know. I was not ready to reveal myself yet, but you taking hold of Kandake? That was a snag I wasn't counting on. It takes a lot to surprise me."

**YouAreTheDarkness.**

"I am many things, little girl, most of which would take you centuries to comprehend, but know this: I am your death. It is the way ahead and nothing you do here today can change that."

**IfThatIsTrueWhyBother**
**ToRevealYourselfAtAll?**

Lil saw Matthias slowly pulling other things out of his pockets, so she did her best to keep Daniel's attention on her by calling bright white light to her hands. It was a simple call since the lights did nothing but glow, but still Daniel watched her hands warily.

"I prefer things to run smoothly. I feel it's pretty obvious that these fools will be no challenge to you. Though now that I'm here—"

Matthias flung whatever was in his hands; it flashed gold in the air and struck Daniel in the stomach, but instead of going through it, the small disc stopped there in his midsection. Daniel screamed and sank his hands into his stomach, trying to pull the metal from his form. The disc would not move; instead, the parts of Daniel's body in contact with it began to stretch and warp. Soon, Daniel's whole form was sinking into the coin. When it was gone, the metal itself winked out of existence.

Everyone looked to Matthias.

**WhatWasThat?**

"A penny that has already crossed all five rivers of the Underworld of the Greeks. It will take a spirit, even a partial one as powerful as Daniel, at least a few moments to cross them again and return to the world of the living," Matthias answered.

"Leave this place. Now!" Arel shouted at the gathered group of enemies facing them.

Lil watched the gathering, and a few of the Antes did turn to leave. She knew that there were Antes in Kandake who had sought shelter with her and that not all Antes were foul, but these were of the Ruling Courts. Most of those gathered were those who had been ruling for far too long to contenance anything challenging them. It would be a fight no matter what.

Both sides were waiting until a single Maasu crept closer, one that looked like a 'dant except for the wickedly long claws and teeth that dripped with something yellow and sizzling. It came too close to Yonas, who reached out a hand and pressed it against the thing's face. It screamed as Yonas burned through its skull and killed it.

The battle was truly joined after that, and Lil struck them down as they came at her. She had already done the base calculation for time and date and location for folding space, so she used it over and over, maiming Ante and Maasu alike as she moved pieces of them back and forth. She could feel the root still hanging in the pouch in her hip pocket. She could feel power leeching into her from where it pressed against her.

Lil pushed her way forward, as did the others, pushing the group back step by step. As other Antes fled, they were confronted with more Maasu.

They suffered their own injuries. She could see where Assan was sitting on the ground, one of his legs bleeding sluggishly, but still aiming carefully with his gun and letting fly. Kima crouched over him, her face covered in scratches that would scar her face in a crisscross pattern for all of her days. If she survived.

One of the foreign 'dants yelled as a clawed hand wrapped around her arm and dislocated her shoulder before she could pull away. Hlani stood over an unconscious Quinn, who had blood covering her face, facing a Maasu that would soon rip her to shreds. Lil concentrated, moving part of it away and letting the other pieces drop, severed and dead. Hlani looked around until she met Lil's eyes and nodded her thanks. She picked up her lover and ran for the doors of Kandake.

Uchel was using her powders like bombs, mixing powders and liquids in clear bladders and then throwing them with deadly accuracy. They burned the Antes' skin, and when they hit the eyes of the Maasu, it blinded them.

Lil turned a corner and found Mayer crumbled behind one of the ruins that used to be buildings. He caught sight of her and fought to sit upright.

"So, it's come to this?"

**ItDidntHaveTo**

**YouBetrayedMe**

**YouForcedThis.**

"No. I think neither one of us could have avoided this," Mayer muttered, looking down at his wrinkled hands.

**IfThatMakesYou FeelBetterAbout**

**YourActionsFeelFreeToBelieveIt.**

Mayer looked up at her. He was now an old man, older than anyone she had ever seen, with his skin barely hanging on to his bones. The peach of his skin had withered to an unhealthy yellow that matched his teeth. He shook his head as he looked down at his hands. The knobs of his knuckles were huge against the twigs of his fingers.

Lil tried to bring herself to kill this 'dant before her; the one who had raised her for almost twelve cycles; the 'dant who had taught her so much, both how to heal and hurt, and most important, how to survive. But Mayer was also the 'dant who had betrayed his people and her, who had brought all this upon himself. She reconciled these two parts of her former Holder very easily, but it did not make it simple to decide what to do. Was it mercy now or foolishness that urged her to allow him to live?

In the end, he had been her enemy. She thought of it and a page flashed in her head. A lesson on war from one of the best leaders of all time, kaSenzangakhona: Never leave an enemy behind, or it will rise again to fly at your throat. She could at least give him some semblance of dignity in death. She worked out the differences.

"Goodbye." Mayer said, looking in her eyes. She managed to smile at him as she put all of the equations together in her mind.

He exploded into the sky, turning into silver light, spreading across the sky as something beautiful. She watched until he faded, mourning the man she had thought him to be, and then went back to the fight. They were winning and pushing the Maasu back, thanks to herself and those from the other place. More and more Antes had fled. Kima had dragged Assan inside and left those more effective against the Maasu to deal with the teeming hordes of black-armored monsters.

Then Daniel reappeared in an explosion of light.

"I did not like that!" With a gesture, the Maasu that Matthias was facing was wrapped in a teeming bubble of shadow. It screeched and screamed as it fell to the ground and the darkness burrowed into it and then went still. When it rose shakily back to its feet it was twice as tall as before. The holes where the darkness had eaten its way in were now covered with sharp black spikes that curled out.

The darkness shot out of the ground all around them, infecting the Maasu and growing them, turning them larger, more vicious, and harder to kill. Lil pulled the moisture from the air again, planning to use it to slow these opponents down and bury them. Before she could do this, something caught her in the chest and sent her flying into the air until her back slammed into something hard.

She fell to the ground, dazed, and looked up to see Daniel looking down at her. She narrowed her eyes.

"You're not within your Athenaeum now, are you? Not even close enough to call on much of its power," Daniel smirked.

Lil reached for her link with Kandake; it was there, but it was not flooding her with the power she'd had only moments ago.

"Your link has made you more powerful, but that power decreases the further you step from Kandake." Daniel came closer.

The shield formed around her without much thought, an older spell Lil had learned very young. She fed all the power that Kandake was giving her into the shield. The root flared and the strength of the shield grew further but she didn't know if it mattered any more. This close, she could feel the power and hunger from Daniel. Lil suspected that even were she in Kandake itself, she would not have the strength to stave off this power.

Lil let out a hoarse cry as the weight of the world came down on her shield, rubble and stone pushing down, trying to pierce her shield and get to her. Then the stone began to glow, heating to red hot, and the heat made its way through the shield. She began to sweat and any part of her touching the shield started to burn.

She struggled to push the shield out further and curled her body down smaller to give herself some breathing room. She brought the moving equations to mind once more and then, taking a deep breath, she applied them to herself.

And appeared on the steps of Kandake.

The increased power from being closer to Kandake helped her stay standing. Daniel turned toward her, flying forward.

Then Erik appeared above the Athenaeum, floating and glowing with power. The sky was ripping apart behind him, showing glimpses of white nothingness. Erik's eyes were nothing but light from lid to lid and he looked at all of them with a smile.

The Maasu that were closest to Erik began to quake and vibrate before cracking apart, their insides spilled out into the street, steaming and turning to mist in the air.

The one they called Daniel did not seem injured, but there was definitely strain on his face where there had only been smug satisfaction before.

"Well, seems like you've learned a few tricks," Daniel remarked.

Erik smirked right back. "More than a few."

Erik looked down and behind him straight at Razel. Then he turned to look at Riana. He pointed at her.

"Traitor. Enheduanna is no longer yours. It belongs to this one." Erik's hand swung around to Razel.

Both women fell to the ground gasping, tears leaking from their eyes. The expressions on their faces were vastly different. Razel smiled, her whole face lighting up. Riana's face was nothing but anger and resentment. She dove for her former apprentice but did not make it. She was lifted into the air until she faced Erik. He reached out slowly and touched her forehead. As soon as his fingertip made contact her mouth opened in a silent scream.

She began to glow a bright white, and a pulse passed from her forehead into Erik's finger. In a flash, Riana was gone.

"What did you do?" Razel asked. There was no censure in her voice, but there was the beginning of fear.

When Erik looked at her, there was no emotion on his face, and Lil felt a shiver. "Do not concern yourself. She has been given the chance to help right what she has wronged."

"Well," Daniel said. "Looks like I have to take you out of the game."

A thick tendril of darkness cracked the ground beneath Erik and shot into the air, wrapping itself around Erik. The man struggled against it and let out a roar as he tore pieces of it in his hands. Before Lil could think to do anything, the tendril pulled Erik beneath and the ground sealed itself over them.

"No!" She turned and saw Matthias screaming and heading for Daniel as quickly as he could.

# MATTHIAS

He watched Erik get swallowed by the earth and a primal scream ripped through his body. He watched Daniel—the darkness that had pretended to be Daniel—smirk as Matthias leapt over the rubble in front of him.

Matthias called on every gift Artemis-Agrotera had gifted him with. His body went light and transparent and he ran. He tore through the creatures that got in the way. He pulled weapons from his cargo pants and used them until they ran out of ammo or got stuck inside some monster or another. He went from handguns to knives to a mace to a sawed-off shotgun. The armor of the creatures was bulletproof or as near as possible, but their eyes were not.

He heard a scream and turned to see Tassi speared through her stomach by a spike of one of the Maasu.

Yonas yelled for her partner and flew to her. Her touch burned through the arm holding Tassi aloft and Yonas caught her before she hit the ground.

Matthias was a pack rat; a collector who used the things he gathered sparingly, but there was no room in his mind for that kind of deliberation today. He pulled things from his pockets and used them immediately after he identified them.

Gems that held moments of frozen time, coins that seared with light, bits of string that came alive and grew to tangle his enemies. When something did not work on a Maasu he just reached into his pocket for another. Finally, he reached Daniel and pulled another penny of the underworld from his pocket, preparing to throw it.

Matthias's body stopped, and the penny fell from his fingers to the ground. He floated in the air and could feel every muscle in his body straining against the power that held him.

Daniel smirked at his struggles. "As amusing as this whole thing has been, it must end. I would devour you, but I have no need of your thoughts inside of me. Take care of him."

There were only a fraction of Maasu left from the initial amount, but they converged on Matthias. The power that held him still released him right before the first one struck. Matthias did not know if it was Daniel deciding to make it interesting or if Artemis was answering his prayers. Either way, he had no intention of letting the opportunity go by. He dropped, letting the first strike go over his head.

Matthias reached into his pockets. Depleted as they were, he still came up with two large wooden sticks lacquered black. Blessed by a friend of Mahrem's line, they cracked across the shells of the Maasu, breaking them open. He ducked and wove his way through the crush of creatures trying to rip him to shreds. Eventually he lost first one and then the second stick. Matthias had no more tricks and so he reached deep inside to the well of his power and pulled more deeply, moving faster and faster.

His skin was burning as he fought them off. His hands were moving faster than they ever had before and glowing a soft silver. His blows, though empty handed, were shattering armor and sending them flying off to die.

"Now we can't have that."

The same power as before tried to take hold of his body but it slipped off as if he were covered in oil.

He smiled up at Daniel, who had a confused look on his face.

On instinct, he held one arm stretched in front of himself and the other bent and pulled back. When he released the fingers of the bent hand an arrow of silver light exploded from his hands. It zeroed in on the first creature and struck, blazing through its body and continuing on to slice through three more before it faded away. He stared at his hands in wonder before doing it again and again. One struck Daniel and the hole it made in his form did not close right away. Matthias's head snapped back and he laughed up into the sky. There were three moons in Corpiliu and all of them were full right now. It seemed like a sign.

*You are burning through, my child.*

He heard her. He heard Artemis.

"Please, I have to punish him," he whispered.

*This is not a fight you can win.*

"But it is one I can help others win."

*My child. Stop. Please.*

Matthias did not. He knew what it meant that he was speaking to his dead goddess directly. He knew that his power levels were so low that he was near death. He did not care. The silver faded from his hands and still he fought, but now he was slower, and weaker. His blows did nothing and he could not block or dodge many of the incoming ones.

They buried him. He saw the others still trying to reach him. Elana flying as quickly as possible. Daya tossing attackers to and fro, Elliot going invisible to try and sneak to him. Yonas had even reemerged from the Athenaeum and had monsters falling like wheat under her death-touch. They were all trying and in that moment, he loved them for it.

The ground exploded somewhere near him and a voice he knew screamed out his name. He felt them ripping into his body; there was a tearing from his stomach, and he found himself tossed into the air. The last thing Matthias saw as he flew through the air was Erik glowing bright as the sun, and he smiled, glad to have seen the man he loved lighting up the night sky.

# ERIK

Erik had never felt such rage burn through him. He had lost too many—Daniel, Tae, and now Matthias. It was too much. It was too far. He blazed across the space between them and struck Daniel in the stomach.

They kept going, higher and higher as Daniel clawed at his hands, trying to push Erik away, but Erik would not stop, taking him into the space between the sky where the whiteness was cracking open. Finally, Daniel managed to slip off his fists and Erik turned to face the monster who had been his first love.

"What are you?" Erik whispered.

"I am what is left of your Daniel, and I am more as well. I am your beginning, the beginning of everything, and so shall I be your end."

"Everyone was right. Matthias was right."

"Deep down, you knew they were," Daniel sneered. "You knew it was too convenient."

Erik said nothing because he could say nothing. He did not know if what the monster was saying was true or if his guilt made him think so. All he could see was Matthias's face, the pain on it as he was ripped in half, the joy on it as he saw Erik and the light dimmed from his eyes.

"It's interesting to . . . interact with you lower lifeforms, instead of just eating you. I haven't shrunken myself down enough to do it since the universe was new."

Erik said nothing, but he felt inside of him for where all this new power bubbled and frothed. He touched Bia inside of him, everything she had gifted him with. He didn't know what to do with it yet, but instinct had served him well so far.

"There is enough of Daniel in me that I do care for you," said the thing in Daniel's shape.

"I doubt that," Erik managed to say, even as he let small tendrils of power out to sew up the cracks around them. He could trap them both in this neverending white. Forever in this space between would mean both safety for those he loved and punishment for himself. The spirit of the darkness must have sensed something, because it began to glance around.

"What are you doing?" Daniel asked as he finally saw that the slice of night sky that showed the Athenaeum was shrinking. He shot for it but Erik went after him, grabbing him by the ankle and pulling him back.

The thing shaped like Daniel swung around and slammed his fists onto the back of Erik's neck. Erik lost his grip and floated for a moment as everything went fuzzy. It was over, though, they were sealed in. Forever.

"Now, I've got to reopen the way," it said in Daniel's voice, sounding like it was pouting. Erik's stomach sank.

"Did you think you would strand me here? This is the nothing between the spaces; this is the place I was born. If there is any place that is home to me, it is this one."

Erik shook off some of his dizziness and managed to move right side up again.

There were pinpricks of black in the white all around them now and some of those widened large enough to be windows. Still fewer widened into doors. He saw Kandake through one of these.

The darkness wearing Daniel stalked closer to him. "You still don't understand. I am everything. I am the father and the mother. I am the god and the goddess. I am the fount from which everything sprang."

"Those people in the mall?" Erik choked out.

"I needed to know of this iteration of your world. I have been gone a long time, waiting for it to grow ripe. I ate my fill but did not want to alert all to my intentions. Some I simply stripped of their knowledge. They did not remember it later. Others I found more long-term uses for."

The darkness touched his face and Erik let some of the power burst out of him and spin him away from the hand. The expression on its face tightened, then relaxed.

"I have touched your father while you are here," the darkness said as it stepped closer.

Erik lunged forward but it was already gone, already behind him.

"I learned from him."

Erik whirled but it was gone again. Daniel's voice sounded in the whiteness, echoed, made Erik feel dizzy and nauseous.

"Don't you want the truth. Erik? Don't you want to know how your mother protected Robert all these years? How she knew what he had done?"

"Shut up," Erik growled and spun.

"Don't you want to know how your father put away your lover? How your mother kept his secrets?"

"Shut up!" Erik cried out as he swung at a shadow. He knew this creature would lie, was probably lying, but the possibility nagged at him and made him sloppy. He had always wondered that Daniel had been convicted at all and then that he was sentenced to jail time instead of probation was also odd. It had seemed harsh, but he was sixteen and heartbroken and didn't look as deeply as he should have.

The punch in his back caught him off guard and he flew forward onto his knees. The next punch came from above him, slamming him down. He tried to stand and the next hit caught him on the chin. Erik tasted blood. The force that drove him down next made him cry out, and he simply kept falling.

He tried to concentrate to bring his powers to bear, but he was in too much pain. Then a hand in his hair stopped him. He screamed as many were pulled from his scalp and he felt blood begin to slip down onto his face. They were back above the Athenaeum. Almost no time seemed to have passed. Everyone looked at the place they had disappeared rather than where they now were for a moment. The hand threaded through Erik's hair and pulled his head back so he could see all the people below him.

"They will all die here, as shall you. As shall this world and then your own."

His world.

He remembered his ancestor's words; his goddess's words. *This place is yours now. Everything that is left in it.*

Erik thought of the ways his powers had grown while here, the way that the earth had shaken around him, and the way that doors and passages seemed to welcome him with no conscious thought on their owners' part. Because it was not the owners' doing, but that of the building, the world. He let his consciousness reach back toward the place where they had met. The room deep in the heart of Kandake. When he touched it he touched Lil's mind. He dove deeper into the room and felt it spread out across the land. Every Athenaeum on the surface of Corpiliu, they held a piece of Bia's heart, a piece of his heart.

He found all the pieces of her heart, scattered. So much knowledge stored inside each one; each was a small version of the goddess, but made completely unique and individual after so many years separated. He opened his arms to them all and asked.

*Come home?*

Erik hissed as the power flooded through his body, and shredded his mind, stretching it in millions of directions.

Somewhere he was screaming. Somewhere the man he could have loved lay dead because of him. Somewhere his friends and allies fought. But none of that mattered to him at the moment, as dozens of women who had been one but were no longer took up residence in his mind. They fought and tore at one another. They loved each other and melted in ecstasy. They were wind and sleet, and the desert sun and the lightning. They came together and flew apart a dozen times in different combinations. They settled in a rough approximation of peace and Erik set to work.

First he made sure his people were safe, pulling those still outside into Kandake. Then he took hold of all the Athenaeums Corpiliu and yanked them from one world to another, slotting them into place as if they had always been on Earth, and in some ways, they had been. Then he took the edges of the world of Corpiliu; of the body that had been his so long ago, and pulled it in on itself.

"What are you doing?" The echoing words came from all around.

He could see the mockery of Daniel, still in Corpiliu, in front of the empty space where Kandake had been. Erik was there as well but he was also elsewhere. Daniel had gathered too much of himself together to devour Corpiliu. Erik could close the edges of this world because unlike the white nothingness this world was his. He could seal Corpiliu and it would hold most of the darkness for a short time. Until it ate its way free.

But it would also mean trapping all those others in Corpiliu, the Antes and 'dants who had not crossed over in time. Who had not sought shelter in any of the Athenaeums or who had tried to escape to other places. He would be closing all of them in with the darkness, all as a stopgap measure. They would die. Be devoured.

He took a breath and made the only choice he could make.

Erik shrunk Corpiliu around Daniel's screaming figure, around all their screaming figures, and stitched the edges of it closed. It would not hold the darkness for long. Even now he could feel it eating away, but by shrinking the world he had made it more dense. It would take time for it to chew a big enough hole to escape and come to Earth. Even as he folded Corpiliu down again he felt as if something of the darkness reached inside of him and tried to stop his heart. It was far too late for that, though.

Erik didn't need his heart anymore; it was vestigial, and its death changed nothing.

# LIL

It was a new world outside those doors. Lil did not need to look outside to know it. She could feel it in the air; in the power that drifted through the world in rivers and streams. The magic here felt fuller, riper. It was as if what she had been dining on all her life was lacking something vital she now had but could still not name. Was it because she now held the Athenaeum in her hand or was it the new world? Lil had been outside, continuing to fight, when something had taken hold of her body and moved her into Kandake. Then she felt that force take hold of Kandake as well and rip it from Corpiliu.

She looked down at Min and Davi who looked back at her with wide eyes. She patted them on the back and rose. They stood with her and followed. The crowd of people parted for her, many of them bowing their heads and holding their hands reverently over their hearts. She saw a crowd of Doors that she hadn't noticed before. Many were dirty but they still shone like colorful birds in their fine colors and sparkles. They saw her and lowered their heads toward her.

Lil wanted to correct them all, but she was too tired. All she wanted now was to curl up in bed with her sibs and sleep; to inhale the scent of family that had been missing from her life for too long now. Instead she let the branch float off her arm and into the air above her.

**EveryoneMoveBackFromTheDoors.**

To everyone's surprise a voice rang through the air. <u>Everyone move back from the doors</u>.

Lil looked up at the branch in surprise. She tried it again.

**CanEveryoneHearThat?**

Can everyone hear that?

There were murmurs of agreement behind her. Lil continued to stare at the wood floating near her head. It looked no different, but it was possible, even likely, that whatever made the magic of this world feel different had given the branch a new aspect as well. The voice it spoke in was not hers. It was stiff and did not emphasize words the way she would have, and contained an odd echo. But it was there.

Lil looked at the branch and forced her will on it. It started to fold in on itself, tighter and tighter, until it was a small tangle of wood no bigger than the palm of her hand. She placed it in her pocket and tried to channel through it. She could feel the wood shifting in her pocket and the voice still rang out.

I will go out and find out what is happening, she announced, glancing around.

She saw Kima and Uchel huddled around an unconscious Assan and a sobbing Hlani shaking a Quinn who was bandaged but might never wake up. She knew Kima would come with her if she asked, but that didn't seem fair. She could ask Arel and Jagi to come as well, but she did not know how the 'dants in this world would react to the Antes. She turned to her sibs.

You two will stay here with Arel and Jagi, okay?

They both opened their mouths to argue, but Lil kept on.

I do not know what is out there. I can promise you I will be safe, but not if I have to look out for you two as well. I promise I shall return shortly.

She knew it was unfair to call on their own guilt, but she needed to get out there fast. She knew things like this often resulted in violence. Lil was Holder now. She had protected these people as they had squeezed through the place between worlds, and she would continue to do so.

Min and Davi nodded and transferred their hands to Arel and Jagi.

I love you both.

They both smiled up at her and returned the sentiment.

This was her duty, and hers alone. She stepped out of the door of the Athenaeum.

Guns, many of them. All aimed at her.

Lil did not like that. She felt through the power floating in the air and found the one that resonated with metal. She pulled on it and their guns flew into the air.

We mean you no harm, but neither will we tolerate having weapons pointed at us without cause.

A woman stepped forward from the crowd of people. “Understood. If you will return my people’s weapons I shall have them holster them.” She was dressed in pants and thick shoes like the ones that had appeared on Lil’s feet. Her shirt was dark purple and her hair was covered in fabrica in the same shade. She was older than she looked. Her eyes looked as old as Uchel, but her skin was almost wrinkle free and she moved without pain.

Another woman walked forward from behind the first and climbed the stairs until she stood one step below Lil but equal to her in height. Lil had rarely met a ‘dant that much taller than herself.

“I am Dayida Jayl of the Agency.” The tall woman who walked like a fighter introduced herself. She was dressed like the other woman, except that her shirt was a bright yellow. “I apologize for the rude welcome. There has been much fighting in the streets lately, and when your . . . place appeared we thought it might be another ploy by the Angelics.” She gestured to the woman in purple. “This is Maestra Luka.”

Lil thought at the shrunken branch in her pocket and the voice rang out from around her. I am Liliana Blackthorn Johns, Holder of Kandake Athenaeum.

The woman, Dayida, looked at her, desperation and interest sparking in her eyes, and nodded.

“From Zebub.”

It was no question, and yet Lil nodded.

“We sent people there recently and we have yet to hear what happened to them. Do you know anything?”

Lil nodded.

There was one: Erik, a young man who led them.

“He is my son,” the woman said.

Lil nodded at her. She could see the resemblance now. Especially around the nose and firm lips.

Your son is a brave man. He helped us save many lives, but I do not know where he is now. He suffered a number of losses. His friend Tae, and then Matthias, his friend who could have been more.

Dayida’s skin went gray, as did the woman behind her. “Matthias?”

Yes, one of the creatures tore him in half on Daniel’s orders. He fought bravely.

"Shit." The voice came from behind them. A young man had made his way toward them while she was distracted.

Who is this one? Lil asked.

Dayida turned and looked at the young man. "That's Tae. He did not die, but was somehow sent here.

It will no doubt bring him some comfort that you survived, but—Lil did not know how to say what she wanted next without sounding cruel.

"But a friend is no substitute for someone you might love?" Tae said with a sad smile. "I understand."

Lil nodded. She turned back to the two who looked to be in charge. We have many 'dants and some Antes inside. All seek shelter. Will you be able to provide it?

"It will take some doing, but as long as they agree to abide by our laws, they are welcome here." Dayida said.

"I'm not entirely sure we have the authority to do that," Luka said, but there was a smile on her face.

"I'm giving myself the authority," Dayida said with a returned smile that had vicious edges. "I deserve it after what we've done here."

There was a series of *pop*s behind them and Lil was calling up her power before she turned. Before she saw them, she felt reassurance from Kandake, who had recognized those who appeared on its steps and knew they were not here to cause harm.

Lil turned and saw those that this woman sought, except for Erik. Except for her child. They all looked exhausted and ready to drop, until one of them saw Tae.

"Tae!" As the others saw him, they seemed to become more excited, three of them coming and surrounding him immediately. The two women, the one who had flown and the one whose touch had meant death for so many, did not approach. One was bleeding from a hole in her torso while the other crouched over her.

Dayida turned to the people behind her.

"We need medics over here! Make sure they call my mother in as well." People hustled forward in a group, some with bandages and others bringing some kind of portable bed to move the bleeding woman.

There was another loud *pop*, and they looked up to see Erik appear in the air and begin to freefall downward. Lil reached out, hardening the air beneath his falling body slowly so that he came to a stop some feet above the ground. She released his form onto the ground.

"Erik."

Tae was already kneeling by him, his hands lightly slapping Erik's cheeks. Erik's eyes snapped open and went wide at the sight of who was slapping him. Erik smiled, the first time she had seen an expression so joyful and free on his face, and embraced Tae. It was then that he caught sight of his mother striding toward him, and his face went blank and stiff.

# ERIK

He let go of Tae, let go of all the other questions that were on the tip of his tongue, and stood to face his mother.

"Is it true?"

His mother stopped in her tracks. She looked into his eyes and flinched, and he knew that his eyes were still nothing but red lightning, lid to lid.

"What?" She asked.

"Did Robert set Daniel up? Did you know?"

Erik could see the answer in her body; see the regret and sadness that filled her eyes. He stood there and waited for her to answer, though. He did not trust his instincts anymore. He had known Robert was his enemy, but not his mother. He had trusted Daniel when everyone had expressed suspicions. He had let his own fear and Matthias's issues keep the two of them apart.

"Did you know?" He asked again.

"Yes." The answer was a whisper that echoed like a shout.

Erik was so angry he wanted to rage; to burn through his mother, to make her feel the same pain that he had felt, but he could really only blame himself in the end. The rage burned out and left behind a bone-deep sadness. Erik looked down at the small world he still cradled in his hand, Corpiliu. He looked at the world around him, so bright and alive and goddamn different from when he left. What did he have left to give it but more mistakes?

He closed his eyes and let it all go.

"Erik?"

The voice that asked was small and tentative and something inside him said that he should know it; that it should be familiar to him, but he pushed that away.

"There is no Erik anymore." No, no more Erik. Erik had been weak; Erik had not been able to protect the people that mattered. He had not been able to figure out who was trustworthy and who was not.

"I am nothing but Wrath now." That was all that he was. Anger and revenge and a burning desire to burn the world down until they hurt like he did. The bile that had replaced his blood burned through him and he disappeared; burned his way away from this world and into one where no one would find him.

MANHATTAN

# ROBERT

All Robert was doing was passing on information, and it wasn't even information that Daniel couldn't get on his own. He just wanted to know what they knew about the movements of those from Anoan and what the folks in the Agency were doing about it. His parents and brothers had woken not long after Daniel had left. All of those injured were offered a place with the Agency. None of his family took them up on the offer, but Robert had.

His official job was field documentation and records, though they were training him on weapons. They needed everyone trained on weapons. Mostly his job was to follow behind a fight; stay in a secure location and document everything he could on the weird tablet they had given him. It sent information to them as soon as he entered it, typos and all. Preserving information for the future, they said.

It had the unmistakable whiff of the expectation of failure and so Robert was not happy about being shoved off. But it was working out well for what Daniel wanted to know.

Now he was standing on the rooftop by himself looking to the right as a whole city block burned. People streamed from the doors of the buildings. The Agents almost blended into the shadows. They hurried around the base of the building, helping those humans who emerged and killing the monsters they could find. He took notes on the types of Antes he saw and any deaths he observed.

Robert looked to the outskirts of the fight; to where more reckless people had gathered to observe. Many of them were trying to find a way off the island. The city was in chaos; there was no place where one did not hear about the monsters that had started to attack the populace. People had tried to leave, but that was when the bridges had suddenly collapsed. Any planes or helicopters that tried to get in or out of the city found themselves swarmed with flying monsters; doing things to the engines and breaking rotors until the machines plunged into the ocean. The waters around the island of Manhattan sported a new coral reef of broken escape vehicles.

Sometimes when Robert walked among them he could hear people cursing the government. Why they had not stepped in to help?

Robert knew that D.C. was having its own problems and, like politicians the world over, they were more concerned with themselves than with their people. It was every city for itself. New York was the most openly attacked, but other major cities were having near daily incidents as well. People were running fromm the cities into the country while they could; where they could be safe. For now.

"Hello again."

Robert did not jump this time. He was used to Daniel appearing out of nowhere by now. He liked to surprise Robert in places where if Robert started, mishaps would occur—urinals, roofs, intersections; anywhere that if he jumped too much he would be embarrassed, if not injured.

"Hello, Daniel. What can I do for you?" Robert asked, not looking away from the scene below.

"Hmm. Well, I need a favor. You see, your son has left me in a little bit of a bind."

Robert's spine stiffened. He had done his best not to think of Yida and Erik; those he had abandoned. He wondered what they thought of him and then tried to forget. He knew what they thought; what they had always thought. Only the things he had given them reasons to think.

"Oh, really?" Robert did his best to keep pride out of his voice, but he thought by the look that Daniel shot him he had probably failed.

"Most of my power has been locked away for a while. It won't take me that long to fight my way free, but in the meantime, I won't be able to be as involved as I would like. I won't be able to keep an eye on things as closely. The war here is well under way. It doesn't need any assistance, so I think you should go home."

"Home?" Robert did not like the sound of this.

"Yes. Back to San Francisco. Back to the side of your poor, distraught son. See, he lost another boy he might have loved. Shame, really." The smirk on Daniel's face said something very different.

"Fuck."

"No, they never got a chance to do that," Daniel laughed.

Robert shivered at the pictures that conjured in his head. He closed his eyes to banish them and when he opened his eyes again Daniel had floated directly in front of him and was leaning close. He caught his breath, but did not move otherwise.

"Is that what it was?"

"What?" Robert asked.

"The thing that made you so uncomfortable about your son and me? The sexy, sexy times?"

Robert flinched. "I know you're not really Daniel," he whispered softly, to the ground. Robert was fairly sure that there was no way this thing was actually Daniel. He'd known the boy for years, and the kind of cruelty this thing reveled in, the pain it like to watch and cause? Those were the kinds of behaviors bred over lifetimes.

"Eh, that's debatable. What's that thing you humans say? You are what you eat?" The smile that Daniel flashed him showed entirely too many teeth for a human mouth to hold. "I mean, it's a little more real with Daniel. I merged with what was left of his spirit before it could be fully devoured. So I guess I am him. And not. Depends on your definition of self, I guess."

Robert was staring in horror at the thing wearing Daniel.

"What? We've all got to eat. And this is what you were all bred for. It's why I seeded this world with life, and why I keep coming back. You're the oldest renewable energy source I know. You humans are delicious and breed like rabbits."

Robert stared at Daniel in horror.

"You said you wouldn't hurt my family." Robert's voice shook, and he swallowed the spit flooding his mouth.

"Don't be a fool, Robert. I have to leave some of you still alive. How would you build yourselves up so gloriously again if I killed too many of you too repopulate the Earth? Don't worry; by the time I come back to devour all life again, you and yours will be long gone."

"So the remnants of humanity have to rebuild society from the ground up. That sounds horrible," Robert spit out.

"Hey, I agreed not to hurt them. Not that they would have a wonderful life. I just need to beat them, not kill them. What they make of the world after that? It's up to them."

Robert turned away. "What do you need from me?"

"Find a way home, Robert. Don't let me down."

When Robert glanced around, Daniel was gone. He finished recording what he could of the fight below. Once it was over, he placed the pad on the ground and laid back on the black tar roof. It was burning hot and he sank into the pain of it. He watched the sky go from blue to red to purple to black.

# OUTSIDE

# MATTHIAS

He was dead. He knew that and it caused him little grief. Everything was muted grays and silvers, and he wondered if that was the truth of the world or all he could see now.

He was close to it; close to the other side, when the power burst across his senses. The waves of the whirlpool were disrupted. Souls scattered back and forth like so many toys. Some cried out as what had been an orderly procession became a chaotic mess that only stopped wailing when they reentered the stream and began circling back to the light.

Matthias stayed out of it. He knew that power and he knew that pain.

*Erik.*

The power called to him; reminded him. The edge of the power was so close now that he almost reached out to touch it, but there was no point, because only moments later it was touching him. And the world exploded into color and memory of a young man whom he loved and never told. He could feel the pain that bound them to one another.

The choice was easy in the end and he sped away from the whirlpool; away from the other spirits and back to the man who needed him.

*You are a gift. He will need you. Take care of my child. He is all of me now.* The voice was throaty and rough and beneath the serious tone he thought he could feel it laughing at him.

Matthias felt himself rushing away from the voice, rushing back through the layers of reality that separated the living from the dead, the holes he tore closing slowly behind him.

He was going home.

This book was harder than the first one in many ways. At one point, I threw away over 50,000 words and had to start all over again, and at certain points I stopped believing in myself.

- Thank you to all my friends for being patient with me and quietly (and, when I needed it, loudly) supportive.

- To all the readers of *The Root* who reached out to me on social media to tell me how much it meant to them and who posted reviews online: you don't know how much it meant to me to know that my words connected with people. Thank you from the bottom of my heart for taking a chance on me.

- For my online community: thank you for the discussions, the commiserations, and the confrontations, all of which helped me grow as a person and as a writer.

# ABOUT THE AUTHOR

Na'amen Gobert Tilahun is a bookseller and freelance writer who had lived on the West Coast all his life until 2017, when circumstances made him decide to pack up and head east. He holds a B.A. in Creative Writing from San Francisco State University and an M.F.A. in Fiction and English from Mills College. He writes in multiple genres, and has had work appear in *Fantasy Magazine, io9.com, Queers Dig Time Lords, faggot dinosaur, Full of Crows, The Big Click, Eleven Eleven, Spelling The Hours, Loose Lips, Endless Ages,* and more. Recently, his debut novel, *The Root*, was named a Rainbow List Top Ten book for 2017 by the American Library Association, and a short piece of his, "Culture House", was selected to be reprinted in *The Best Small Fictions 2017*. You can find him on Twitter (@Naamenism) when he should be writing.